YESTERDAY'S
HERO

YESTERDAY'S
HERO
JONATHAN WOOD

TITAN BOOKS

YESTERDAY'S HERO
Print edition ISBN: 9781781168080
E-book edition ISBN: 9781781168141

Published by Titan Books
A division of Titan Publishing Group Ltd
144 Southwark Street, London SE1 0UP

First edition: September 2014

10 9 8 7 6 5 4 3 2 1

Did you enjoy this book? We love to hear from our readers. Please email us at readerfeedback@titanemail.com or write to us at Reader Feedback at the above address.

To receive advance information, news, competitions, and exclusive offers online, please sign up for the Titan newsletter on our website
TITANBOOKS.COM

For Tami, Charlie and Emma.

As ever. Forever.

1

"I don't suppose there's a chance," I say, "that we get the day off on the grounds of, you know, saving the world yesterday?"

Felicity Shaw, director of MI37, sworn defender of Britain's sovereign borders from threats thaumaturgical, supernatural, extraterrestrial, and generally batshit weird, arches an eyebrow at me.

Which is pretty much the answer I expected.

And then a zombie T-Rex tries to bite my head off.

AN HOUR AGO

"I don't suppose there's a chance," I say, "that we get the day off, on the grounds of, you know, saving the world yesterday?"

Shaw looks up from her newspaper and arches an eyebrow at me.

It's not like it's a lie. We genuinely did save the world yesterday. Hell, it's barely been twelve hours since I was helping banish an alien the size of Texas back to its own cold and desolate dimension. And now I'm on a train to London to try and put down a zombie T-Rex.

"It's barely the whole world this time, Arthur," Felicity points out to me. "It's just the Natural History Museum."

"Oh, well then," I shrug, "I'm totally up for risking life and limb again. Forget I said anything."

Shaw appears to take this more literally than I'd hoped.

Not that, in fact, I am too worried. Hell, I saved the goddamn world yesterday. A creature so alien it almost turned my sanity into a small squeezable plaything was involved. And I was on the winning side. How much trouble can a T-Rex be?

But complaining about it is easier than dealing with the other thing I did yesterday. Which was sleep with Shaw.

Sleeping with your boss, my television has reliably informed me, is rarely a wise decision. Relationships, especially new ones, are tenuous things with only a frail grip on life. Like a newborn monkey on the Discovery channel—adorable and sweet one moment, flinging shit at the camera the next.

When you add on the fact that you and your boss work for a clandestine government agency that deals with threats to national security that are a little more than mundane, the whole not-sleeping-with-your-boss thing seems to take on an extra layer of urgency.

Not that I regret the act. Not at all. Far from it. And it's not just the usual gratitude I'd feel towards anyone looking to get Biblical with me. Shaw is a genuinely smart, funny, and attractive woman. She is... well I could get sappy, and there's the rub, as Hamlet probably wouldn't have put it. Because Shaw isn't a sappy woman. She's a highly trained monster killer.

A highly trained monster killer who seems entirely unfazed by the whole bedding-of-a-subordinate thing. There again, since I met her, my life has been on an oddly accelerated track. Forget saving the world for a moment, it's barely a week since she recruited me from the Oxford police force where I was happily chasing down a serial killer. My entire training for this job has consisted of a lifetime's dedication to Kurt Russell movies.

The fact that the aforementioned serial killer is now my co-worker, Kayla, and that her superpowers are only outnumbered by her psychoses is entirely incidental at this point.

Still, the fact that Shaw's out in the field is odd. The directorship is a largely behind-the-scenes role. She hired me as the field lead.

Not for my own mad monster-slaying skills—that's a little

bit of a work in progress—but rather my mad cat herding skills. Kayla is not Shaw's only troublesome employee.

So—the question niggles in my brain—why exactly is she on the train with me? What exactly happened in Shaw's bed last night?

Aside from… well… I am intimately aware with the mechanical aspects. It's the other…

Well…

And of course, I should just ask her. I saved the world yesterday. I can now confidently say that Felicity Shaw is not the scariest thing I have ever faced. But still the train rattles on, and I rattle about in it, and we continue to avoid the subject.

NOW

"You know," I say to Shaw, "I sort of expected this to go better."

She doesn't reply. She's too busy kicking in a door and looking for an exit route.

I take aim with my pistol and provide covering fire. To be honest though, the aiming thing is barely necessary. The T-Rex is the size of a bus and is heading straight for me. Moldering flesh hangs off its massive head. Gray, gelatinous eyes roll in that head. The bullets ping and pop off its cheekbones, exposing the yellowing skull.

It takes another thunderous step in our direction.

"You getting on any better with that door?" I take the time to ask.

"You getting on any better with slowing that fucking thing down?"

I try aiming for its kneecaps.

Another footfall like a grenade going off.

"Oh sod it." I'd be doing as much good with a popgun. I turn and lend my foot to Felicity. We both kick the door at the same time, and the hinges decide to give before the lock. It crashes to the floor revealing a narrow corridor lined with precious-looking things.

Despite the years of human cultural history packed along the walls, what really appeals about the corridor is that it's a sort of not-T-Rex-width narrow. Right now that's my favorite kind of narrow.

Felicity and I break into the sort of run Olympic sprinters

would be proud of. A roar crashes after us. Massive vases—priceless testaments to mankind's artistic achievements—shatter in our wake.

Felicity dives around a corner and I follow her. I slam my body up against the wall. I decide to tell myself I'm taking cover. It sounds significantly better than "cowering."

FIFTEEN MINUTES AGO

It's raining when Shaw and I head up from the Underground station. A police car and several chaps in uniform are arranged around the museum gates. A small crowd of tourists is gathered before them.

We flash ID and the uniforms let us through the cordon. I get to learn epithets for queue jumpers in fourteen different languages.

A man in a beaten-up brown suit is waiting for us beyond the museum gates, trying to look inconspicuous against a backdrop of rhododendrons. He peers out at us from beneath a sagging umbrella as we draw close.

"You military intelligence?" he asks us. His voice is all cockney.

"Yes," we both answer at the same time.

"Inspector Chevy." He grimaces as if the sound of his name upsets him. "Don't ask me much, 'cos I don't know bollocks." He seems to be struggling to decide which one of us he should be addressing. "All I have is that something went down about two hours ago. By the time I get here, we're clearing folks faster than curry clears the colon, and some civil servant is telling me no one's allowed in, including my lads and lasses. Folk are on their way, I'm told. In the meantime, civilian militia is slowing stuff down."

"Civilian militia?" I double-check I heard that right.

He stares right back. "I bloody told you," he says. "I don't know bollocks." He wrinkles his nose. "Anyway, I sit here, twiddle my thumbs, and then Glum and Glummer show up and give everyone the creeps, and now you're here."

He nods at the steps that lead up to the museum's grand portico. Two figures huddle together in the rain, one improbably tall and slender, the other shorter and improbably pissed off at the world.

A smile crosses my lips. More co-workers: Clyde and Tabitha.

"Just go in, sort it out, and don't tell me nothing." Inspector Chevy shakes his head like a dog shedding water.

"Thank you, Inspector." Shaw gives him a warmer smile than he deserves. "We'll take it from here."

"Bloody right you will." He makes a hunched retreat back to the uniforms at the gates.

"Britain doesn't have a civilian militia, does it?" I thought I knew the answer to that, but assumptions haven't done me well since I joined MI37.

"No." Shaw nods.

It turns out there is a wide gap between affirmation and reassurance.

NOW

"That's not a good sign."

I stare at the approximately T-Rex-sized hole in the wall of the Hall of Mammals. I look down at my pistol. "No chance MI37 has a stash of much bigger guns hidden somewhere on site, is there?"

"Arthur," Shaw looks at me, "we had to take the train to a national emergency. What on earth makes you think I have the budget for better weapons?"

"Saving the world. Like we did yesterday." And that really does seem relevant here.

"At what point in between you taking my clothes off and now did you see me debrief the budgetary committee?"

I shrug. "All I'm saying, is that this would go significantly better if someone gave me a bazooka."

God, I would love to have a bazooka. Though I think I'd be tempted to just frame it and hang it on the wall of my apartment, which would rather defeat the point. So, I suppose I want two bazookas. One for aesthetic purposes, and one for blowing the living crap out of zombie dinosaurs.

Still... I look down at my pistol.

What would Kurt Russell do?

God, that question gets me in so much bloody trouble.
Still, it does simplify matters. I step through the hole.

TWELVE MINUTES AGO

Tabitha and Clyde wait on the museum steps. Tabitha—five feet of angry Pakistani goth largely covered in white ink tattoos. MI37's researcher, and computer expert. A walking, talking... well, cursing database of forbidden knowledge. She appears to have shaved half her head since I saw her last. The remaining hair is dyed a deep maroon. The newly exposed skin is pale, like coffee with too much milk in it, covered by a fine grain of stubble.

Man, I wish I hadn't just thought of furry coffee...

Clyde is harder to get a read on. This is largely because of his recently adjusted physical status. When I first met Clyde he was a scruffy, nerdy-looking man in tweed who kept talking about electricity as the universal lubricant between realities, and who put batteries in his mouth to do magic. Then his head was invaded by an alien. And then I shot him, which I'd rather not think about. But he was dead. And then... God, this is complicated. But there was an ancient, magical, Peruvian mask that he'd written his personality onto. There was a good reason for it at the time, I'm sure. But we had that, so we had a back-up Clyde. So now Clyde is a blank wooden mask strapped to the body of an impossibly tall, impossibly thin, elfin-looking man.

And that's actually one of the more normal things that I have to deal with.

Clyde, though, has decided to compound the mind-buggering by forgoing his traditional collegiate attire in favor of a decidedly un-Clyde-like hoodie, a leering skull emblazoned across the front, bisected by a zipper. The hood itself is large enough that it could be used to smuggle small children through border checkpoints.

I raise both my eyebrows. "I know. I know," Clyde says. "Fully aware of the wardrobe situation. *Compos wardrobis.* Not real Latin that, of course. I mean the real Latin would be..."

Shaw adds another raised eyebrow, making a triumvirate.

"Well," Clyde continues, "it's just... All my old clothes were back at my flat, and last time I went there I wasn't a wooden mask strapped to a lanky blond giant. Not that I should be demeaning about a chap's physical appearance, of course. Rather impolite as I am sort of wearing him. Not exactly self-deprecation anymore. But anyway, the thing is, Tabby rather wisely pointed out that the whole mask thing may lead to some concern amongst civilians, the uninitiated, plebs, muggles, et cetera, and that some sort of hood device might be in order. And then, I did rather fancy the idea of some sort of cowl with moons and stars and such, proper Gandalf gear, but it's Sunday, and I'm suddenly seven feet tall."

"Friend of mine," Tabitha adds. "Owed me."

Clyde gives one of his profoundly expressive shrugs that seems to sum up the whole story of how the hoodie was acquired. And Clyde may now be a digital copy of the deceased man I called a friend trapped in an ancient Peruvian mask, and he may not look like my friend, he may not even sound exactly like him, but Clyde is somehow undeniably himself. It's good to see him. I smile.

"I'd be lost without her." Clyde turns his head and the mask stares blankly down at Tabitha. I imagine it's meant to be a tender gaze.

Tabitha rolls her eyes.

But, yes, I was not the only one to celebrate saving the world last night.

"Excellent," Shaw says in a slightly perfunctory way. "Good thinking." She clears her throat. "Any actual insight on the situation?" She looks from Clyde to Tabitha.

Tabitha whips her laptop from a shoulder bag with the speed of a Wild West gunslinger. "Not much," she says. "Extra-reality animating force. Most likely. Summoned. Invested into T-Rex skeleton."

"Wait," I say, because I need time with these things. "An animating force. From another reality?" Tabitha nods to let me know I'm keeping up. She looks bored.

"An animating force," I repeat, "from another reality. And jammed into a T-Rex skeleton."

"Invested into it, actually." Clyde corrects my nomenclature.

I mask my inner bewilderment with balderdash. "So not really a zombie T-Rex then," I say. "Just a skeleton."

"Disappointed?" Tabitha asks.

And I have to concede it isn't quite as cool as I'd hoped, but that's not an entirely professional thing to admit. So instead I go with, "Do we have any idea who did the whole summoning and investing bit yet?"

"Quintessential bad guy," Clyde says. "Nefarious plans and all. Ready to be thwarted."

"Well." Shaw claps her hands. "No time like the present."

I look around at the gray day, the dripping bushes, the gaggle of angry tourists. "Anybody know Kayla's status?" I ask. Because if your team does include a supersoldier, it seems to make sense to have her around. There's nothing like a superhuman swordswoman to make the animated T-Rex skeleton blues go away, I find.

"Oh," says Shaw with a shake of the head and another pat on the arm, "she probably jogged here already. Takes her half the time the trains do."

"Probably taken care of everything already," Clyde says. "Knowing her."

TWO MINUTES AGO

I would be the first to admit that Kayla and I have not always seen eye to eye. Take the time she stabbed me in the lung, for example. That said, I am more than willing to be the bigger man, to move past our differences, and face evil side by side.

Or, to put it another way—where the hell is she, and why the hell is my bacon not being saved?

Instead of waiting for an answer, I start running.

I'm not sure it's exactly what Kurt Russell would do, but sometimes self-preservation has to win over your traditional eighties action movie muse.

Behind me the T-Rex's jaws slam shut. A triceratops skeleton that formerly resembled excellent cover starts to look more like matchsticks. Stringy flaps of moldering T-Rex skin quiver at the impact of the monstrous jaws.

Shaw comes up from behind a bench, firing. Chips of bone and rotten flesh spatter away from the T-Rex's chest. It doesn't even turn to face her.

I definitely thought we were going to make it further than ten feet into the museum.

Clyde stands in front of Tabitha, arms out, protective. She seems oblivious, tapping madly away on her laptop. I'd love to take the time to appreciate the sweetness of the moment, but I'm too busy crab-crawling backwards over the ruins of an information booth and trying to keep the T-Rex from bisecting me. I take a few potshots at the zombie's eyes. The T-Rex seems to have maxed out on fury, so they don't even serve to piss it off anymore.

Clyde grabs a battery from his pocket. With elegant, piano-player fingers he slips it up under the surface of the mask, into his mouth. He bows his head. The T-Rex advances. I hit the back wall. Shaw reloads desperately.

Tabitha says something inaudible to Clyde. His arms explode outward, violently flinging fistfuls of nothing at the ragged dinosaur skeleton.

It squeals, staggers sideways, trips over itself. Its head smacks against a mezzanine walkway with a spattering of plaster.

Behind Clyde, Tabitha fist pumps.

I'm back on my feet. The T-Rex struggles to gain its own. Head down, I scramble toward Shaw.

The T-Rex bellows again. Clyde balls his fists, pulls them into his chest, preparing the next blast. I imagine I can hear him muttering magical gibberish underneath his mask.

The T-Rex arcs round. Its tail blurs, traceable only through the wake of destruction. A vase becomes so much powder. A brontosaurus femur becomes a complicated jigsaw puzzle.

Tabitha and Clyde become rag dolls.

The tail connects, lifts them both into the air, slaps them carelessly away. Clyde barrels over Tabitha in midair. He hits double doors. They swing wide. Both figures tumble through. Dismissed.

The T-Rex peers at where I'm hunkered beside Shaw. I aim at its nostrils and attempt to widen the holes. The T-Rex screams, its undead breath wafting over us, filling my nose with the scent of decay. It is definitely more of a zombie T-Rex and less of a skeleton T-Rex.

I am less enthusiastic about this fact than I was a few minutes ago.

Shaw fires. The bullet ricochets off the T-Rex's ribs with a whine, buries itself in a wall somewhere.

The T-Rex paws the ground with a massive foot.

I pop my pistol's magazine, slam a fresh one home. I turn to Shaw. "I don't suppose there's a chance," I say, "that we get the day off on the grounds of, you know, saving the world yesterday?"

2

NOW

The T-Rex is gone from the main hall. Priceless artifacts crashing to the ground mark its progress a few halls distant.

Tabitha and Clyde stagger through the door on the hall's opposite side, arms around each other more for support than to display affection.

"Well," Shaw says. "That wasn't exactly according to plan."

Maybe we should claim the plan was for us to have our arses handed to us. Still, a new one wouldn't go amiss. Step one: dealing with information gaps.

"Didn't we agree it was going to be a skeleton?" I say. "It's... fleshier than I expected."

"Showing off. Bad guy is, " Tabitha says, without even opening her laptop. "Glamour."

I love the way this job just keeps finding new concepts to totally mess with my head. "English version?" I request.

"Illusion magic," Shaw supplies.

"OK," I say, processing that. "Obviously the kicking-everyone's-ass plan has issues. Probably time for a more nuanced approach." I try to think at the same rate my heart is beating. "While the T-Rex is the only thing trying to nibble our legs off, it's a secondary problem." I nod to myself, and hope the others come with me on that one. "Whoever created it is our primary target. We take him down, the T-Rex falls too."

"Agreed." Shaw nods. Which is nice.

Tabitha rolls her eyes. Which is not.

"Excellent," Clyde says. "Totally agree. Except... well, not really an objection, just a question. Seeking clarity on just one issue. Probably just being dense. But this chap we're trying to find. Or chap-ess. Villainy is gender neutral, I'm sure. But anyway I was really just wondering, how do we find him? Or her?"

I open my mouth. Close it again. I look to Shaw to see if she wants to leap into the leadership breach, but she doesn't seem to have anything to add.

I'd rather come up with a better plan than following the T-Rex. The further we can keep from that bastard the better. I scan the hallway in search of inspiration. It looks like a bomb went off. Rubble is strewn everywhere—chips of marble, porcelain, bone, and pottery. I see the remnants of the information booth that I stumbled through—the tattered entrails of a computer, discarded ballpoint pens, a crushed security camera...

Security cameras...

"Security cameras!" I say.

Everyone looks at me. There's a familiar moment of panic that I should have gotten over by now. "The T-Rex can't have destroyed all the security cameras in the museum yet," I say.

"Good thinking." Shaw nods tightly. I get a moment of warm fuzzies. "Tabitha," Shaw turns to our researcher, "a floor plan."

A few moments and violated firewalls later, Tabitha says, "Basement."

We move in a tight diamond. Shaw takes point, Clyde tails behind. I can hear the coppertop clacking against his teeth beneath the mask. I walk next to Tabitha, the shaved side of her head. She catches me looking.

"Nice haircut," I say. I try to breathe enthusiasm into the compliment. I am not so good at that.

Tabitha gives me the finger. It's rather sweet for her.

She guides us to a locked door marked "Staff Only" and

Shaw produces a rather complicated-looking key which opens it without protest.

"That legal?" Tabitha asks.

Shaw ignores her. Which pretty much confirms that Shaw is apparently the type to carry around rings full of illegal skeleton keys.

This is the point where I should be charmed to find out something new and previously hidden about my new girlfriend. Being intimidated... well, I'll pretend that's close enough.

Stairs lead down. I go to take a step, but Clyde catches my elbow. I stand aside, but suspect chivalry probably isn't his motivator for letting Shaw and Tabitha go first.

Clyde shuffles his feet and doesn't say anything. It's a maneuver his new body doesn't seem designed for. A movement from his old self.

"So," I say, taking a stab at the most obvious topic, "you and Tabitha."

"Yes," he says. He doesn't sound as enthusiastic as I'd imagine he would, given the length of time he let the crush fester.

But I suspect I know the fly in the ointment. Devon. The girl, not the shire. Because, I've no idea how Clyde feels about the south-west of England, but Devon-the-girl is Clyde's ex of about ten hours. I also suspect she's the main reason Clyde didn't go back to his flat and try to find more suitable attire, no matter what he says to the contrary.

"Well, I'm sure..." I start. "I mean... I assume Shaw's going to declare you dead. Which obviously—"

"Oh," Clyde says. The sort of "oh" that means that something unpleasant is going to happen to my assumptions again.

"What?" I say.

"I may have phoned her."

That one actually rocks me back on my feet. I have to take a step backwards.

"You did what? You're in a new body. You've left her for another woman. Why did you...?" I can't finish. I can't comprehend the logic. Why would you do that to a nice girl like Devon?

"Well," he twists his long elegant hands, "I didn't sort of in any way take into account the declaration of death thing. And, anyway, the really important news, I thought, and maybe my judgment was clouded at the time by the, erm, well, I don't want to go into details. But Tabby was involved at the time, and if we could leave it at that..."

God, please let us leave it at that. And this is hardly the most appropriate time for this conversation. Except Clyde is our big gun, the only one who the T-Rex even seemed to notice. And, more importantly, he's a friend. Plus, for a man without a face, Clyde looks remarkably shame-faced.

"You see," he twists his long elegant hands, "the thing is, well... I was thinking... Usually a mistake, I realize. But Devon wasn't aware of the entire situation vis-à-vis my sudden reduction in corporeality. And I thought, well, Tabitha suggested, helpfully I think, though maybe in retrospect I should have reconsidered, but... Well I didn't want to have to muddy the waters while clarifying the whole relationship point by having to clarify the whole being-a-wooden-mask point, so I sort of, maybe, perhaps, and, like I say, hindsight, twenty-twenty, all that stuff, but I sort of broke up with her over the phone."

Wow.

Such... Devon... Just a nice girl. And why would you...

Except, maybe he wasn't wrong. At least if he didn't realize we were going to declare him dead. In that situation, how can you both show up on someone's doorstep as a mask, and dump them in the same conversation? But holy hell.

"How long were you guys dating?" I say, which is not an entirely politic question.

"Twelve years," Clyde says with remarkable succinctness.

"Jesus."

I can picture Devon—an impregnable fortress of happiness in sudden and abrupt defeat. I feel bad for her. She deserved better. But I don't know exactly what better would be in this situation.

I start down the stairs. "Assuming we make it out of this place in the usual number of pieces," I say to Clyde, "you want to grab a pint later?"

"That does sound like a rather good plan."

So that'll make at least one today if the security camera thing doesn't work out.

Above our heads, the T-Rex roars. A rattle like gunfire replies. I remember Inspector Chevy talking about civilian militia. And where are they in all this? Who are they? Remembering the way Shaw's bullets ricocheted off the T-Rex's bones, I rather doubt I'll get to meet any of them.

The security room is a poorly lit, low-ceilinged room with far too many TVs coating one wall. Three are blank. Others show the rooms above us, some still whole, some less so. But no T-Rex. No villainous spell-caster.

I rather expected an array of colored buttons and glowing panels worthy of James Tiberius Kirk and boldly going where no man had gone before, but instead there is just one desultory-looking computer the same shade of brown as the seventies.

"Tabitha," Shaw says, and nods at it.

And should that be my line? Not that I should begrudge my boss taking charge. And I don't really know why I should object to someone taking the pressure off me. Give me more time to concentrate on not being eaten. Except… Does she not trust me? Is she just being protective of me, now that we're an item? Is she thinking of taking me out of the field?

Am I just over-thinking things?

Tabitha sits and starts pressing buttons. The TVs switch images with little spits of static. One by one by one. Another hall. Another. The same hall from a different angle. The same shots of nothing and nobody.

"Faster," Shaw urges.

"This is it." Tabitha seems unsure of whether to give her evil eye to Shaw or the computer. "My Google fu: strong. My security knowledge: excellent. My supernatural ability to overcome shitty programming: not real. Could rewrite the program. You got a spare half hour?"

Shaw shakes her head, more in frustration than in answer. Tabitha keeps clicking. The images drag through their cycle. Another hall. Another. Another. Nothing. Nobody.

From the corner of my eye, I catch Clyde standing next to me, twitching. I look at him to be sure, to try and work it out. Tabitha clicks. An image changes. Clyde twitches. She clicks. He spasms.

Every time she hits the button—a tremor running through his body.

"They're wireless," he says, catching my eye.

"Come again?"

"All the cameras," he says, gesturing to the screens with a trembling hand. "No wires. Pinocchio-esque, one might say. Well, one probably wouldn't. Horrible adjective, but you get the idea."

Tabitha looks up from her console. "How do you know that?"

Clyde tilts his head, saying nothing. I try to read him. He used to be so obvious, every emotion writ large across his face. But now there's nothing. Utterly blank. He looks... inhuman feels like the wrong word. But suddenly what he's lost is very apparent.

"I can feel them," he says. "I can..." He trails off.

"What?" Shaw urges. "Information, Clyde. Keep the team in the loop." She sounds like she's summarizing a training manual.

There's a decent chance that instead of worrying about why she's in the field, I should be taking notes.

Still Clyde says nothing. Tabitha is watching him, some distant cousin of concern on her face, finger poised above the keyboard of the computer. The televisions illuminate us in wan light.

I'm trying to think of something incisive and commanding to say when all the TVs go white. Tabitha is a black gothic silhouette framed next to the computer. The edges of Shaw's face are shown in sharp detail.

Clyde's body snaps up like a dancer's. He's balanced on the tip of his toes, body arched back. Like a live wire is stuck to his spine. A violent shudder runs down his spine, through his arms, his legs. He starts to shiver, a violent tremble.

"Clyde?" Tabitha has cranked up the volume of her concern.

The blare of light from the TVs is unrelenting. And then something flickers, a trembling shadow from the monitors. Everyone's gaze twitches. Clyde twitches. An image appears on one screen. Then on another. Clyde twitches again. He starts to jerk. Another image. Another image.

"Not me," Tabitha says, her professional calm definitely abandoned now. "It's not me."

Still Clyde twitches. Still the images change. Faster now. One image. Another. Another. My eye tries to track the images but they pick up speed. Clyde is shuddering, no gap between each jerk. His mask shakes, precarious on his head. The spasms grow larger, more violent.

"Clyde!" Tabitha is out of her seat, reaching out to him.

"Clyde, stop." Shaw's bark is intended to be obeyed.

But he doesn't. His fingers blur. His wrists.

Electrocution? Except there are no wires. No electricity. And I've seen Clyde electrocute himself in the name of magic. This is different. Something stranger.

A seizure?

I move toward him. I grab his hand, try to calm that at least. It's like trying to wrestle a runaway jackhammer. I scan the desks for a ruler, something I can jam in his mouth to try and stop him from chewing his tongue off.

Suddenly Clyde stops. The TV images stop. Clyde stands still, panting hard.

You could hear a pin drop. At least you could if Clyde would stop panting for two seconds. We're all staring at him. I let go of his arm. It seems a little odd all of a sudden.

Clyde flips an exhausted hand at the TVs. "There," he says, and there's a smile in his voice even if it's not on his face. "Got them."

His mask is focused on the TVs.

Our eyes flick there.

Sixteen images. Sixteen continuous feeds. Not a flicker on them. A shattered door. A wall with a T-Rex-sized dent in it. A T-Rex denting walls. An Asian woman, early thirties, firing a semi-automatic pistol. A teenage girl with headphones the size of soup cans over her ears and a revolver in each hand. A middle-aged black man with… wait, is that an assault rifle? Seriously?

And more. A bullet-pocked security bench. Shattered glass on a mosaic floor. And there—Clyde's quintessential bad guy. A stocky, hard-faced woman. A substantial amount of robotics strapped to her left side. A vast spark arcs from a wall toward her, then leaps away from her outstretched palm and beyond the limits of the camera's vision. In another screen the black man leaps sideways. The screen goes dark. The image blinks, another angle of the man sprawled out, a smoking scar in the floor behind him.

And I don't know how—I'm actually a little scared of "how"—but Clyde's right. He's got them.

3

We all take a moment to be a little stunned. Which is a nice change of pace, I think.

"I didn't know I could do that." Clyde sounds as shocked as the rest of us look.

Tabitha is staring at the computer. "You did that? How?"

"I…" Clyde shakes his head. "I could feel them. In my head. Like thoughts. And then… I don't know. Just thinking about them differently. And on the screen…"

"You, sir," I say, wrestling my confusion under temporary control, "are one useful bugger, aren't you?"

"But, was it…? Are *you* wireless?" Tabitha asks.

"Not now," Shaw's voice cuts through. She points to the screen. "We will work this out. But not now. Now we go save the day." She slides the action back on her pistol to emphasize her point.

She is so obscenely badass at that moment I have to admit I am briefly distracted by thoughts of some very naughty things indeed.

But, she's right. Now is not exactly the time for that sort of thing.

"Where are they?" I ask, pointing to the three people with guns. Surely the militia that Inspector Chevy was talking about.

Clyde bows his head. A shudder runs down his spine. Some of the cameras start panning about, zooming in on pockmarked displays and wall posters.

And OK, that's a little creepy.

But still useful. "Minerals," I say. There are large crystalline chunks of rock scattered everywhere. A picture of a volcano against one wall. It's not the hardest piece of detective work I've ever done.

"Route incoming," Tabitha says. She moves even as she taps on her laptop. "Got it." Shaw kicks the door open and we're off again.

TWO MINUTES LATER

Finally: Kayla. She's waiting for us in the lobby when we get there.

Except… The word "supersoldier" obviously has some baggage that comes with it. The captain of a certain nation across the pond is probably responsible for that. There are images of thick-armed men with can-do attitudes, patriotic shields, and Lycra outfits that laugh in the face of fashion laws.

Our supersoldier kicks disconsolately at rubble. Her hair is greasy, disheveled, reminiscent of someone who either just got out of bed or out of a high-end Soho beauty salon. Her shirt is more wrinkled than an octogenarian's elbow. I'm pretty sure her shoes are on the wrong feet.

To be fair, this is worse than normal. And, considering her week has probably been worse than mine, she's doing pretty well.

I, at least, am not down two foster children. Kayla on the other hand is dealing with the fact that one of hers had her brain eaten by aliens, and that the other became a demigod who popped the first one out of existence. Basically, she's been through a lot lately and if she wants to take it out on her wardrobe I'm not going to comment.

"There you are," I say, as gentle and supportive as it's possible to address a woman you once believed was a serial killer and who popped your lung one time.

"Situation?" Shaw ignores the softly, softly approach and cuts straight to the chase.

Kayla shrugs. "Just got here." Her Scottish brogue is so thick right now, individual words are barely discernible.

"You OK?" I ask. It's a stupid question. Kayla's not been OK since she was twelve and the aforementioned aliens took over her family and she had to kill them all to survive. I can't think of anything that could have happened recently to have improved that situation.

Kayla doesn't even tell me to feck off, though, which rather underscores the severity of how not OK she is.

"You need to sit this one out?" I ask.

Shaw gives me a sharp look. Apparently that is not the plan. For her part, Kayla gives me a lack-luster middle finger.

"That's the spirit," Clyde says.

I can hear roaring and fully automatic fire and explosions, and the clock ticking. And we do not have the time to counsel Kayla now. And I know Shaw thinks we need her. And I know Shaw is probably right. She usually is. But, punctured lung or no, I do not want to see Kayla come to harm because her head is so far out of the game it's in another building.

"Kayla?" I say.

"We need her." Shaw's voice has an edge. I think it's a testament to our budding romance that she doesn't just directly tell me to shut up.

Kayla sticks with the sullen silence. She doesn't even disappear at superhuman speed looking for something to stab. Just shuffles into line behind Tabitha.

It's a bad call. I can feel it. If Kayla doesn't get hurt then someone relying on her will.

"I think—" I start.

"We need her." Shaw's voice is a rod of iron coming down on the floor. And I get the feeling that's what it's like when she pulls rank.

I consider pushing it, but it seems early in the relationship for open insubordination.

Shaw turns her back, leads the way. Tabitha saunters past, a little smile on her lips. "Just fuck her," she says. "Not with her."

MINERALS EXHIBIT

The floor is a glittering death trap. Shards of rock attempt to turn my ankle every step. One slip and I'll come up studded with more gems than a rapper's necklace.

The gunfire has risen from a background crackle to an insistent thunder. Bowel-shuddering roars underscore the soundtrack of violence. We break into a run through the detritus of the battle. Double doors mark the line between us and harm's way.

"OK," I say, trying to think it all through as we accelerate. "Clyde, you're the only one the T-Rex seems to notice. You focus on that. Tabitha, you stay here. Give Clyde the info he needs. Stay out of harm's way. And Kayla—" I glance over at her. I'm still unconvinced we can rely on her. But I can't think of anyone else here who can deal with the T-Rex's full attention. "—you buy Clyde the time he needs to take it out." Which leaves. "Felicity—" I start.

"You and I are on the primary. Take out the wizard responsible for this. Defending the Weekenders is secondary. They got themselves in this mess."

She's the boss. But who are the Weekenders? Then there's no time to ask. The doors fly wide. Shaw slides through them like Rooney sliding in to put it over the goal line. I shove my earpiece into place. Clyde barrels after Shaw, his substitute body shifting up to ridiculous speed. I elbow my way through. Sweep my pistol in a large arc.

Destruction. Pure and simple. The T-Rex stands at its heart, head pressed to the ceiling. It twists, fixes its piggy eyes upon us, scrapes great swaths of plaster free.

It's meatier than the last time I saw it. For all the ammunition emptied into it, it's somehow got more flesh on its bones. Scabs of green skin stretch over the exposed muscles of its barrel chest.

Lightning lances across the room. A display case disappears in an explosion of steel and splinters.

I blink in the aftershock, seeking the source. The far end of the room is raised, separated by a few steps and a low stone wall. Bullets chew the wall's surface, while I scan for signs of life.

Clyde and Shaw huddle behind the remnants of another display case. The top has been sheared away, glass scattered about them.

I run. Head down. The T-Rex roars. The glass on the floor jumps and rattles. By the time I crash into the display case I've sweat through my jacket. I peer around the corner. The T-Rex is lowering its head. Where's Kayla? Isn't she meant to—

The double doors swing wide and Kayla saunters through. Like

John Wayne with a hard-on for gunslinging. Except Kayla is about a hundred and fifty pounds lighter than John Wayne. And has no guns.

Lightning strobes past her. A crater appears in the wall behind her. Stone shards fly. She doesn't even flinch. Her sword blade trails her, bouncing and skittering off the floor.

The T-Rex unleashes another shuddering howl. Kayla stops walking. My pulse finds a higher gear.

The T-Rex paws the ground like a bull with 'roid rage. I swear it curls a lip in a sneer. It reveals teeth. Sharp and glistening now. Teeth for slicing, for tearing. Kayla just stands there, unflinching.

The growl builds like an oncoming train. The T-Rex paws the floor. Its talons tear great chunks of rock free.

And, seriously, is Kayla ever going to look up? It just doesn't seem safe at this point.

The T-Rex charges, each footfall an earthquake. Its jaws stretch. And stretch. I open fire. Everyone opens fire. Its flesh ripples as bullets pour into its sides. It doesn't deviate an inch. Just barrels on. Death and dust billow in its wake.

It's not slowing. It's yards from Kayla. Feet. Inches. She stands so still. The T-Rex brays in victory.

And then, finally, she moves. The sword flies out, my heart leaps, my stomach drops—

Kayla bats the T-Rex's head out of the way. The dinosaur skids past her, slams into the wall. It sways, dizzy. Kayla looks like she never moved. Standing, sword loose at her side. Barely watching.

The T-Rex recovers fast. It spins. Its tail races toward her. She ducks. But… well, it's too fast to call it lazy exactly, but by Kayla's standards it's barely moving at all.

The T-Rex spins again, lunges. The flat of Kayla's blade drives its head up. The ceiling plaster crunches under the impact, hemorrhages wires and air conditioning. But there is no follow-up. There is no death-defying leap, no stabbing, or slicing, or dicing. Just these halfhearted dismissals.

The T-Rex comes at her again. Again. Again. She slaps at it, twitches aside. Again. Again. Again.

"You know," says Clyde, crouched beside me, "I'm not sure that is the spirit after all."

Damn it. I should have said more to Shaw. I should have stood my ground. Except... Where is the line now? Which side of the bed?

"Kayla!" Shaw yells, trying to break through, trying to snap her out of the funk.

Another lightning bolt. The three well-armed civilians on the other side of the hall dive for cover. Chunks of ceiling rain down on them.

"Plus side," I say. "The T-Rex is distracted." Lead with optimism, I figure.

Shaw nods. "We move on the primary. Clyde, prepare whatever you've got. Arthur, get close. I'll cover you."

Ah, point man, my favorite. Still, I need to put in more time at the range if I want to be a good enough shot to hang back and snipe at things.

A couple of deep breaths, then I go for it. Head down. Arse out. Break cover. Scramble forward.

Bullets fill the air. Knowing they're not aimed at me doesn't make it any better.

I make it to one display case, spot a pile of rubble that looks like cover, dive for it. Behind me, the T-Rex bellows. I want to turn, to look, to make sure it's not closing, not chewing on Kayla while she stares at its teeth, a look of boredom on her face. But I can't because here comes the lightning storm.

I'm half running, half dancing. And screw cover, it's down the middle of the hall now. I fire blindly. The room explodes around me in strobe flares of light. Stone and wood and glass score my cheeks. I scream obscenities, and then just scream. I'm barely on my feet now, skittering forward. I can't see. I can't—

The blast lifts me off my feet. It feels like being the center of the world. A great, tearing change in perspective, slamming me into the very heart of creation. Suddenly all there is, is white, is pain—a great hollow sphere of it surrounding me.

And then back to reality, to flying across the room. A sprawl of limbs as graceless as balled paper tossed at a trashcan.

4

I land. The impact jars my bones, blurs my vision. My teeth chomp on the inside of my mouth, draw blood. I roll like a rag doll. My limbs are distant memories.

Instead of the wall ending my passage with a crunch, it's a person with an "oomph." They collapse on top of me. My eyes focus for at least a second. It's the pretty Asian woman with the automatic pistol. She sits up, shakes plaster from her hair. My head is in her lap. She smiles down at me, curiously calm in the middle of the madness.

"Hello," she says, "I'm Aiko. Nice to meet you."

I go with the more casual, "Gnnnfgg nnn."

I try to roll off her. There's a blinding pain in my left shoulder and my left foot. That whole side of my body feels loose—skin and bone turned to so much jelly.

"Arthur! Arthur!" Someone's calling my name. I go to turn my head but decide to spasm helplessly instead.

Shaw skids across the floor. Clyde flails his way through lightning strikes behind her. Shaw grabs me off Aiko's lap. Claims me.

"You're alive?" Shaw says. She runs a hand over my forehead.

I'm blinking a lot and twitching so that seems to confirm it for her. She does the thoughtful thing, turning away and emptying a magazine in the direction of the lightning-slinger. It's rather sweet.

Another lightning bolt blasts past. Clyde yells. Shaw curses, tugs another magazine from an inside pocket. I struggle to bring my limbs online, managing to use my right elbow to get upright.

The Asian woman, Aiko, leans forward, puts a hand on my shoulder.

"You should probably—" she starts.

"Get off him," Shaw snaps. "And get out of here. We don't need casualties."

Aiko bristles visibly. She removes the hand from my shoulder. That's good—bearing the extra weight was a little much for me right now. "Where were you while we staved off a double-digit body count?"

Shaw fires in the direction of the lightning-slinger without taking her eyes off Aiko. "I am more than happy to arrest you for illegal weapon possession." She wears a tight smile.

Another different decision from the one I'd have gone with. And I'm going to have to call her on one of these, but right now I'm playing the twitching injured guy, so I let her have it.

The T-Rex interrupts the nascent feud. Its tail sweeps overhead. Display cases detonate. Glass shards and mineral missiles fill the air.

"Will somebody make that fucking dinosaur extinct already?" Shaw yells. She looks distinctly less cool than when we arrived here. For people who saved the world yesterday, we're looking spectacularly outclassed.

"Clyde," I manage, "what have you got? Anything that can evict an animating force?" The words are strained.

Clyde touches his earpiece. "Tabby," he says. "Trying to think of a way to remove an animating force. Anti-magic doo-dad. Wondering, if you have a moment that is, if you could check the database."

If she has a moment? What the hell does he think she's doing out there? Crocheting mittens for any reanimated triceratops she happens across?

Kayla still bats at the T-Rex's head as if disciplining a troublesome dog. Shaw mutters her name along with some select curse words.

"Animating force," Tabitha's voice comes back. "Invested in

skeleton." Though the T-Rex is hardly a skeleton now. Skin covers most of it, exposed muscle and gristle the rest. "Rather than removing force, remove skeleton. Nothing for force to cling to."

Filet a T-Rex. Well that should be easy.

"Explosive kinetic force, located centrally?" Clyde says.

I like the bit where he uses the word "explosive."

Tabitha grunts.

Clyde nods. Then he looks to Shaw. "Excuse me," he says. "Don't mean to interrupt—"

"Spit it out."

"I don't suppose you happen to have a grenade on you, do you?"

Which is a slightly more mundane solution than I was thinking we'd go for. I could have thought of blowing it up with a grenade.

Shaw reaches into another inner suit pocket and removes a thin steel canister. I am beginning to think I should never go through her pocket book.

"Excellent," Clyde says lightly as more of the room disintegrates around us. "Just need to get it inside the T-Rex now."

And, I admit, I would not have thought of that bit.

Shaw blinks. "All right then," she says, and goes to stand up.

I'm not entirely sure if it's because I have tender feelings for Shaw, or because of a sense of duty, or because of the blows to the head, but I reach out a hand to stop her.

"No," I say. "You're still a better shot than me." I manage to get my face muscles to stop spasming long enough to smile. "Primary objective and all that. You stay here, shoot the evil cow with the lightning, protect Clyde. I'll go."

"Arthur—" she starts.

"Oh," I smile, "I can't have been that good in bed."

That line clearly sounded cooler in my head. Even Clyde's blank mask looks shocked.

I rather hope the T-Rex does get me now.

To cover the moment, I grab the silver grenade and run toward imminent death.

5

Running is harder than I'd hoped. My left side still feels numb and weak. My feet skid on discarded rubble. I fear I look like I'm creating my own Olympic event—half hopping, half limping.

I hug the left-hand wall, desperate to avoid the T-Rex's gaze. It thrashes back and forth, dominating the central aisle. Kayla thumps it desultorily on its head. It roars, spraying her with prehistoric phlegm. The grenade is a solid weight in my hand.

"Its mouth! Open its mouth!" I scream at Kayla. I don't know how else to phrase the absurd request.

Kayla turns slowly, arches an eyebrow. The T-Rex lunges, jaws snapping. She sidesteps casually.

"Its mouth," I yell. "Open!"

Kayla gives a heavy shrug.

"Please!" I'm close enough that I don't want to get any closer. I can smell its breath, foul as a charnel house.

The T-Rex lunges again. Kayla sidesteps again. The gaping mouth of the T-Rex whistles by her. Toward me. Knife blade teeth lancing at my head.

I try not to close my eyes. I hurl the grenade at the beast's tonsils. It bounces off one tooth, drops into the wide red maw.

Without much seeming care, Kayla slams an elbow into the T-Rex's jaw. The mouth shuts very suddenly and very fast. Instead of the T-Rex's teeth scouring my flesh from my bone, its nose thuds into my chest, sitting me down on my arse. The roar turns to a choking cough.

For a moment I think the grenade is going to come out the other way, coughed back at me in a fiery ball of death. And then, as the T-Rex rears backwards, I see a tiny flash of silver disappear down its throat.

It worked.

It actually bloody worked.

I'm so stunned I actually sit there and stare before remembering to scramble for cover.

The explosion rips through the room. Through the guts of the dinosaur. The rib cage distends, bursts through the rotten skin. Vertebrae, claws, bone shards embed themselves in the walls, a mess of reptilian shrapnel. The creature's head barrels over the pile of splinters I'm pretending is cover. Its teeth slash the air one final time.

I stay there, waiting to be certain. Waiting to make sure the Grim Reaper has left the building. Eventually I uncurl, my ears ringing. The back of my jacket has been flayed, but I'm remarkably whole, just a few grazes along my back. Smoke billows through the room.

"Oh! My! God!" It's the young girl with two pistols and enormous headphones. She paws them down around her neck, still holding the guns. Two platinum-blond pigtails bounce as she skips forward, almost prancing through the massive pool of blood that's spreading across the room.

"You guys!" She stares at me, at Shaw, at Clyde, at Kayla. "You are *so* freaking awesome!"

To be honest, I am not entirely upset with that response. Modesty be damned. That looked pretty cool.

The job's not done though. Shaw walks past the girl, heading toward the stairs. Clyde and I head after her, drawn warily into her wake, pistol out. Kayla stands watching us walk.

The blond girl dances after us. "I mean, did you guys see that?" she says. "With the grenade! And its head! I mean holy Jesus, I have never seen anything close to being half that cool. Not even on TV." She pauses, thinks. "You guys should totally be on TV."

She nods to herself. "You would be massive."

I wonder if I can get this girl to be a character witness at my next performance review.

We're at the foot of the stairs. Shaw signals with her gun for me to go wide. I start edging along the wall and Shaw starts edging up the stairs. Clyde stands and watches us.

"Batteries?" Shaw says to him.

He gives an embarrassed shrug—proving that such a thing is possible—and slips two AAs under the lip of his mask.

She pauses at the top of the stairs, in line with the wall, not yet visible to anyone crouched behind it. I see her take two quick breaths.

I realize I *really* do not want to see her get shot. That I would be very upset. More than if it was Clyde, and despite the brevity of our association I'd already count Clyde among my best friends. And I realize that maybe I'm not so sorry about the joke about being decent in bed. Not as sorry as I ought to be anyway.

Shaw holds up three fingers, then two, then—

I move before she finishes the countdown. There is no way I'm going to let this wizard cow put holes in Felicity Shaw. I vault the wall. It's not a maneuver that's going to win me an Olympic gold, but I keep my gun arm free. I sweep the pistol along the length of the raised platform.

I point it at nothing. At no one.

"Shit!" Shaw, snapping around the corner, curses at the empty platform. She scans back and forth. There's just one door. One route away from here, easily taken in the confusion. Shaw points to it. We start running.

The door flies open onto a corridor. More display cases line the walls. The stocky woman stands beside one. She has bad skin, bad teeth, and a bad perm. She looks a little like my mother. Admittedly my mother's left jaw, shoulder, arm, and side aren't encased in metal, but it's still a little embarrassing that she's the one who's been handing us our arses so tidily.

The woman raises a hand. Sheets of steel shift with an electronic hiss. Engines whine. She extends the hand protruding from the metal arm. A ring of LEDs shine blue and bright around her wrist. With a quick movement she smashes a glass case. She grabs something large and silver—a sizable chunk of metal or mineral—off a velvet board.

"Put it down," I say.

Shaw points her pistol. I mirror her movements.

The woman starts shouting, defiant. But I don't start understanding. The language sounds familiar, though. Something eastern European? Russian perhaps?

Shaw cocks the hammer on her pistol. "He said put it down, you Russian bitch."

So, definitely Russian then.

The woman laughs at us.

"I'm warning you," Shaw says, but perhaps not loud enough to expect to be heard.

Lightning arcs out of the wall. Shaw yells, fires. But she's not as fast as the Russian woman. The bullet whips through a white electric blur, slams into the wall. The corridor is abruptly empty.

Another electric blue-white light flashes from through an archway to the right.

"Fuck!" Shaw yells.

I'm already running past her. I skid at the archway, bunch my knees ready to put on another spurt of speed—

It's a little dead-end room, an alcove with dreams of grandeur. It holds a great carved rock, a few spotlights, some poorly chosen wallpaper. And no Russians at all.

Shaw joins me, pistol still pointing. She thrusts it at empty space. We stare at each other. There was nowhere for the Russian to go and she's totally gone.

6

"Oh. My. God."

I sit on the floor next to Shaw, my head on her shoulder. My hands are still shaking.

"Just, like, wow."

Clyde seems unable to sit. He keeps glancing over at us, shrugging and turning away awkwardly. We seem to be making him uncomfortable. Right now I'm willing to be selfish.

"I mean, just like, totally..."

Tabitha strolls up through the devastated minerals display, her laptop held under her arm. She gives Shaw and me a look that lies somewhere between disgust and admiration. Kayla falls into sullen line behind her.

"This is so completely awesome!" the blond girl squeals. "There's totally more of you."

"Jaz," says the large black man. He has the assault rifle slung over his shoulder. "Jasmine." He speaks calm and slow.

The girl ignores him as he approaches, staring wild-eyed at Tabitha, who looks back as if she's just discovered an all-singing, all-dancing turd.

"Jasmine." The man lays a large hand on the girl's shoulder. She looks up in surprise. "Calm down," he says in the same slow way.

"But... But... Didn't you see? They..."

He stares at her, impassive.

"You're totally oozing over this one and you know it," she tells him. "This is totally emotional repression on your part."

"I'm squee-ing on the inside," the big man deadpans. He nods his head in miniature greeting. "Malcolm West," he says. "This is Jasmine."

"Hi!" Jasmine pipes, bouncing on her toes.

"Hello," I say, raising my hand. "I'm Arthur."

"Awesome," breathes Jasmine.

The Asian woman stops pulling bits of plaster out of her hair and looks up at me. "Aiko." She smiles. "We already met."

"Agent Arthur Wallace," I say, smiling.

No one else from MI37 says anything. It seems a little unfriendly. I'm fairly sure we were all just fighting the same giant slavering T-Rex.

"So, how did you guys—" I start.

By my shoulder, Shaw clucks her tongue. I glance at her.

"The British government," she says, not looking directly at me or the strangers, "does not recognize the Weekenders as a legitimate militia group. They do not endorse their activities. Its members are not privy to documents or information protected by the Official Secrets Act. They have not received any form of government-approved training." The man, Malcolm, grunts at that. "Their possession of firearms is illegal, and it is the duty of British officials to hunt them down and arrest them before they harm others or themselves."

She rolls her head to look up at me.

"Wait… We have to arrest them?" It seems like a pretty shitty way to treat them. "That's not right."

Shaw looks back at them, the Weekenders. Aiko shrugs at us.

"Maybe later," Shaw says. "I'm tired and I need a shower." She stands slowly, stretches, grimacing. "Come on, let's get out of here." She takes a step, then looks back at the Weekenders. "You are going to get yourselves killed. Maybe you're going to get us killed."

I'm going to give Shaw the benefit of the doubt and assume she's still pissed about the middle-aged Russian woman making us look stupid in front of an audience. That's no fun for anyone.

"Next time," Shaw continues, "I will arrest you before I even bother taking on the threat. For your sakes. For ours." She shakes her head. "Bloody amateurs."

I don't want to totally break rank, and Shaw's made the official MI37 line pretty clear, but I would like to soften the blow if I can. I try to take everything that Clyde has taught me since joining the department, and I shrug apologetically at Aiko.

She sneaks me a grin when Shaw isn't looking.

We file out. Shaw and I lead, Clyde and Tabitha hand-in-hand behind us, Kayla at the rear. Unfortunately there's only one real way out of the building, so the Weekenders walk with us. Everyone seems to be rather pointedly ignoring each other.

Almost everyone.

"Is that, like, a real real sword?" I hear the girl Jasmine ask Kayla.

Considering Kayla doesn't gut the girl, I imagine that an exploding T-Rex hasn't cheered her up any.

Aiko falls into step with Shaw and me. "So," she says, "what did the Russian grab?" She gives me a cheeky grin.

My eyebrows bounce up.

"I mean," she goes on, "at first, I had it pegged as a pretty basic heist. Use the animated T-Rex to clear out mundane security, then use the window until the specialists arrive," she nods to me and the rest of MI37, "to go for the precious stones, et cetera. But then," she knits her eyebrows, "she goes for minerals and takes her sweet time getting there. And it also strikes me that maybe a T-Rex is a bit flashy. I mean, if she knew her stuff, and she surely seemed to, she could have swiped some jewels and been out of here without anyone blinking. But, like I said, she didn't even go for jewels. So what did she swipe? What did she want you to see?"

For an amateur, that strikes me as pretty bloody good detective work.

"You on the police force?" I ask on instinct. Shaw clucks quietly.

"I teach first grade," Aiko says. "It gives me profound insight into the way twisted minds work."

I can't help but chuckle.

"I believe I mentioned that you're not privy to information

covered by the Official Secrets Act, didn't I?" Shaw says to her.

I stop chuckling.

At the entrance hall, Aiko says, "Probably better to go our own way from here." She gives me a friendly wave. Shaw is quasi-glaring at me. I leave off returning the wave. Maybe it's time to prioritize the women in my life and follow Shaw's lead.

THE 2:34 FROM LONDON TO OXFORD

Rain graffitis the train window. Shaw and I are alone again, Tabitha and Clyde opting for the intimacy of Clyde's Mini, and Kayla opting for solitude.

Shaw's been quiet since we left the museum, wrapped up in herself. She hasn't even chewed me out for the being-good-in-bed joke. That might be a good sign, but on the other hand my subsequent attempts at witty banter have been met with the same polite nods most people reserve for village idiots.

As Reading rattles past our windows, she finally looks up at me.

"We didn't do very well there, did we?" she says. She looks anxious, small in her suit. Very un-Shaw-like.

It's technically true, but I'm still feeling pretty buoyant about yesterday's world-saving and today's more explosive moments, so I say, "We blew up a zombie T-Rex. I think that was why we went there."

"But the Russian who summoned it got away, didn't she?" Shaw says. "We failed our primary objective, and she achieved hers. She stole whatever she was looking to steal. One woman defeated us. All five of us."

"Cheer up," I say, laying a hand on hers as I avoid the specifics of the argument. "We saved the world yesterday."

Shaw looks out the window and then back. She's smiling but there's no humor to it. "But don't you think," she says, "that maybe we shouldn't have let it get that far? Shouldn't we have stopped things before anyone needed to save the world?"

Which is a tricky question. Because of course we should. But—

"Nobody else was trying," I say. "Without us there wouldn't even have been an eleventh-hour victory. Just no victory at all."

"Hmmm," Shaw says. I'm not sure I've convinced her. There again, I'm not entirely sure I convinced myself.

7

MI37 HEADQUARTERS, OXFORD

Conference room B has changed in some indefinable yet profound way. Without losing its plastic chairs, or its cheap vinyl veneer-covered table, it has somehow become comfortable. The environs of MI37 have become reassuring. I think something might be wrong with me.

Shaw sits at the head of the table, once more the woman in full command.

"First impressions?" she says.

"Theft," Tabitha says, without taking a beat. "Get us all excited about the T-Rex. Nab rock. Scarper."

Shaw nods. But, something feels odd about that assessment to me. I remember what the Weekender, Aiko, said as we left the museum.

"This T-Rex," I say, "wasn't it the opposite of a distraction? Didn't it draw attention to the theft rather than away from it?"

Shaw appears to weigh this. "Care to expand on that?"

"It's just," I say, "this Russian woman is a magician, so a zombie T-Rex seems like overkill for just doing some thieving. Why not a more surreptitious route? Just teleport the stone out of there or something?"

"Can't teleport," Tabitha interjects.

"What?"

"Teleportation," Clyde says, "magico-physical impossibility."

"Really?" I'm kind of surprised to find out that there are things that are still impossible.

"Oh yes," Clyde nods enthusiastically.

He's about to slap me with magical theory, I realize. I brace for impact.

"You see," Clyde says, "I think we've established that magic works when human will, shaped by specific syllabic constructs, or spells, powered by electricity, punches a hole out of our reality and into another one."

He's building up, relying on lessons taught before, but I've been trying to avoid the specifics of magic and let all the other "what-the-fuck" percolate. I wrestle my way through memory to the specifics. There are multiple realities. Magic involves reaching out of our reality. Punching a hole, Clyde calls it. And you need electricity for it. The universal lubricant. Not the nicest term. But apparently it's using electricity that stops the whole project from going boom in the spell caster's face.

"So, the magician, or whatever," Clyde continues, "reaches out of our reality, and into another one. And he or she pulls something out of the distant reality through the hole and into our world. For example, an animating force that they want to slap into a T-Rex skeleton, or maybe some kinetic force that they want to use to cave in that T-Rex's skull. Theoretically simple if a little tricky in practice."

I nod. "You told me all this." Which is my polite way of saying, "I remember you gibbering all this at me once before."

"Well," Clyde says, "teleporting, that's passing instantly from one place in one reality to another place in the *same* reality. Which you know. Of course. Definitional. But it's important. You want to tear a hole in one part of reality, and step out of another hole in the *same* place you punched out of. Can't do it. When you punch out, you're punching *out*.

"I mean, say, for example, you're in a paper bag. Not a likely scenario, I realize, but imagine, attack of the giant paper bags. Swallows you whole. Oh no. Need to punch your way out. So you punch. Easy job really. It's only a paper bag. One reason paper bags will never take over the world, I assume. Anyway, when you punch out of the bag, you punch out into whatever environment is surrounding the bag. You don't punch back into the bag."

I knew it was going to happen. I've gone cross-eyed.

"Intradimensional magic," Tabitha chimes in, just to baffle me more. "Name for it. People tried it. Remember Chernobyl?"

More memory wrestling. And I'm surprised to find I actually do remember this discussion. I'm quite pleased with myself.

"Chernobyl wasn't a nuclear explosion," I say, dredging the brain trenches. "It was experimental magic gone awry. The Magic Arms Race. It was ballsy communist wizards trying to experiment. To pioneer their own spells."

"Indeed." Tabitha nods. "Intradimensional magic. Them. Trying it. Wanted to get a nuke into Times Square. Some such. Instead blew bits of themselves around the place."

"All right," I say. "No teleporting." I think that sums up their point.

"But," Shaw says, finally pulling us back to the discussion at hand, "Arthur, you're basically saying this woman wanted us at the museum?" She's not dismissive, merely curious.

"I'm saying if she didn't, she did a piss-poor job of keeping us away." I'm pretty sure I'm right, but what experience I've had in the supernatural world has taught me to avoid something as simple as a straight "yes."

"I'll buy that," Shaw says, pushing back in her chair. "But then why did she want us there?"

I try to think. "What if the point was just to impress us with what she's capable of? Territorial pissing?"

"Not really a message. That." Tabitha looks irritated, I'm not sure if it's at my argument or at the world for not shriveling up in self-hatred yet.

"Indeed." Shaw nods along with Tabitha.

"Did she say anything?" Clyde asks.

I think about that. "Yes." I nod. "Well, at the end she shouted angrily and tried to scare me with magic." I look at Shaw. "You said it was Russian?"

"I understood a few words." Shaw looks suddenly worried again.

It's not wholly reassuring. "Here and there." She lapses into silence.

"Any examples?" I ask once it becomes apparent that no one else is going to leap in. Apparently, if you sleep with the boss then you get to ask her the hard questions.

Shaw grimaces. "What I understood was, 'time,' 'we will,' and 'bomb.'"

"Bomb?" My eyes widen. I don't disbelieve her. I just want to.

"Yes."

There's silence in the room.

"Ballsy Russian," Tabitha says finally. "With a bomb. Or wants a bomb. Or needs a part for a bomb. Wants us to know about it."

Not the prettiest picture anyone's ever painted for me. And while we did save the world, this Russian woman didn't make us look exactly like we operate in the world-saving league. Having seen her with magic, I'm not sure I want to see her with a bomb.

"I just want to check," I say, "but it's still a no on the days off, isn't it?"

8

Shaw doesn't reply, so I decide to pressure test the new bomb hypothesis for holes. I find one, but not one I expected. "We said she can't teleport, right?"

"In detail." Shaw is rubbing her temples.

"So how did she get away?" I ask. "We had her in our sights. Then she wasn't there."

"Glamour," Clyde says. "Illusion magic. The same sort that was used on the T-Rex. The magical and mysterious art of making something appear where it isn't. Not stage magician sleight of hand, obviously. But it has that same sort of underhand sneaky feel that leaves a bad taste in the mouth. Of course, your opinion of illusionists might depend on how badly disappointed you were by Dynamic Dave, Master of the Seven Deadliest Illusions on your eighth birthday." He catches himself, and shrugs twice. "Anyway we were talking about glamour magic. Totally going to stick to that. Basically, duping people. Obviously that's simplifying it quite a lot. Visual distortions is closer. Bending light is closer still. Summoning refractory space from other realities is almost nail on the head."

"Oh," I say. It's actually kind of flattering that this Russian woman seems to be going so far out of her way to impress us.

"Well," Shaw puts both palms down on the table, "whatever her motives with the T-Rex were, we do know for sure that she stole that stone. What's so special about it? *Can* it help her make a bomb? Tabitha, I want you on that." She pushes back a stray lock of hair. "Now, Clyde—"

A small black phone on the desk interrupts her. She scowls at it. Unfortunately, the inanimate object refuses to be cowed. She grabs the receiver and puts it to her ear. "Yes?" she says, irritated. "Who?" She flicks a look at Clyde, then Tabitha. "What does—OK. And you said?"

Shaw's face darkens. She looks at Clyde more and more. "Yes," she says finally. "Thank you." She doesn't sound grateful.

The phone hits its cradle. "Clyde?" Shaw says. Her voice is the audio version of a thunderhead.

"Yes?" Clyde seems to be trying to work out how nervous he should be.

"Would you care to explain exactly why your ex-girlfriend is banging on the door to the office?"

Clyde settles on very nervous indeed.

9

"Forgive me if I'm wrong, Clyde," Shaw uses his name as the verbal equivalent of a club, "but shouldn't Devon believe you're working as an accountant on Jericho Street?"

"I... I..." Clyde stammers. "I..."

"Let me guess," Shaw interrupts his stuttering. "When you broke up with your girlfriend, that seemed like a good time to reveal highly privileged information to her, didn't it?"

"I... I..." Clyde starts again. "I'll go out to her." Shaw's accuracy has reduced his shoulders to random desperate waggling. "Lay out the whole A-to-Z process that occurred," he says. "I'm sure she'll understand—"

"When she sees your seven-and-a-half-foot tall, wooden-faced self?" Shaw arches an eyebrow. "No. I'll go." She stands up. "In the meantime, you..." She looks at us all, and for a moment her shoulders sag. "Just try not to reveal our existence to anyone else would you?" And then she's gone.

A moment later Kayla is heading for the door. It's the first time I've seen her hit full speed all day. There's nearly a sonic boom.

And I'd wanted to ask her if she wanted to talk about things. She wouldn't have, but I think she might have appreciated someone asking.

Clyde puts his wooden face in his hands. "I did it all wrong," he says. "With Devon. Didn't I?"

Tabitha is looking far too pleased with herself, sitting next to him.

And honestly the answer is yes, but that's not going to help here. So instead I go for the more vague, "I think Shaw is just tired."

"Shagged out?" Tabitha raises an eyebrow.

And I know Tabitha is abrasive at the best of times. I know the professional thing to do, the thing the team leader would do, is take the higher ground. But instead, I go with, "Oh yeah, because my office romance is totally the one causing issues right now."

Clyde clutches his head again.

So that wasn't the right thing to say either. It's mildly concerning that I'm starting to get more comfortable in life-or-death situations than in conversational ones. I'll need to watch that.

I grab around for a subject change. Tabitha remains looking stalwartly smug.

"So," I try, "Clyde, when did you start being able to commune with security cameras?"

Tabitha scowls.

"Oh." Clyde takes a moment pulling his thoughts together. "I… I'm still not sure about that. But I got my personality onto this mask via a wireless internet connection."

The incident replays in my mind. Deep beneath the earth in a Peruvian temple. Kayla actually being fought to a standstill by ancient monks who'd stored their personalities on masks half magical and half electrical. And then Clyde using Tabitha's laptop's wireless connection to astrally project. Overwriting one of the monks' masks, so Kayla could kick his arse and turn the tide of the battle.

"I imagine I'm basically digital now," Clyde says. "I mean, this mask is all electronics. Magical, Peruvian electronics from the dark ages, but still… But I guess there's a two-way connection. In and out. I just… It's weird." He shrugs, helpless. "There's a lot to get used to," he says. "This whole body…"

For the first time I really think about the trauma Clyde's been through. Yesterday, his meat body was possessed by an alien. Yesterday, I killed him. Yesterday. That's got to take its toll.

Yesterday was a really busy day.

I check my watch. "You should probably clear out," I say. "Let this whole Devon thing blow over." Neither Tabitha nor Clyde seem to need any more prompting.

I sit alone in the conference room for a while and let my head spin. Clyde is wireless. Russians are trying to bomb us. Kayla seems abruptly unable to punch her way out of a paper bag. Not even the world-invading kind. Devon is in the building.

We saved the world, but I'm no longer entirely sure that we put it back right.

I'm still chewing on that one when Shaw appears in the doorway with her coat on and a pocketbook over her shoulder.

"So," she says, "what do you fancy? Curry or Chinese?"

I weigh my options. "Which one is less likely to be transformed into a life-threatening monster by rogue wizards?"

I'm beginning to get concerned about how work is affecting my decision-making process.

Felicity smiles. "I think I have a good place in mind."

10

You have to give it to the Mongols. Fabulous at both invading China and takeout food. Kudos to them.

Shaw takes me to a place near work and her apartment where we pick up a steaming feast of noodles, vegetables, and meat. Later, we sit about in her living room surrounded by trapezoidal cardboard boxes and I get to demonstrate my inability to use chopsticks.

"So, how'd it go with Devon?" I say, giving up on the whole process, and just trying to spear a piece of pork.

"I hired her," Shaw says through a mouthful of noodles.

Having just placed the piece of pork in my mouth, I then spray it halfway across the room.

"You what?" My incredulity is a zombie T-Rex smashing through the room.

"Would you be better off with a fork?" Shaw's face is the picture of innocence.

"You did what to her?"

"Hiring someone is not a violent act, Arthur."

"It is to bloody Clyde," I say. And I believe I have a point.

Shaw puts down her chopsticks. "What should I have done, Arthur? Clyde had told her everything. Literally everything. In fact he briefed her so extensively I think I should have him date and break up with all new hires. Tabitha's in the process of stepping up into more of a field agent role. We need a good researcher in the office, and I suddenly have one sitting in my lap."

"She's going to work for Tabitha?" My voice leaps up to an octave I didn't know it could reach. "Her ex-boyfriend's new girlfriend is going to be her boss?"

Shaw shakes her head. "She won't report to Tabitha. I don't think Tabitha's entirely ready for that sort of responsibility."

"Not exactly my point." Jesus. Shaw is sensible and steady. How can she be letting this happen?

"Look, Arthur." Shaw grimaces. "I didn't recruit her. Clyde did. My hands were somewhat tied."

"This is going to be a disaster," I say. Which is maybe not diplomatic of me.

Shaw puts out her hands, calming rough waters. "We saved the world yesterday," she says. She's smiling. "How bad can we do at this?"

Considering the arse-whopping the Russian woman gave us, the depths are starting to seem deeper than I'd previously imagined.

But Shaw is leaning over the boxes of noodles to kiss me, and that exact point gets lost for a while.

LATER, AFTER A FORK IS FETCHED

Given the long girlfriend drought I suffered through prior to this relationship, I am intimately aware of that moment when there is nothing left on TV except infomercials and made-for-TV movies about hepatitis. The time when there is nothing left to do but hang around. It's usually around two in the morning.

But having already crashed headlong through the sex-with-my-boss barrier and landed, tangled in the sheets, on the other side, there's no bloody way I'm waiting around that long tonight.

I slip my hand off Shaw's and onto the remote. The news credits roll out to Big Ben's farewell bongs. I press a button on the remote, and the TV dies with a little electronic sigh.

I turn, look at her. She turns, looks at me. She has her hair down, has her legs tucked up under her. She has a spot of soy sauce on her chin that I think is cute enough to not tell her about.

I smile. And I know exactly what Kurt Russell would do.

Shaw reaches out a hand, touches my chest. I lean toward her. But there is no give in her arms.

As much fun as kissing is, I am abruptly aware of how stupid someone looks in the split second before it all happens, eyes half-closed, lips half-puckered.

I pull my face back into the semblance of a non-idiot. Shaw is smiling.

"I'm not stopping anything," she tells me. "This isn't me wishing you good night. Far from it. But…" She looks away for a moment. "I just want to make sure we both know what we're doing here. I… I get that this could be weird. I'm the wrong side of forty. I'm divorced. I work a lot. I'm your boss." She shrugs. "And the thing is, I'm not going to stop being any of those things."

"I don't mind those things," I say. And it's true.

"Except I think you might have minded a bit in the museum today. With the way I handled Kayla. And the Weekenders. Sometimes I'm going to make calls you disagree with. And I'm going to stand by those decisions despite you. And it won't be personal, but I think sometimes it'll feel that way."

And that's true too. But… "I'm willing to work with that," I say.

Shaw smiles. "I am too. I just wanted to make sure… Relationships aren't perfect. They're messy. People aren't perfect. I know I'm not. I'm messy. And I know you're not, but that's not me saying I want you to change. I don't want you to stop being funny, or good-looking, or decent at a really fundamental level."

"OK," I say. I can feel her elbow weakening.

Shaw furrows her brow. "Will you say pretty much anything now if you think it's going to get me into bed?"

"Not anything," I say after a moment's consideration. "But I should warn you that we're pretty far from where I draw the line."

She slaps at my shoulder. A playful rebuke. One that means her hand isn't between us anymore. I close the distance.

She pulls me closer. She smells sweet and spicy, of far-flung lands, and horseback riders conquering the known world. Her hair falls forward onto my cheek. Her lips brush mine.

We manage to make it to our feet, she pulls me after her, through the unfamiliar apartment, down a corridor I should surely remember from this morning. Through a doorway. She pushes me onto a bed. Her bed.

The idea of sex, to me, is always a graceful, nebulous act. Limbs, and pleasure, and afterglow. The act itself always seems to involve more issues about getting my tie over my head, and trying to find the correct moment to take my socks off, and negotiating the mechanics of bra hooks. And then there's the choreography of where to be when, and there is always more sweat than I remember, and I'm pretty sure it can't be comfortable with my weight there, but I'm not sure how else to rest it.

But then, somewhere along the way, I finally lose myself. And there is just Shaw's body, and mine, and the point where we meet, that tiny spot of pleasure that grows to eclipse the whole world.

And then, shuddering, and gasping, and grinning, it's over. She kisses me. I kiss her. We lie next to each other, panting.

"I know," I say, looking up at her ceiling, gripping her hand tight in mine, "that this won't always be easy. But I believe some things are worth fighting for. The right things. The good things." I turn, look at her. I want her to see that I am, for once, at least, sincere. No dissembling frivolity. No shield of humor. "I think you're a good thing, Felicity."

"You'll fight for me?" Her finger plays across my chest, the corners of her lips curl.

"Well," I say, "that is basically what you pay me to do."

11

ONCE THE AFTERGLOW HAS FADED

"Fucking with me. Seriously. You are."

Cold war has broken out in conference room B. On one side of the iron curtain, Tabitha sits next to Clyde shooting fiery daggers from her eyes. On the other sits Devon, Clyde's ex, large, buxom, and red-cheeked, with an expression of unadulterated hatred carved into the soft surface of her face.

Kayla and I perch in no-man's land, bathing in the backwash of enmity. Except, for once, it doesn't seem to be just washing over Kayla. She looks back and forth from woman to woman, slowly chewing her lip.

I should probably say something, but putting words out right now seems like an invitation to be kicked in the gut so I keep my mouth shut for a change.

Still, I am going to have to have a word with Shaw. Her, "You head into the meeting, I'll be along in a minute," seemed so innocent at the time.

I keep calling her Shaw in my head. Not Felicity. Surely we're on a first-name basis at this point.

And then she opens the conference room door. "Ah." She smiles warmly at Devon. "Punctual. Excellent. Very happy to have you aboard."

"About that," Tabitha says.

Shaw… Felicity smiles at Tabitha in much the same way a Great White smiles at a minnow. "If you have a problem with the staffing situation, Tabitha, I suggest you work on being promoted to a position where you actually get a say."

Clyde lowers his wooden face to the table. It lands with a slight thunk. Devon twitches. At first I wonder if she's gone wireless. Then I think that there is probably a significant difference between Felicity telling Devon about Clyde's new corporeal state and Devon seeing it for herself.

Shaw… Felicity, damn it… lets her breath out in a controlled, slow fashion. "Now, I was hoping to deal with the more pressing issue of Russians trying to blow up London. Is everyone fine with that?"

"Not really," Tabitha says. Because she apparently has far larger balls than I do.

"Unless you have information on the stolen mineral deposit," Shaw suggests, "be quiet."

Tabitha opens her laptop, still glowering. She reaches to tap a key, but next to her Clyde spasms violently. The laptop screen blinks, and a file opens. Tabitha looks over at Clyde and finally lets her frustration boil over.

"The fuck?" she snaps at him.

"Sorry."

As soon as he utters the first syllable, Devon seems to shrink into herself. Again I hear how it's not quite Clyde's voice. See how it's not quite his movements when he gestures. Everything is in translation.

And my relationship with Felicity is not the first one I've been in. I know that when someone leaves you, you hope they'll come back, you hope they'll be regained somehow. But given how much Clyde's changed, "the way things were" must seem like it exists on a different planet to Devon. The impossibility of a way back must be slapping her in the face.

I'm debating if it's my place to do something about it, when Kayla reaches over and pats Devon's hand.

There is utter silence in the room. We all stare at Kayla. She glares back.

"Thanks," Devon mumbles.

"Well then…" Felicity starts but doesn't seem to have anywhere to go.

I try to think of something to say to cover the moment. "Clyde," I say, grasping at straws, "did you just open a file on Tabitha's computer with your mind?"

Clyde turns his head, studiously ignoring Devon. "Well, I sort of figured out how last night."

"Boundaries," Tabitha hisses.

Clyde says nothing, while Devon's stare looks like it's causing his sperm to detonate one by one.

Felicity massages her skull. "OK," she says. "On the off chance we can actually get down to business. This stolen mineral deposit."

"Not of terrestrial origin." Tabitha sounds almost glad for the opportunity to change the subject. "From a meteorite. Hit earth about a thousand years ago. High percentage of antimony. Odd element. Not much of it here on earth."

A voice cuts Tabitha off. "It's mostly used for flame-proofing actually."

Every eye in the room flies to Devon. She is attempting to look breezy and detached while engaged in a life-or-death staring contest with Tabitha.

"Was saying." Tabitha curls her lip between sentences. "Main uses are flame-proofing, producing synthetic fibres, and lead-acid batteries. Not typical for bombs. But, of note, Chernobyl came up again."

Russians. Chernobyl. Bomb. Not the most reassuring triumvirate of words.

I glance up at Shaw but she's watching Tabitha.

"Big component of Chernobyl experiment," Tabitha says. "Thought it'd power intradimensional magic. Russians did."

I look over to Devon. "Magic that doesn't punch out of our reality," I say to her in a way I hope sounds more knowledgeable than rote. Then I realize more backstory is required. "There's magic, by the way. Did you cover that?"

My respect for Clyde's explanations suddenly grows profoundly. He makes explaining this stuff seem much easier than it is. Still, Devon finally unlocks her gaze from Tabitha and beams at me with a megawatt grin.

"Thank you, Arthur," she booms. "Very helpful to know. Don't really understand a word of what you're talking about but common courtesy is really just… Well, it's not that common at all really. Actually a bit of a misnomer. I mean if it's common courtesy then why mention it? But people are always mentioning it. Well not always. Due to the uncommon-ness." She glances away. "Yes," she concludes.

Then she levels her death-stare at Tabitha once more.

I look from Devon to Clyde. God, there are two of them now. My chances of understanding anything at all ever are rapidly diminishing.

"Was saying." Tabitha's pointed statement has grown claws. "Antimony. Used by Russians at Chernobyl. Catalyst metal. But we know Chernobyl doesn't work. So: coincidence."

"That seems a bit of an assumption," Devon starts, still booming but with even less friendliness, "in my opinion that is, which, well I realize I'm still proving the usefulness of that, being the new person and all. No one wants to lick the new flavor of lollipop until a friend has tried it. Not that I want to be licked. Horrible image. Just making a metaphor. Licking always seemed a dirty habit to me, anyway. Always preferred a soft chewable candy myself. Why make food you can't bite? Doesn't make any sense." She pushes her hair back from her eyes furiously. "Anyway, I was just saying that it seems to me that making assumptions about coincidences without fully investigating all the angles may be a little shortsighted." She blinks. "As I understand the situation."

I'm not sure she knows what she's talking about, but I am pretty sure that she doesn't care.

Tabitha remains unfazed. "Coincidence because Russians know intradimensional magic doesn't work. Which you'd know," Tabitha sneers, "if you'd done any fucking research."

Kayla makes an odd noise. A sort of click of the tongue.

Did she just tsk Tabitha?

For some reason Felicity doesn't seem about to step in. But, because it feels like MTV's *Real Life: Supernatural Horrors* is about to be unleashed in the conference room, I think someone has to. I open my mouth and say—

"Well, you can't trust the bloody Russians to do anything right."

Except I don't say that. Someone else says it. And I don't recognize the voice.

"Incompetent buggers, the Russians," the new voice adds.

Every eye in the room turns and stares.

A tall, heavy-set man stands in the doorway. I'd peg him in his late fifties. He wears a brown tweed suit and a red tie that hangs awkwardly to where his waistline is losing its integrity. Ruddy brown hair is cropped close to the sides of his skull and a mustache the size of a seal pup balances on his upper lip.

"Oh God," Felicity says. "Oh no."

"Still," the man says, apparently oblivious to the impact of his sudden presence, "can't trust the sneaky bastards. Always up to something." His voice booms as loud as Devon's but is muddied by the sheer volume of his mustache. "You," he points to me. "Tall, dark, and ugly. And you, the one with the Halloween mask." The sausage finger points to Clyde. "Next to the weird chick." I have to imagine he means Tabitha. "Off to the British Library, would you? We need the Chernobyl papers."

"What the hell?" I manage through my confusion. I sure as shit don't move.

"Come on," the man snaps. "*Ondelé, ondelé*, or whatever it is those bullfighting nancies say. Chop-chop. Queen and country. Go, go, go. London. Library. Lots of books. Can't miss it." He squints at Clyde and me. "Spreken zee English?"

"George," says Felicity, her voice like a knife's blade. "What are you doing here?"

She knows him. The collective stare swivels to her. It registers. She swallows. "This is George Coleman," she says to us. "He works for MI6."

The man called George smiles. "Not anymore actually. Bit of a promotion. Top brass seem to think brinksmanship with aliens isn't the smartest of plays. Steadier hand at the tiller and all that." He thumbs his own chest. "Co-director of MI37 as of about," he checks his watch, "thirty minutes ago. And now," he points to Clyde and me, "directing you two to London. Fucking yesterday already."

"No." I shake my head. It's a denial aimed as much at the universe as it is this unpleasant stain of a human being. This seriously can't be. We save the world and this guy is our reward? "Shaw is the director," I say. I demand.

But, apparently, the universe is about as interested in my assertions as it usually is.

"Lippy bugger, are we?" Coleman shoves out his chest. "And evidently not at the top of the food chain when it comes to information dispersal. Maybe because you've forgotten this is *military* intelligence. There is a chain of command. Information and orders flow big man to little man. And you are a little man and you would do well to remember that."

It doesn't happen with any degree of regularity, but I think I am about to lose my temper. I open my mouth—

"George, please." Shaw, the placatory voice of reason, trying to find the balance point in the room. Sensible. Rational.

"Yes," I say. "Please piss off."

Felicity turns to me. She has a pained expression. "Arthur," she says. Something between an order and a request.

And this is one of those moments she talked about last night, where I don't like her lead.

But I'm not willing to break my promises this early. I'd like to wait at least six hours before I kick out one of the foundations we're building this relationship on.

I bite back my bile.

"Come on, George," Felicity says. "We can do this without the territorial pissing match." She forces a smile out. "This news is a bit of a shock to everyone, that's all. I'm sure we can all find it in ourselves to act like mature adults."

Coleman finally retracts his chest, apparently mollified.

"Now," Shaw says, "perhaps we can have a brief word in private."

Coleman's mustache quivers like an enormous electrocuted caterpillar, then he turns on his heel and stomps out of the room.

Felicity hesitates for a moment, her professional mask flickers. A glimpse of a woman worried and worn. I want to reach out to her as a colleague, a friend, a boyfriend.

Except there's rather a large audience for that.

"You shouldn't take this," I say, restraining myself from stepping toward her. "This isn't right."

Her lips twitch in the imitation of a smile. But she doesn't answer me. She just slips out the door after Coleman.

"This isn't right," I inform the room in general. Not that anyone seems to care. They're all too busy shooting daggers at each other.

And that's not right either. Something just happened that's bigger than personal battles. Some ground shift.

Of course getting anyone to see it is going to involve stepping into the middle of the Tabitha-Devon divide. And to be honest I think I'd rather face another zombie T-Rex.

Screw it. I'm field lead. In the office, I'm not touching this crap with a ten-foot barge pole. "I'm getting a cup of tea," I say as I head toward the door. That's my story and I'm sticking to it.

For a moment I think I'm going to get away clean but then Devon says, "I'll come too." I can feel Tabitha's scowl scouring the back of my neck even as the door swings closed.

The MI37 kitchen is a small nook of one corridor with an electric kettle balanced on top of a microwave, balanced on top of a mini-fridge. A few mugs, a box of tea bags and a jar of instant coffee sit in a sink waiting for everything to fall apart.

I shove a bag into a cup. Everything seems to be speeding up just when I'd like it to slow down. Just a few days to wrap my head around my new reality. To get to grips with this relationship thing. Except now there are Russians, and bombs. And it's not just my relationship that needs to be adjusted to. And on top of it all, this Coleman prick. He has to be someone's idea of a joke. A very, very, very bad joke.

I stare at the tea bag. Just five minutes to get my head together. "Did you know?"

Devon, it seems, has no intention of letting that happen.

But... God, I can't send misplaced aggression her way. It's Coleman who really has me on edge, not her. She doesn't even sound like herself. She's being quiet.

I flick on the kettle. Take a moment to brace for the admission. "Yes."

It's an awful thing to say. A terrible acknowledgment of complicity.

"Does he... Does he..." There's more swallowing. "Do you think he loves her?"

I grab two sugar packets, tear them open. I suspect I'm going to need to switch to artificial sweetener, though, if I want to get over the bitter taste of this one.

"I…" I hesitate. Would a lie be better? Would that be the right thing?

"Please. I just want to know the truth." Devon is turned away from me, hiding her face.

"I think so," I say.

The water in the kettle starts to work itself into a froth. I reach out to turn it off.

"I don't know why I came here," Devon says, freezing me. "It was a really stupid thing to do. And now I'm trapped here. Looking at him. At what he's become. At her. I'm caught and it's awful and I don't feel like me. I feel like some mean terrible person who wants to do terrible things. And I've never done a terrible thing. I'm a good person, Arthur. And that sounds like an awfully conceited thing to say, but, well, maybe now is the time to be conceited, just a little bit, if it helps. But I try. I really try to be a good person. I try to be happy. I was happy. And I'm not. He's taken it. She's taken it. She's taken my happiness. And… And…"

She's crying now. Really crying. I step so I can see her, so she can see me. And screw the politics of it, she needs to see she has a friend here.

"Starting here sucks," I tell her. "But I promise it gets better."

Another wracking sob from Devon. Then she lunges forward and clamps me in a bear hug. All the oxygen exits my lungs. I gasp like a fish flipped to shore.

"Thank you," she says. "Thank you."

My ribs creak.

"Ahem." Behind us, someone clears their throat. I twist my head as the corners of my vision go dark. Kayla stands there.

"Oh," Devon says, and releases me. I stagger back, gasping.

Kayla points to Devon's face. "Your make-up," she says, a little gruffly. "Should fix that. I'll show you the bathrooms."

"Oh!" Devon says again, clapping hands to her cheeks. "Oh gosh, I must look terrible. Really silly of me. I mean, well, this is an emotional time, of course. But still, a tighter rein might be necessary. Keep myself in check. There's acting the fool and then looking like one afterwards. Compounding the problem. You are very sweet to point it out. I'm Devon by the way." She sticks out her hand. Then her brows crumple. "You know that." Her lip starts to tremble. "Silly of me."

"Bathroom," Kayla commands. And the two of them walk away, leaving me with a screeching kettle and the sense that no one is really who I thought they were.

BACK IN THE CONFERENCE ROOM

In the absence of other targets, Tabitha is staring daggers at me now.

"Look," I say, "I know being hideously insensitive to everybody is kind of your 'thing'," I even give her the air quotes, "but if you could lay off the woman whose boyfriend you stole that'd be just lovely, all right?" It's not the most diplomatic way to handle it, but I'm really not in the mood.

To my shock it's not Tabitha who responds.

"Hey," Clyde says. Then, uncharacteristically, he seems to run out of things to add.

Tabitha rolls her eyes at him too.

I close my eyes. I don't want fights. I want to be happy and in a new relationship and my only concern to be a Russian that wants to blow me into very small pieces.

"If we could all just... act like we're adults, and not stare venomously at Devon, and not avoid her eye with our heads on the table, then maybe this might be easier, that's all I'm saying."

The daggers continue from Tabitha. Whether it's in spite of or because of what I've said, I'm not sure.

I'm about to try a new tack when the door opens and Felicity pops her head back in. My heart does a little leap. Hopefully this is to announce Coleman has been sent back to whatever circle of hell he had the temerity to crawl out from.

But instead she says, "Clyde. Arthur. If you could pop down to London and pull papers on the Chernobyl incident that would be very convenient."

She sounds like she's asking. It's very unlike her.

"Are you sure?" I say. Something else feels wrong now.

"Please." She nods.

OK, something else is definitely wrong.

"Do you need us to—" I start.

"Just go to London," she says. "It'll be fine."

But as Clyde and I stand, I know she's lying. Something is shifting. And it's not some towering monster, not something from outer space or out of our reality, it's something small and mundane. And I know for certain, all of a sudden, that when we put the world back together, we did it wrong.

12

Clyde and I manage to maintain silence for at least two corridors. Then he turns and looks at me.

"Did you know?" he asks me.

Here we go again.

"About Devon?" I ask, just to confirm this is going to be as uncomfortable as possible.

"Shaw told you?" He's working his long piano-player fingers against and between each other.

"I…" I start, then fail to think of a way to change the subject mid-question. "She told me last night."

"You could have called me."

He's right, of course. I should have. It was cruel to let him walk into that this morning. But I was… otherwise engaged last night.

"It was late," I say rather than get into the sticky details of it all.

Clyde taps the mask that is not his face with a finger that is not his. "I don't seem to really sleep anymore. Little bit shy on the old zees. With this." He doesn't sound overjoyed about it.

"You OK?" I ask.

"Me?" He cocks his head again. Shrugs. "Been better, yes. But I've been worse. Been dead actually. Albeit briefly. So, you know, on the scale of things, pretty much always going to be able to say things have been worse. But you know, reincarnation and all that, so things can pick up. Sleeping in the bed I made. And it's Tabitha's bed, so..." He trails off, hangs his head. "I feel like a bit of a shit, Arthur."

And he should. But that's not the sort of thing you say to a friend. "You followed your heart," I say instead. I try and make it sound like an excuse.

Clyde nods. "Not the smartest organ out there, is it?"

"Not the stupidest organ I've ever been accused of thinking with." I twist my mouth into a smile for Clyde.

Clyde chuckles, then he laughs. And he shrugs, and a little of the morning tension sloughs away.

"What do you reckon's going to happen about this Coleman bloke?" I ask. Not that either of us really know. But a problem shared... well, it's not halved, but maybe it's... well, it's someone to talk to about it.

"I'm sure Shaw will sort it out," Clyde says.

In Shaw we trust. And I have to trust her. Except I already have misgivings about how she's handling it.

"Come on," Clyde says. "Let's get off to London. See the sights. Revel in the sense of history. Maybe buy a T-shirt. Or look for hoodies without skulls on them. One of the two. Whatever takes your fancy."

"Sounds like a plan." I nod.

"There's just one thing we need to pick up along the way."

OUTSIDE THE BODLEIAN LIBRARY

Clyde's Mini is parked, engine running, in an empty back street near the massive copyright library. I watch Clyde staggering under the weight of an enormous cardboard box as he exits. He sets it down by the car with a grunt. A large and rather eclectic collection of books. I look at Clyde confused. His mask is—obviously, I suppose—unreadable.

He goes to the trunk, pulls out two jump leads and passes them to me.

Ah, the regalia of the supernatural. Screw cauldrons and smoking test tubes.

"If it's not too much of an imposition," Clyde starts, proving he's the only man who can use those words and not make it sound like it's the beginning of an insult, "would you pop the hood, and then on the word '*Arcum*' slam these down on the car battery?" He takes a firm hold of the metal clamps on his end.

How exactly *I* managed to kill Clyde before he did it to himself, I'll never know.

"Any chance of you telling me what's going to happen when you say that?" I get nervous whenever Clyde works magic. It always seems far too closely associated with someone trying to tear off parts of my body.

"He's good with books," is all Clyde says, and then he's off muttering to himself. "*Entok um jessun. Lom niem mor cal anum. Eltoth mok morinum.*"

And because I've seen what happens when magic isn't powered by electricity, I pop the hood and jump out of the car.

Violently exothermic, Clyde called it. Magicians getting turned into bloody smears on the ground seems a little closer to the mark.

"*Cathmartum mal ellum. Etok mol asok.*" Clyde intones nonsense syllables, a voice that is not quite his own issuing from behind a mask that... that is him.

What if I took it off the body? What would be left? Some mindless fellow? A vegetable? So much human meat?

"*Melkor al malkor. Mor tior. Arcum—*"

And then there's no time to think. At the requisite word I slam the contacts on the battery.

"*—locium met morum um satum Winston.*"

Wait. Winston?

Sparks fly. The world darkens, blue light spitting from the battery, crawling up the wires toward Clyde. He keeps chanting as it racks him, working its hissing, burning way over his body.

Clyde convulses. His gut heaves. I worry about him dropping the clamps. About violently exothermic results that blow me halfway to China.

Then Clyde hawks out a great white gob of lightning. His throat bulges with it. His face behind the mask distorts, distends. I can see his cheeks bulging. Then it flies out and under the mask as he gags. It smashes into the box. Books explode out, scatter. They fly through the air, slap into the walls. But they don't fall. They just spin. Faster. Faster.

Clyde chokes up another lightning ball. He spits and gags. His body doubles over. Another. Faster.

The books slam around the corridor. All in the air. All caught in the maelstrom of detonations.

The lightning batters at the books. Balls of the stuff smash into them, force them together. Tighter, tighter. A ragged cylinder of crackling paper.

Clyde chokes again. More lightning balls. Faster.

The mass of books changes shape. Is refined. Gains defined edges. Then the realization hits me. This isn't just Clyde blowing off steam in a fit of adolescent arcanum. The lightning is molding the books. This is magical sculpture.

Hardbacks stack into legs. Papers and encyclopedias jostle to form a chest. Paperbacks and dictionaries become two roughly hewn arms. At their ends, books clack open and shut like lobster claws. A head starts to appear. A book on its side for a mouth. Children's books with finger puppets for eyes.

A jagged silhouette of a man, limned in crackling white.

Clyde collapses, the spell done. I pull the clamps off the battery, blinking away the shapes that have bleached my retinas.

The book man lets out a racking cough. "Oh fuck me sideways," he says. "That stings like a bitch."

Oh God. I wonder if becoming incorporeal might have seriously damaged Clyde's judgment.

"Seconded," Clyde coughs.

The book-man takes a stumbling step forward, catches himself, takes a second, more confident stride. "Arthur?" he says. He has a thick cockney accent. "Is that you, mate?"

Winston. Clyde's book golem. His inside man at the Bodleian Library. Scanning for thaum... thaw... thaumer... spell books. Living in the stacks. Owner of a filthy mouth.

"Hello, Winston," I say.

Pages ripple in Winston's face. I think he's smiling. "Well bugger me," he says. "Looks like we're getting the band back together."

13

Clyde pilots his Mini out of Oxford. Winston sits in the back seat. "So," he says to Clyde, "the kiddie murderer look is big right now, I take it?"

"Sensitive," I say.

"Honesty, mate," Winston says in very serious tones, "is a valuable commodity in this day and age."

"I probably should have thrown in an etiquette manual this time, shouldn't I?" Clyde says.

Winston, as it has been explained to me, derives some of his personality from the books that constitute his physical form. Too much Dickens and Irvine Welsh, I seem to remember Clyde commenting. Why he failed to revise the mix this time, I have no idea.

"Harsh, mate," Winston says. "Fucking harsh."

I look from Winston's paperback face to Clyde's wooden one. I feel like the odd one out. "Why did we summon him again?"

"Charming fucking company this is," Winston grumps. "Like bloody tea with the Queen it is."

I shake my head. "Not what I meant." I suspect it's all bluster with Winston, but Clyde's right, he is good with books and I'd rather not piss him off. "Just, weren't you summoned already?"

"Oh, well." Clyde shrugs. "There was a small break in the spell binding Winston to this reality. Spell interruptus, so to speak.

Breach of magical contract on my part. So old Winston toddled off to his natural plane of existence. Just a blip, really."

"Nice to see the old country," Winston assures us.

"What sort of blip?" I ask. Magic and blips seem to be a combination that ought to be avoided.

"Oh." Clyde shrugs as if wrestling out of an uncomfortable jacket. "The whole dying thing."

There is a long and very uncomfortable silence in the car.

Winston breaks it by clearing his throat. "Tabitha any good in the sack?" he asks.

Silence, mercifully, returns as Clyde drives on.

LONDON

The British Museum appears around a corner, and I say, "Bollocks."

"No need to brag about them, mate." Winston gives me a papery smile.

"No," I shake my head, "I just… I didn't know you were coming to the library, so I didn't… There's no plan. How do we get you in? Can't just walk up to the front desk with an animated pile of books, and ask for the way to the reading room."

"Books?" Winston says. "Is that all I am to you, Arthur? All surface with you, isn't it?"

I flap a shushing hand in his direction. He harrumphs.

"Well, I've got a handcart in the trunk," Clyde says. "Should be fine."

I puzzle over this one. "Are we going to use the handcart to bash in the brains of anyone who asks us about Winston?" is about as good as I can get.

Winston cackles. "Nah, mate. Same way we got me into the Bodleian. I stand to attention and we use old Tabitha's bogus paper trail to sneak me in as a donation of books. Subterfuge. Like a bleedin' ninja."

"Tabitha's false paper trail?" This is the first I've heard about it.

"Oh," Clyde says. It's no longer possible to catch his eye, but he still turns his head so I can only see the edge of his mask. "About that. Yes. Well I was sort of thinking, by which I mean, I was very precisely thinking, that perhaps, I, by which I mean… well, myself. No one else I could mean really. But I was thinking I, me, might be the one to create the paper trail. Perhaps. Maybe. Except, well… sort of connected to their system and doing it right now." He shrugs. "Wireless and all that. Terrible security if I can break it."

"Wait," I say. "You're connected to the internet right now?"

"Well," Clyde shrugs, "come back from the dead with computer superpowers, seems a shame not to use them."

And of course, Clyde violates the laws of the universe on a daily basis. That's basically his job description. And I work with him. I watch, and I nod, and I smile while he does it. So really, connecting your brain directly to the internet shouldn't be a big deal. But somehow Clyde has blown my mind again.

"Didn't accessing the internet almost give you a seizure yesterday?" It's probably not the most important question to ask, but it's the one that's easiest for my mind to form.

"Well, yes." Clyde nods. "But practice and its correlation to perfection and all that. And, I concede, Tabitha did advise against the practice. Bit of a sticking point. That and my first attempts lost her a lot of her files. Total accident, of course. But, in hindsight, I probably should have waited until the caffeine sank in this morning before mentioning it to her. But she took it pretty well, I think. Could have gone a lot worse, and we also happened, along the way, to learn certain lessons about the durability of the mask. So, you know, in overall terms, a positive experience." He shrugs. "But yes, sort of stayed up all night working on it." He taps the mask, and, again, there's something odd about the way he does it. As if the feel of it makes him uncomfortable. "Might as well make myself useful, I figured. I want to be useful."

There's something off about the way he's saying that word, but without an expression to go from I can't quite work out what the problem is.

And I was so totally planning to use this time to be weirded out about him just being a mask now… I'm going to have to make time in my busy freaking-out schedule to gibber about this too.

"It's amazing," Clyde is saying, "how many people use 1-2-3-4 as their computer password. Tabby told me about it, but I didn't imagine they'd all be such silly buggers."

Looks like I'm going to have to revise my computer security plans then...

Clyde twists his head sharply to one side, looks up, then back at me. "There we go." He gives a satisfied nod.

"You sure you're all right?" I ask him. I seem to be asking that too much recently.

"Of course." Clyde pops the car door, bounces out. "Now let's get Winston loaded up. We have a delivery to make."

14

That definitely should have been harder. The security guard at the service entrance barely looked at us. I mean, admittedly, it's not like we're breaking into Fort Knox, we're pretending we're donating books to a library, but still... well, OK, maybe it shouldn't have been harder.

Clyde is wearing his hoodie again, head bowed to hide everything in its shadows. I trail after him with the handcart. He stops suddenly and I almost rear-end him with Winston. "Oh wow," he says.

"What is it?" I spin around, trying to work out what he's looking at. It's tricky when the gaze you're following doesn't actually originate from eyes.

"Oh. Sorry." Clyde pulls his head down between his shoulders. "Rude of me. It's just... Well, I was still on the servers for the British Museum. And, well, there's some first-rate scans of some really rare Dickens on there. Obviously a terrible time for it. Realize that now. Like reading at the table. Terrible habit. My mother was always on at me about that. Definition of rudeness she called it. There again, she never had an alien take over her body and lay its eggs in her mind, so her frame of reference might have been smaller than mine. But definitely up there with the ruder things one can do."

I close my eyes. I don't know why this bothers me so much. Why should a wireless internet connection be more upsetting than violating reality at its most fundamental levels?

Except, violating reality seems at its core a human skill. The mind and the words intersecting with power. A wi-fi connection is so much more… mechanical. Inhuman.

I think I'm going to have to find a better word than that.

Clyde looks around. "You know, I've no idea where we should be going. Do you?"

"Again, my original plan had been to go in the front door," I say. A bit catty of me, but I'm never at my best when people are rearranging my view of reality.

"Ooh!" Clyde's hand shivers and he cocks his head. "Blueprints."

Post-human?

Superhuman?

Somehow, no name for it makes me feel even slightly more comfortable.

THE READING ROOM

The sense of history is palpable in the room. It seems to bow heads over books, to color the light that slants in from the high windows. Gandhi studied here. Mark Twain. Karl Marx. H. G. Wells.

"Lovely librarian ladies," Winston mutters to himself. "Glasses and skirts, nom nom." A copy of *Lady Chatterley's Lover* has worked its way loose from his pile of books and is waggling lewdly.

"Jesus," I say.

"That's what all the ladies say."

I am sorely tempted to slap Winston, but there's a slim chance that might look odd in public.

"OK." Clyde nods at a balding man behind a counter polishing his glasses on a maroon vest. "That guy should have a backdated email from George Coleman with the request for the papers."

"Any reason why it's him?"

"Oh," Clyde digs deeper into his hoodie. "Slim chance that perhaps, I found someone on the email server talking about their cat a lot. And then, you know, hypothetically the cat's name was that person's password. So, again, it would be within the realm of possibility that it was easy enough to get into his account."

Again there's that creeping sense of wrongness. "So, basically," I say, "you're saying it's within the realm of possibility that you broke a bunch of privacy laws."

"Just," Clyde hesitates, "trying to be useful." He shrugs with a certain amount of violence.

That word "useful" again…

"Greasing wheels is all," Clyde continues. He is, at least, reassuringly bad at being succinct. "But totally see your point. Like reading at the table."

Like reading someone else's book that you stole at the table. But I don't say that. Instead I go to the desk, ask for the material, reference the email, and the man says he's sorry he missed it, and he'll have stuff pulled right away.

Again, easy. Even if Clyde does look like he's trying to work out where the metal concert is, and Winston is singing Hot Chocolate's "You Sexy Thing" under his breath.

And then someone catches my arm and says, "Well fancy seeing you here."

My hand immediately goes for my gun. It's a slightly frightening instinct to have developed. There again, my left side still stings from being electrocuted.

But the voice doesn't belong to a cyborg Russian schoolmarm. Instead it's a pretty, smiling Weekender from the Natural History Museum. "Aiko?" I say.

She nods. "Nice to see you again, Agent Arthur."

I let go of the gun, but not before her eyes travel to its momentarily exposed butt.

"Paranoid moment?" she asks. "Totally understand. Happens to me in the classroom all the time."

I smile at that. Clyde stands a few yards away, shaking his head. Winston is waggling *Lady Chatterley* again.

I ignore both of them. If I'm the lead field agent, and I believe I am, I'm not going to lead with rudeness. "So," I say, "what brings you here?"

"Oh," Aiko grins, "Chernobyl. Same thing as you, I imagine."

Clyde starts shaking his head more violently. I can almost hear Felicity enunciating, "Official Secrets Act."

"No," I say, jumping for the nearest denial. "Totally different reasons. Totally." I'm not completely convinced the academy is going to give me the Oscar for that one.

"Yeah," Aiko gives me the look a first grade teacher gives to the innocent-eyed child with the crayon and the wall covered by a Jackson Pollock interpretation.

Clyde steps forward at that. "Different reason," he says. He sounds nothing like himself. Harsh and sharp.

It is not a mechanical glitch, I tell myself. It's just the Weekenders. They just did something that got them enormously deep underneath everyone's skin.

But what the hell was it?

Aiko gives Clyde the same indulgent look. "So," she says, "trying to pump me for information, Agent Arthur? Shame on you."

There's an edge to the question I can't quite read.

"You know I can't tell you why we're here," I say. While I refuse to be openly rude, I should probably toe the party line.

"Fine then." Aiko rolls her eyes. "We'll do our time magic research, you do yours."

"Time magic?" That one genuinely is new to me. And I totally get that I'm not supposed to like these people, but they do seem all kinds of helpful.

"Sure." Aiko nods, though I get the impression she still thinks I'm playing the fool. "Zombie dinosaur regrowing its skin," she says. "Russian magician. Chernobyl is the biggest space-time experiment of them all. We may not make a living doing this, Agent Arthur, but we know what we're doing."

I'm about to explain that I'm genuinely confused, but a new voice interrupts.

"Oh, totally," says someone behind me. "Totally just hit on guys and let me do all the work. Because you know how much I just love analog research. Urban ninjas in the library. Totally where it's—"

I turn around and see Jasmine, the blond, pigtailed girl from the Natural History Museum. She's still got headphones on, these ones pink and emblazoned with a stylized skull. She's added a pair of reading glasses and a Hello Kitty T-shirt. Malcolm, the large black man, stands behind her looking like he's been listening to this monologue since approximately the dawn of time.

Then the girl sees my face.

"Oh. My. God!"

I wince a little as the girl hits the high note at the end. People look up from their books.

"You guys! I love you guys!" She rushes Clyde and clasps him in a sudden hug. He stands startled, hands trapped down at his sides by the embrace. Some onlookers start to glare. Clyde tries to bury his head deeper into his hood.

"Jasmine," the black man behind the girl finally rumbles. "Let him be."

"Has your therapist talked to you about repression, Malcolm?"

The big man shuffles his feet. "I don't... Not the therapist. Not to strangers." He sounds embarrassed, avoids our eyes.

"They're not strangers!" Jasmine squeaks. "They're," she looks around warily then lowers her voice, "MI37." The word sounds hallowed in her voice.

The big man looks back and forth from me to Clyde then back to me. He holds out a hand. "Good to see you," he says. My hand disappears into his, but he shakes gently.

"So," Aiko says, "if we're being all friendly, is there anything you can tell us?" She has a sweet, hopeful smile.

"Official Secrets Act," Clyde intones.

I shrug.

"Fine then." She waves a dismissive hand. "We'll try not to get in your way."

I seem to have ended up being rude without meaning to. And I still feel like these people, these Weekenders, could be useful allies.

"It's not like that," I say.

"Is it like something you *can* tell us?" She cocks her head to one side.

"You know I can't tell you anything." I try out a smile on her. Try to get the tone right. "It's the law, and it's my job."

"So we should piss off and leave you alone." Aiko smiles with her mouth but her eyes have gone cold. "I get it."

"No," I say. Why is it so hard to get myself understood some days?

"No?" Aiko's eyebrows are doing the yo-yo thing I feel mine do.

"No?" Clyde echoes Aiko, only he doesn't sound so pleased.

"All I'm saying is I can't help. Everyone else is telling you to piss off. I figure that's more than enough people without me needing to chip in." And God knows if that's the smartest thing to say, but it's the most honest. I feel she deserves that at least.

Aiko seems to weigh that for a while. Then, "All right," she says. "All right, Agent Arthur. You get a pass this time."

"You seem like a nice person," I say. "All of you." I nod at Jasmine and Malcolm. "I honestly think you can help with this. I just can't help you. My hands are tied."

"Nice?" The edge I don't quite understand is back in her voice. "You think I'm *nice*?"

I shrug. "Am I wrong?"

She smiles at that, then reaches into a pocket and pulls out a notepad and pen. She scribbles something and hands a page to me. "My number, if you ever want to play with other kids." The edge to her voice is still there. She smiles. "Good luck finding whatever it could possibly be that you're looking for."

I am, most definitely, in the process of getting myself in trouble. I can just feel it.

But then, just like that, the balding man with the spectacles and the maroon vest is back with a stack of manila folders, saying, "Here it is," and I smile, and Aiko smiles—

—and then a Russian voice says, "Well fancy seeing you here."

I turn, already reaching for my gun. She's standing there, short, heavy-set, steel glistening along her jawline. Beside her stands a taller man, dark-haired and pale-skinned. He has hangdog eyes, hollow cheeks, and more stubble than a rock star. His smile reveals chrome-coated teeth.

I've got the gun halfway out of its holster. The tall Russian tuts. The short one mutters. Then the world goes white. Gravity goes away. And I sail through the air as the room around me explodes.

15

I remember hearing once that one of the worst things to drive your car into is a tree. Worse than a brick wall or sheet glass. No give in trees apparently. Big thick oak buggers just stand there and take it and laugh at your crumple zones.

Apparently it's very much the same sort of situation with people and bookshelves.

For a minute I do a very clever impression of a man lying on the ground incapacitated by pain. In the meantime, the British Museum Reading Room takes the opportunity to pretty much go to hell.

People scream and run. Light flashes. Wood splinters.

If you ask me, the bookshelves had it coming.

I manage to make it to all fours, breathing hard, spitting blood. The world tilts and I haul on the bookshelf that did my spine in, grasping for my bearings.

Then there's a sound like the world grinding to a halt. A deepening "bwoom" of sound like the audio track on a video slackening to a quarter speed. I see the tall Russian standing, metal arms stretched out toward me. Between him and me is a great ball of rippling space. A bubble of heat shimmer.

I dive sideways, crash over chairs. The ball rolls past my head. Missed me, you bastard.

But the Russian is smiling. And I start to worry, but then he disappears as Malcolm West pile drives him to the ground in a flying tackle. And special government training be damned, that is how you solve a problem.

"Arthur! Get down!"

I spin to see who's yelling at me. Aiko, I realize. And then I think that instead of working that out, I probably should have gotten down.

Something crashes into my shoulder. I spin across the floor. I slam down on my back. The world shudders and shakes as my head bounces off the floor.

Apparently, the bookshelf hasn't finished with me yet. Wooden spikes are growing from its shelves, its sides. One lances out, spearing the ground between my legs. It is inches away from putting a serious crimp in my relationship with Felicity Shaw.

The spike shudders. Its surface fractures. Tiny thorns burst forth, stretching out.

Time to move.

I perform something close to a backwards roll. When I come up, the pole has turned into a fistful of wooden spikes. It rises up before me, and I scrabble back, desperate to get out of range of the oncoming strike.

But the wooden fist doesn't come down. It rises and rises, growing, thickening. It sprouts leaves. I stare, confused.

It's a tree. It's a bloody great tree growing in the British Museum Reading Room. And it's not alone. Back where the bookshelf stood—there's a whole bloody thicket of the bastards growing there.

I don't understand what's going on. I stagger to my feet, staring, clutching my injured shoulder. Blood soaks through the fabric. I can see Clyde, hood thrown back, a halo of sparks around his wooden mask. He flings his arms about like a deranged semaphore operator. The world explodes around him. The girl, Jasmine, has produced two pistols. She fires them, one then the other, then the other, the other.

My gun. I grab for—

"Get down, you silly bugger!"

I wish people would stop shouting that at—

Winston collides with my midriff, removing the air from my lungs and my feet from the ground.

We land in a tumbling crash of limbs and pages. Winston is yelling, "You'll rip me! You'll fucking rip me!" and I'm trying to get the breath to say anything.

We crash against something. My head rattles. I'm lying on top of Winston. Back where I was standing there's a tree tearing up through the ground, splintering the floorboards. And what the hell is going on?

"Get off me, you big nancy," Winston says. "You're not my type at all."

I comply as best I can. I roll off, still shaky, vision blurred.

"Get up! Get up!" Winston barks at me.

I look around. A forest. How did this place turn into a forest?

Another bubble of sound. A grinding of the universe. Another tree rips upwards.

"What are they doing?" I ask, still trying to clear my head.

"Getting away with those Chernobyl papers. What's it fucking look like?" Winston is already running back to the fray.

I grab my gun. It feels reassuring and heavy. I sweep around in a circle. My sight lines are for shit. Trees block everything, new branches expanding into space. A shadow moves and I fire. Nobody yells. Neither friend nor foe.

I hear gunfire to the left, wood splintering.

I start forward. Movement is getting difficult, the trees jammed tight together, trunks fused. There are narrow woodland passageways floored with torn maroon carpet. The still extant bookshelves are caught between branches spilling their contents like ruined birds' nests.

They are turning the bookshelves into trees. That's the only explanation that makes sense. Which is one of those messed up pieces of logic that this job forces upon me.

I hit a dead end, push back the way I came only to find a new tree blocking my path. I'm in a tight little clearing. No way out. I spin. No exits. I hear a yell. A scream.

Up. I look. Trunks giving way to branches. The space less dense. And I didn't so much spend my youth climbing trees as I did playing video games and reading books, but there's no time to learn like the present.

I stick my foot in a fork of trunk and branch. And it's surprisingly easy, everything is so tightly jammed it's not hard to find the next handhold, the next place to put my feet. Up I go. Five feet. Ten feet. Fifteen feet. I am swaying in a tangle of twigs and leaves.

Even as I make my way forward, the trees don't stop growing. The press of the place intensifies. I am briefly stuck and have to leave my jacket behind. I push through a net of thin branches and a trunk closes the path behind me. I wriggle, panicked, between two encroaching trunks. I don't care about Russians. I just want to get out. There is sunlight distantly above me. Windows. Maybe I could get out through the windows.

And then suddenly space. Suddenly I am teetering, the branch beneath my feet bending, bending, creaking. I scrabble back, drop my gun. I watch it tumble away. One rotation. Two. It hits the floor with a sharp crack.

A woman turns. Steel glints.

Oh shit.

I'm twenty plus feet in the air. I try to push back, but the branches resist me.

The Russian smiles.

Twenty plus feet. The fall probably won't kill me.

The Russian won't give it time to do that.

And I don't know what Kurt Russell would do. He wouldn't be stupid enough to get in this situation.

White light and the smell of ozone fill the air.

Sod it.

I jump.

16

I leave my perch as lightning arcs. A stark white line playing dot-to-dot from wall, to her, to me.

No. To where I was. Splinters scour my heels, tear my trousers. I skid through the sky, the shockwave slamming into me, skewing my trajectory. I strike branches. They crack and snap as I punch a hole through the forest.

I'm only six feet off the ground when I finally hit clear air. I plummet into a low clearing. My head cracks off the floor. Everything spawns a twin.

I roll, clutching my temples. It takes me a minute to realize I've come to rest with my head in someone's lap.

"Seriously?" Aiko says. "Again? Seriously?"

My lips try to smile but even that hurts. "I think I left half my skin up in the trees," I say. It seems relevant at the moment.

She shakes her head reassuringly. "Quarter of it, tops."

I push off her, still groggy. Malcolm and Aiko are in the clearing too, crouched low, bristling with weapons. I reach for my gun. Then I remember it's gone.

"Shit."

"Malcolm," Aiko calls. "You got any spare toys on you?"

"Always," Malcolm says to Aiko and holds out something smooth and black and deadly.

"Safety's off," he says as I take it. "One in the chamber."

I realize that underneath Malcolm West's long-suffering exterior there is someone who is quite possibly very frightening.

"How did you get these in here?" I ask. Nothing seems to be making sense.

"Not really the relevant question right now, is it?" Aiko says. And she does have a point.

"We're going to have to move," I say, even though it seems rather a shame. I think I could grow to like taking cover here. But I nod up at two bookshelves I noticed caught in the trees above us as I made my way down. "They hit those and we run out of space."

"Where do we go?" Jasmine says, looking eager and excited, which seems rather inappropriate for a life-or-death battle. I blink. Too many blows to the head.

"Clyde," I say. "We find him. He's the biggest gun we have."

"The skinny dude?" Aiko looks uncertain about this plan.

"Trust me." And from their expressions, I genuinely think they do.

"You know where he is?" Malcolm asks.

And then, conveniently enough, Clyde comes flying through the hole I made in the trees, and lands with a sickening crack on the floor.

17

Clyde bounces like a rag doll. He spins and skitters. His mask flies off, spins across the floor.

The tall pale man whose body Clyde controls lies unconscious on the floor. I'd forgotten that face. Too oddly proportioned to be handsome, but a face you would remember. Delicately boned. Skin pale enough you feel you should see the bone beneath. No fat. No excess. Cheekbones and skin.

The eyes are open. They see nothing.

"Clyde!" I shout. I start running—to the body at first, but then I remember that's not where Clyde is. That's not who he is. I run to the mask, scoop it up.

For a terrible moment I think it's going to be cracked, spilling circuitry and Clyde's soul. But, thank God, it's still in one piece. I scoop the mask up, head over to the body. I flip it roughly onto its back. Then, as carefully as I can, I slip the mask back over the head.

"Clyde?" I say. "Clyde?"

Nothing. The head lolls. And does he need time to re-establish control? To reboot?

"Clyde!" I say again, my voice rising.

"Shhh!" Aiko hisses. "He's unconscious."

And what is he doing? How long does rebooting take? Any time at all is too long right now.

So that's our biggest gun down. Time to rely on the little ones.

"OK," I say, suppressing the expletives that want to spill from me. "We need a good firing position. Somewhere—"

"Move!" Malcolm bellows.

Above us the universe grinds on its gears. A shimmering bubble of space engulfs one of the bookshelves.

A branch lances towards us.

The clearing's exit is a low tunnel. I back into it, hands under Clyde's shoulders, heaving. The clearing is disappearing fast, thick wooden walls closing off our exit.

Everything is dark and close. I'm scooting backwards on my arse, bumping up against someone's heels, Clyde a dead weight behind me.

Another clearing. Malcolm shouting again. Another loose bwoom of sound. Another tunnel. Clyde's feet bumping over roots and shattered floorboards.

"They're going to crush us." It's Jasmine talking, her voice climbing the octaves. "There's no way out. They're closing the exits."

And I'm not one for pessimism, but it is starting to look like I'll be getting a closer look than I might want at how pâté is made.

"Quiet." Malcolm's voice is a low roll of thunder. "Need to work out where they are. They're giving us a lot of cover." There is a brief tense moment of silence. Then, "This way," Malcolm rumbles.

We shuffle on. Everything's quiet now. No more lightning cracks. No more... well, whatever the hell the other thing is.

We come to something that, relatively speaking, seems like a clearing. I wedge my way into the tangle of brambles, branches bending and cracking.

"Shhh," Malcolm hisses. He's lying on his belly, clutching a gun with a barrel long enough to suggest that he might be compensating for something.

I twist, trying to see what he's looking at. We're near the edge of the trees, I realize. Just a thin web of branches separates us from open space. A few yards of open floorboards, and then a doorway. A sign glows above it, letters bright and red: EXIT.

The woman is still there, her back to us. She's bent over a desk studying something. A few bookshelves still stand between her and us. Malcolm holds the pistol in both hands, drawing a bead on the back of her head.

Shooting her while she's so completely unaware will not exactly be a sporting move, but the other team is using magic so I think the rules of gentlemanly conduct have been cast pretty far away.

The whole world seems to narrow, seems to become the two points of focus. Malcolm. The Russian. I can see the sweat on his forehead. I can see the light of the LEDs around the woman's wrist reflecting off the sheet of paper she holds up. I can see Malcolm bring his breathing under control. Slow and steady. One. Two. The Russian's hair moves slightly as she changes the angle of her head. Three. Four. Malcolm's finger starts to tense.

"No!" a voice howls. "Run! It's a trap! A fucking great ginormous trap!"

A pile of books explodes out of one of the shelves. A leg concertinas out of the whirling mass. An arm. Winston.

Then the tall Russian stands up behind him, from where he was taking cover. Between bookshelves. Between us and the woman. Staring and smirking over Winston's shoulder.

"What the f—" someone is yelling, but then the Russian's arms bunch. Lightning flares off the ground. I dive backwards, half-dragging Clyde, half-falling. Aiko rolls through branches. Malcolm catapults forward, into Winston's path. Jasmine pulls her guns, too late, too late.

The lightning hits the tall Russian. Winston flails his arms, still running. The Russian flings his arms forward. The air coalesces around them, becomes a ball of gel that slops forward and rolls through the air. Winston hits the tree line. I hit the floor.

The ball of gelatinous space hits Winston.

Bwoom.

Winston stops, staggers. He drops to his hands and knees.

He manages to raise his head, trembling all over. He looks through the trees, looks me right in the eye.

"Bugger, mate," he says. "Balls and buggery-fuck."

18

I dive away from Winston, my gun out, finger squeezing, barrel barking. It's not as easy to hit things while doing that as they make it look in the movies. Flying through the air, body thrumming with adrenaline—it's not exactly good for the aim. Still, it's satisfying to see the Russian dive for cover.

The others scatter through the maze of branches. Lightning slams through the trees. Fire licks at fresh leaves.

A branch bursts out of Winston, a wooden tentacle, thickening, widening. He screams, his mouth open so wide his whole head hinges back on the spine of a book. One leg is growing, lengthening. I see bark spreading over his chest.

And shit and balls. Oh irredeemable buggery-fuck. They're turning Winston into a tree. They're turning him into… Jesus.

He screams again. It's muffled. Leaves burst from his face even as it's lifted into the sky by his suddenly colossal legs.

Lightning arcs. He staggers round, smashes a wooden arm into the newly grown forest. Branches fall like rain, rattling and snapping their way down. He sways again. The top of a tree falls down beside him, obliterating another bookshelf. The tall Russian dives for safety a second time.

I scramble for cover. Crouched behind a tree, I'm unable to look away. I wait for it to be over, for stasis to seize Winston, for him to die.

Turns out he's a bit of a persistent bugger.

"Oh fuck me backwards!" Words start to emerge out of Winston's senseless yelling. "Oh Jesus."

He smashes into more of the newly grown forest. I heave on Clyde moments before a tree limb slams into the space his head just occupied.

"I'm a fucking Ent!" Winston yells. "I'm a Tolkien fanboy's wet dream!"

He stumbles forward. The Russians scatter as he mashes towards them.

"What have you bastards done to me?" He sweeps an arm clumsily in their direction. Furniture is obliterated. Chairs fly across the open space, shatter against the walls. The woman turns, a look of fear on her face. She stretches out a hand.

"No you bleeding don't."

Winston's massive foot comes down. Lightning flares—

—and dies. There is a crack and a crunch. A sickening wet snap of bone and blood.

"Ow! Jesus!"

Winston's foot is on fire. He hops backwards, trips, comes sprawling towards us. The tall Russian is scurrying for the door.

"No." Malcolm is calm and furious all at once. He opens fire at the Russian. I join in. Bullets chew through wood, spatter among bookshelves, embed themselves in Winston's leg.

"Timbeeeeeeerrrrrrrrrr!!!"

And gravity finally wins. And Winston comes down.

19

"Move!" I haul hard on Clyde. He is a sack of skin and bones. Branches fight me.

Winston hits the tree line.

The world shudders. Explosions drum against my sternum. Noise eclipses my senses. Everything is shattering and cracking and creaking. Everything is falling apart. My face is full of leaves and tree.

Somewhere, between my heartbeats, silence returns. Only the whistle of damaged nerve endings in my ear and the heave of my breath to listen to. I am pinned in branches. They give way one by one. I half collapse, half slither to the floor.

Clyde has been thrown to the very edge of the trees. He's still unconscious. Missed the whole thing. Lucky bastard.

He better just be bloody unconscious. I do not want to have that conversation with Tabitha.

"Bastards," says a basso cockney voice. "Bastards made me a bloody treeman."

Winston's voice. Winston is still alive, still here. His form's changed, violently and unmistakably, but the animating force that is Winston is still invested in it.

No breach of contract. So no death. So Clyde is definitely still alive.

Well thank God for that.

I bend down, start heaving my friend up. Aiko emerges from a nearby thicket. Her clothes are torn and blood from a cut on her forehead is matted in her eyebrows.

"Come on," she says. "Let me help you with him."

"You OK?" I ask as we pull Clyde free of the trees.

"Not really." She shakes her head. Then she lets go of Clyde. I stagger against the sudden increase in weight.

"Shit." Aiko sits down hard. "This is twice in one week. Normally the worst I have to deal with is a six-year-old calling me a poopyhead." She starts to cry.

"Oh Aiko." A voice from behind me. I turn, and Jasmine and Malcolm are emerging from the trees. Jasmine's headphones have been mangled. Malcolm hobbles, a deep gash in one leg. Jasmine pulls ahead of him, goes to Aiko, wraps her in an embrace. And shit. Aiko really is a first grade teacher. Jasmine really is just a teenager. And if I'm what passes for a professional, I can only imagine how much of a toll this takes on an amateur, enthusiastic or otherwise.

Felicity can say what she likes about the Weekenders, but these guys have my vote of confidence any day of the week.

I look over at Malcolm. He shrugs. There's no trauma on his face. Stoic, maybe a little nonplussed by Aiko and Jasmine. He has to have been military or something. Balls of steel.

As he approaches, something catches his eye. He peers and looks behind a smashed bookcase. He blanches. And if there's something that makes a man as hardened as Malcolm turn pale, why do I have the sudden urge to look?

But look I do.

Oh Jesus.

My guts heave. I choke down bile.

A bloody mess of skin and bone. A mangled red silhouette, limbs horribly distorted. Metal mashed into the mess of bone.

The Russian woman. The one who electrocuted me. The one Winston stepped on.

"Jesus," I say again. I close my eyes but the image remains. I close them harder.

"Arthur."

Winston calls my name and I look up.

"Arthur, look what they did to me, mate."

Winston is struggling up out of the trees. I stare at him. All of him. Twenty-five feet or more, towering and tottering. His face is inscribed in bark, knots for eyes, a twisted crack in the wood for a mouth. Leaves burst in an ugly mop above the half-hewn face. His legs are ivy-strewn trunks and his arms are branches. One foot is blackened and charred, leaking sap, leaving sticky glistening footprints tinged with red.

"What they do to me, Arthur, mate?"

"They turned you into a tree, Winston," is about as much as I can manage. But I think he had that bit figured out.

He shakes his head. A few twigs tumble around him.

"It's time magic."

Winston and I look over. It's Aiko, rubbing tears from her cheeks with the back of a fist. She swallows, re-establishes control. "Same as with the T-Rex. Turn back the clock. The books, the shelving—all wood. So they go back to being trees. There'll be other stuff too. Statues back to rocks, that sort of thing."

"No..." A new voice cuts in, then dissolves into coughing. We all spin, looking. Malcolm yanks out his improbable-looking pistol again.

"No such thing as time magic."

"Clyde!" I run to him, skid down on my knees. Another cough wracks his body.

"Yeah," I hear Winston rumble. "Don't worry about me. I'm fine. No psychological trauma suffered here."

"Shit," I say to Clyde, eloquent as ever. "I was worried about you."

"No need," Clyde says. He reaches up a trembling fist and taps the mask. "Flash memory, I think. Very durable."

I laugh. Clyde doesn't. I'm not sure if it's not a joke, or if it's just not as funny as he thought it was going to be.

"Time. Magic," Aiko says again, emphasizing each word.

Clyde shakes his head but doesn't sit up.

I don't blame him. My head's spinning and I was conscious the whole time. Time magic. Magic that looks like time magic.

Chernobyl. Bomb threats. Stolen meteorites. It's like someone cut lines out of a newspaper and scattered them in front of us.

Admittedly it'd probably have to be the *Fortean Times*. But still…

Chernobyl is the connection. It has to be. But Chernobyl is broken, a mistake. But if that's a false lead, why did two Russians just turn the British Museum Reading Room into a nature reserve to get their hands on our documents about it?

I look down at Clyde. "I just don't understand how the bomb is involved," I say.

Clyde starts shaking his head again.

Jasmine looks over at me. "Oh my God, did you just say bomb?"

"Maybe, you know, ixnae on the omb-bae," Clyde says, but he's ten seconds and fifteen years too late for that to be relevant.

Crap.

Aiko looks over at me. "A bomb?" she says. "There's a bloody bomb involved in this?"

"No," I say. "Not at all." I just can't generate enough effort to make the lie convincing.

Aiko shakes her head.

A shudder runs down Clyde's body. "Just sent an instant message to Tabby," he says. "She says you're an idiot."

Instant-messaging. With his brain. I shudder almost as hard as he did.

"Tell her to stop flirting with me," I say. "It's inappropriate." Here's hoping passive aggressiveness plays better than straight-up aggressiveness.

"Wait." Clyde holds up a hand. "Shaw's hijacking the conversation."

Oh God, there's going to be a debrief. And that prick Coleman is going to be there. I wonder how many sick days MI37 gives me.

"Shaw says, and I'm sure in a very loving, tender way, that you're an idiot too," I smile at that, "and that we need to haul our collective arse back home pronto."

"Shit and balls." This is by far my worst trip to the library since my mother caught me with an inappropriate tome during the years of my puberty.

Slowly, painfully, I clamber back to my feet. I offer Clyde a hand and haul him up.

"So that's it?" Aiko has her hands on her hips. "You guys bugger off and leave us here?"

It does seem a bit callous now she puts it that way. "How about I say thank you first?"

Clyde harrumphs. Aiko smiles. I prefer the latter.

"Look," I say—and surely some kind of concession has to be made here; we can't keep pretending these guys aren't helping us—"I'll talk to people back at the office. There's got to be some way we can work together on this." Aiko doesn't look so convinced, and, to be honest, I'm not either so I decide to throw a bone. "And yes," I say, "there is a bomb. And, yes, we were looking up Chernobyl."

"Arthur!" Clyde explodes.

"Oh what?" I turn to face him, because, seriously now, what part of that did they not already know? "Next time you're conscious through a fight you can tell me who deserves to know what, OK?" It doesn't sound as placatory as I was hoping it might. "Without them we wouldn't have arses for Felicity to kick."

Clyde's blank mask gives me nothing. No sympathy, no condemnation, no understanding. Eventually he says, "Felicity?"

"Shaw," I say.

"Oh." He nods.

There's a sound from the door. All of us turn. We point guns.

A short man with a pinched gray face wearing blue overalls shoves open a door, pushing aside the remains of a bookcase and peers at us. He sees the guns. "Oh Jesus bloody Christ." He puts a palm to his brow.

I look to Clyde but he doesn't see my look to return it.

"Excuse me," I say, lowering the gun, "but who—"

"What in the name of all that is holy are you still even doing here?" The man throws up his hands, then finally forces his way into the room. "Jesus, they expect me to..." He shakes his head. "You understand the situation, right? You're aware, right? You're undercover." He points to Clyde and me. "Hush-hush." He pushes his hands through his hair, leaving visible grooves. "There are coppers on the way, funders on the phone, librarians trying to upload crap to YouTube, hackers in the email." He kicks a book. "I'm trying to run a bloody cleanup operation here."

He stares at us. We stare back. My life was just threatened by trees. This seems like an odd moment for a scolding.

"Scarper!" he yells at us.

"Who are you?" I ask. Because I still haven't quite got that bit straight.

The man slaps a hand to his forehead. "Unappreciated, that's what it is. You chaps all bugger about blowing stuff up and never really think about the man sticking it all back together." He walks up to me. He comes up to my chin. He screws his face up even more so that it more closely resembles a drill bit than I thought was humanly possible. His stiletto of a nose does not help the impression.

He thrusts a hand at me then retracts it before I have time to take it. "Ogden Beauvielle, cleanup operations. Don't really have time for this, but I know that people who get guns are apparently just oh-so-important, and I'm just a little cog does bloody vital work that everyone is utterly dependent on. No need for anyone to have mentioned me."

"You work for us?" Surely a sixth member of MI37 would have come up. I look to Clyde, but he just shrugs.

The little man abruptly drops to his knees. I stare at him, nonplussed. "Please." He clutches my knees. "Leave. Just leave. Bugger off. Fly away. I don't care. But if Shaw has to get you out of Scotland Yard's nick then it'll be your hide as well as mine."

I take a step away, shaking him from my legs. But it does sound like he knows Felicity.

"You do the cleanup for us?" I ask, still trying to work it all out.

"Oh God." The little man drops his head. "I'm begging you. Just walk out the door. Please. Leave. Leave. Leave."

"Leaves? You talking about me?" The trees rustle. With a crack of branches, Winston sits up.

"Oh," I hear the little man moan. "Oh bugger. Oh that's just bloody typical that is. Bloody typical."

In the end, I suppose, it's always a little bit reassuring to know someone's job is worse than yours.

20

AN HOUR LATER

"Come on," I say to Clyde, "out with it." For a man without a face, he certainly can pout.

He maintains the silence that's lasted through the London suburbs and halfway around the M25 ring road. The Mini's wheels thrum over potholes. A chirpy woman on Radio Four tells us that rain is coming, and it's going to stay until sometime around the apocalypse.

I turn the radio off.

"Talk to me, Clyde," I say. "We're on the same side, remember. Team members. Friends."

Clyde nods his head. Once. Twice.

"Arthur," he says eventually, "I completely understand, you know, full three hundred and sixty degree perspective on the subject, and I know you're trying to do the right thing..."

There's a "but" heading towards me like a jack-knifing truck.

"But there are things you don't know."

"Such as?" I'm caught between defiance and trepidation. This is going to be about the Weekenders, I know, and I think MI37's official attitude so far has been unfair. But Clyde is not a person who naturally tends toward chewing others out, so if he feels the need to speak up, there's the serious possibility that I've taken a misstep somewhere.

Clyde sighs and switches into a slower lane. "The Weekenders," he says, "have existed in some variety since the seventies. Obviously not the same folks we saw today. That would be absurd. Or the product of some sort of phenomenal skin cream. And, well, most experimental thaumaturgists through history have been men. Not an observation on gender that, just testament to a biased system. But yes, crinkly old men—not big on the whole magic skin cream research as far as I'm aware. But, basically, what I'm getting at is that only that Malcolm chap has been doing this Weekending thing for any length of time, and that only dates back to the millennium according to records." He gives a little shiver on the word "records." I think he's pulling this data from somewhere.

"Anyway, going back to my whole, you know, point, the original seventies group was founded by some folk who didn't make it all the way through the vetting process for MI37. The Magic Arms Race was heating up, and our side was recruiting with a certain… well, I don't want to speak ill of people who aren't here to defend themselves, though, I mean, that does put certain unrealistic limitations on speaking ill of people. Because, really, some people deserve it whether they're present or not. I mean, take Hitler, for example. Not that I'm trying to compare anyone in MI37 to Hitler, just trying to say that maybe if you're recruiting people to become participants in a clandestine cold war, then maybe an anyone-will-do attitude isn't a solid strategy. And so they basically let some ill-equipped people find out too much before cutting them loose. And some individuals are of a disposition—and this isn't a criticism, just an observation—but once certain people know a little bit about the certain sort of stuff we deal with, well they certainly won't give up on it.

"Anyway, these folk had all failed the vetting for, and this is important, I think, for a reason. It wasn't just, you know, random capriciousness. Significant factor in the universe though it may be. But there were reasons. And those reasons, well it's why we don't know anyone who was on that original Weekenders team. They're not in the fight anymore. Not because they stopped believing. Not because they got tired. They died, Arthur. They were killed. Not metaphorically, or in a manner of speaking, or as an exaggeration. It's just, this is a dangerous job. I know you know that. I'm not trying to speak down to you. I mean in a literal sense, yes, given my height, I am speaking down, but now I've gone back to colloquialisms and idioms and all that. And, what I'm trying to say is that the people in the Weekenders, they're not right for this sort of work. It kills them.

"And—and this is really my point, Arthur, I'm getting there in the end—every time, every single time they've been involved in an MI37 operation, one of our people has died too."

He takes his eyes off the road, looks straight at me. I can feel the gaze through the mask. "They kill us, Arthur," he says. "They don't mean to. They have the best of intentions. But they mess up. And they die. And we die. So the only decent thing to do, the only right thing to do, and that's why I started this whole thing by saying you're a good chap, a chap trying to do the right thing, but the only thing to do is to try and stop them."

Finally he falls silent. He stares at the road. After a minute's silence he puts the radio back on. Someone talking about the best way to baste a turkey.

They die.

We die.

I don't want to die. I don't want anyone to die. But—and I'm probably going to regret this... But I've never in my life trusted absolute statements. In this world, it seems to me, there is nothing that is totally certain. Especially these days, when reality seems to break every five seconds.

"Look," I say, "you're telling me Aiko, Jasmine, Malcolm—they're all brand-new Weekenders, pretty much." I suspect I sound like I'm grabbing at straws. Maybe I am. "So how do we know working with these ones is going to kill us? It's a generalization. It doesn't take the individuals into account."

What pass for Clyde's eyes leave the road again.

"The individuals?" he says. He sounds slightly incredulous. "Arthur, I mean, again, not to condescend, but that girl Jasmine, she's seventeen years old. She's not been to school since she was thirteen. Malcolm West—"

Another tremor in his arm, I note.

"—was dishonorably discharged from the military, and then was kicked out of Blackwater in disgrace. You know how messed up you have to be for Blackwater to declare you a disgrace?"

I do have to concede the straws are beginning to get a little harder to grab now.

"What about Aiko?" I say. Of all of them, it seems hard to object to her.

Another violent shiver from Clyde. "Honestly? I'm surprised they let her near children."

"What?" Are we talking about the same woman?

"She's a total conspiracy theory nut. And, well, I realize 'nut' is a pejorative term, and maybe I should be more understanding, but she logs an average of sixty hours a week on internet forums and chat rooms talking about how JFK and Elvis are the same person."

"Oh." Not the most reassuring things to hear. And, well, Clyde does have a case against them. A good case even. Might even hold up in court.

But it's not like MI37 is made up of the most balanced people either. And they helped save my life. Clyde's life too. So I remain that obstinate juror demanding a smoking gun.

"What about time magic?" I say.

"It's impossible, Arthur." Clyde sounds almost exasperated. Like he thought better of me. "It's just another form of intradimensional magic. Trying to punch out of a reality's timestream and then into the same reality's timestream further along. Trying to change time within one part of one reality. It's not possible. It was all part of Chernobyl. It all ended in a big smoking hole that no one can live in and which causes terrible things to happen to wildlife. Sort of like the anti-RSPCA. Apart from the smoking hole bit. I don't know what the opposite of that would be. Maybe if the RSPCA started building mountains. But, what I'm saying is that sort of magic doesn't turn back time or turn shelves into trees. It just kills people."

Jesus. With that sort of glass-half-empty attitude, no wonder he looked so grumpy.

I shrug, still not entirely cowed by logic. "It just seems like we're making a lot of generalizations without taking the specific events into account."

"Crazy people," Clyde says. "Illusion magic." It is a remarkably succinct summary of his arguments. If he wasn't using them to argue against me, I'd compliment him.

"Illusion magic," I argue, "is like an argument get-out-of-jail-free card. You didn't break into the bank, some other guy did it, it just looked that way because of illusion magic."

"Time," Clyde informs me, "was concretized back with the establishment of Greenwich Mean Time as an international standard."

It seems a mean debating technique to just go and pull reality out from under my feet again.

"Time was concretized?" I ask. I almost don't want to, but in the end not knowing this stuff just leads to... well it leads to this sort of conversation.

"Oh." Clyde shakes his head. "Well, you see, when Greenwich Mean Time was established as an international standard there was this clock built. Ceremonial thing. But time sort of got tied to it. Still not wholly sure how that happened. Poses some interesting questions about collective perception and the nature of reality. How expectation influences probability. Really interesting fringe math in that area actually. Maybe I can access a few papers..." His right leg starts to quiver and we veer slightly.

"Clyde..." I'd rather his leg tremors didn't send us into oncoming traffic.

"Right." Clyde nods. "Read those later. But yes. Time. Concretized. In a clock. Called the Chronometer, actually. Not the most original name really. Might as well just have called it 'The Clock' and be done with it. But polysyllables make some folk feel smarter I assume. Anyway, yes. Time. The Chronometer. Inexplicably linked. Wind the Chronometer forward, time goes forward. Wind it back, time goes back. So nobody does really."

I intend to say something like, "What?" or possibly, "Why?" but instead I let out an ugly sort of grunt. I'm beginning to notice that having my preconceptions beaten out of me seems to affect my speech centers first.

So... time travel *is* possible. And we haven't...

"Hitler?" I manage to say.

"Yes," Clyde says and leaves it at that.

"Why didn't we...?"

"Oh! Sorry." Clyde shrugs twice. "I meant, yes, that is the obvious application. But, well, you know, the possibility of reality-annihilating paradoxes causing the Chernobyl explosion to happen at an atomic level throughout the entire universe. That sort of thing."

Which does seem like a good reason really.

"Where is it?" I ask. Because it's as good a question as any I have.

"They put it in Big Ben," Clyde says. "Sort of symbolic I suppose."

"Wait." I try to wrap my head round that one. "Big Ben? The tourist attraction? The first thing to get blown up in every terrorist movie set in London ever?"

"Well," Clyde says, "to be fair to the chaps that put it there, it's in a massive, lead-lined titanium room, with its own anti-magic field, surrounded by about a hundred fully-armed SAS ninjas."

"We have ninjas?" It's possible that's not the most important point, but I just have to know.

"Oh," Clyde says. "I just sort of figured. I mean, if you're an international power player, shouldn't you have ninjas?"

That's something I would have dismissed out of hand not so long ago. Now I'm genuinely worried he may have a point.

Actually, I'm a little worried he's right about everything. Time magic. The Weekenders. I could have put them in danger. Put M137 and my friends in danger. My girlfriend.

George Coleman can be in danger. I'd be fine with that.

But, Jesus, can I be so off on this? I was never a cop to go on gut instinct. Follow the evidence. Follow the paperwork.

But there's something about this... I don't know. I just don't know.

Clyde drives on, and the rain begins to fall.

21

MI37 OFFICES, OXFORD

"That's it?" Coleman barks at me. He paces back and forth across the conference room floor, puffing his chest out like a preening peacock. Actually, you can lose the "pea."

I remain looking at Felicity, the primary recipient of my report on our London escapade—the Russians, Winston, the Weekenders, the conversation I had with them afterwards, theories of time magic. She remains, impassive, against the wall.

"Did I miss anything, Clyde?" I am trying to play it cool in the face of Coleman's bluster.

"What?" Clyde shudders. "No. No." He shrugs then says it again. "No."

And thanks for joining us, Clyde. I think the ability to read at any time is going to seriously damage his social skills.

"So?" Coleman examines his corpulent fingers. "You didn't get the papers I sent you for." One finger up. "You didn't capture the Russians." Another finger. "And you told unauthorized individuals about military secrets." The third finger. "What do you do for an encore, Wallace, fuck my daughter?"

He steps forward on the last. A schoolboy bully. But if he wants me to kowtow, Coleman's going to have to try harder.

"George," Felicity interjects into the tense little space between us, "you don't have a daughter."

Coleman flaps a hand at her. "It's an expression, Felicity," he says. Only I call her Felicity.

"Well?" Coleman shoves his finger at me. "What do you have to say for yourself? What mitigating circumstances permitted such a colossal fuck-up?"

I stare at that finger. Not exactly the scariest thing that's been pointed at me today.

"Where exactly were you during the mission?" I ask. "What support did you provide?" I will not be intimidated by him.

Coleman's cheeks go beet red. "Mission?" he spits. "Mission? It was a request to go to the fucking library, Wallace. I asked you to get a book out. I didn't think you'd need an armed guard. Next time I'll just send my goddamn grandmother."

"We were attacked," I enunciate clearly, "by two Russian wizards. They ambushed us. And we killed one of them."

I'd not usually use the death of another human being as demonstration of a victory. No matter what someone does, killing them always seems a little extreme. But Coleman is pushing me to an edge here.

"Yes!" Coleman says. "You even let the retarded treeman stomp on our one potential witness. I mean, bravo, Wallace. A real clean sweep of fuck-ups." He turns his back on me.

I throw up my hands. "Is there even a point to this?" And I know the point, I've seen this before on wildlife documentaries. This is a pissing match. Establishing patterns of dominance. Coleman wants us all to recognize him as an alpha dog. Big man on campus. And I am far from an alpha male, but that doesn't mean I want Coleman pissing on my lawn.

He wheels around. "What's that?" he barks.

"I said," I speak slowly, and instead of looking at him, I look at Felicity, "is there a point to all this?"

Coleman approaches me slowly, predatory. And I get to take note of the fact that, while he is getting heavy at his waistline, he is a larger man than me. He invades my personal space, fills it with his bulk.

"How do you think you'd fare, Agent Wallace," Coleman asks,

"against one of the Russians on your own?" There is a bite beyond conversational to his tone now.

"You mean without the wonderful support you provided today?" I'm not going down without swinging a few conversational punches of my own.

"From what I gather," Coleman continues ignoring my defiance, "you did pretty much zippo to actually defend yourself. Your country. Faffed around a bit. Pulled your gun. Shot a tree. Lost your gun. Without a bunch of untrained, unprofessional, un..." he spits and froths, "...idiots, you would have died."

Another sneer. "But on your own, Wallace, would you contribute anything other than a few pints of blood to a fight?"

And he does, unfortunately, have a point. Combat is hardly my field of expertise. It's worked out so far, but it's because I am with surprisingly competent people, like Clyde, and Kayla, and Felicity, and Malcolm West from the Weekenders.

"We won today," I say, refusing to go down under one conversational punch.

"I think you're dead weight, Wallace," Coleman spits. "You're not a leader. Not a fighter. Not a researcher. You know only jack and shit. You bring us nothing. And if you don't find something soon, Wallace," my name has become an insult, "if you're not a team player, if you can't keep your mouth shut around civilians, if you so much as utter a word to those idiot Weekenders again, if you don't shape up, Wallace, then alone is exactly how you'll find yourself. In the dark. Cut off. With no one to help you when the bogeymen come knocking." He peers in close once more. Voice barely audible even to me. "And I think I know exactly how that'll go," he says. "And you do too." He turns his back. "You pathetic excuse for an agent."

And screw him. I want to hit him. To feel his nose break. God knows if I could break his nose, but God I'd love to feel it. Except he's pulling rank. He's saying he could fire me. And there's a chance he could. Jesus, there's a chance that most of what he's saying is even true. I mean, I certainly didn't kill anyone today. And I basically let Clyde run the mission. But to deliver the news like such a complete jackass. No, I will not stand for that.

"We'll see," I say, "who's standing at the end of this."

Coleman laughs. An ugly laugh. Too confident for my liking too.

And nothing from the peanut gallery. Clyde, still blank and silent. Too close to a meat statue for real comfort. Kayla, disconnected. Tabitha pissed at both of us for wasting her time. And nothing from Felicity. No leaping to my defense. No putting Coleman in his place.

And then: "What..." A voice breaks the thunderous silence, then trails away. We all turn to stare.

Devon seems to suddenly grow very small indeed. She clears her throat. Then she looks at me, and swallows, and says, "Well, I mean, I realize, you know, new girl on the team. Not completely up to speed on everything. Still wrapping my head around the infinite realities part of the day. But, well, that bit, where Arthur mentioned the time magic. Well, it rather... You know, you'll be cooking scones and spam, for example. Well, maybe you don't, but I do, and say I am, for example, of course, but there you are, elbow deep in dough and spam grease and time is just whipping by you, half the day gone in a blink. And then there's ten minutes until *Whose Line Is It Anyway* and suddenly that takes up the second half of the day. And, well, I suppose my point is, in a roundabout sort of way, that time is a slippery little chap, like some sort of pixie, or elf. At least that's how I've always imagined him. But yes, doesn't that make sense? The bit that Arthur said? About the time magic? I rather thought, you know, now that apparently I live in a world with zombie T-Rexes that that sort of all added up a bit. Maybe."

I want to run across the room and hug Devon and kiss her dimpled cheek and pump her hand like an oil prospector dredging up the last gallon from his well.

But, well, public decorum.

Kayla pats Devon on the arm in another very un-Kayla-like moment, which shows that she must have woken up at some point.

"Ha!" Coleman brays a phlegmy half-laugh. Devon sinks further into her chair.

"I say," he booms at Devon, wiping froth from his mustache, "I rather think it'd be a better use of that pretty face of yours to try and convince me to buy you dinner than it would be to try and convince me this prick is even halfway right about anything."

The silence is absolute. The sound of a momentous and collective, "what the hell?"

Did Coleman just... Did he seriously just proposition Devon in the middle of all this?

She turns first red then almost purple. Then confusion wins out over embarrassment and rage. "What?" she says. "I just... what?"

And then, out of nowhere—the icicle making its triumphant return from hell—Kayla steps forward and says, in no uncertain terms, "You better mind your feckin' manners."

Better men than Coleman—a term which, admittedly, encompasses all men throughout space and time—have tried to stand up to Kayla and failed.

"I—" he starts. He puffs out his cheeks.

Kayla narrows her eyes. "I'll have no more of it."

And I don't understand. And I have misread Kayla before, almost to the detriment of the entire world, but I have never seen this from her. Such defensiveness. Such loyalty. Almost... mothering.

Oh...

Oh, that I have seen after all. Except her girls...

Oh, that's not going to work out well at all.

Coleman opens and shuts his mouth at Kayla. He runs his hands down the lapels of his jacket. And then, he turns on his heel and stomps towards the door. "That'll be all then."

He opens the door. Pauses. "Oh, and tomorrow," he says over his shoulder, "we'll be relocating to London." Another round of silence and bewilderment.

"Wait," Felicity finally pushes away from the wall. "We'll do what, George?"

"London, Felicity. I'm sure you heard me." Coleman doesn't even bother turning around. I can still see the bright spots of red on his cheeks, though.

"Russians are there. Obviously," he says. "We should be there. Obviously. And there's free space at MI6. I've already made the arrangements. Pack up. Tonight. Shouldn't take long considering the state of this shithole."

And then he's gone, through the door, leaving confusion and outrage behind him.

22

FIFTEEN MINUTES LATER, IN FELICITY'S OFFICE

"You know, Arthur," says Felicity, "it is generally considered unseemly for a man in his thirties to sulk."

The look I give Felicity is not a charitable one. I feel more worked over and bruised from the encounter with Coleman than I do from the one with the Russians.

"Come on," she says. She carefully lifts an orchid off one of the shelves that line her office and places it into a cardboard box. "Work's over. Get it off your chest."

But now is not the time. Now whatever I say will be confused, and mixed up with other unfair emotions. Really the best thing to do is to hold my tongue and wait until I've calmed down a bit.

So I say, "Is that how it is then? We turn off the relationship from nine to five. Then, oh wait, time to head home, let's be friends again?"

Not my finest moment of heeding my own advice.

Shaw shakes her head and unclips a daylight lamp from the shelf. "We spoke about this, Arthur. I'm your friend. Your," she pauses over the next word, "girlfriend. But I'm your boss too. We can joke, and laugh, and shoot monsters in the face, but in the end I have responsibilities to my position here. You have responsibilities to your own. The fate of the world. Life, liberty, and the pursuit of happiness. These are not little things, Arthur. They're not things lightly set aside. So, when we're at work, I am going to put that first when I have to. Only when I have to. But I will. That's going to be part of this."

She is calm and collected, reasonable and rational. It makes me less so.

"Oh," I say, dumping a stack of folders into a box with an unceremonious crash, "so sitting by and watching Coleman treat me like his new favorite piñata was a responsibility that came first? I see now."

And part of me knows that I'm acting like a prick, but unfortunately it's not a big enough part.

"Coleman is really not worth it, Arthur. He's really not."

"You're not the one whose ass he's riding."

She looks away at that. I smell blood in the water.

"One word," I say. "Just one of support, would have been nice."

"He was right, Arthur," she snaps. She turns to look at me, holding her orchid, a beautiful complex architecture of purple petals. "He was right."

And that shuts me up.

"He may have been a jackass about it. But you screwed this one up."

I'm holding more folders. I slowly lower them into the box and don't stand up. Just sit and let that sink in.

"We won," I say. But the enthusiasm has been kicked out of my defiance.

"The Russian got away with the papers." Felicity shrugs. "That's not a victory."

I stare at the floor. It's much harder to fight back when someone is being so nice about letting you know how much you screwed up.

"Come on," Felicity says. "It's not like I haven't had to chew you out for failed missions." Her voice is softer now, her expression softer, the shadows of her face deep as she unplugs another daylight lamp. "They come with the territory. This is hard work and there's little margin for failure. And you're up against hard odds. Though I should say, talking to the Weekenders was totally on your own head. That was completely within your control."

"They're good people," I say. Still stubborn.

"Good people is not the same as competent people, Arthur."

Except I really hope it is.

"It's just…" I shake my head. "Coleman's been here less than twenty-four hours and already it seems like he's calling all the shots. You're the boss. Not him. It's bullshit you letting him strut around the way he is."

Felicity sets down the orchid, reaches a hand out to me. "Coleman is really not worth worrying about, Arthur," she says, pulling me up to my feet. "He's a little man who likes to throw his weight around. MI6 was not a promotion for him. And he's only back here because everyone else from the eighties has managed to move on to something bigger and better. He was never anything other than a middling field agent. He's the tail-end of the good old boys' club, nothing more. I need to tread a little carefully around him for a while. Give him enough rope to hang himself. Just remember, if anything, he's intimidated by you."

I laugh at that. A caustic bray. I'm comfortable enough to be honest here. "Me? How on earth would I intimidate him?"

I stand, grab a bundle of folders and put it in the box. I grab another and then I notice Felicity still hasn't answered. I don't have to be an ex-detective to spot she's holding out on me.

"Felicity?" I say, half-formed anxiety nudging my stomach. "Why would he be intimidated by me?"

Her back is to me.

"Oh," she says, then stops there. "Well." She clears her throat. "I mean… It's just… You know…"

It's like Clyde's taken over her speech patterns.

Jesus, that's suddenly become something I feel like I might one day actually have to worry about…

"Felicity?" I say for the third time. In the fairy tales they have to answer you the third time you ask.

"Well," she pauses again, then takes the plunge, "you know how I mentioned I had worked with exes before…?"

And just… no. No. She can't mean that. She can't. She mustn't?

"Coleman?" I say, and my voice climbs to a pitch I haven't

managed to access since I was eight years old. "No." I shake my head. "Not Coleman. Not Coleman. Please tell me—"

"It was a long time ago."

She's still not facing me.

And that's it. The final kick to the nuts that this day can deliver. The lowest of the possible blows.

Didn't I save the world the other day?

"You have to be kidding me." I'm begging really. I don't care if she lies or not. I just want her to take it back.

"I was young. It was a bad mistake. It was the mid-nineties. I'd just come into MI37. And, well, he presented a certain aura of confidence. And I was taken in by that. Literally taken in. It was essentially a confidence trick. He duped me for a while. But I see him now. I learned. That's what we do when we make mistakes. We learn. We learn not to repeat them. And what he and I had…" She hesitates again. And the horrors I fill that pause with. "It was just a stupid physical thing, really. That's all."

And even I didn't go to those depths of depravity.

"That's all?" I say. "That's all? That's all?" I'm a record skipping. I want to get past the phrase, past this, but I think I'm going to be stuck here for a while. All I can picture is the ends of Coleman's mustache flopping rhythmically up and down.

I think I'm going to be sick.

"No, Arthur. No." Shaw steps forward, puts a hand on my shoulder. I almost flinch away. "I meant…" She trails off. She's flustered, searching for words. It should be adorable. This should be a moment where I smile and feel the warm and fuzzies take over my soul, but instead all I can do is listen to the claxon siren in my head screaming, "Mistake! Mistake! Mistake! This was a mistake!"

"What we have, Arthur, it's more than that. It's the physical thing *and more*. That's what I meant. Coleman has nothing that you don't also have. That's what I meant."

And that's a nice thing to say. A sweet thing. I look and meet her eyes. Her face is unguarded, a little defiant.

"This doesn't change who I am, Arthur. This was all as true yesterday as it was today. This doesn't change where you should sleep tonight."

There's an invitation there. And... I don't know.

Some things are worth fighting for. Worth sacrificing for.

I swallow, and I nod. She steps forward and holds me.

And still in my head I see the ends of Coleman's mustache. Flop. Flop. Flop.

23

ONE NIGHT TOGETHER LATER

Felicity and I take her minivan down to London. She double-parked outside my apartment last night while I threw things into a suitcase. Jackets, pants, shaving kit. Simple enough. Easy enough. But it was an evening defined by us working in parallel rather than together. The companionable awkwardness of the previous night was missing. Coleman seemed to loom over everything. His mustache draped over the night.

Flop. Flop. Flop.

Stop it.

We pull up outside the hotel Her Majesty's government has deigned to pay for. From the looks of it, it's time to raise taxes again.

"The Virginian" appears to have been press-ganged into wedging itself between a long chain of grease-stained restaurants, and an industrial-sized pet store which I suspect supplies them with their better cuts of meat.

A teenage boy, who appears to have had all his personality surgically removed, stands, pasty-faced and impassive, behind a crumbling Formica desk in a lobby that makes a postage stamp seem roomy.

"Shaw," Felicity informs him. "We're sharing." She uses what available space there is to turn and nod in my direction.

My eyebrows bounce up. I suppose I hadn't really thought about sleeping arrangements. Or if I had, that Coleman would have booked us separate rooms.

And… Well it's not exactly that I object, or that she really needed to consult with me, I suppose. Except, aren't we only on two dates? Shouldn't there be the courtesy, "You want to shack up?"

The boy grunts, in what could be a profound insight into the effect of the liberal attitudes of the sixties upon modern culture and acceptance, or a belch. It's hard to say.

"Need a hand with bags?" Clyde appears on the stairs. Or at least as much of him as will fit in the lobby. He has his hood cinched so tight only a square inch is open. I have the feeling that just wearing the mask openly would be less suspicious.

Then we all take part in an odd shuffling dance that involves getting poked in the ribs by as many elbows as possible as I try to get the bags to the stairs and Clyde attempts to ascend them without breaking his neck. I think the Russians might actually be less hazardous to our health than this place.

The room I'll be sharing with Felicity turns out to be slightly smaller than the lobby. Through some space-folding trick twin beds separated by a shared bedside table have been crammed into it.

"Shaw amenable to the whole cohabitation thing?" Clyde asks, twisting his head about in the confines of the hoodie as he dumps Felicity's bags on one bed.

"Her idea, actually," I say, opening my own bag to see how many of my possessions have been ruined by a spilled shampoo or soap or some such. An unavoidable byproduct of travel in my experience.

Clyde nods and hums a bit. "Bit touch and go, my end," he manages eventually.

"Really?" I say. Could there be trouble in paradise this early? Not that my relationship is free of its early day screw-ups.

"The whole reading at the table thing."

"The what?" I ask. Clyde is being oddly minimalist in his answer.

"Definition of rudeness." He makes a circling gesture with his hand. Something almost impatient. Waiting for me to catch up. A very un-Clyde-like gesture.

"Oh right." I remember the conversation at the museum.

"Well, you know, it rather turns out, the whole digital thing—" He taps the mask. It's unlike the other times he's tapped it, I notice. Not a sullen gesture. It takes me a moment to place the emotion. But in a story about how Tabitha's pissed at him, Clyde's abruptly excited.

"I can speed-read," Clyde says.

This story is taking an odd tack. "Congratulations?" I try.

"I mean, I don't wish to brag," he continues, clearly lying, "even worse habit than the table reading. But, well..." Clyde actually rubs his hands together. Only Clyde could have a Scrooge McDuck moment over the number of books he's read. "I may have read one thousand seven hundred and thirty-six books last night."

"Holy crap," I say in a moment of great eloquence. That's... It's not a possible number. It's... Jesus, it's...

Inhuman.

God, I've been trying to avoid that word.

I see that tiny square of wood peeking out from the pinched hood.

"You know what I found really fascinating though?" Clyde asks me, bringing me back to the conversation.

I shake my head. I have no clue what Clyde found fascinating. I don't have a clue about anything anymore. About how to define the existence of my friends.

"How very good John Grisham is." Clyde nods. "Blew me away. *The Pelican Brief*. Impressive stuff."

That snaps me out of it right there.

"Grisham?" I say, failing to keep the incredulity at bay.

"Master of suspense," Clyde replies.

"Out of seventeen hundred books, Grisham was the author that stood out?" I really can't let that lie.

"Oh yes." Clyde nods. "Totally engrossing."

I cannot believe we're having this discussion. I cannot fathom any aspect of it. I cannot believe Clyde enjoys such tawdry crap.

Somehow I need to find a way out of this conversation, back to some sort of comfortable ground.

"But Tabitha wasn't so impressed?" It's a low blow, but it's for the sake of my sanity so I'm going to call it fair play.

I imagine Clyde's face falls beneath the mask. Assuming his face does anything beneath there. He shuffles his feet at least, picks at the baggage handles. "Yes," he says. "While reading... The whole talking thing, I sort of fell down there. Arse over elbow to be precise. She..." He shrugs furiously. "She doesn't sleep as much as, well, as Devon did. Which is not a criticism. As I explained to her last night. Repeatedly in fact. Thought I was quite clear on the matter. But anyway, that was always reading time for me, and, of course, I recognize that with the advent of never sleeping ever again, spare time will be more abundant, but I just... well, let's just say I was excited. Like a small child on his birthday, for example."

"Tabitha, not so much?" I'm not comfortable with any of this. I can't even imagine the response of someone dating him.

"Not so much." Clyde nods.

I think about that. About Clyde. About what he is.

What is he?

A friend. I need to treat him like the friend he is. Stop tripping over myself. "It's early days." I clap him on the arm with the sort of camaraderie that seems to be natural to people cooler than me. "Teething problems is all," I tell him.

Clyde nods. "Yes. Negotiating new terms and all that." His knee gives an involuntary shake. "Living together is just a period of adjustment. I read that. Tried to explain the whole thing to Tabitha actually. Never been one for self-help books before, but the author seemed quite insightful on the subject. Tabitha wasn't overly receptive to the theory."

"Just give it time," I say. Another platitude. But I've got nothing of substance here. I need time to clear my head.

"Plenty of that." Clyde taps the mask again, not so excited this time.

We begin the complicated maneuvering that will allow us both to escape the room. I head downstairs, Clyde to his room.

In the lobby, Felicity is waiting. "That took a while," she says. "Everything OK?"

"Clyde read seventeen hundred books last night."

She raises an eyebrow. "The mask?" She looks concerned. I find that reassuring. Concern seems like a more appropriate reaction than excitement.

I nod.

"You worried about him?"

And yes, I am. But maybe I should be more supportive of a friend.

"I don't know," I hedge.

Felicity nods. "He's been through a lot. We should keep an eye on him. Make sure he's OK."

I nod again. It's a simple enough solution. Except it doesn't feel like a simple problem. But how do I just come out and say that I'm scared my best friend is losing his humanity?

"Would you stop fussing!" A booming voice from the top of the stairs interrupts my mental circling. Devon's voice.

There's a muttered response. Then she booms again. "I am telling you that this is how shoelaces work. How it has been done for thousands of years. Well, not thousands. But for a very long time. I imagine Robert Burns did this exact same thing just before writing his godawful poetry, not to insult a Scottish legend, of course, except well... what do you lot see in him?"

There is another pause, another barely audible response.

"No I do not need a cookie!"

Silence.

"Yes, I do like cookies. Obviously this figure does not come without a certain amount of help from the Pillsbury dough boy, delicious little bugger that he is. But now is not the cookie moment. Eleven o'clock—yes, that would be lovely. Right now, I am digesting an ample breakfast. About the only healthy meal I have in the day."

Another pause as we collectively digest this surfeit of information.

"Well, if you insist I shall take the cookie and eat it later. Probably at eleven. As I mentioned."

Felicity and I exchange a look but no words. And I think I know who Devon's talking to but I can barely believe the conversation.

There's a clatter of feet on the stairs. Felicity and I quickly try and find something to stare at.

"There you are!" Devon booms. "And here I am. All unpacked. All settled. Snug as a bug in a very tight and cramped rug." She clomps down the stairs. "Hello Arthur!" She flings two meaty arms around me and attempts to crack my ribs. "Lovely to see you. Lovely to be here. Seat of the empire and all that. Not that empires have to sit down, I suppose. Silly anthropomorphism. And not that London would really be that comfortable to sit on. Big Ben poking up your jacksie. Terrible place to rest I imagine. But, well, all the same, excited."

She casts a vaguely baleful look up the stairs. "Kayla informs me she will be down in a minute."

I nod to myself. I'm in a room with Shaw. Clyde's in with Tabitha. So… Devon in with Kayla. Just as Kayla seems poised to unleash every ounce of mothering on the poor unsuspecting woman.

Perfect.

Someone clears his throat behind Devon. Devon turns. "Not excited to see you, of course. You shit," she informs Clyde.

Oh wait… *now* this is perfect.

I would move closer to Felicity for comfort but it's not actually possible in the confines of the lobby.

And just as the tension starts to congeal the door flies open.

"What in the name of fuck are you all still doing here?" Coleman booms. He aims an umbrella at us all, then singles out Felicity. "Communication. Command. The basics, Felicity."

"I'm sure you'll grasp them all soon, George."

I check the flowers perched on the front desk to see if her scorn has wilted them. It's good to hear the acid back in her voice.

"Email, Felicity." Coleman waves a phone at her. "The twenty-first century. Priority communication."

"If you'd set us up in a hotel that had—" Felicity starts, then cuts herself off. She takes a breath. "What's the message, George?"

And why did she bite back on the aggression?

Flop, flop—stop it.

"Russians, Felicity," Coleman snaps. "Trafalgar Square. Now." He looks at me, at Devon, Clyde, at the others jammed behind him on the stairs. "Go!" he demands. "Go now! Go!"

24

We bundle out into London and rain. Felicity throws open her minivan door. Tabitha and Clyde pile in one after the other. I step aside for Devon, but Coleman grabs her elbow.

"This way, my lovely." He tugs her toward a sleek black penis extension with a BMW logo on the hood.

Devon resists. Inside the van, Clyde gets his legs tangled with the seatbelt. Devon closes her eyes. Coleman tugs again and she goes with it.

And Devon had my back in the conference room in Oxford; there's no way I'm abandoning her to this fate.

"Wait—" I start, grabbing her other arm.

Then Kayla comes out of the hotel at the sort of speed that puts the fear of God into world-stability-threatening creatures from every plane of existence.

"You," she points a finger at me, "don't get her wrapped up in your feckin' trouble."

"You," she fixes Coleman with a deadeye stare that would shake even Clint Eastwood on a main street at high noon, "keep your dirty feckin' hands to yourself."

I'm not sure if Coleman or I swallows harder.

"I'm all right." Devon's voice is small, but she meets Kayla's eye—a feat I'm incapable of. She shakes off my hand and Coleman's.

The intensity of Kayla's gaze slackens from "flame broil" to nonplussed.

"But," Kayla says, "the Underground. We can take—"

"I'm all right." Devon's voice has gained in strength. She turns to Coleman, grimaces. "Let's get on our merry way then."

Coleman recovers. "Step into my parlor," he says. He even manages to leer as he opens the car door.

"But—" Kayla says to the closing door.

"But—" I echo.

"Come on, Arthur!" Felicity calls from the front seat. Coleman slams his door and revs his engine.

I get into the van. Kayla swings up behind me, settles disconsolately beside Clyde and Tabitha. Felicity stamps the accelerator to the floor. Tires screech. Rubber burns. We spin out into traffic.

And then the seatbelt nearly chokes the life from me as she stamps on the brakes.

Black taxis. Red buses. Red lights. London traffic.

"Shit!" Felicity loses control of her temper if not the vehicle.

In front of us, Coleman lays on the horn. I hope Devon's OK in there.

I glance back over my shoulder at Kayla. Our resident swordswoman is chewing on her collar, staring blankly out at the rain-spattered streets.

I need to explain to Devon what's going on. What Kayla's going through. So Devon can explain to Kayla that making her a surrogate daughter is not a healthy or fair thing to do.

So I don't have to explain it myself.

Ahead of us the lights flicker to green. We gain approximately six inches of blacktop. And red. A herd of pedestrians swarms across the road.

Felicity's phone buzzes. She flips it open, one eye on the traffic light, foot ready to pounce on the gas. She punches a button.

"—cking bullshit lights. Fix this, Felicity. Sirens. Police. Anything," Coleman's voice barks.

"Clandestine organization, George," she says, sugary sweet.

"Fix it!" he barks. The rest of the car grimaces at the phone. I think I can see Kayla reaching for her sword.

"Tabitha?" I fight my seatbelt and call over my shoulder. "Any chance you could help us?"

Tabitha is already unfolding her laptop. "Course," she says. "Hack into the grid. Rejig the algorithm."

"Oh wait!" Clyde pipes up. "I think—"

"No," Tabitha says. There is no debating that word.

"But I think I can—"

"No," Tabitha says again.

Even my balls retract at that one. Clyde says nothing.

"Clyde?" says Tabitha. She sounds suspicious.

Still nothing.

And then: the jingling of change.

I strain to look around. Even Felicity takes her eyes off the light.

"Oh you stupid silly fuck!" Tabitha's fingers suddenly blur across the keyboard.

And I see Clyde's hand. His hand in his pocket. It's vibrating, rattling the coins.

Man, Clyde has some stones.

My eyes fly from his pocket to the traffic light.

"What are you silly bastards playing at?" Coleman says over the phone. "Fix it already."

Red. Red. Red.

"Lives on the line, you incompetent fucks!"

"Oh yeah," I snap, unable to bite my tongue. "Well that sort of encouragement is definitely going to help save them."

"The day I start taking leadership advice from an incompetent fuck like—"

Green.

Cars lurch forward. Pedestrians scatter. Coleman is cut off. We all brace for the slamming on of brakes.

And it doesn't come. Green. Green. Green. Light after light.

"Got it," Clyde says. "I got it."

He sounds like a man who just ran a marathon. Who just ran it and won. He's breathing hard, lying back against the seat. It's the moment in the movie where Kurt Russell would roll the girl off him and light the cigarette.

"More bloody like it," comes Coleman's disembodied voice from the phone.

London passes in a blur. Record stores. Theaters. Pubs. Accounting firms. Law firms. Government buildings. History. Far too many tourists for anyone's liking.

Tabitha still types furiously.

"I got it, Tabby," Clyde says. He finally seems to have noticed that she's pissed at him. He reaches out a hand to her. "I got it."

"Stupid," Tabitha says, shrugging off the arm. "Silly. Fuck."

"But I—" Clyde starts. "I fixed it. We'll get there."

"Yes," Tabitha snaps, finally looking up from the screen. Her fingers don't stop moving though. "You cleared a path. Fixed the lights. But, I mean, for a moment, did you think to put them back afterwards?"

Clyde is very, very quiet.

Which gives us a chance to hear the concert of car horns sounding in our wake.

"Not your job." Tabitha enunciates the words very carefully. "For a reason." She doesn't speak loudly. Not even forcefully. But every word is a body blow that rocks the car.

And paradise is most definitely in trouble.

25

Trafalgar Square. Nelson's Column. The National Gallery. History. Gravitas. A thousand bloody pigeons. They take off in one great flapping mass as Felicity's minivan bursts through a police cordon. Officers yell. Car sirens squeal.

To be fair it was a very unexpected roadblock.

Coleman plunges out of his car waving a badge. Devon is more hesitant, her arm held high as pitiful protection against the rain. Kayla falls into step next to her as the others and I tumble out of Felicity's van. Devon ignores Kayla and pointedly steps toward me instead.

"Aren't we meant to be all secret and undercover?" she says. "This seems a touch bombastic for cloak-and-dagger stuff. Not my area of expertise at all, of course. Could be that John le Carré's been telling me terrible fibs all these years."

"They'll bill it as a feckin' terrorist threat," Kayla answers, not giving me a chance to display my ignorance. "Then a poorly conceived feckin' publicity stunt. Always do."

Devon turns and finally acknowledges Kayla. Complicated emotions play out. "Thank you, Kayla," she says finally.

"There are the primaries," Felicity interrupts our little soap opera. She points.

Misted by rain, framed by the monumental lions that guard the square, four figures stand in a loose group at the base of Nelson's Column. I squint, trying to make out details.

There's the tall bastard from the British Museum. The tree-maker. Or the warper of time, depending whether you adhere to the logical theory or my one. He's wearing shades, and a trench coat, and generally trying to look like I did when I was fourteen, and discovered cyberpunk, and didn't know any better.

To his right is a rotund little man in what appears to be an anorak and cords. If it weren't for the fact that his right hand appears to be encased in the sort of power glove sci-fi artists drool over he'd look more like my dad than a threat to national security.

To the left of the group is the only one of the Russians who looks younger than forty. He has a scruffy goatee beard, little round glasses misted with rain, and an irate expression. The collegiate proto-Lenin look worn fifteen years too long.

Hanging back is a blond woman with a pretty, angular face. High cheekbones outlined in steel. Half her head is covered in long sweeps of blond hair. The other half is bald metal that creeps down to encase a frighteningly Terminator-like eye. She appears to be wearing a lab coat.

All in all, I feel like I've faced more frightening foes and lived to walk away. Plus, we outnumber them. If it wasn't for the fact that it only took one of them to kick our arses at the Natural History Museum, I might have made it all the way to feeling confident.

Tall, dark, and Russian holds a bullhorn. He barks curt phrases into it, then glares at us. Behind him, the blond woman cracks her knuckles.

"They're saying things?" I say. "No one mentioned that they're saying things." It seems like the sort of information it might have been useful to have.

"No hostages." Coleman disengages from irate policemen and the tatters of their roadblock. "No reason for us to listen. So round them up. Standard delta formation."

We all stare at him, confused by this last utterance. Felicity clears her throat.

"Oh bravo, Felicity." Coleman gives her a withering look. "Not even the basics of field training. I understand your attraction to the incompetence of Wallace a little better now."

And there, right there, that should be the moment when she tears the balls from his body.

"Is delta formation the one where Kayla goes and attacks everyone with her sword?" Clyde ventures.

Felicity's head definitely goes down. And is there a chance that Coleman is right? That Felicity isn't everything I believe her to be?

No. No, that way lies madness.

So instead I pipe up with a persistent, "You didn't think it might be important to know what they're saying?" I'd rather go on about the holes in Coleman's thinking than in Felicity's training. "Is this lack of field information going to be a constant thing?"

Coleman wheels on me. His arm comes out and, to my great shame, I flinch back. But he's just holding out a smartphone. He smirks at me.

"Use the bloody MI6 translation app if you're so fascinated, toy-boy. And keep out of the way of the real agents."

"Hello? Researcher. Right here." Tabitha rolls her eyes.

"That's me too," Devon pipes in. "I remember that. I'm a researcher too."

Coleman pats her on the arm. "Oh don't worry." He smiles. Shows too many teeth. "No one really expects anything of you, gorgeous."

Kayla takes a step toward Coleman, and he takes a step away.

By the shade of Devon's cheeks, a large number of her new teammates are now dangerously close to clambering above Clyde on her shit list.

"Right," Coleman says, "over by that bloody fountain."

He pulls an improbably long, silver pistol from inside his jacket, crouches, and runs toward one of the fountains that lies between us and the column with its guardian lions. Rain patters off the back of his expensively cut suit. The Russians watch him warily, shifting positions slightly. The tall one continues talking into the bullhorn.

"Oh come on then." Felicity starts moving. Then looks back at me. "Find out what they're saying," she tells me. "It's a good idea."

I smile at that. A little late for the praise, but I'll take it.

Then Felicity's off. Tabitha follows, then Clyde, all with the same doubled-over urgency—like victims of a bad buffet covering the final yards to the bathroom.

Devon remains standing next to me as I examine Coleman's phone. Kayla doesn't move an inch from Devon's side. And to be honest, this is about the time when an overprotective Kayla becomes a very, very good thing.

"What do we do?" Devon asks, a look of concern on her face.

"You stay here," Kayla says. "And I beat down every feckin' one of them that comes this way."

"Oh." Devon's eyes are wide. Apparently she's still getting used to Kayla's particular brand of doting. "Did not... hadn't really considered that an option. But I suppose—"

I skim through a few pages of apps on the phone trying to find one that says something as obvious as "translate."

Over by the fountain, Coleman, Felicity, Tabitha, and Clyde are all crouched in a large puddle. Coleman and Felicity have their guns drawn, Tabitha has her laptop on her knees. Clyde slips battery after battery under his mask.

And *there* is the translation app. I have to believe it was Coleman who named it "Foreign jabber." I get the thing running and select "Russian-to-English" from a menu.

"—until the seventeenth of this month," says a robotic voice from Coleman's phone. I stare down in surprise. The translation app. It talks.

"If our demands are not met," the thing continues, "then we will destroy London in its entirety."

It talks, and it says the most awful things.

Over by the fountain Felicity pokes her face and her gun around the curve of stone to get a clear look at her target then ducks back. She nods to Clyde. I want to get over there. I don't want Felicity out there alone. No matter how many big guns she has around her. I want to be one more.

The Russian says something.

"I repeat," the phone says, "our demands are the complete and unconditional surrender of the West to the Union of Soviet Socialist Republics."

Wait. Their demands are what?

Devon stares at the phone. "Are they serious?" she asks.

To be fair, despite the madness, they probably are. This seems a little far gone for an improv comedy routine. But still, that demand's a little eighties cliché, even for a fan of the decade.

I mean, "The surrender of the West"? What is "the West" anymore?

I look back at Felicity. She is out there with Coleman, and two people going through relationship trouble.

"I've got to get out there," I tell Devon. "You'll be safe with Kayla."

In fact, I'd be safer with Kayla. It seems a little late to convince everyone to come back here, though.

I start toward the fountain but Devon catches my arm. She gives me a quick, savage hug. I look at her, confused. Kayla lets out an irritated hiss.

"Thanks," she says.

"Whatever for?"

"Well," she says, "it's just... in a manner of speaking... I think they're probably going to kill you." Devon looks sad and slightly embarrassed at having admitted this. She gives me a rather pathetic-looking thumbs-up. "Good luck, though."

Funny. That doesn't make me feel any better at all.

26

I start to cover the ground with the same doubled-over run Felicity performed, but when you've seen other people do it, it's hard not to be self-conscious about the whole thing. I cover the last ten yards at a light jog.

Coleman fixes me with an uncharitable stare. "And to think," he says, "I always thought that late was better than never."

"You could always go back to MI6 if this is bothering you," I say.

"—expect declarations of surrender to be delivered to the nearest available embassy by six p.m. on the evening of the seventeenth, local time." Both the Russian and the phone drone on, unperturbed by our argument.

"That." Tabitha points at the phone.

"Oh," I say, as nonchalantly as I can, "the Russians are demanding the total surrender of the West to the now extinct USSR. Nothing much."

"Wow," Coleman says, sounding decidedly un-wowed. "Completely unreasonable demands from the bad guys. Good job finding all that out, Arthur. Great detective work." My former profession has become an insult.

"And to think," I say, "I always thought assumptions made an ass out of more than just you."

Coleman and I then engage in a bout of light death staring.

JONATHAN WOOD

"Just a thought," Felicity interjects, "but the people trying to blow up chunks of the capital are just over our shoulder."

Coleman harrumphs. I spend some time fantasizing about the Russians maiming Coleman in some academically interesting ways.

"All right," Coleman strokes his mustache, "we know they're heavy hitters, so we go in quick and decisive. Shock and awe and all of that. I want at least two of the bastards spitting out their intestines from the initial strike. So I'm thinking we have to drop the column on them."

My eyebrows shoot up. The column? Nelson's Column? Drop a national monument on them? Has Coleman been hitting the crack pipe? There again, it may be fun to let this play out just to see Coleman come up hard against reality.

"Sounds workable." Felicity nods.

It sounds what?

"What have you got, Clyde?" she asks.

No. This can't be.

"Databases. Warming them up." Tabitha has her laptop open.

"Wait," Clyde starts, "I can—"

"Fucking Bobbitt you if you try." Tabitha doesn't even look up from her screen.

"Oh," Clyde says. "Well in that case then, maybe..."

Is this all part of Felicity giving Coleman enough rope to hang himself?

"If upon the seventeenth," the phone continues, "our demands are not met—"

"Elkman's Push. Not enough," Tabitha says. "Need more power."

"—we will utterly annihilate the city of London."

None of this makes any sense. We're trying to deface the capital. The Russians seem to care more about their demands than the bunch of armed agents crouched nearby. I mean, they know who we are. We've taken one of them out. There's cocky and then there's cocky.

"A modern Chernobyl," the Russian continues. My eyes snap from the phone to the drenched foursome standing calmly demanding something they can't ever possibly receive. Chernobyl again.

"Oh!" Tabitha lets out a little exclamation. All eyes snap back to her. She looks up at Clyde. "We could try the Sinsdale."

"Oh!" Clyde echoes the same excited little noise.

"Sinsdale?" I ask.

"Sinsdale," Clyde confirms. "As far as we can tell it pulls, well basically, high barometric pressure. But in very specific places. Very interesting experimental thaumaturgist from the late 1800s is Sinsdale. Really plays with language. Ended up accidentally fileting himself of course, but we get to walk in his footsteps now."

"English?" asks Coleman.

"Swiss actually," Clyde says, "though his grandfather was—"

"Explain it, you jackass," Coleman demands, cutting him off.

"A blistering hole in this green and pleasant land," the phone responds.

"The column," Tabitha interjects. "Chop it down."

Coleman rolls his eyes.

"You know," says the phone, suddenly conversational. "We can hear you."

It takes a moment for the meaning of the statement to fully sink in. "We"—the Russians, the bad guys. "Can"—are able to, possess the facility. "Hear"—auditory sampling, soundwaves striking eardrum, turned into neurological impulses resulting in understanding. "You"—me, Felicity, Clyde, Tabitha, Coleman. Or, in other words, the Russians are listening to us, to what we're talking about, to us discussing how to attack them. And they're doing nothing. Which means...

"Oh fuck," I say.

There is a white flash, the crack of thunder. A thousand pigeons leave the ground.

"Move!" Felicity bellows even as she does. Her arm catches me around the waist, tearing me away.

Proto-Lenin and Anorak-boy are off the ground, speared by lightning, backs arched, heads thrown back. They spasm, curl up around their guts, then jerk spastically, rigidly out again. Proto-Lenin gags, hawks up a ball of lightning. It flies across the square, detonates against the lion to his left.

My feet hammer the ground. Rain lashes me, each footfall a detonation of spray.

Behind me I hear Coleman scoff, "Damn Russkies couldn't hit a bus."

But he's wrong. I know he's wrong. As Lenin chokes up another ball of lightning and spits it in the same direction. As pigeons wheel away. I've seen this before. I've seen Clyde do this.

In front of me, Felicity pauses, aims her gun.

"Keep moving!" It's my turn to pull her along.

She fires wildly. "Fuck!"

Behind me there is the sound of bronze grinding on rock. A dull dry scrape in the middle of the monsoon. Something growls.

"No time!" I'm trying to explain it all, all the danger, my fear, my need for her safety as I pull against her. As my feet slip and slide over wet stone.

"What in the name of shit?" I hear Coleman shout.

"Sinsdale!" Tabitha is yelling for no apparent reason. "Sinsdale!" It sounds like she's taking the name of a very interesting experimental thaumaturgist in vain.

The tall Russian is still talking into his bullhorn. "We only need one of you alive to deliver the message," the phone tells me. I don't need it to tell me he's chuckling.

"Let go!" Felicity struggles against me. "Let me fucking go."

I let her go.

"I need a clean bloody shot, you imbecile."

"I need you not to get gutted." I know what's coming. A body shot isn't going to cut it.

She turns, goes down on one knee, sights down the barrel.

A roar obliterates the world. I turn. From the left. It's coming from the left. A lion. The symbol of the empire hewn in glistening bronze. Spray makes a white halo around its metal mane.

Felicity doesn't even flinch. It's coming right at her, and she doesn't move a muscle.

She's going to get her shot and then she's going to die.

27

I slam into Felicity. My full body weight. She sprawls. The lion doesn't hesitate for a moment.

Time grinds then. As if the tall Russian hit me with one of his gelatinous balls of messed up space. I can see the bronze muscles rippling in the lion's back as it closes on me. I can see its metal skin stretching as its jaws open. The rain spattering against its back. I can hear Shaw cursing as her shot goes wide again. I can hear Tabitha still shouting, "Sinsdale! Sinsdale!" over and over again. I even have time to wonder if the stress has finally gotten to her.

And Clyde too. I can hear him, something barely audible under the crackle of lightning, the bark of the gun, the shattering echo of the roar. Nonsense words. Syllabic salad. The language of magic.

"*Mel forum kel ashtium fer fillum.*"

There is a horrendous scraping noise. A screech. A scream from the lion. Its jaws widen further, further. They do not stop. The seam of its mouth goes back, back, back, stretches down the length of its body. A great gash from mouth to tail. Like a blade slicing the thing in two. Like it collided with an enormous, invisible knife.

Sinsdale.

That's what... Tabitha... Clyde... Sinsdale. That trio just saved my life.

Except while Sinsdale chops, he still can't stop several tons of bronze from careening on through the sky.

Two inert slabs of metal fly at my head. One falls, one rises. There is no time to crawl away but I try it anyway. All I have time for is falling backwards, toppling. As the top half of the dead lion skims over my head. The world rings from the collision. A hot line of blood and grazed skin across my scalp.

The bottom slab hits the ground, the edge driving into the paving slabs in a great spray of rainwater and stone chips. The slab tilts up, a great black monolith teetering before me. I stare at it bewildered, dumbfounded.

Gravity does its thing. It starts to fall.

Something hits me from the side. Felicity. She kicks me. Both feet. Right in the side. And I'm winded, and I'm falling, skidding through puddles, and I'm still a little bit wounded she called me an imbecile when all I was doing was trying to save her life. And then I'm hitting the floor, my cheek and nose mashing against the rocks, as the second half of the lion slams to earth.

Two tons of bronze lies between Felicity and me. Cold, dead, rain strafing its length.

And I am alive, to stare at it. And Felicity is alive, on the other side of it, staring back at me.

And then behind her…

"Duck!" I yell.

And she does. The ball of warped space, and time, and whatever rolls over her head. Behind her, I see the tall Russian, hands outstretched.

Missed again, you fuck.

Not that that really matters. As the ball collides with the slab of metal.

Metal. What did metal used to be? Ore?

The slab ripples, cracks. Enormous waves of heat suddenly coming off it. A red glow emanating from the widening cracks, spreading, infusing the whole thing. Steam boils off it. And still it ripples, wobbles, like jello.

A blob of steaming red metal falls to the earth with a hiss and a splat. A paw oozes toward me.

After it was ore. Before it was a statue. Molten metal. Solid metal was molten metal.

I scramble away, crab-crawling backwards. Through the steam and the heat I see Felicity rolling away from the spitting red mess, toward the Russians, away from me.

Lightning flares again. Again. I hear another roar. Another.

Four lions, one at each corner of the column. We've only taken one of them down.

I've said it before, and I'll say it again, but I bloody hate magic.

28

I take cover behind a plinth that once held a lion. Rain drips down my nose. I hold my gun up next to my head and unsuccessfully try to imagine this is a scene from *Escape from New York*.

There is a scuffle of limbs from above. I kick back and away from the stone. A decidedly unheroic grunt bursts out of me. A grunt and a half yell from someone out of sight. I blink water from my eyes and try to stare down the pistol sights.

Clyde's head appears, his hood pushed back, sodden hair matted to his mask. He collapses over the plinth into an untidy pile of limbs. I collapse next to him.

"Magical metal cats," I say as he unfolds. "Last week extra-dimensional brain parasites used them to attack us, and now these sodding Russians. I can't believe our bloody luck."

Flippancy is a good way to keep the fear at bay.

"The aliens used panthers, though," Clyde says. "These are lions. Kings of the jungle. Totally different ball game."

"Panthers?" I say to him. "I always thought of them as tigers."

This is the conversational equivalent of hysteria. Things are going to shit fast. I need to focus, need a plan.

"We get any of the Russians yet?" I ask him. Gather information. Ask the right questions. Do detective work. Of a sort.

Clyde shakes his head.

"They get any of us yet?"

"Not for lack of trying. Enthusiastic bunch, I have to say."

I nod. A plan. Shock and awe. That's what Coleman said. It's what the Russians used. Worked for them too. We did not anticipate the lions. We probably should have, but we didn't. We need to do something they're not expecting.

I poke my head around the corner, try to assess the scene. Coleman and Felicity are crouched together near a fountain taking potshots at Proto-Lenin but the amazing anorak boy is holding them down with lightning. Kayla is set apart, battling with the blond woman who has apparently strayed too close to Devon and the van. She flicks her sword lazily at the woman, batting her away.

Stab her, I find myself willing, but Kayla seems satisfied with slaps of the blade, knocking the woman off-balance, beating her back, but refusing to advance.

"You see Tabby?" Clyde asks. "I'm trying to remember the words to the Wall, but I've forgotten them."

"I'm pretty sure they involve them kids being left alone by teachers." I'm not helping, I know.

Clyde shakes his head. "That came about four hundred years after the version I'm looking for. Not Romanian enough either."

We need to get back to Felicity and Coleman, to regroup. To get Kayla to actually fight. And where *is* Tabitha?

Shock and awe.

I need to take one of them down. I have to. I have to find a way to get close. Except they're standing in the middle of an empty square and they've got most of the cover prowling around and attacking us.

"You a hundred percent sure there's no way for you to teleport me next to someone?"

Clyde says something which is less sarcastic than I deserve, but I'm not really listening. The tall Russian is in the center of the square. The ringleader, I think. And if there's no way to sneak up on him… Well I only see one way to get close to him.

"Clyde," I say.

"Yes?"

"Cover me."

"Whatever with?"

I'd reply, but apparently I decided to hurdle the plinth about two seconds too early. Now all that's left to do is put my head down, charge, and regret it.

29

The Russian sees me coming when I'm five yards away. I'm closer than I thought I'd get.

Lightning flares.

Two yards away. I leap. A full body tackle.

The lightning doesn't stop. It hits me as I hit the Russian. There is a crack like the world ending in my face. Everything is white and weightless.

Then I come down, crack against the stones. My head rings. Pain floods me. I can see the tall Russian lying on the ground twenty yards away. His jacket is smoking.

And what the hell was that? Some transmutation spell to turn all my muscles into spaghetti? I flop over onto my belly. Rain stops running into my nose. God, I knew I was going to get electrocuted again.

Footsteps. I try to twist, see who's coming to finish me off.

It's Clyde, crouched low.

"Arthur? Arthur?"

I grunt at him.

"I think you may have attracted some undue attention." Clyde suddenly looks over my shoulder, flings out his arms. I watch as the tall man flies ten feet back through the air, lands in a haze of rain spray.

And that seems to take care of that problem.

Except...

The first lion comes out of the rain to my right. Clyde hauls me to my feet, stoops to let me put an arm over his shoulder. We turn. And there's another. We turn. The third.

They circle us. Metal tails stretched out behind them, whipping back and forth. Heads down low.

I remove my arm from Clyde's shoulder. It turns out my knees still work. I rest my hands on them, doubled over, still breathing hard. Everything hurts. How can everything hurt all at once?

Clyde circles me.

"You think a gun would work?" I say, glancing down at the pistol.

"Not really."

"You know," I say, "sometimes a little false optimism wouldn't go astray."

God, I hate these Russians. I mean, yes, we saved the world the other day, but these guys look like they're operating in a whole different league. All of them are magicians. We have Clyde. And Clyde... well, as much as I like him, the Russians animate stone lions, he animates Winston...

"I think I'm going to try that wall spell." Clyde has his back to me, looking at a street leading away from the square.

"You remember the words to it now?"

"Not really."

"What happens if you get it wrong?"

"Depends how wrong I get it."

"Best-case scenario?" Though in my experience there is rarely a best-case scenario with magic involved.

"The lions eat us."

That may be a worse best-case scenario than usual.

Clyde slips another AA under his mask. A lion roars. The circle tightens.

"They don't like that, Clyde." I'm surprised to find I can still sink deeper into fear.

"Then they really won't like this." He lowers his head, collapses in on his chest, knees bending, body sagging. "*Fellum mahrat mel cthok*," he mutters.

The lions stop pacing. Slowly they start to turn.

"*Messum ex locinun.*"

The lions are done circling. This is it. I aim my gun futilely. One bunches its back legs.

"Clyyyyyde!" My voice rises in volume and pitch.

"*Tellat al reium.*" Clyde straightens, stiffening his body violently, flinging his arms out. "*Masrat!*"

A line of spray races out from Clyde's body, billowing up from the ground. There is the sound of rain drumming against something invisible and massive.

But then the time to ponder what Clyde's done is over. A lion roars. Leaps. Another leaps.

Bronze jaws. Bronze claws. Closer. Closer.

Three feet from my face it slams into something. Stops dead in the air, arse tumbling over shoulders. The second one collides with it. Metal sparks and squeals.

Clyde reels back as the lions slump to the ground.

"Nice!" I'm still staggering, legs struggling to bear my weight, but I clap Clyde weakly on the shoulder.

"Still got the third one behind us."

"Oh shiii…" I turn. It smiles at us. And grandma, what big teeth you have.

"Run!" Clyde yells. "Run!"

It's very good advice. I ignore it.

I open fire. Bullets whine off the thing's muzzle. One chips a tooth. It keeps on grinning.

"RUN!" Clyde bellows.

But the thing is, I can't hurt this lion. I brought a pistol to a metal lion fight. I am seriously out of my weight class. The only person here that can make the lion take notice, I think, is Clyde. Which means it's important Clyde doesn't get turned into someone's dinner. Which means that I have to distract the bloody thing. Which unfortunately means upping the chances that I'm today's appetizer of choice.

The lion roars. The force of it blows back my hair, blows rain drops off my face. And when it comes to shock and awe, well that is how one does it.

I glance over at Felicity still trading potshots with the other Russians.

"Clyde," I say, "you better not screw this up."

In defiance of every urge in my body, I step toward the lion.

30

"Arthur," Clyde says, a warning note in his voice. "I'm relatively sure that's not the whole running thing I was advocating. I mean, not an athletic expert here, but—"

The bark of my pistol cuts him off. I aim for the lion's eyes as best I can. I have no idea if it needs them to see, but it's the most annoying place I can think to target.

"Come on, you big bastard." I know it can't understand me, but saying it makes me feel better. "Come to poppa."

My knees still feel weak. I would feel much better about this plan if I had, say, dedicated the past thirty-four years of my life to actually exercising on a regular basis.

The lion roars once more.

I put a shot down its throat.

And that does it.

It comes at me. No warning. No final growl. Just uncurls into action.

"Fuuuuuuuuuu…" I never make it to the end of the expletive. I turn and flee, fast as I can. I can feel the ground shaking beneath me. Can feel the thing a yard behind me. Gaining. Eating up inch after valuable inch. Just like it'll eat me.

Save me, Clyde. Please. Take this moment I'm trying to buy you and save the crap out of me.

A noise from behind me, vast, squealing, but still that rhythm of metal paws doesn't cease. Head down. Push on reserves of adrenaline that I'm not sure are there. A breathless, ragged push to flee. To get *away*.

Everything around me disappears. Even the sound of the lion. Everything narrows down into the action of placing the next foot, the next one, pumping my legs that little bit harder. My whole world reduced to a single action.

And then I trip, I sprawl. Hands out, too late. I grind my chin on concrete, bite my lip, spit blood. I roll. Arse over head. Feet over arse. Crashing down. Arms splayed. Wrist slamming down. Skid and stop.

And this is it. This is—

—I don't die. I lie on my back, puffing, wheezing, trying desperately to suck air back into my lungs. Trying to widen my vision from the two narrow points it's become.

I am not in Trafalgar Square anymore. I am in a dull back street. All brown brick, and black, wet asphalt. Somehow in my mad dash, I have managed to fully clear the field of engagement. I must have looked like a lunatic, sprinting madly away.

Jesus, I have to get back there.

I check my gun. My hands are shaking almost uncontrollably. Too much adrenaline in the system. Too much having my life threatened by things that shouldn't be. I am going to go back to that square and I am going to execute me some Russians. Shock and bloody awe.

"What's Katerina's situation?"

Who the hell? I spin around. But the street's abandoned. No one here.

"Pardon?" The voice again, quiet and bland, barely audible. "Is she on location?"

A little voice that seems to be coming from my pocket. I reach in. What the hell do I have…?

Coleman's phone. It's still on, still translating.

"She's at Big Ben now."

Russians. Russians are talking. Near me. Audibly.

"And they're all here?"

Russians talking about Big Ben. I was just talking about Big Ben the other day. Something to do with all this. What was it?

"The MI37 goons? They haven't a clue."

I spin around in the street. And there's no one here. A couple of parked cars. An empty Fiat. An empty Ford. Some workmen's white van.

Wait... the van. The window is rolled down. I take a step toward it. I hear a voice. Syllables I don't fully catch.

"Ivan has given his performance?"

I look down at the phone. Take another step.

More mumbling.

"What was that?" asks the phone.

I look at it. What was what?

"Do you hear that?" asks the phone.

I waste about half a second wondering how on earth I triggered paranoia mode on Coleman's phone before I realize I'm rumbled. The Russians know I'm here. I back up ten fast paces and flatten myself against the rear of the van. My breathing is coming fast. I put the phone away, slip it into the inside pocket of my jacket. Time to concentrate on my other hand and the gun in it.

I hear the van door open. A heavy foot falls.

Breathe slow. I make my mouth a little "o," concentrate on controlling each exhalation.

Footsteps move away from me. Four, five, six. They stop.

I grip my gun in both hands, the cold wet barrel pressed to the tip of my nose. Like I'm praying to the god of gunslingers.

The footsteps stop, reverse direction, come closer. Four, five, six. As quietly as I can, I thumb back the hammer on the pistol. More steps. Seven, eight, nine. Still coming. I can hear a slight motorized whine with each one. Ten, eleven, twelve. They stop.

I stop breathing. Slowly, so slowly, I stretch out my arms, point the gun at the corner of the van.

Get back in, bastard. Get back in.

A woman's voice comes from the van. Someone calling to the figure in the street. An incomprehensible stream of Russian syllables.

"Come back, Leo. There's no one there."

I stare in horror at my pocket. What sort of hellspawn put a microphone with the sensitivity of a hummingbird in this bloody thing? Who would do that?

I hear the scuff of the man's heels. I take a step backward, brace to pull the trigger.

A flash of light, like a camera going off. Then my world spins. I stagger.

Behind me. Someone just hit me from behind. But he… Did the woman climb out of the van?

Groggy, I spin, bring up the gun. But I'm just staring into a flash of light.

Another blow. From the right this time. From down back the way I'd come. And how many of the bastards are there? How long have they been watching me?

I spin again. A foot crashes into my kidneys. I stagger, go down on all fours. I try to hold onto the gun but it spills from my hands. I watch it scatter uselessly away.

A cold hand grabs my chin. Cold like the barrel of my gun against my nose. It heaves me up, an unforgiving grip on my jaw, lifting me to my knees, my feet.

A man in his forties. Good-looking. Elegant Slavic features. Straw-blond hair matted to his scalp by rain. Disgust in his eyes.

He pushes me back, and I fall. I land on my arse in a puddle. My hands grind against the blacktop. Everything is spinning.

The Russian, Leo I heard him called, says something I don't understand.

"You think you are clever?" asks the phone.

Not particularly, no.

Another question in Russian.

"You think you have us now?" the phone translates. "I do not think you are clever, little British man. I do not think you have us, little spy." The Russian takes another step toward me. Still talking.

I scrabble toward my gun.

"I think you are dead," says the phone.

I'm beginning to think that Coleman's phone is as big an arsehole as he is.

31

The Russian reaches me before I reach my gun. His boot in my gut once more. I grab onto the limb, try to haul myself up. He shakes me off—a deft punch to my sternum that makes me wheeze. I stagger back. My gun is still yards away. The Russian steps between me and it. I ball my fists.

The Russian grins, takes a step back, beckons to me with one hand. And I don't need the phone to translate that cocky little gesture. *Come on then, if you think you're hard enough.*

And screw this guy. Screw all these Russians, and their superior fucking attitude. Winston trod on one of you bastards. I'm going to do the same.

All the fear, and pain, and exhaustion of the day, I ball it all into my fists. I crush it between my hands. And I swing. Because, yes, you Russian bastard, I think I'm hard enough.

And I swing. And I miss.

He's not there. There's a flash of light and my fist flies through empty space. He's simply not there. I stumble forward into abandoned space.

And then a blow out of nowhere. Hard knuckles colliding with the side of my head, sending me staggering.

I spin, and he's there. Where he wasn't. Grinning at me. And fuck. This. Guy. I lower my shoulder, charge.

A flash of light. A bright-blue line from van to man, and then I'm sprawling through empty space, tripping and slipping. I splash down, grind my chin against the blacktop. He's not there.

His foot crashes into my ribs. I fold in around his boot, fail to absorb the blow. Another. Another.

I manage to pull myself together enough to spin my legs at him. Not really a kick. A kick's inbred cousin. But again—an electric blue flash, a spark from car to man, and I strike air.

His boot comes in again, again. I make it to all fours. I can't see. Water and blood in my eyes. His foot catches me in the gut. I'm off the ground. Smacking down. Hands and knees. My head down. Water filling my nose. Grunting. Waving my arm. Not really a punch. Not much of anything. All I've got left is hurting. A flash of light, and the boot comes from the other side. There's a rhythm to it. Pain. Pain. Pain.

I collapse. The road pressed to my cheek. An unsympathetic shoulder to cry on.

Pain. Pain. Pain.

"Leo," I can hear the phone in my pocket saying. "Leo. Leo." Damn thing isn't even talking to me anymore.

"Leo, you'll hurt yourself."

Wait. He'll hurt *himself*? But I'm too concussed to be truly indignant.

"Leo, stop it."

More of that please.

The world has become a very small place. A tiny point of rain and pain that swirls before me. It seems very far away. Each kick knocking me further away, further darkness, until, finally, everything goes black.

32

Consciousness returns in strobe flashes. I see the street. It fades. Rain falls. It fades. Hello world. Goodbye world. See you soon. Even the pain sinks into darkness for a while.

Next time I come to, the world is bleached away. Everything brilliant and white. I try to get away from the brightness, but my body won't respond.

Should I go into the light? Has it come to that already?

"Not as dead as he looks," says a voice.

Probably stay away from the light for now then.

"Arthur? Arthur?" It sounds like Felicity. It's nice to know she's here.

"All right, all right. Hold your bloody horses." It's the first speaker, the one so keen to shine light into my eyes. He sounds familiar but I can't quite place the voice. "I'll give him a shot of the jolly juice."

There is a pinch in my neck. And then the world suddenly grows very bright and very light. My body grows light. I gasp and air, cold and sharp, rushes into me. Fills me. Makes me buoyant. I sit up. Blink. I feel like I'm in the middle of a bubble.

"Calm down. Calm down." A hand on my chest. "Don't get bloody carried away." I look over. A man in a paramedic's uniform. A tight little face pinched around a needle-like nose.

I've seen him before. At the British Museum. The connection feels simple, easy to make. I laugh. "The cleanup crew."

Felicity is there too. The others. I go to stand up. The hand on my chest grows heavier. I push against it but I can't make it move. I look quizzically at the cleanup man.

"Look," he says, "I know you're all special and a field agent and what have you, but right now you're on quite a lot of morphine, a fair few amphetamines, a little bit of caffeine, glucose, and a lot of stuff for the swelling. And I know you feel more like Superman now than ever, but when you crash it's not going to feel any better than when this was done to you the first time.

"The jolly juice'll get you off site and through the debrief. It'll speed up the healing but it'll suck you as dry as an ex-wife. Take it easy." The needle-nosed man rolls his eyes. "Not that you'll bloody listen to me."

To be honest I just didn't. I feel kind of spacey right now. But I nod.

"All right," he says, "on your feet." He reaches out a hand to me. So does Felicity. She looks pensive. I try to give her a reassuring grin.

"I'll be OK," I say. She doesn't reply.

"Oh," says a loud voice from behind me, "there he is." Coleman. He doesn't sound overly pleased to have found me.

I turn around, look at the little shit. I sneer my contempt at him, but I think the effect is hampered by the dizziness. No matter.

He stands in front of me, chest puffed out. "Well?" he says, "what do you have to say for yourself?"

I blink at him, trying to work out exactly what he means. "Ouch," I say. In case he is talking about the beating I received.

"Probably want to give him a minute before you start—" the cleanup man says. But Coleman waves a hand at him.

"Hmm?" He peers at me. "What happened, 'ey? 'Ey?"

"Russians," I say. I say it like he would say it, loud and pompous. See how he likes it.

"I know fucking Russians, you imbecile," Coleman seethes. Apparently he doesn't like it very much.

"No, no, no." I shake my head. Then I do it again more gently, because that makes me feel dizzy too. "No. Just one Russian. Leo.

Leo the lion. Except he wasn't a lion. He was just a chap."

I'm vaguely aware I sound like Clyde, swimming around my subject. I should probably be concerned but it's kind of funny, and thinking about how it's funny when it should be concerning is funny too. I snort.

"Might have given him a tad too much," says the cleanup man.

"Leo," I say again. "Teleported about. Jumpy, jumpy, jumpy. And he hit me." I frown. It is not a pleasant memory. "Quite a lot actually."

Coleman leans in close. His breath is not lovely. "I don't give a flying fuck what happened to you in this alleyway. Anything that did, you had fucking coming. I want to know what passed between the two neurons you pass off as a functioning brain when you ran from the field of fucking engagement and left your fellow agents to die."

It feels like someone just burst a balloon in my head.

"You," I say, looking him right in the eye, "are a shit."

For a minute I think he's going to punch me, right there in the street. I'd go down too. I know that much.

Instead he just jams his finger into my chest. Hard. I rock back a step.

"I'm a shit?" he asks. "I'm a shit? Then I'd rather stay one than be a fucking coward." His finger strikes me again. Pushing me back. "I'd rather be a shit who stood with his men. I'd rather be the shit who didn't turn and run." Each statement punctuated with a finger push, with a step backward. "I'd rather be the shit with honor and spine. I'd rather be a shit with agents at his side when the Russians come so I don't end up alone and bleeding in a London street."

He's pushed me back against one wall of the street. I look down at his finger. Up at him.

"I was being chased by a bronze lion, you fuck," I say to him. Small, petty man that he is. And I bet he'd love to see me torn limb from limb. "And I had a pistol, and itty bitty little bullets that did fuck all."

"And Clyde?" Coleman doesn't give me an inch. "What was he going to do?"

"Clyde knows magic! I was buying him time!"

I look around. Clyde stands at the end of the street, arm wreathed in bandages, not meeting my gaze. Tabitha is next to him, matching bandages on her left leg. She does look at me. It's not the friendliest look she's ever given.

Devon, at least, has a smile for me, but Kayla, standing behind her, looks like I shit in her porridge.

"And once that was bought?" Coleman stares at me disdainfully. "You thought you'd done your part."

"Oh, yeah," I throw up my hands and sway back a step, "I just figured I'd lie down for bit, have a nap." I look down at the blood on my arms. "You have any idea where all these bruises came from?"

"It's good to know, Wallace," Coleman says, "when push comes to shove, whose life you're really concerned with saving." There's a sneer on his face. "Good to see your true colors."

"Oh go screw yourself, you bloody idiot."

It is, I realize after about a second's retrospection, high as I am, not the smartest thing to say. Because no matter how low my opinion is of Coleman, other people with far more power than me have a high one. Or a higher one than they have of me. So Coleman has more power than me. And Coleman is going purple.

"You're on probation, Wallace," he says. "Officially. Thirty days to shape up. To contribute. Or you're out."

I stare at him. This has to be a joke.

"Felicity?" I say. I look at her. She is standing off to the side, looking concerned, and completely bloody failing to express it. "Felicity!"

Coleman shoves me. Hard. I stagger backwards, only held upright by the wall I collide with. "Fucking her won't save you now, toy-boy," Coleman hisses.

I take a swing at him.

Screw it. Screw consequences.

He bats my fist away. It's a pathetic attempt on my part. I can barely feel my elbow, let alone my fingers.

"He's on drugs." Felicity finds her tongue, finally steps in. Too little, too bloody late.

I feel very sober now. "There were Russians," I say. The pain is starting to leak back in. "Back here. In a van." Neither Coleman nor Felicity are really looking at me as I say it.

"They were talking about this as a distraction." Screw this. I'll do my damn debrief, then I'm out of here. "They were saying this wasn't important, that something was going on at Big Ben."

Coleman starts to walk away.

"Nothing's going on at Big Ben," Felicity says. "Nothing's happened there."

"It's what they said." I shrug. I don't know what she wants to hear. I'm not asking for forgiveness. "They beat the living shit out of me for hearing it."

"We'll look into it, Arthur." She's still not meeting my eye. I don't know whether to believe her.

"He teleported, Felicity," I say. "I know Clyde and everyone says it's not possible, but I saw it. He wasn't there when I went for him. When I tried to fight him. He got hit by lightning or something, coming from the van, and then he was somewhere else. Space magic. Time magic. Impossible magic. He was doing it."

"We'll look into it, Arthur." The same flat tone. And she doesn't believe me. And I don't believe her.

"It's the truth." I can't make it any plainer. I can't make it any more convincing. This is what I have to give them.

"OK, Arthur." She nods. A small woman in a small suit. Hardly Felicity Shaw at all.

God, I'm on drugs, and I'm in pain, and someone should be taking bloody care of me. And instead I'm trying to explain how I did exactly the right bloody thing in the rain. To my girlfriend.

Three days. Three days since I helped save the world. Three days since I snuck into Felicity's bed. And now she's watching as I'm put on fucking probation. And I'm sure she has reasons, but right now none of them feel good enough.

I push off from the wall, start walking away. Away from Trafalgar Square. Away from Coleman and Felicity and the whole MI37 crew.

"Where are you going, Arthur?" Felicity asks me.

"I don't know," I say. Away. Trying to find the space to put my head back together.

"Come back to the hotel, Arthur. You need to rest."

"I need…" I hear my voice rising. All my anger and frustration starting to boil up and over. I take a breath. "I need a little while," I say.

"Don't drink on it," calls the cleanup man. "Lot of drugs in your system right now."

Not enough. Not enough by half.

33

I don't know London. It's just streets. Just strips of gray stretching off into a rain haze. I walk them. Get lost in them. And it's good to concentrate purely on taking this left. This right. To feel the litany of directions overwhelm memory, obliterate thought, obliterate what just happened. I just concentrate on getting lost. In this city. In my head.

I push my hands through rain-slick hair, then shove them into my pockets. There's a piece of paper in one. Another distraction. I pull it out. A phone number. Eleven digits all lined up.

Aiko's number.

Aiko. The Weekender. And from there it's just a short step to work. To the absurdity of the last scene. It's all the fault of that poisonous shit Coleman. Why else would they think I abandoned them? They found me lying down beaten up. It wasn't like I'd chosen to remain out of action.

And, yes, looking back on it, I can see how it might have looked like cowardice, fleeing the field. How I might have kept on going too long after Clyde removed the danger. But I was running for my life. If I went too far then... I mean, surely that's bloody understandable.

And seeing that situation wrong isn't the only mistake they're making. This isn't just about a bomb. This isn't just about the surrender of the West to the USSR. Something else is happening.

And they're not seeing it. I just wish I knew what it was, had enough vision to make it undeniable for them.

I look down at Aiko's number again. And would she dismiss my theories so completely? Or would she listen?

I shake my head. I need to remember that I'm on a lot of drugs right now. I need to remember that calling this number would be a stupid idea. A really, really stupid idea.

THIRTY MINUTES LATER

The Lamb and Flag is warm and steamy, full of thawing tourists and locals already five pints into their supper. I remember the cleanup man's advice and just order a coke and a bag of salt and vinegar crisps.

Aiko looks at me across the table. "Jesus," she says. "Tell me you got the number of the truck at least."

She's wearing jeans and layered T-shirts. She pulls her hair out of a ponytail and peers at the bruises distorting my face. "I'm starting to think you hang with the wrong crowd, Agent Arthur," she says. "An unsavory bunch."

I laugh. It sounds worryingly bitter. "I'm starting to think you're right," I say. I don't know how much I'm joking.

Still, what about the crowd I'm with now? I could lose my job over this. Felicity told me not to do this.

Felicity is smart and sensible.

Felicity also just watched as I got put on probation.

Felicity also slept with Coleman.

I look at Aiko across the table. She's looking right at me, open eyes, clear face. A little bit of concern. A little bit of a smile. Some secret joke I'm not sharing. I need to work out what I'm doing, how big a mistake this is. And how do I broach this delicately?

"Clyde says you're a conspiracy theory nut."

Probably not like that.

But she smiles as she rolls her eyes. "You know," she says, "they're only theories if you don't have evidence."

I laugh. Because she's making fun of me, and she's doing it pitch perfect.

But she doesn't laugh with me. She doesn't even crack a smile.

"You're serious?" I say.

"What do you mean by a conspiracy theory?" she says.

"Well…" I shake my head. It still feels loose with all the drugs. I can't believe we're having this conversation. "The moon landings," I say.

"First one's totally fake. You can smell the epochal fear coming off Kennedy through the tapes. They were showing TV images of that come hell or high water. But they got the third Apollo mission up there, for sure."

"Nine-eleven?" I ask.

"Perpetrated by the US government. Because of oil money. Obviously."

Oh Jesus, she's serious. She's totally serious. "The assassination of JFK?" I try.

"You think I'm going to say the CIA did it, don't you?" She's smiling. I'm not though.

"It was actually organized by the Gnomes of Zurich," she says.

She can't have just said that. She can't. Not to my face.

"The who?" I ask.

"Cabal of financiers living in Switzerland. They control about ninety percent of global wealth. JFK was a destabilizing factor for them. See they were heavily invested in Nixon. So they worked with him and the CIA to take JFK out. It's funny, but it was actually the elder George Bush who was the trigger man. He denies it now, but he was secretly working for the CIA at the time. Which, I mean, totally set him up for the legacy presidency." She squints off into the distance beyond my shoulder. "The US is really messed up with shit like that."

She's serious. She's totally dead serious. "You really believe all this, don't you?" I say. I put my head down on the table. And Clyde was right. Felicity was right. They're all right. Even Coleman. I'm such a fucking imbecile.

"Belief implies faith," Aiko says. She's taking my skepticism pretty well. On the other hand this is probably not the first time she's gotten this reaction. "Faith implies a lack of evidence."

"Evidence?" I say, not quite managing to look up. "Don't you think if there was evidence to support all this then we'd know?"

"Arthur." Her tone brings my head up. She looks at me as if I'm a child. "There's about a thousand documentaries on the internet demonstrating how nine-eleven was an inside job. It's out there. It's just people don't listen. They don't look. They take the accepted cultural view."

"I don't..." I shake my head. I have no idea what she's talking about. I don't know why I'm talking to her.

"Do you believe in gravity, Arthur?" she asks me.

"What? Yes. Of course." I'm not sure if it's the non sequiturs or the drugs, but this is getting hard to follow.

"Why?"

I blink at her. "Why?" I repeat. I'm not sure I understand the question.

"Because it's the best explanation for events, right?" she continues, careless of my confusion. "Things fall down. A force attracts objects with mass. It makes sense. Doesn't it?"

And yes, of all the things we've covered so far, that is the one that does make sense. So I nod.

"Have you ever read Newton's paper on gravity? Have you ever read any papers on it at all?"

I think about it. Mr. Carper teaching me physics. Me sitting by the window and fantasizing about Sandra Watkins in the row in front of me. Not many primary sources involved in any of that as far as I can recall. I shake my head.

"Then you're a believer in gravity, Agent Arthur." Aiko fixes me with a dead-on stare. The sort Kurt Russell gives the bad guy just before he pulls the gun and blows the man's stone-cold heart out his back. "You've accepted a common cultural belief. You don't *know*, no matter how deeply you believe you do. You've taken gravity on faith."

I feel like I should have issues with that argument but I'm having trouble finding them through the fuzzy edges of my thinking.

"I'm not criticizing you, by the way." Aiko lets her face soften as she watches me try to puzzle through her logic. "I'm with you. I'm not hunting down the original paper. I'll accept the popular theory. Maybe if I was into quantum physics or some such then

I'd be motivated, but I'm not. But when one of these big cultural beliefs looks like it's really having a serious effect on my life, on my ability to live the way I want to, then I'm motivated to go and find out the truth. I'll do the research, look at the evidence, be open-minded. And I've seen proof. And I don't believe in anything. But I know a whole number of things that don't agree with those common cultural beliefs."

It's a good speech. It's delivered with conviction. It's delivered calmly. She's a rational girl who happens to subscribe to a bunch of theories people have labeled as irrational. And considering what I've seen maybe I shouldn't be so quick to judge.

"Shall I tell you why I think you're here, Agent Arthur?" says Aiko.

She's taking charge, I notice. The way Felicity does.

I bat that thought away. It seems errant and ill-advised. Instead I just nod again.

"I think you're here, Agent Arthur," Aiko says, leaning in and pilfering a handful of my crisps, "because you've got proof that a cultural belief is wrong, and you're bumping heads with people who don't want to hear it."

She snarfs the fistful of crisps and leans back, a satisfied expression on her face.

I, on the other hand, just look generally perplexed.

Aiko rolls her eyes. "Time magic," she says. "Conspiracy theories. I'm making a comparison. Creating common ground."

"Oh!" The penny drops.

"Are you really high right now?" She seems genuinely interested.

"Just a little," I say. "I think. Mostly painkillers."

She smiles. "You're kind of fun when you're high, Agent Arthur."

"You can just call me Arthur, you know."

"I know." She's still smiling. I'm being toyed with. The mouse while she's the cat. And, as I understand it, the mouse rarely comes out of these things well. Time to change the subject. Get back to why I'm here.

"Time magic," I say.

"Of course." Aiko smiles. She still resembles a Cheshire cat.

"So," I say, "and as a caveat I really shouldn't be telling you this."

"Understood." A nod from her. She finally lets the smile fade, playing the attentive student.

"The Russians were in Trafalgar Square today," I say.

"I know that." She looks as if I just revealed to her the great and wonderful secret that the sky is blue.

"You do?"

"I've just gone on and on about how I am relatively adept at navigating to the truth and avoiding cultural misdirection put about by such things as government-sponsored mass media. I'm perfectly capable of working out what's a set of demands by magical terrorists and what's a publicity stunt gone awry."

In some ways it's reassuring to know that our cover stories are seen through. I always feel more effort should be dedicated to duping the public. When it's easy, I lose a little bit of faith in my humanity.

"All right," I say. "Well the Russians and MI37 also had a bit of a disagreement. It got physical." She rolls her eyes. "I know you know," I say. "I'm just giving background. Anyway, I became..." I hesitate over the wording, "separated from the main fight." She raises her eyebrows but I plunge on, ignoring her. "I came across two more Russians," I say. "They were hanging back. They were talking about events in Trafalgar Square being a distraction. The whole thing about nuking London being a distraction." And now I do have her attention. "They were talking about a woman called Katerina being at Big Ben—"

"Where the Chronometer is," Aiko interrupts me.

And that was it. That's what I'd been talking about. Clyde and I. The Chronometer. Located in Big Ben. Protected by an anti-magic field and ninjas. I remember now.

Time magic. Again. Around and around it goes. And I still can't find my way to the center of it all.

Which brings me back to why I'm here.

"There's more," I say. "This," I wave at my battered face, "happened because of a fight with one of them. And I'm not the world's greatest fist-fighter, but normally I don't suck this bad."

Aiko looks more doubtful than I think is kind.

"I look this way," I say with gravitas, "because he was a *teleporter*." I let that word hang there.

Her eyes go wide. And she gets it. She gets the significance of that word.

"You saw it?" she says.

I nod. And this is the reaction this sort of news should get. This is appropriate. And even though the pain is starting to cut through the drugs, I smile.

"They've done it." Aiko is nodding to herself. "They've actually done it. Intradimensional magic." She's wide-eyed with wonder.

"You realize," I say, because I need to check, "that that's not a good thing, right?"

"No, no, of course not. I know. But still… Christ." She bites her bottom lip.

And this is it for her, I realize. This is what it's all about. Where her involvement in this supernatural world circles back to her love of conspiracy theories. Hidden knowledge. That's her personal crack, and I just gave her a hit off the pipe.

"You believe me?" I ask, just to double-check. I feel I should partly because now I know her personal issue with belief and partly because I'm decreasingly familiar with the experience and some verbal confirmation would be good.

"Well." Aiko looks up at me, bites her lip again. "I haven't seen it with my own eyes, but let's say you're a credible source. I don't see why you'd just come here to mess with me."

I smile again, a small one, but it runs deep.

We sit there silently for a while, she basking in her newfound knowledge, me in my newfound belief. A cult of two.

"You going to eat those?" She indicates the crisps.

"All yours." She takes the pack, pounds down another fistful. "You know what I don't get?" she says. I shake my head. "If they've worked out how to bend time and space, why would they be interested in the Chronometer? They don't need it. Why go to the bother of luring you guys to Trafalgar Square just so one of them can sightsee?"

I shake my head. Try to think through the fog of fading drugs and blossoming pain.

"There has to be some limit to what they're doing," I say. "They have to need the Chronometer instead. Maybe they can't travel so far, or…" I stare into the depths of my coke.

"When would they want to go back to?" Aiko asks.

"Chernobyl?" I venture. It's the vaguest of guesses. It just seems like it has to be the answer to something.

No response from Aiko. I look up from the coke to see if she's looking at me like I'm an errant child again. Somehow it's both an aggravating and an endearing look at the same time.

But she's not giving me a look like that. Instead she's giving me wide-eyed fear.

"Oh my God," she says.

"What?" I glance over my shoulders looking for Russians, for a pissed off Coleman with a shotgun. There's nothing there.

"Chernobyl," she says. She's seeing something I don't. "The space-time experiment. The definitive one. The one that would have allowed the USSR to win the Cold War. They know how to do it right. That's what we're saying, right? That they figured out how to do space-time magic."

And it hits me then, the fullness of it.

"They want to go back," I say. "Back to Chernobyl. They want to do it right. They want to rewrite twenty-eight years of history."

34

We spend the rest of the evening stress-testing the idea. Double-checking ourselves for paranoia.

But it holds water. It makes sense. No matter how we come at it, the facts actually tally with this theory. There's only one last objection I keep butting my head against.

"They can't do it," I say.

"Why not?" Aiko looks a little frustrated at this blanket statement after three hours of solid discussion and napkin diagrams.

"Because they'll be killed. There's about a hundred soldiers in there."

"So they just teleport past them. Go right to the Chronometer itself, wind it back, and goodbye goes today."

"They can't," I say, remembering the conversation with Clyde clearly now. "There's an anti-magic field of some sort around the Chronometer."

"An anti-magic field?" Both her eyebrows bounce up.

"Not my words." I wave my hand.

"And I'm the conspiracy theory nut?"

We're off-topic. "They can't teleport in," I repeat. "They have to face the guards. And several hundred or so of them. Special forces ninjas or some such. And I don't care how good the Russians are, they won't get past several hundred guys," I catch her look, "or girls."

"So why was this Katerina at Big Ben today?" she asks. "Why

give you guys a deadline of the seventeenth? I mean, that's only seven days away now. Why go public at all?"

"I don't know," I say. "I don't know." I shake my head. I genuinely feel like crap now. I slump against the booth and regret the platter of fish and chips.

"You OK?" Aiko asks me.

I shake my head.

"You want me to give you a lift? My car's not too far from here."

"No." I shake my head again. "If I'm seen with you..." I trail off, not sure if the imagined repercussions will really be worse than the actual ones.

"Agent Arthur," Aiko says, "are you cheating on MI37 with me?" That cat-and-mouse smile is on her lips again.

I smile too, despite myself. But I'm stopping things right here. I'm still pissed at Felicity, but I'm neither angry nor high enough to get stupid. "I should catch a cab."

She comes out and helps me flag one down. It's still raining, but I'm rapidly losing the use of my arms.

"We should talk more about this," she tells me as I climb into the car.

"Yes." I nod. We should. But... "I'm going to have to run this past the others at MI37," I say. Aiko deserves to know. Because when I tell them I won't be able to mention her. And I don't know what will happen to her role in things after that.

"Sure." She nods, like she was expecting it.

"I'm not trying to shut you out of this."

She nods, resigned to the fact. "They won't believe you," she says, "just so you know."

She thinks the worst of them, and I can't truly blame her. But maybe I know them better. "They're not bad people," I tell her.

"You're not a bad person, Arthur," she says, "but do you believe me that powerful financiers in Switzerland organized JFK's death?"

She's got a point.

"You planning on actually going anywhere tonight, mate?" asks the cabby.

I make my apologies, say my final goodbye to Aiko. "I'll call you," I say.

"I know," she says. Again, the cat-and-mouse smile is back.

35

NOT ENOUGH HOURS LATER

"Wake up, Arthur. Wake up." Soft but insistent words. Each one like a velvet-wrapped brick trying to cave in my skull.

I crack an eyelid. Light lances in and tries to spear my brain.

A silhouette—the only patch of blessed darkness—resolves itself into Felicity. She gives me a quick, tight smile. "We should talk," she says. "But you needed sleep, so I let you go as late as I could. You've got ten minutes."

"Uuh," I reply, and roll off the bed.

The previous night slowly resolves out of the pain of waking. The beating. The conversation with Aiko. The startling wisdom of sneaking into my hotel room and going to bed without discussing the day's events with Felicity while crashing off a potent cocktail of drugs.

But now I'm sober, what do I say to her? I'm in no state for a fight.

Felicity touches my arm as I find my feet. "Just..." She stops. Complicated emotions move beneath the surface of her skin. "You'll do better today, Arthur. I know you will."

* * *

MI6. OCTOBER 11TH. THREE MINUTES AFTER NINE

"What the hell is this, you tardy fucks?" Coleman eyes the collected mass of MI37 as we file into a conference room deep in the bowels of 85 Vauxhall Cross, the home of MI6.

I feel my blood pressure climbing. My head is still thundering. But I need to roll with the abuse. I need to make nice and convince this gargantuan arsehole that what he believes to be impossible is real.

Flop. Flop. Flop.

That's not helping.

The MI6 conference room is nicer than the one we have in Oxford. There are no coffee mug rings on the table. There is, to my wide-eyed disbelief, a window.

"All right, all right," Coleman blusters. "Shut up. Listen. Big waggly things on the side of your head. Better-looking on some than on others." He winks at Devon. "Use them."

Kayla harrumphs.

"Wait." I hold up my hand, taking advantage of the brief pause this causes Coleman. He looks at me like I'm a turd that just crawled off his shoe and asked to perform for the crowd.

"No," Coleman says.

"About yesterday," I start, ignoring him. Coleman takes a step toward me, but Felicity holds up a hand. Finally. Finally she has my back. And Coleman backs off.

I keep the smile locked down, tight in my gut. I can't afford to spoil this now.

"I know we've talked about it before, about how teleportation is impossible. About how intradimensional magic is impossible."

From the corner of my eye, I see Felicity, almost imperceptibly, shake her head. But she's backed me to this point. She'll listen.

"But I saw it happen yesterday." I lock my eyes on Clyde and Tabitha. "A man teleported in front of me yesterday. Whatever science needed to be worked out—the Russians worked it out. They know how to do it."

"No, Arthur," Tabitha starts.

"It all goes back to Chernobyl." I plunge on. I am not going to be shut down by denials. This is too big, too important. And I lay it all out for them, piece by piece, just the way Aiko and I went through it last night. Until it's all there, before them. Definite. Undeniable.

"Are you kidding me, Arthur?"

Felicity says it. Felicity who has my back. She's staring at me, incredulous. And no, she has to see this. She has to.

Coleman chuckles quietly to himself.

"Glamour, Arthur," Tabitha says. "Illusion."

"We covered this," Felicity says, exasperated.

"That's not how it was." I shake my head. I look at Felicity. "You said you would look into this."

"I did, Arthur." It's Clyde who replies. "Took me all of two minutes to scan the literature. Gift of incorporeality and all that. It's still impossible. There's not a single dissenting voice in the thaumaturgic community. And that's not a crowd known for being unanimous about things. Except perhaps the wonderfulness of beards. But, you know, Occam's razor and all that. Look for the simplest solution. So rather than it being the impossible answer, maybe there's something more obvious. Maybe, whatever you thought you saw…"

He hesitates, looks to Felicity, who nods. "I looked up head trauma symptoms too, Arthur," he says. "They can be terribly nasty buggers. Much like ferrets. Never saw why people keep those as pets. Teeth with furry tails and attitude problems if you ask me. Not the symptoms, that is. Ferrets. But the symptoms, they include altered memories and changed perceptions. Which could account for everything you think you remember. How you interpret it. Seems a little more likely. Wouldn't you say?" He nods encouragingly.

Goddamn it. This is… I shake my head vehemently. "I am not remembering this wrong." I try to make it sound undeniable, but I fear I just sound petulant. "I saw what I saw. He moved. He teleported. It's real. The game has changed. They're going to change it. They're going to go back and give teleportation technology to the Russians in the eighties. During the Magic Arms Race. They're going to change it so that they win."

Coleman keeps on smiling like the mouse who got the whole fucking Edam. I look to Felicity, imploring.

"Stop it, Arthur," she says. "Just... Jesus, I thought you were going to apologize."

I throw up my hands. "I have nothing to bloody apologize for! I bought Clyde time. I had the shit kicked out of me."

And... I don't know. When does fighting for what's right just become banging your head against a wall? I look at the door.

"Feel free," Coleman says. He steps aside, proffers the exit with one sarcastically gracious hand.

"George..." Felicity starts. But she doesn't finish. Leaves the line and me hanging.

"He's your mistake, Felicity. Not mine."

And just because it will piss him off, just to piss on his goddamn parade, I pull out a chair and sit down.

Devon, sitting next to me, reaches over and pats me on the back. I know she's trying to be supportive but being patronized doesn't exactly help.

Coleman arches an eyebrow, then snorts and turns to the others. "Now we're done with the clown's performance," he says, "maybe the adults can talk about what's really going on."

36

It's Clyde who speaks. "Lightning strikes," he says.

I have a moment of, "*Et tu*, Brute?" Not happy with just dismissing my theories and damning all of western civilization, now he has to back Coleman up?

It's not a fair thought, of course. But God I preferred it when he wasn't a mask.

Clyde reaches, with a certain temerity, for Tabitha's laptop. She spins it around to face us, but doesn't let him touch it. Clyde's hand tremors and Google pops up.

"We thought," he says, "that the Russians were using lightning primarily as an offensive tool." On the screen fifty tiny images of forked lightning appear. "However, we've all noticed, at least I noticed, and Co-Directors Shaw and Coleman noticed, and Tabitha did too, and I'm assuming other people did, but, well, the appearance of lightning doesn't always correlate with an actual attack. Plus the Russians are frequently hit as well. Not totally the way I'd attack people. I mean, it's subjective, I'm sure, but the less crispy I am the better, I always think."

Tabitha is sitting next to Clyde, not looking at him. She stares at the back of the laptop and chews her hair. Even Kayla looks more relaxed right now. Wasn't there a day just last week when she would have been staring rapturously at Clyde?

And I'm not the only one it seems, who misses the man behind the mask.

Clyde's hand shakes again. More images on Google: yellow signs with black lightning, a plug, a light bulb.

"Electricity," he says, "is the universal lubricant between realities. Allows us to breach this reality, reach into another, pull through a force, have an effect. Why I drop about seven hundred pounds on batteries a month. But the Russians," a few images of Moscow appear on screen for no clear reason, "have worked out something very tricky."

My stomach lurches. And I know, of course I know, he's not going to say intradimensional magic. But he should.

"They're pulling ambient electricity from their surroundings," Clyde says. "From wiring, from passing cars, laptops, anything that has a charge really. Which is, I think I should really point out, some frighteningly cool physics. I mean it's a virgin science. We all thought it was practically impossible at this point."

Another stomach flip. "Wait," I say. "This we're OK with believing? This impossibility we permit them, but mine is one too far?"

Felicity puts her head between her hands.

"Oh do be quiet," Coleman says.

And, hell, normally I like to spread the abuse I receive evenly throughout the day. Front-loading like this is really going to throw me off. But I open my mouth to bite back.

"Wait…" Devon raises a hand slightly. "I mean, isn't Arthur… Didn't we just dismiss an impossible thing?"

And, God, I could kiss her.

"Oh," Clyde says. "Well. Erm…" He works his hands, can't quite bring himself to meet her eye.

"Practically impossible," Tabitha cuts in smoothly. Her lip curls, superior, and cruel. Apparently a chance to one-up Devon is just the thing to cure the my-boyfriend's-an-inhuman-mask blues. "Versus actually impossible. Practically impossible equals theoretically possible. Actually impossible equals bullshit. We tend to avoid bullshit. Professionals at work."

I realize I'm only an incidental target of her bile, but it doesn't stop it stinging.

"Watch your tone." Kayla's voice is barely above a whisper but everyone hears.

Devon's cheeks are burning. "Quiet," she hisses at Kayla, loud enough for people on the floor above to hear it.

Somehow, Tabitha meets Kayla's death stare head-on. "Know what?" she says. "Way you handle a sword these days, I might be willing to pick that fight."

And, I never thought I'd see the day, but Kayla actually averts her eyes.

God. We put the world back so very, very wrong.

And why didn't Kurt Russell ever make a movie where he handily dealt with an awkward staff meeting? I could really use some life lessons here.

"OK, shut up everyone." Coleman stands up, dismissing Clyde and any additional comments with the back of his hand. "So," he says, "in summary we've got ourselves some militant Russkies with insane demands that an unidentified 'West' surrender to the USSR even though it's about as alive and kicking as the dodo. And the stick for that charming little carrot is the threat of a Chernobyl-level explosion in London. And they've given us six whole days to comply. Because the Russkies are a generous people and all that PC hog crap." He cracks his knuckles. "That said, while the demands are bullshit, the threat's credible."

I'm disappointed to find myself forced to agree with everything the bastard just said.

"The original Chernobyl," he insists on continuing, "took a nuclear reactor to power it, so normally I'd start looking at major power sources. But they've got this whole wireless access to electricity, so that plan is viciously buggered."

He looks around the room, locking eyes with everyone but me. He gives Devon double time to make up for it. And despite his attempts to mentally fling Devon's clothes all over me, I'm again confronted by the unavoidable accuracy of his summation of the information.

If only he wasn't drawing completely wrong conclusions from it.

"Not that any of that's much of a problem, of course," Coleman says with a shrug.

And that conclusion seems the furthest from reality that we've achieved today.

"Always been a short-sighted people, the Russkies," Coleman informs us. "Their plan is still dependent on power. Just on a broader scale. But we can still deny it to them." He claps his hands together as if that's the case closed.

My quizzical expression remains. And what the hell, I'm playing the role of village idiot anyway.

"We can what?" I say.

Coleman grunts as if my thick-headedness causes him physical pain. "Power, Arthur." He speaks slowly and loudly. "To London. We cut it. They can't have it. No bomb."

"*All* of London's electricity?" I want to be sure I've got that quite right because something niggles there. And not just the obvious implausibility. Something I was saying earlier if only I could put my finger on it.

"Why are you still talking?" Coleman's expression has evolved from distaste to full-blown disgust.

"Actually," Devon raises her hand if not her head again, "I was sort of, well exactly really, but I was wondering about the same thing."

Why on earth would Clyde ever leave someone as wonderful as Devon?

"Well, sweetheart—" Coleman's tone is suddenly sugary smooth "—basically we put out some announcement about sun activity and a danger to all electrical items for the next week. Whip the media into a frenzy. Government issues panicked warnings, etc. Then we EMP London. Take out anything the Russkies are packing. Simple enough."

"EMP London?" It's Tabitha's turn to ask questions now.

"Yes, yes," Coleman snaps. "EMP. I thought you were meant to be the smart one."

"Know what it is." It does my heart good to see Tabitha's painted nail (white with a black skull) rise at Coleman. "Electromagnetic pulse. Wipe out anything electrical."

"Problem solved then." Coleman turns away.

"No." Tabitha's voice is a stiletto blade between the ribs. Coleman is forcibly stopped in his dismissal. He looks rather nonplussed. But Tabitha stared down Kayla today. Coleman doesn't stand a chance.

"Clyde," Tabitha says. She reaches out and taps his mask twice with her knuckle. She suppresses a grimace. "Electronic. EMP London. You EMP him. And you kill him again. And I kill you." She's not joking. We can all feel it. And it's not malice, and strangely enough it doesn't even feel like love. It sounds like a woman stating the terms of her existence as she's negotiated them.

Coleman purses his lips, momentarily knocked from his stride.

"Actually…" Every eye in the room snaps to Clyde. "Well, I mean, what I was thinking," Clyde hedges towards his noncommittal comfort zone, "there's a chance, well something I've been reading up on… and, obviously some existential thinking has occurred recently. Clear why, I suspect. But I've dived into a lot of philosophy, and more computer theory than I originally anticipated. Artificial intelligence, that sort of thing. Quite a lot of anime, truth be told, but I'm wandering off-topic.

"What I'm trying to say, in a roundabout sort of way, is that I am not in a carbon-based meat body these days. Probably noticed. Hello, elephant in the room. But obviously that means some of the more comfortable assumptions about corporeality and mortality no longer apply."

He shrugs several times, seemingly trying to gear himself up for something. "Which, admittedly," he says, standing, "is all rather just a sort of preamble to explaining that I'm pretty sure I can do this."

Abruptly Clyde's head goes sideways. His arm snaps out. His legs kick. For a moment I get to wonder if Clyde has spent the evening reading texts about avant-garde art movements and is now treating us to a postmodern deconstruction of the traditional dance show aesthetic.

Then he keels over and his head cracks sharply against the floor.

37

"Clyde!" Tabitha barks.

"Clyde!" Devon shrills in unison.

They both step toward him, then Devon catches herself. This is not her watch anymore. She turns away and I glimpse the pain and confusion on her face. Kayla moves toward her.

Clyde starts to tremor on the floor. Felicity, efficient as ever, seizes a first-aid kit from a wall mount.

"Hello?"

Tabitha's laptop, lying ignored and open on the desk. It speaks. It has an absurdly cheery tone. I stare at it. For a moment I seem to be the only one who's noticed.

"Can you hear me?" it says. "Are the speakers on? Do you need me to turn up the volume?"

A familiar tone.

It takes a moment for the realization that Clyde's voice is coming from the laptop to permeate the room. One by one the others turn and stare with me.

"Clyde?" Tabitha, kneeling by the body, says. Her voice is shaking. She swallows hard. "Did you just download yourself onto my laptop, Clyde?" Her question doesn't so much have an edge as it has a 9mm barrel.

"Well…" the laptop starts.

And then Clyde sits up and rubs the back of his head. "Bugger," he says. "Need to be doing the whole horizontal thing next time I try that."

Felicity does the full-on comedy double take. Clyde, laptop. Laptop, Clyde.

Tabitha is shaking. Visibly shaking. Shudders quaking up her arms and spine.

"Just trying to explain the whole thing," says the laptop. Apparently to Clyde. So maybe Clyde says it to himself.

"Oh marvelous!" Clyde nods. "Want to finish up?"

"Oh no, you go ahead," the laptop tells him.

Something's wrong with reality again. I can feel it. That odd sideways slipping feeling where my brain has to perform gymnastics it was not really built for.

"Well," Clyde—the meat Clyde, the real Clyde—says, "it's all fairly simple. I'm a digital file. Big complicated one. But I can be copied. Rewritten. Backed up." He sits up straighter. "Just a data compression problem really, but I've mostly solved that. Handy really."

Abruptly, and with a certain violence, Tabitha scrabbles away from him, crab-crawling on hands and feet. She hits the wall, slithers up against it, trying to maximize the distance between herself and her boyfriend.

"What?" she manages. Her quaking hand points at the laptop. "What the fuck? Clyde, what the fuck is going on?"

"Tabby?" Clyde sounds genuinely disturbed by her reaction. Genuinely upset. "It's just a copy. Just another me. So I can't die. When the EMP goes off."

"On my laptop?" Her head is twisted on one side. She's near tears. And this is too much. This is a step too far.

"Yes," Clyde says. "I thought that would be a good place to keep it. So I'm always with—"

"Which one of you am I fucking dating?" Tabitha screams it, her voice breaking on the last syllable. "Which one of you is my fucking boyfriend?"

"Me." Clyde taps his chest as if it's obvious.

"Him," the laptop says.

Tabitha lets out a noise that's half shriek, half moan.

And how could he have thought this was all right? How could he have not considered this as an outcome? Clyde's a smart man.

Was a smart man?

Is a smart... what? God, what is he?

Quickly, decisively, Felicity leans across the table and slaps down the lid of the laptop.

"Hey!" it says, and then the voice is cut off.

"I am not dating a computer program." Tabitha has her head in her hands. "I am not dating a computer program."

"No," Clyde says. "Of course not. It's just a copy. Just in case."

"Away," Tabitha moans. She slides along the wall, keeping the maximum distance between herself and Clyde. "Need air. Need fucking space."

"This could be terribly useful, Tabby," Clyde says.

Useful. God I hate that word.

She keeps backing away.

Everything about Clyde slumps. And he really didn't see this coming. "I was just trying to be useful." He reaches out to her.

"Feckin' stop it." Kayla finally steps away from Devon. Three strides quick enough they blur together. She catches Clyde's hand. An iron grip. "You've done e-feckin'-nough already."

"Leave him alone!" Tabitha spits her rage and confusion across the room. All the emotions she's trying not to unleash on Clyde, all the pain—she dumps it on Kayla. "Fucking psycho bitch. Don't need you. I'm not someone for you to defend. They're gone. Your girls are gone. Fucking face it. I'm not one. Devon's not one. Can't just grab us and make us belong to you. You're fucking alone. Fucking insane. Fucking pathetic."

And then she's out the room in a storm of black lace and tears.

There is silence in her wake. Absolute and utter. Kayla stares after her, still holding Clyde's wrist. He starts to writhe and twist. His hand turns an ugly shade of purple. Then she releases him, and his gasp of relief is still the only sound. Devon is looking back and forth from Kayla to the doorway. And I really should have taken the time to explain to her what was going on. But I didn't say a word. And now, no one is.

And in that silence, from nowhere, it suddenly comes to me:

what's been bothering me about the plan to cut power to London.

Not Clyde's mortality.

Not the horrifying impracticality of the plan.

Not the potential chaos of blacking out the nation's capital.

Big Ben. The Chronometer—protected by its anti-magic field. The field that prevents the Russians from bypassing the mundane security and teleporting in. The field that is completely and utterly dependent on electricity.

The Russians wanted us to see them. Wanted us to see them pull electricity from thin air. They wanted us to extrapolate. This is everything they've been planning for. We're giving them exactly what they want.

And no one will believe me. If I tell them, no one in this room will trust a single word I say.

And so I stand here, and I don't say a word.

38

"Is everyone quite done?" Coleman's booming voice echoes in the room. He has his eyebrows raised, is fiddling with one end of his mustache.

Still not a peep from anyone. Devon is staring at Kayla. Kayla is still looking anywhere but at Devon.

"Hello?" Coleman says to us all in general. "Anybody home?"

I think I might kill him. Right here and right now.

Felicity snaps into life before I do. "Clyde," she says. "Clearly you and Tabitha need to talk about this." Clyde leaps towards the door, but Felicity interposes herself. "But give her time to calm down," she insists. "Nothing good will be achieved now."

For a moment I think Clyde's going to ignore her, going to move to push around her. But then he buckles, collapses in on himself.

"Killing Russkies before chasing skirt." Coleman nods as if this is a pronouncement worthy of Confucius.

Felicity massages her brow. "George is right," she says.

God, I hate the way she uses his first name.

"The most possible good that can be done now," she says, "is catching the Russians before their deadline. Before the seventeenth. And we still know very little." She pushes her hair back behind her ears. "I need you all to take deep breaths and go back into the field. Back to Trafalgar Square. Why did they pick that place? What did they do there before we arrived? We need as many answers as possible."

Coleman is nodding now. I look back and forth between them. Both of them working so well together. Everything in sync.

And maybe I should be proud of Felicity for handling this all so well. Maybe I should tell her that I'm impressed by her ability to still do her job so well in the face of adversity.

But she didn't back me up. She hasn't backed me up once in the office. Not since this all began.

Jesus. I mean... how long have we even been dating? Life in MI37 seems to be on some absurdly accelerated timeline. It's not even been a week. With her, what am I fighting for exactly?

Except that thought brings an unexpected sting. My... connection with Felicity has been brief but... God, I don't know. I'm no good at putting this into words. But if things keep going the way they are it won't matter how hard I fight for a relationship.

Something has to give.

Someone has to.

"We'll do it," I say.

For now I let it be me.

TRAFALGAR SQUARE

After some silent but fraught negotiations, I end up sharing the back seat of the car with Devon on the drive to Trafalgar Square. Clyde drives. Kayla sits dissatisfied in the passenger seat beside him. She keeps peering over her shoulder at both of us. Whether she holds her tongue because of my presence, or because Devon is staring resolutely out the window I can't tell.

We arrive, flash IDs at policemen, and stand in the morning drizzle regarding what's left of the square. The plinths—where the lions stood before they decided to enter the business of shortening my lifespan—are covered with heavy green tarpaulins dragged over hastily constructed faux-lions of wood and chicken wire.

We stand, silent and awkward for a minute. Clyde clears his throat. "So," he says, "should probably, you know, discuss some sort of plan of action—"

"Shut up, Clyde." Devon's voice is unusually quiet.

"Ah." And that is apparently all Clyde has to add. But Kayla picks this as the moment to finally bite the bullet.

"Devon," she says.

"No." Devon is as definitive as Tabitha. "You're a very nice person, one of the few people to be nice to me since this whole nightmare began, and I appreciate it, I really do. And I am terribly sorry about whatever it is that happened to your daughters. It must be awful. But not now. Thank you but I need a little time."

She steps away, walks toward Nelson's Column. She stands at the base, facing the way the Russians did, looking up at the National Gallery. We follow loosely in her wake. Nobody says anything. I've stopped knowing what to say.

Wasn't I good at this at some point? Back when the world was a known quantity.

I shove my hands back in my pockets. And there's Aiko's phone number, still there. And I had the words last night. It all seemed so clear. There was a plan then. When did it slip away?

And then, fingering that slip of paper, I find the right words.

"Right now," I say, pushing damp hair from my eyes, "there is evidently a lot of shit going on. More personal stuff than even this square can hold." No one looks at me. I plow on and hope there are points for honesty. "But there's a bigger problem too. Russians are threatening to wipe this city from the face of the earth. And if that happens then we're all going to feel pretty bloody stupid that we let it happen because we couldn't get past our own personal crap." Rain runs down the back of my collar. "That is assuming we're in enough parts to still regret things."

Devon and Clyde shuffle their feet, and there's a chance I've got their attention at least. Kayla's looking up at Nelson's Column. I think I'd have to pull out a gun and start shooting to get her to notice.

I sweep my hand around the square. "So why here? Why in such a public place? Why show their hand so completely?"

"A public show of strength." Clyde has thought this all through. The answer comes out quick and concise. Not like Clyde at all, really. Par for the course these days, though. Beads of water stand out clear on his mask, not entirely hidden in his hood. "To get us to agree to their demands."

I wait for the "I think," or the "perhaps," or the "maybe," but it doesn't come.

Maybe he's read books on interpersonal communication and has taken those lessons to heart.

Maybe.

"But," I say, pushing those concerns away, "the demands are bullshit. Even Coleman and I agree on that point." I pause. I have to control this carefully if I'm going to make headway. "Why show us how powerful they are and then ask us to do something so bogus. It's misdirection. It has to be. It's smoke and mirrors. Either they want us confused or they're trying to provoke a specific response out of us."

Silence. Either they're chewing it over, or working out the most tactful way to dismiss everything I'm saying.

And then, finally, Clyde nods. "I," he starts, "I mean, yes, that makes a certain degree of sense." He looks for confirmation, first from Kayla, who's still staring up at the column, then from Devon, but only for about a nanosecond.

"And, on top of that," I say—*carefully, carefully, now, Arthur*—"whether they teleported or not, I was beaten up by Russians hiding away from the main fight."

Clyde examines his hands first. "Well," he starts.

"Yes." Devon cuts him off. "That's true."

Another awkward silence. It's broken by Kayla.

"That pigeon is funny," she says to nobody in particular, still staring upwards.

"Right," I say to that, because I'm not sure what else to say, "well, if we have Russians trying to confuse us, and Russians hiding down side streets, shouldn't we at least check out the place where I was attacked?"

"That one." Kayla points at a distant flock of pigeons milling about the top of the column. "It's no' right."

I take a deep breath.

Clyde gives me a second nod. "We should check the square too," he says.

"Of course." I nod quickly, play nice. I know Clyde's smart enough to know I'm maneuvering him. But still, he's conceded. The first small victory. Now I just need to build on it.

A really handy follow-up would be finding some critical evidence, but fifteen minutes of searching the square kills that hope. My biggest discovery is that England really needs to take better care of its national monuments. One corner of the base of Nelson's Column is in a shocking state, almost crumbling away to dust at my touch.

The others come up similarly empty-handed. Aside from the fact that the square is arguably the most public place in London, there seems to be little else to have drawn the Russians.

"Side street?" I say.

"Erm," Clyde says.

Again I feel the resistance when I push him on this, but then Devon says, "Yes," in a voice that echoes off the buildings that surround the square. She starts marching off towards the edge of the square. I follow promptly because, basically, I am not above trading on Clyde's guilt. Kayla dawdles along in our wake, eyes still on the pigeons.

It's not too hard to find the spot where seven shades of shit were beaten out of me. Some of the parked cars are the same. The facades haven't changed. And yet…

I look up and down the road.

"Is something wrong?" Clyde asks.

I can't read his voice, can't work out if he's looking for a way to validate my arguments or an excuse to get out of here.

"The road…" I say, kneeling down. Most of it resembles any other London street. Dirty pitted blacktop, dotted with gum. But in places the surface is almost crumbling—potholes like craters. And then, right next to them are areas where the road is almost perfectly smooth, as if newly laid. And I've seen workmen do bad patch-up jobs before but this is absurd.

"It wasn't like this yesterday," I say. "It was just…" I pull a Clyde and shrug, "typical road."

"Have you considered that, well, that you might not remember it clearly?" Clyde asks. "Blows to the head and all that."

"Or Arthur might be right." Devon inserts herself between Clyde and me.

Clyde gives way faster than a wet tissue before a semi-truck. He bobs his head, backing away quickly, examining the nearby cars.

As for Kayla—she orbits us like a lazy moon. The spat between her and Devon has clearly not been good for morale.

I stay staring at the odd road surface. Because maybe there's a kernel of proof here. I remember the crumbling, aged corner of the column's base. Could there be a link?

"Is there any way we can find out when these roadworks were done?" I say. Because if I'm going to keep Clyde's trust I need to play this like a cynic. And because if roadworks weren't done... Yes, maybe that might be something.

"There's some wireless connections here," Clyde says. "Shouldn't be overly difficult to find out." His arm starts to shake.

"There's that feckin' pigeon again." Kayla's staring at a tight flock of birds above us.

And it's a testament to how far she has fallen that I find I have the nerve to say, "Seriously? Seriously with the pigeons? Which one are you even talking about? It's impossible to tell any of them apart. They're bloody pigeons."

"No." Kayla shakes her head, emphatic. "That's just one feckin' pigeon."

I look closely at her, on the off-chance that madness has a visual manifestation.

"That flock of pigeons?" I say. "Up there?" I even point. "That's one pigeon?"

Reality testing, I believe the professionals call it. Endurance testing delusions against what's plain as day. Of course they probably do it with a slightly less derisory attitude.

"Why the feck do you think I'm concerned about the feckin' pigeon?" Kayla looks at me like I'm an idiot. "Devon," she says without missing a beat, "head back to the car."

"Look." Devon places her hands on her hips. The drizzle has set her coiffure slightly askew, giving her a mildly comical appearance. "I know you mean well, but I am an adult woman and have been for several years now, more than I'd prefer to admit, truth be told, and I am beyond the point that I simply do as I'm told. I'm happy to do as I'm *asked*. More than happy. Please and thank you go a long way. But I am not a child. I am a woman and—"

"Get movin' to the feckin' car!" Kayla unleashes the words on Devon.

There is a moment of stunned silence. Even Clyde seems to emerge from his twitching reverie long enough to stare.

And then Kayla leaps, actually physically leaps at Devon. As if she means to drag her back to the car. And I think I should stop her, that madness has taken over. And I think how screwed I am, going up against Kayla.

Then a scream. At first I think it's Devon. But the sound is more raw, more wild. The sound is from above.

A shadow falls over the street.

I turn, see it coming down, falling, screeching. A clot of feathers. A tumor of beaks. A storm of wings. Down it comes. The flock of pigeons that is not a flock, that is something massive and wrong. A writhing, shrieking mass of bird. And suddenly, yes Kayla, yes, I agree, there is something profoundly fucked up about that pigeon.

39

The once-pigeon blasts through, and around, and over Clyde. He is bowled to the floor, collapses in a tangled heap. One hand flaps spastically, drums against the ground.

Then the bird-beast is on me. A moment of beating thunderous darkness. Its stench engulfs me. It batters at me, tiny feet scraping, beaks gouging. And the sound—above the flutter and twitch—the screeching of its calls. A horrifying chorus. One shriek, echoed, changed, repeated, but undeniably one sound, one utterance.

And then it's off me and over me. It barrels toward Devon and Kayla. Devon stares, open-mouthed, wide-eyed, horrified. Kayla steps in front, sword drawn. And then they are lost to me, swallowed by the thing.

It swirls around them, pulsing, distorting. Wing after wing after wing unfolds in a great swath. A limb made of limbs. Each individual component flaps madly. Each one in desperate need of a body. Feathers and bone unfold then dissipate, fold back into the mass. Something like a head rises up. A hundred heads. A hundred pairs of black eyes twisted in pain and fear. A hundred gray beaks. The thing writhes and twists. I hear a woman screaming at the heart of it.

Then it rises. It swarms upwards, elongating, fluttering. Kayla and Devon lie in a heap, streaked with blood and guano. Devon is clutching her arm to her stomach, face twisted in pain.

Kayla's sword is still drawn. But the gleaming blade is free of blood. Not a single avian body part lies upon the ground. And surely, even on an off day, Kayla could filet that bird and serve it up for barbeque in under eight seconds.

And when exactly was the last time I saw her actually stab something?

Above us the pigeon wheels, screeches, circles back for more.

I can't rely on Kayla. "Clyde!" I yell. "Clyde, get something between us and it. That wall spell. Go, go, go!"

He lies there on the ground.

"Clyde!"

His arm spasms.

"Clyde! Offline now! I need you here!"

The pigeon is almost on us.

"Clyde!"

Then it's too late. The mass of bird hits me in the gut, drives me back and down. I roll, face mashed against smooth and fresh asphalt. The stink of tar fills my nostrils. I feel my jacket tear, feel the shirt beneath giving way. I'm dragged by the momentum of the bird, tumbling, grazing down the street, barreled over and over.

I come up on my knees, haul my pistol bodily out of its holster. I point it at the thing as it swarms over Kayla and Devon. Lift, you bastard. Lift up so I can fill you full of holes.

"Clyde!" I scream. "Clyde, get out of cyberspace now, you bastard!"

"Sonics." Clyde's voice is barely audible as the pigeon-thing shrieks and lifts to the sky. "High-fr—" And then the roar of my pistol cuts him off.

The gun kicks in my hands. Blood and feathers explode out of the mass of pigeon. I bring the gun to bear again. It's easy to hit something this damn big. I fire. Again. Again. The pigeon twists through the air. Up and away behind a building.

I'm sweating, breathing hard. My hands are shaking. I turn, sitting back on my heels. I stare at Clyde, still lying on the street.

"Sonics?" I ask him. "Are you fucking kidding me?" Not our usual near-death-experience banter, I admit, but I'm a little on edge right now.

"High-frequency sonics," Clyde repeats. "Should drive it off."

"Should? Should?" I can't believe what I'm hearing. "You know what *would* drive it off? Spearing the fucking thing on a spell. Now—"

But it's too late for more chastisement.

It's down at ground level, streaking along the street towards us. I drop onto my stomach, sight past Clyde, pray that I can aim at least that well.

Boom. The gun kicks. Boom. Again. Die you fucking thing. Just die. Boom, boom, boom. The clot of birds spins and careens, sheds parts of itself. Chunks of bird fly loose, folding in on themselves as they spiral away, folding into nothing, non-events.

The pigeon slams into Clyde, barrels him over. Regardless of internet connectivity, sonics, or spells. Then it's over him, storming into the muzzle of my gun. I fire. I fire. I fire. I stare into a thousand beaks stretched wide. Boom. And then, moments before beaks and wings strike, it pulls up and away, keening.

Click. My gun runs dry. Click, click, click. I keep firing anyway, finger spasming.

A fresh magazine. I need— I tug one free. I can hear someone sobbing. Devon curled up, fetal, Kayla standing, impotent over her. The old magazine falls away from my gun. There are police sirens in the distance. Too far away.

"Clyde," I say. "Clyde, I need—" But then I look at him. A tall pale-skinned man lies, face staring empty-eyed up at the sky.

Where is it? Where's the goddamn mask?

The pigeon swoops down. And there. Caught in a jagged tangle of feet. The mask is coming down at me.

I slam the new magazine home. I aim. I try to think of something that Kurt Russell would say.

"Oh shit and balls."

40

I close my eyes. It's coming at me like a storm. Like a bolt from Zeus's hand. I stretch out my arms, my gun. The once-pigeon is screeching, is screaming, and then the sound of my gun eclipses everything. I fire. Over, and over, and over. Pulling the trigger for as long as I can. Until it's on me. Until I'm overcome.

But then, still standing, the screeches crescendo, breach even my pistol's barrier of sound. And then: a crash, loud and meaty.

I open my eyes. My finger still twitches. My gun still fires. Bullet after bullet slams into the brickwork of a house.

The mass of pigeon lies on the floor, convulsing, shedding parts of itself. Clusters of wings, torsos, feet roll away, shrink, twist down into nothing-ness. Not all parts stay fresh as they go. I see mold bloom in fast-forward in some, flesh flake away, exposed bone blacken and fragment. It's like watching stop-motion photography. Months of decay in moments.

I manage to stop firing.

And still the central mass of the bird shrinks. It becomes something more like a single pigeon. And then it is just a bird. Just one, lying dead in the street, its head mashed by a bullet. My bullet.

I killed it.

It takes a moment for that to sink in. It's over. I took this thing down.

I'm still breathing hard.

I took this thing down. Single-handed.

Well suck on that, Coleman.

The pigeon is still moving, still twisting and contorting. Not quite dead. Despite the bloody wound that used to be its cerebrum.

And then I realize, it's not the last spasms of life, but something else. One of its wings contracts, sheds feathers, becomes a stubby furry thing. A chick's wing. A leg falls off, and rots away before my eyes.

Jesus. I've never seen anything like this. What the hell happened to it?

And then... some lateral leap in my head. The bird's corpse. Parts of it accelerating through time. Parts of it moving backwards. The road. Parts brand-new. Parts so old. Unstuck in time.

And also—the way the pigeon moved. Existed. A wing here. A wing there. Unstuck in space.

Space and time.

Russians.

More proof. This is more proof.

I spin to seek out Clyde. He still lies in two parts. His unconscious body lies in the street. His mask lies a few feet away. I seize it. And maybe with too little concern for his health, and too much enthusiasm for his corroborating story, I jam the mask back on his body.

He arches back, an almost feline contortion of the spine. Beneath the mask I see the jaw muscles stretch, the mouth opening wide. A noise like static blasts from Clyde.

I reel back. That noise. It's so... it's... Jesus. Again. Again that word.

Inhuman.

Slowly, the sound becomes something more recognizable, more guttural than electronic. Clyde gasps, collapses, pulls in his legs, folds himself up, and rolls onto his side. He lies that way for a moment.

"Clyde," I say, reaching out a hand toward him. "Clyde, are you OK?"

"Oh," he says, the word small and hurt. "Oh." He staggers onto his front, coming up on hands and knees, head down, blond hair hanging down around the mask. "Oh, that is why they tell you to shut down all the programs before you turn off the machine. Ow." He shakes his head. "Ow, ow, ow."

"Clyde?" I say, as much confused as I am concerned now. He twists, sits. His arm is tremoring hard, I see. "Is everything OK?"

"Just…" He shakes his head a few times. With his good hand he puts the shaking one between his knees, holds it tight there. "Shouldn't take the mask off while I'm connected to the web apparently." His arm is still convulsing despite the pressure of his knees. "Give me a moment."

I glance over my shoulder. Kayla is over by Devon, trying to coax her to her feet. Devon is proving resistant to her efforts.

"Get off me. Get—" Devon shakes, then moans, clutching her arm again. Her clothes hang in tatters. I realize I'm in no better shape.

The police sirens. I remember them now. They're becoming more insistent. They are very close, I realize.

"Quite frankly, the last person's help I want right now is yours!" Devon's voice booms out of the whispered argument she is having with Kayla. She turns, sees me looking at them.

"Arthur," she says, as matter-of-factly as it is possible to say anything when you are streaked with blood, bird shit, and mascara, "please come over here and help me up."

To my chagrin, I hesitate. There again, given the look I'm getting from Kayla, I think it's understandable. All the violence I wished she'd do to the pigeon she appears to now be wishing on me.

"We have to get out of here," I tell them. *We have to go back and tell people this story. Prove I'm right.*

Devon nods. "As soon as I'm on my feet."

I swallow. I just need to remember: Kayla didn't hurt the bird. Surely I'm less of a threat to her. I get close enough to extend an arm out for Devon to reach. She heaves herself to her feet. She's still clutching her arm.

"Are you OK?"

She shakes her head. Kayla circles us, on the edge of being predatory.

"OK," I say. "Clyde, can you—"

"Team back at the office, all fully appraised." He's standing now, still clutching his shaking arm. Something seems off in the way he's talking. Something less Clyde-like.

But the sirens sound less than a minute away. We have to leave.

We have to get back and wipe that bloody smirk off Coleman's face.

"Back off!" Devon snaps at Kayla who is still circling us, sword drawn. "And put that bloody thing away if you're not going to use it for anything useful. I mean," she looks at me, "what is the point of carrying around such an absurdly outdated weapon if you just wave it at stuff like a duster? Not the most effective deterrent. Certainly nobody enjoys dusting. Well, maybe yes, someone does, I imagine. But, I think if we were to get properly scientific here. P-values and hazard ratios, and all of those marvelous little numbers, well, I believe we'd find that the only people who thought it was an effective defense against physical attack were missing a few of the more critical IQ points. Don't you think, Arthur?" She grimaces as she reclasps her bad arm.

I pretend I'm too busy steering her toward another side street to get involved. And thank God, I can see an entrance to the Underground.

"This way."

And even as I herd the cats, my head is spinning. Proof. Proof that they all saw. If I can get them to acknowledge it. To see it the way I'm seeing it.

Despite it all, I have a grin on my face as we duck out of the rain and beneath the earth.

41

85 VAUXHALL CROSS—TEMPORARY MI37 HEADQUARTERS

In the confines of the conference room it is increasingly obvious that Clyde, Kayla, Devon, and I smell very strongly of bird shit.

"You're sure it was you that shot it?" Coleman, standing by an open window, sounds incredulous.

I don't deign to answer.

"Yes," Clyde finally says, still trying to hold his right arm steady. "Yes, he did."

His responses to queries have been getting shorter and shorter as time goes by. To be honest, I'm scared for him. I'm a little scared of him. He is changing…

And of course there would be changes. He died. He's a digital copy of a person, but… but… I don't know what exactly. In some ways he's the biggest barrier between me and acceptance of my theory. It was his voice that took my argument apart so definitively. It's his argument that Felicity and Coleman are picking up and running with.

But he's a friend. And now, with the proof of the pigeon, I have a chance to win him back onto my side. I just need the right opening.

"Kayla?" Felicity stands at the door, hands on hips, not providing the opening.

Kayla works her jaw several times, something between anger and self-loathing. "I used my sword," she says. "Drove it off."

"But did you cut it?" I think Felicity is trying to get to the reason behind Kayla's non-involvement, but it sounds a little like she's as unbelieving of my active role in the pigeon's defeat as Coleman is.

Kayla says nothing.

By the window, Coleman is looking smug.

God, I need this opening to come soon. I need us to unite around this proof. We're falling apart. Felicity's team. And she is where our buck stops. Our mistakes become hers. And each time one of us makes her look worse, Coleman looks better.

Felicity exhales, hard and angry. "And you, Clyde?" She wheels on him. "What's your excuse?"

"I was just…" Clyde starts. "I was already online. The frequency plan would have worked. I needed more time."

"Spells, Clyde." Felicity's complaint echoes mine. "Would that have worked quicker?"

"Perhaps." Clyde finally gives a shrug, but it seems perfunctory.

"We are a team." Felicity looks at us. "You are a team. You have roles. You work because you work together." I nod along. Neither Clyde nor Kayla move a muscle. "Is that clear?" she asks the room. I nod again. Still nothing from the others. "Is that clear?" She barks it, tendons suddenly stark in her neck, red spots on her cheeks.

And I want to go to her then. I still do. I want to comfort her. I want that prick Coleman with his fat, smug grin to fuck off back where he came from so we can do this right, do this our way, fumbling and stumbling as it may be.

But Coleman pushes off the wall, like a mustachioed shark smelling blood in the water. "So this bird," he says, "this terrifying pigeon." He shakes his head. "Describe it again."

"It was…" I look to Clyde. This would sound better coming from someone else. Someone else should say space and time. Because if anyone is going to believe those words, they can't come from my mouth.

Clyde gives me nothing. I don't even bother double-checking with Kayla.

"It grew," I hedge. "And shrank. Not all of it. Not one giant wing. Bits of it multiplied, divided. A wing made of lots of wings. Of other bits of bird." It seems ridiculous to be describing such a thing in the confines of such a neat, tidy conference room.

Coleman nods his head in a way that utterly fails to communicate any sort of agreement.

"And when it died?" he asks.

"It sort of folded away. Shed bits of itself." Again I look to Clyde. "Bits of it seemed to rot very fast. Other bits regressed, became chick parts."

Coleman works his jaw. "As if bits of it were moving through time, Agent Wallace?" He rolls his eyes. "I'm sensing a tediously familiar theme."

Fuck. Shit, and balls, and fuck. The problem with Coleman, well, one of the myriad problems, is he's not as stupid as he looks.

I shrug at him. "What can I say? I see a spade. I call it a spade." I look again to Clyde. Come on. Please. Help me out.

Nothing. Not even a twitch of the mask. Just his arm.

And then, "Was a regular bird at first."

I start slightly at the voice from behind me. Kayla's Scottish brogue. Low, mumbling.

"Went under one of the tarps covering where the lions had been. Saw the wee bugger do it. But when it came out it were... It were like he said." She nods my way minimally, a look of distaste on her face. "Weren't as big then. But more bits of it. A pigeon collage. Sort of. And it went up and up, and it got to growing. More bits and bits. And I thought, I thought to myself, that's a bad thing. And I thought maybe I should kill it. Climb up the pole, slash it while it was still small. And then I thought about that and, well, it's a life isn't it? It's all life. And where does one life stop and another begin? Who gets to weigh those feckin' decisions? Why is it always me? And what if the Russians are right? What if it would be better with them in charge? So maybe we should all feckin' die. Or maybe we should all live. I don't know. And I thought, well maybe I can just keep one person safe. Maybe I can turn that streak around. If I couldn't save two girls, maybe just one this time. Just defend her. And I did that. I mean, I shouldn't have thrown the stone at the bird. Just trying to drive it off. But I did. But then when it came at us, I did save her. I stopped the harm from being too bad. But she doesn't want that. No one wants just that." She works her jaw. "Stupid feckin' idea. All of this."

"You threw a rock at it?" I don't know why that stands out the most from everything she said, indeed this should probably be a moment of pathos for a poor woman lost in her grief, but... a rock? You have to be kidding me.

Kayla's eyes flick up at me. She drops her shoulders, her mouth tightens, her knuckles whiten.

Suddenly I am very afraid. Very afraid indeed.

And then Kayla slumps. Folds back in herself. "Don't think this excuses you, you feckin' waste of space. You still didn't protect my Ophelia. You're as feckin' guilty as me."

I close my eyes. The world back—all wrong.

"Well." Coleman claps his hands. "That's just marvelous, isn't it? A swordswoman who refuses to use her sword." He snorts. "A real team of winners you have here, Felicity." He sneers even harder around the room. Kayla seems to recoil from the gaze. Clyde's hand drums uncontrollably against the side of the chair.

God, it's not just the team that's falling apart, it's each of us. This was meant to be my moment of triumph, but everyone's too locked in their own disaster to stand back and see the big picture.

"At least she put a team together," I say, "rather than just pick one apart." I've put up better defenses to accusations, I have to admit, but right now, his argument doesn't seem too far off.

Coleman shakes his head. "You're the big man, is that it now, Wallace?" He looks at me with disdain. "The Russians either got the drop on you and enchanted some bird while you weren't looking, or they left a booby trap and you wandered straight into it. And just because you didn't die, you think you've redeemed yourself." He sneers. "Personally I just see more of the same." He stomps out, even gives us a gratuitous slam of the door.

Felicity stares around the room. "Thanks, guys," she says. She doesn't mean it.

And what to say to her? What to say to my boss? My girlfriend? I don't know if I have anything she wants to hear. He's wrong. You're wrong. If we follow your plan then the whole of western civilization is doomed to, at best, a life of slavery.

"Why do you give in to him?" If she could just answer that for me. If she could just give me a reasonable explanation. Maybe I could understand.

Felicity looks at me, slightly incredulous. "Here?" she asks. "Now?"

I just look back at her. There seems to be something that happens to words after they leave my mouth, something lost in translation.

She waves at the door. "Clyde, Kayla... Just go, and... find something out. Anything. Where that meteorite from the Natural History Museum went. Who the fuck those Russians are. Come back with something other than a beating from a mutant bloody pigeon." She can't even look at us as she says the last few words.

Silently they head for the door. I stand my ground. Felicity watches me. Two gunslingers facing each other at high noon.

"Right then," Felicity says as the door slides closed, "you and I need to talk."

42

"You know what's at stake, don't you?" she says. Her eyes are fixed on me, deadly intent. "I know you're not as stupid as you've been acting the past few days."

So that's how we're going to do this.

She has her hands on her hips, mouth drawn into a sour line. Her hair is pushed back awkwardly, defying her part. Her suit is rumpled.

And I feel bad for her. I feel sorry for all she's going through. The part of me that is boyfriend wants to comfort her. But we're in the office now. She defined these rules.

"You know I'm right," I say. I stand tall and stiff, matching her inch for defiant inch.

"It doesn't matter if you're right!" She throws her hands up like this is the most obvious thing in the world.

And... what the... "Are you shitting me?" Suddenly I find a vent for my words. "The fate of the western world is at stake. I think a little thing like addressing the correct fucking problem might be important."

Maybe I should bite back my bile. Should play this game with a little decorum. But my meditative calm has been somewhat ruffled over the past few days.

Felicity puts her hands to her head. "You were a police detective. A successful one. Surely you must know something about politics."

"Sounds like the sort of thing that got innocent men convicted," I snap back.

"It doesn't matter," Felicity repeats slowly, enunciating carefully, "if you're right, if no one's listening to you."

"So listen to me!" I reach Devon decibels.

Felicity sits down then. Just collapses into a chair. "Who on earth, Arthur, do you think is listening to me?"

And, I have to concede, I do not have a comeback for that. I sit down hard. Smacked by a vision of how the land lies.

Felicity runs her hand through her hair again. If she does it anymore she's going to wear a groove.

"I'm on the thinnest of ice, Arthur. No one wants me in this position. Especially Coleman. And my only hope is that he'll hang himself. He's done it plenty of times before. But right now all he has to do is do nothing. And he knows it. Because if we fuck up, just once, he's won. And, God, Arthur, you are not helping."

I sit and dwell on that. She sits silently opposite me. And she is the closest thing I have to an ally. Jesus… she's still my girlfriend. Whatever else has been fucked up in the past few days, that is still true.

I think about reaching out to her, taking her hand. I don't know if it's too soon. But if I'm not willing to take a risk here then what am I willing to take risks for?

I take her hand. She stiffens. But then she relaxes.

"It's the truth," is all the defense I have.

"Clyde doesn't think so." She meets my eyes, face open. It's as much a comment as it is a challenge.

"I know." I shrug. "I don't know why."

Felicity echoes my shrug. "He's the expert, Arthur. He might not always seem it, but trust me, he is one of the smartest thaumaturgists in the world. He is very good at what he does. And knowing magic is what he does, it's his role on the team. You can see why his word has more weight than yours, can't you?" She's almost imploring. "You can see why Coleman will believe him over you?"

"What about you?" Because that's really the crux of it. Maybe it's not the most important point in the grand scheme of things, in the overall fight for survival. But here, now, it's the most important point to me, for the survival of "us."

Felicity closes her eyes. My heart clambers handhold by handhold up into my throat.

"You'll need proof," she says after a long while. "Incontrovertible proof. Not supposition. Not something that looks a lot like proof. Actual, real, undeniable proof. Proof that not even Coleman can piss away. That's the only way I'll be able to move on any of this. To even openly support any of this. You understand that?"

She's side-stepped the question, and she's done it neatly. I see the move, but suddenly I don't want to call her on it. Not at all.

We sit there looking at each other. A table between us. A table and so much more. And maybe that's what this whole thing comes down to, in the end: what's worth fighting for.

"Hey," I say, taking another risk, "at least I killed the pigeon."

Felicity's face shudders. Her mouth works. And then… a smile.

"A mutant pigeon, Arthur?" She shakes her head. "In the history of this department only you could have gone face to face with a mutant pigeon."

She's told me I'm on my own out in the field. But at least I'm not in here.

"How'd you feel about dating a pigeon killer?" I ask her. I'm smiling too. A sudden boldness seeping into me. It's good to have friends. Even secret friends.

And there's a thought in that phrase. The barest edge of a plan. I remember the phone number in my pocket.

I know, Aiko said when I told her I'd call.

"I'm surprised," Felicity says, "I chose to date someone who smells so much of bird shit."

I smile at that. But already I'm slipping away from this moment. Slipping toward a plan. Toward doing something Felicity really wouldn't approve.

"I should get going on this whole saving the world thing." I squeeze her hand.

She rises. I rise. We meet at the end of the table. She catches my arms, holds me as close as the smell will allow.

"The next time I see you," she says into the inches between us, "you better have at least killed a mutant squirrel."

I can't help but smile.

"I promise."

She kisses me gingerly on a clean inch of cheek.

"Go on," she says. "Shower. Work out where the Russians are hiding. Save the world."

"Yes, ma'am." I nod deeply, almost a bow.

She holds the door open for me. We smile at each other, long, maybe even a little lingering. And now, having earned Felicity's trust, it's time to totally betray it.

THE LAMB AND FLAG PUBLIC HOUSE

"A mutant pigeon?" Aiko looks at me as if I just pissed in her pint.

"So. Totally. Awesome." Jasmine emphasizes this point with a spectacular popping of her gum. She's even slid her headphones down around her neck. Something with more beats per minute than a jackhammer emanates tinnily.

Malcolm greets the news stoically and takes another sip of his Guinness. I'm not sure what would faze Malcolm.

Maybe if I kissed him?

Not really worth finding out.

They sit opposite me, like three witches ill-met on some Scottish hilltop at midnight. At least they would if that hilltop had a cheap leather booth and a jukebox that was about to play "November Rain" for the third time in a row.

I asked Aiko to bring them along. If I'm going to be running my own sub-operation then I'm going to need as much manpower as I can get my hands on.

It's four in the afternoon, still technically work hours, and the withered stump of the policeman I used to be feels guilty as I sip my beer. But Aiko refused to buy me a coke when she offered to buy the round.

"A mutant pigeon?" she repeats.

"A pigeon," I say, as significantly as it is possible to say the word, "unglued in space and time."

She shrugs. "We already knew the Russians were messing with this stuff. It's just corroborating evidence."

How can it be so obvious to the Weekenders that this is evidence and so difficult for everyone at MI37 to grasp?

"Something was off with how it happened." This has been playing in my head since leaving Felicity. I describe it to them as Kayla described it to me. The pigeon enters the tarpaulin normal, exits with a definite normality insufficiency.

Malcolm gives me a long troubled stare. "The Russians," he starts, then examines the white froth of his Guinness, "they booby-trapped a pigeon?"

And I thought that was odd as well. So I describe the crumbling corner of Nelson's Column, the strange pattern of repair and decay on the street.

"Some sort of residual effect," Aiko says ruminatively. "Whatever they're doing, it's not clean." She plays with her ponytail, twisting and untwisting the hair.

"But," Jasmine looks almost apologetic, "what about, like, a trap?"

Malcolm nods. "A planned counter-operation."

I try to consider that fairly. As if I'm not simply averse to the idea because Coleman suggested it.

"It seems too random for that," I say. Aiko nods along as I speak. I'd forgotten how nice it was to have someone do that.

"Pockets of disturbed space-time?" Malcolm chews his lip ruminatively. "That's your theory?"

And yes, I suppose it is.

"Anyone else back at MI37 believe it?" Aiko asks.

I shake my head, and then pause. "Well," I say. "Devon might, if I tell her. She's been generally supportive."

"Devon?" Aiko arches her eyebrows.

"Oh." I shrug, slightly taken aback by her tone. Almost... accusatory? "She's a researcher. New. Probably very good at her job." I realize I'm not totally sure what Devon has researched for us so far. "Probably," I repeat, due, apparently, to my desire to emphasize my lack of clarity on the issue.

"Is she good-looking?" Aiko asks, which seems oddly off-topic.

I blink. "Well, erm…" I look to the others for help, but Malcolm is abruptly taking a large draft from his Guinness and Jasmine seems to have suddenly found the straw poking out of her Diet Coke more interesting than I'd have warranted. "I mean, she's a bit…" I flounder. How to put this? "Well I'm dating someone. But, you know, if I weren't. Well, I… wouldn't… date Devon." I limp to an end. I am not sure that's really what I meant to say or if it's what anyone wanted to hear.

Somehow Malcolm is still working on that same sip.

"Girlfriend?" Aiko's eyebrows are still up.

"Leave him alone," Jasmine says, slapping Aiko's arm with the back of her hand. But Aiko doesn't stop looking at me.

I have a horrible feeling I might know what the cat-and-mouse smile was all about last time I saw Aiko here. But I think I'd rather pretend I don't.

"Err… yeah." I take cover behind my pint. "You met her. At the Natural History Museum. Not the goth girl. That's Tabitha. The smartly dressed, pretty woman."

"The ice queen?" Jasmine's eyebrows meet Aiko's up in the stratosphere.

Malcolm finally puts down his pint. "Jasmine," he rumbles.

"Oh." She toys with her headphones. "Sorry. I just… Totally not what I meant."

"It's OK," I say. "She can be brusque at first." I smile a little. I think I thought something similar about Felicity when I first met her.

"Does she know you're here?" Aiko asks. She's going to give herself frown lines if she keeps her eyebrows up there much longer.

"Oh," I start, then go back to my pint.

"What will she do if she finds out?" Aiko asks, all sweet innocence.

I need a "get out of jail" card really badly right now. And then I realize that out of all the people I know, Coleman has provided me with one.

"Oh my God," I say, "I haven't even told you the worst part yet."

"So tell us," Malcolm says with unusual quickness.

So I tell them, or at least I tell Jasmine and Malcolm, without really risking a look at Aiko, about Coleman's mad plan to EMP London.

"Wait." Jasmine holds up a hand. "Like, seriously?"

"Completely." I nod.

"No." Aiko shakes her head. "No, he can't do that. That's too big. Everything? The financial district…" She shakes her head again. "He can't."

"He says he has approval." I shrug.

"Do anything they damn want."

I glance at Malcolm. Either his Guinness has done something to piss him off or it's getting the brunt of a glare meant for someone else.

"You remembered to take your meds today, right, Malcolm?" Jasmine reaches over and pats Malcolm's arm. He shrugs it off. This is not a joke, I realize. I flash back to my conversation with Clyde about the unsuitability of the Weekenders as colleagues.

"Still got the right to be pissed," Malcolm mutters.

"Wait." Aiko half drops her pint onto the table. She stares across the table at me. "Wait. Hold on a fucking minute. No electricity." All the playfulness is gone from her. She looks stricken. "Big Ben."

"Big Ben?" Jasmine looks dismissive. "Like tourists won't be able to tell the time for…" Then she gets it too. "Oh shit."

And again, they see it so quickly and so clearly. Something that no one at MI37 seems capable of seeing. And how do I bring that vision across?

"The Russians will be able to teleport into the Chronometer," I say. "They'll be able to take time apart."

"Oh fuck," Aiko says. She teaches small children with that mouth.

"This Coleman guy is, like, a complete prick, isn't he?" Jasmine says. "Like, just totally."

"Like, just totally," I say.

"It's worse." Malcolm's baritone sweeps under the rising sense of panic at the table like a riptide. We all turn to stare. "They might want to turn back time," Malcolm says, "but they won't. Nobody will be doing shit after they go in there."

"Malcolm," Jasmine sounds as stern as her years will allow, "you *did* take your meds today, didn't you?"

Malcolm turns to her, slow as thunderheads rolling through the sky. "Residual. Effect."

And... Oh shit. Oh balls.

"What?" Aiko doesn't see it.

"We were just talking about it." I try to keep my head up, to support it under the weight of the colossal fuck-up in the Russians' plans that I now see. "The residual effect of these spells. Things coming unstuck in space and time. And what if one of them teleports in right next to the Chronometer? What if the very thing governing time comes unstuck?"

43

It's difficult, I find, to fully hold in my mind something enormous. Even something like an elephant. Ears, trunk, tail—I have to break them down into small manageable parts.

Time itself, unstuck in time. That's enormous. I can't... I give it one more try. No, I can't quite grasp that.

"Bits of the world." Aiko shakes her head as if trying to clear it. "Bits of everything. Some moving forward in time. Some just in stasis. Some slipping back. It wouldn't... You couldn't live in a place like that. It would be the end of everything."

A phrase of Clyde's slips into my mind. "Standard end-of-the-world scenario."

There's silence at the table. Around us the pub patrons carry on drinking, and laughing, and talking about lives, and loves, and all the petty bullshit that we seem to fit in between the important moments. And it seems briefly wondrous because it suddenly seems so fragile, so close to not being.

"I don't want to be a total downer," Jasmine breaks the silence, "but, like, a lot of your stories seem to involve the Russians kicking your arse."

I shake my head. She's right. "We can't take them alone," I say. I know the enormity of what I'm going to ask them. "We need more people. We need MI37. I need you to help me prove to them that this is real." And I have to remember that this was my plan all along. This shouldn't seem so daunting. Nothing has changed. Except the stakes.

"And why," Malcolm rumbles like the warning of an earthquake to come, "would they listen to us?"

"Evidence," I say, earnest as a preacher man. "Undeniable evidence."

Malcolm isn't done. "And why," he says, "would we want to work with them?"

"Because," Jasmine answers before I can, "they're totally awesome."

Malcolm does not appear convinced. But instead of answering him, I look at Aiko, the tie-breaker.

"What are you thinking, Agent Arthur?" she asks me. This time I think less of a Cheshire cat and more of a sphinx.

"We need them," I say. "You saw what just two Russians did at the British Museum. And there are so many more."

"And what," she asks, "makes you think that MI37 will want to work with us?"

And that's the million-dollar question, in the end. "If you're the ones that go to them with the evidence," I start, "undeniable evidence—"

"They'll cut us out." Aiko finishes for me.

"I won't let them." I'm defiant.

She smiles, a little sad, a little sweet. "If you had that much pull, you wouldn't be here in the first place."

And she's right, of course. I massage my temples. Suddenly it feels just like being back at MI37. "So," I say, "we let the Russians win because of pissing matches?"

Aiko lets out an exhalation of amusement. "No." She shakes her head. "We'll fight with you, Agent Arthur. But if you're planning to lead on this one, I'd rather you had your eyes wide open."

And, God, I could kiss her.

Except… well, I totally have a girlfriend. Just a figure of speech. Nothing else.

"Can I just say," Jasmine interrupts my mental backpedaling, "that this is totally awesome."

Malcolm rolls his eyes.

And, OK, this is on. This is happening. There is traction, forward momentum. And it has been so long since I felt that way.

"We need to go to places the Russians have been," I say, "back to Trafalgar Square, the British Museum, the Natural History Museum, places we know they've used intradimensional magic. We need to find out more about its effects. We need to research the meteorite they stole. We need to find out everything. And Chernobyl. We have to know more about Chernobyl. That's the key to all this, I think. The lynchpin."

And they're nodding. All of them are nodding. Even Malcolm.

We divvy up the duties, we buy more drinks, and in that moment I'm even deluded enough to feel like it all might be possible.

44

OCTOBER 12TH. ONE DAY CLOSER TO THE DEADLINE

I ride down the elevator to the basement of 85 Vauxhall Cross, trying to rid myself of the mild nausea the last MI37 staff meeting has given me.

It was all going so well. A status meeting. One Coleman had blown off via email as "a waste of fucking time." It almost didn't matter that none of us had anything. I'm not sure I really expect us to find anything until we start chasing the right leads. The Russians have gone to ground most thoroughly.

But then... just after Tabitha told us the past ten years of records on Russian spies were giving her nothing, just after Felicity had given us her version of a pep talk, Clyde stepped forward.

"I just want you to know I can help," he'd said. "I can be useful."

God, a vacuum cleaner is useful. Not a person.

Then, across the table—sliding them with those long elegant fingers that don't really belong to him—four flash drives. "If you need help," he said. He looked at Tabitha, but she didn't look at him. "It's a copy of an application based upon some personality algorithms I've been working on." He spoke carefully, no margin for error in his words. No margin for himself. "So if you want a digital personal assistant, a pretty advanced one, like the one I downloaded onto Tabby's laptop, then you can just run it on your machine at home."

Devon had balked. "These are copies of you?"

Clyde again looked to Tabitha. "No," he said. "A digital personal assistant based upon personality algorithms—"

"Yeah," Tabitha cut him off, voice an octave below its usual pitch. "It's a copy of him."

Devon left hers on the table. I wanted to do the same. But how do you do that to a friend? To what's left of a friend?

So now, I'm riding down in an elevator, with Clyde in my pocket, and a bottomless hole in my stomach.

SUBBASEMENT 3

The elevator doors ping open. The corridor is gloomy, has a musty, abandoned smell. It reminds me of the MI37 facilities back in Oxford. I feel abruptly homesick.

I'm following up on an idea I had last night. Someone wrapped up in all this that no one seems to have thought to question.

The guy at the MI6 front desk gave me an office number. But now I'm down here, the labeling of office doors seems to have been carried out by drunken preschoolers. It's only after fifteen minutes of walking in circles that I find the right one.

I knock. There is no reply. I try the knob. It turns easily and the door swings open.

My jaw swings open a little bit too.

I am at the top of a flight of gray aluminum stairs. They take angular turns, leading fifteen feet down to a small concrete platform jammed full of rickety metal shelving. The shelves are covered in toolboxes, battered textbook-sized instruction manuals, scrolls. A small desk covered in novelty ashtrays has been jammed into one corner. Beyond the platform the floor drops another six feet, and beyond...

I stare out over a vast subterranean warehouse.

There are more shelves, bigger ones. Some loaded down with pallets and plastic yellow crates. Bronze statues, ankhs, glittering crystals, chipped marble busts, odd gnarls of machinery, strings of dirty jewelry, dried plant stalks, candlesticks, crucifixes, unidentifiable chunks of wood, tiny glass vials—all overflow from the containers, spilling onto the shelving. There's a forklift parked down there. There are wider spaces. Glass tanks filled with amorphous shapes floating in ochre fluid. Cages full of stuffed animals with too many heads, too many limbs, too many species mixed into their forms. I can see the two halves of the Trafalgar Square lion Clyde kebobbed the other day leaning up against one wall.

And a tree. In the middle of it all, a tree reaching toward the cavernous ceiling.

A tree that's waving at me.

"Arthur, mate. You are like a vision of bustiness to a sex-deprived man."

"Winston?" Jesus. He's still a tree.

"Meant that in a totally heterosexual way," Winston qualifies. "Not that there's anything wrong with the other way." He shakes branches at me trying to fix my attention as he wrestles his own under control. "You have got to get me out of here, man."

"Winston," I repeat, still trying to recover. He isn't the person I was looking for. "What are you doing here? What's going on?"

"What's going on? What's going on?" Winston throws up his branches, almost toppling a column of precariously stacked wooden crates. "I'll tell you what's going on. I'm bloody wilting is what's going on."

It takes me a while to realize that this is meant literally. I seem to have trouble keeping up with the recently metamorphosed. But yes, I'll admit his leaves do look pale and droopy.

"Daylight bulbs aren't cutting it, man. And the bowl of water this dick has me standing in is hardly bloody sufficient for root growth. I need a park. I need greenery. Wind in my hair. Somewhere I can really settle in." The bark whorls of his face knot together, a look of pain. "I need some bloody company."

I start to descend the stairs, sorting out the signal from the Winston-generated noise, trying to get to the facts. "*Who* put you in a bowl of water?" I say just before I enter into the warren of bookshelves.

"I bloody did."

I almost fall the last four feet of the stairs. The short man emerges from around the corner of the bookshelf, almost seems to detach himself from it. I feel like a cloud of smoke and a rimshot on the drums wouldn't be amiss.

Two beady black eyes regard me from either side of the knife-edge of a nose.

"Wallace," he says to me. He looks suspicious.

I nod, in what I hope is an encouraging way. "You shot me up with drugs after Trafalgar Square. You do cleanup for us." I know he's told us his name, but honestly if my life was being threatened by some interdimensional name-collecting alien, I would end up as an entrée. Something beginning with O.

He wrinkles his nose. It might be a sign of recognition. I might not have fully shed myself of the smell of bird shit. It's hard to tell. He thumbs back at Winston.

"Thinks I want to bloody keep him. Like I'm fond of his bloody company. Because all I have to do is sit around listening to him bitch and moan. Soundtrack to my life that is." He rolls his eyes. "Probably thinks this place is so roomy it could really do with a tree in it." Another roll of the eyes.

"So you'd like to—" I start.

"Get rid of him? Love to." The little man hugs himself in paroxysms of fake delight. "Ship him off to a park? My wildest dream. But he talks, and he talks." He spins as he says this last, to face Winston's towering bulk. "And he talks. And he talks." The volume rises. "AND HE TALKS. AND HE TALKS. *AND HE TALKS!*" The little man turns back to me breathing hard. He puffs out his cheeks, blows it out. Forces up a smile like a supermodel forces up her last meal.

"How the flying buggery fuck am I meant to put him in the middle of the park when he won't shut up? I'd put him in the middle of a forest but there's hikers. I'd put him," this last said with another acidic glance over his shoulder, "in the middle of the bloody rain forests if I had jurisdiction in Brazil, but they're still pissed on account of the bloody monkeys." He doesn't elaborate further.

"You love it," Winston bellows from the back of the room.

"You never had it so good as now I'm here. You can't bear to be bloody parted from me."

"Are you fucking kidding me?" The little man turns away, purple-cheeked.

"He touched me, Arthur! It was inappropriate!"

My mind blanches at that one. How in God's name—

"It was with bloody pruning shears!" the little man bellows back at him.

"He's into the rough stuff, Arthur! You've got to get me out of here."

Oh my God. I can't… I can't… We put the world back wrong. So very, very wrong.

"I was really hoping," I start saying, wondering if I can just pretend that exchange didn't happen, "that we—"

"He's here to see me, not you!" the little man shrieks viciously over his shoulder. Then he turns back to me with an ingratiating smile. "Go on."

"OK," I attempt, "I wanted—"

"*Et tu*, Arthur?" Winston breaks in. "Abandoned is it? Only ever interested in me for my research skills?"

"I just wanted," I persevere, "to ask you about—"

"Clyde too, I suppose," Winston goes on. "Digital over the analog, I suppose." Somehow, and I really have no idea how, Winston manages to sniff.

"Shut up!" the little man screams over his shoulder. Tendons in his neck quiver. Again he turns back to me, cheeks the color of beetroot. Again he smiles, simpering. He gestures with his hand. "Go on."

"Was wondering—" Everything feels very surreal, very fake. "—if perhaps you could let me know if there had been—" I keep waiting for the interruption but it's not coming. "—any oddities you'd noticed at the British Museum, or the Natural History Museum. Especially any that seemed to involve some sort of spatial or temporal component."

The little man gives me an abrupt but seemingly genuine smile. The first one so far.

"You're not having me on are you?" he asks.

I'm not entirely sure what tack the conversation has just taken.

"No," I say tentatively.

"You're interested?" he asks.

I nod.

"No one's interested in you and your shit!" Winston bellows.

"SHUT UP!" The little man then turns back to me and offers up the same anxious smile. "No one ever asks about me," he says.

"Well, I just wanted to know—" I'm trying to get things back on track.

"I stopped sending reports back to people five years ago and I'm still waiting for someone to complain." He sniffs a little bit.

"That's a shame," I say.

"No it bloody isn't!" Winston yells across the room at us.

I've sort of given up hope on finding an answer at this point. I'll be lucky to get out with my sanity intact.

"I used to put a lot of effort into those reports," says the little man. "Used to be works of bloody art." He looks at me, trying to still a quivering jaw. "I used bullet points."

"That was, er… very thoughtful," I venture.

"He's only interested in himself, Arthur! He's a hollow, self-centered, little man."

The cleanup man turns around, fists shaking. "How would you know? How would you ever realize? It's you, you, and always you! Always you!" He turns back to me. "I miss writing," he says.

"Maybe you should take it up again," I suggest.

"But why bother?" he asks.

"Give up!" Winston chips in, slightly too enthusiastically.

There are moments in life where things come out of my mouth and I am not entirely sure why. Some poorly programmed autopilot fulfilling an anticipated piece of conversation. The insufficient survival instinct that got me working for MI37 in the first place. But against all reason, I say, "I'll read them."

"What?" Winston bellows.

"What?" The little man is clutching himself again, but this time the delight is real. "You would?"

"Erm—" I say, thus committing myself fully to the madness.

The little man actually claps his hands. He starts skipping.

"You've doomed yourself, Arthur, mate," says Winston. "You'll regret this moment for the rest of your life."

I have a worrying feeling that Winston is being unusually prescient.

"I'm going to write one," the little man says to me. "I'm going to write one right now." He looks away, then back at me, a look of devilish glee on his face. "I've got a good one."

He makes towards his desk.

"Wait," I say. One last desperate attempt to get the information I came for.

The little man turns, an eyebrow raised.

"Odd effects," I say again. "Spatial or temporal. At the British Museum, the Natural History Museum, Trafalgar Square." I give him my best you're-crazy-but-I'm-going-to-treat-you-fairly-decently-anyway smile.

"But... But..." the little man sputters. "My report. I was going to put it in my report." He looks crestfallen.

"No one wants to read your bloody reports," Winston yells. "I've had it up to here with your reports. All I ever hear about is your reports."

Purple clambers up from the man's collar again. He spins on Winston. "He wants to hear them! He's bloody begging for them. They're masterpieces in miniature. You're just jealous because one day you'll be chopped down and turned into paper for me to write one on!"

He turns back to me. "I was going to write it down." He's almost begging me.

"Oh," I say, doing the social arithmetic. "I don't want the full thing now. Just a... a..." I struggle for the word. "A verbal abstract of the full paper. An overview. An appetizer." I smile as winningly as I am able.

"An appetizer?" The little man contemplates this. There is at least a fifty percent chance that I've just pushed him into a murderous rage.

"To pique my palate." Which is probably taking it all a little too far.

The little man nods. "Oh." He rubs his hands. "Yes. Yes. I understand."

Thank God one of us does.

"Well," he stands conspiratorially close to me, "as I would have put in my report," he smiles, corrects himself, "as I am *going* to put in my report," he lets out a little chuckle of pleasure, "there have been some unusual circumstances in the aftermath of the Russian attacks." His tone starts to lose some of its jollity. "In fact," he says, "I am fully planning on including a comprehensive appendix surrounding the issues of funding and the expectations of my job. I mean take the library. I'm slipping a hypnotist in as a grief counselor to confuse witnesses. I'm hijacking press releases. I'm undercover vetting the repair crew. And then on top of that I have to take a librarian and keep him undercover in a hospital while I wait for the bloody doctor I've got on retainer to get back from bloody Majorca so he can amputate an arm that's suddenly gone fetal on the poor bastard and then look the other way."

"An arm that's gone fetal?" That sounds both awful and exactly like what I'm after.

"That's just the bloody tip of the proverbial fucking iceberg. I've got replicating bookshelves. I've got folks going to pull a book off one shelf, finding it won't move, but that they've ransacked a shelf across the other side of the room. I've got a candle that never burns itself out. I mean I'm having to deal with a veritable perpetual fucking motion machine, I'm having to contend with something that's defying Newtonian laws of physics. Defying space and time? That's the least of my bloody problems."

I think this must be how a pirate feels when his shovel strikes the treasure chest.

"So," I say, trying to keep my voice under control, "that's pretty much a yes on the spatial and temporal disturbances."

The little man eyes me, suddenly suspicious. "Maybe."

"Wait—" I say. "But you said."

"You'll have to read the full report for me to actually confirm that."

"He's mentally unhinged, Arthur! Fear for your safety, mate. He's waiting for an opening!"

I try to block Winston out.

"I swear to you," I say. "I am totally going to read your report."

The little man regards me from one bulging eye, then backs up. "All right then."

"And when will the report be coming?" It's my turn to be suspicious.

"Well," the man hedges. "It's not like I can just vomit up three hundred and fifty pages of—"

"Three hundred and fifty!" My incredulity cuts him off.

"I knew it!" he gasps. "You're not going to read it! You lied!"

"No, no, no." I hold out my hands, try to preserve the charade of sanity.

"It's the pruning shears for you! Run, Arthur, run!" I wish Winston didn't sound so gleeful.

"I explained." The little man is wringing his hands. "I explained, I'm overburdened. It takes a long time to write a proper report. It's not something that can be rushed. I have a lot on my plate."

"The lithium's wearing off, Arthur. Five, four, three…"

"Shut up!" the little man screams at Winston.

"I'm going to read it. I'm going to read it." My hands are still out, fingers spread wide. But I'm glad I remembered to wear my gun today. "I promise you I'm going to read it."

The little man is breathing hard. He looks at me. "Swear on your mother's grave?"

"Of course." Thank God my mum's still alive and kicking, albeit in Australia.

"I'll know," he says. And in this place who knows if he's lying or not.

"You will receive a full written response," I say. Because we've clearly entered fantasy land at this point.

This appears to mollify the little man somewhat.

"It's just," I continue, "it's very important. As quickly as it's possible for you to get something to me is all. Allowing, of course," I decide to cover my arse in case Winston isn't exaggerating, "for the appropriate levels of quality to be met."

The little man regards me from under his narrow eyebrows.

"I'm making no promises," he says finally.

"Whenever you can get it done. But it's very important."

He nods, still wary.

"I have to be going now," I say.

"Oh yeah, course you do," Winston yells at me. "That's it, abandon me. I never helped you out. I never trod on a Russian for you. You ever cleaned a person off your foot, Arthur? You ever had to do that?"

"I cleaned your bloody foot, you whinging bastard!"

The bickering chases me even after I firmly close the door and retreat down the long corridor to the elevators.

45

THE TEMPORARY OFFICE OF MI37 CO-DIRECTOR FELICITY SHAW

"Hello, Arthur." Felicity looks up distractedly from her computer monitor. She pushes her reading glasses up her nose, then pulls them off with a sigh. She pinches the bridge of her nose.

"Is now not a good time?" God I hope it is one.

"No worse than any other."

I smile sympathetically and take a seat. She's set up her office the way it was in Oxford. Filing cabinets along one wall, plants along the shelves on another, daylight bulbs clipped in place. It's a reassuringly familiar look.

"This is nice." I gesture around. I'm itching to get to the point here, but I feel I need to give Felicity time to get into a receptive mood.

She tries to force a smile and ends up grimacing. "It's hard to appreciate it when I'm reviewing Coleman's proposed cost-cutting measures."

"Ah." I try to think of something more meaningful to say but I'm finding it hard to make small talk. So I just cut to the chase. "I've done some digging," I say.

Felicity shifts her weight, perhaps sits up a little straighter. "Something I can bring to George?"

The way she says his name puts my teeth on edge, almost

deferential, but Felicity made it clear—that's the nature of the game now.

"I think so," I say. Except I don't just think so, I know so. I have my smoking gun.

"Tell me," she says.

So I tell her. I describe my journey to the storage room, my meeting with the cleanup guy, my questions. And then, in excruciating detail, I go over his answers. By the end, I'm tapping my hand against my thigh, emphasizing each point.

"Residual," tap, "temporal," tap, "and spatial disturbances." Tap. "Everywhere he looks." Tap. "He can list them." Double tap. I'm grinning like a child.

Felicity is not. "Arthur," she says, slowly, carefully, "how much do you trust Ogden?"

I'm not too carried away to notice something is clearly off. "Who?" I ask.

Felicity nods, as if this was expected. "Our cleanup man in the subbasement. His name is Ogden Beauvielle. You didn't know that, did you?"

I clap a hand to my head. "Oh, that's it. I'd forgotten. But I don't see how that's important."

Felicity contemplates a coffee mug. "You don't know much about him."

I shake my head. My stomach is sinking faster than a holed battleship.

"But you trust him as a source? Nothing seemed odd about him to you?"

Felicity reminds me of defense lawyers I've seen pick apart my cases in court. Go after the validity of the witness first.

"He had no reason to lie to me," I counter, dodging Felicity's precise question.

"I'll take that as a yes then," Felicity replies, her bullshitometer as effective as ever.

"He didn't lie to me." I try to say it calmly but I'm getting belligerent. And I really should play nice, but I'm getting sick of this. How many times can my evidence be ruled too thin? "He's reporting exactly what he saw."

Felicity spreads her hands palms down on the table, stares at them for just a moment before looking up at me. "I'm just asking you to see this from Coleman's perspective. How will he respond to this?"

And it's right there. Right in front of her. It's plain as goddamn day. The smoking gun. All she has to do is pick it up and show it to the world.

Except…

She doesn't believe me.

I mean… I've known that. Always known that, I suppose. But it's not an easy thing to admit. And she's trying to pretend she has an open mind, and I've been playing along, but she doesn't. And… God… I should leave well alone, but I just feel fucking sick right now. It doesn't get more obvious than this. They're throwing the whole world away.

"Why is it so hard for you," I say, "to imagine that I might be right on this one? Why do you have such a problem with it when other people can see it plain as day?"

Shaw cocks her head. "Other people? What other people?"

Oh shit. My heart doesn't so much sink as it goes through the floor, heading for Winston's subterranean branches. Oh shit and balls. Oh, I should not have said that. That was really—

"You mean, Devon?"

I try to keep the relief off my face, out of the heaviness of my breath.

"I mean," Felicity carries on, "she's nice enough, but talk about wet behind the—"

And then she stops.

And apparently I didn't keep the relief off my face.

"No," she says, and she shakes her head. "Not Devon." Her brow furrows. "Who did you tell, Arthur? Who did you talk to about this?"

I close my eyes. And I am such a shitty liar. I have no idea how to get out of this. And I was so not prepared to fuck up this bad.

And then I don't have to lie, because Felicity is smarter than that.

"Oh no," she says. "Oh no, Arthur. Not them. Not the Weekenders."

Clyde probably knows a spell about having the ground swallow you up. I should ask him about that.

"Fuck!" The curse explodes out of Felicity. She seems rocked by the force of it, flinging herself back in her chair, her arms going up. I take a step back. "Fuck!" she shouts it again. It seems so foreign coming from her, from this neat little woman, so foreign in this neat little room. She stands up, kicking her chair back. It slams off a filing cabinet and careens into a wall.

"Was I not fucking clear, Arthur? Was I not explicit enough for you?"

"You know—" I start, but Felicity has no time for my answers.

"You're out, you know that, right?" She spins, seems constrained by the enormity of her rage. This room is hardly big enough to hold it. "Coleman will have every inch of your arse for this. He'll have mine too. We're fucked. We're both fucked. Because of you." She holds her head in her hands, as if trying to contain the thoughts, as if to hold everything together.

And it was bloody her that put me in this position. She has to see that. I step toward her. Try to get her to see one last time.

Her palm whips out. It crashes into my sternum and I stagger backwards, trip, sit down hard.

"Don't you fucking touch me," Felicity says to me. "Don't you fucking dare."

And... Jesus. That's what it comes down to? That's how this all ends? Me sitting on my arse in the remnants of my career and my relationship, staring at the end of everything.

And, God, is it really my fault? What exactly have I done wrong here? I'm the only one in MI37 who sees this threat for what it is. I'm the only one doing the right thing.

"What the fuck?" I'm yelling suddenly. Bug-eyed with anger, sitting on my arse. "Are you really so fucking blind?" I pick myself up. "I'm trying to do the right thing. I'm trying to save the bloody world. But Coleman, and Clyde, and, goddamn it, you, Felicity, you keep standing in my fucking way. You keep making mistakes and slapping me down when I try to fix them."

"This? This is fixing a mistake?" Her laugh is bitter as coffee laced with lemon juice. "God, I'd love to see it when you really screw up."

I close my eyes. She's not just capitulating to Coleman, her psychology has been colonized by him. She's as bad as him. "You're handing the Russians the Chronometer," I say. "When you cut the power to London, you're serving it to them on a fucking platter. You!"

Felicity seizes her head again. Her mouth is stretched in the rictus of a smile on a face that's been robbed of mirth. "And whose theory is that, Arthur?" she asks. "The Weekenders'? Whose life are you looking to end, Arthur? Whose do you want on your conscience? Clyde's? Tabitha's? Devon's? Mine?"

And God, it's as plain as goddamn day and she cannot see. She will not see.

"Do you want six fucking billion lives on yours?" I step in closer. Keeping just out of striking range.

I'm the only one here trying to fix this. It's suddenly clear. MI37 is done. It's finished and useless. Coleman has broken it irreparably. Whatever I do here, it will be too late.

"No, Arthur," Felicity says. "I don't want any lives on my conscience." Her voice changes, is calm—an ice field crystallizing. "That's why I'll have your gun and your badge."

And God, it's so fucking cliché. It's so the absurd echo of every action movie I've ever seen. It's like Felicity and I are playing at cops and robbers. And what can I do? What else can I do, but what Kurt Russell would do?

I pull my badge from my pocket.

"Agent Arthur Wallace," Felicity's voice is shaking with anger. "You are hereby suspended—"

I fling the badge at her, hurl it in the face of her bullshit. "You know what?" I say. "I fucking quit."

46

And there it is. Out there. Said. Done. And I don't even regret it.

I move toward the door.

"Arthur!" There's a warning edge to Felicity's voice.

I keep moving.

"Arthur Wallace, you get your arse back—"

She's cut off as I slam the door behind me. Calling me by my full name stopped working about the same time as my balls dropped.

That said, Felicity knows a lot more kung fu than my mother ever did.

Just in case, I start to run.

THIRTY MINUTES LATER

Finally, exhausted, sides heaving, I collapse, land on the sidewalk. A few people look at me. A bedraggled man clutching his sides, rain spattered and puddle stained.

Holy crap. I just quit. I just ran out of MI37. Literally ran.

It was the right thing to do. I had to do it. I don't know what else I could have done. My movie viewing has not prepared me with any other response.

God, I'm on my own. Really on my own. All the resources I enjoyed thirty minutes ago, gone. All my friends. My colleagues. Not mine anymore.

I just ran out on Felicity. On our relationship.

I quit. I really quit.

I could go back, of course. I could beg forgiveness. I could deal with my suspension. I could sit on the sidelines. I could see if Felicity and I could pick up the pieces.

Except that then the Russians will win. And I'll be as culpable as Coleman.

So if I don't turn back? If I do the right thing?

Onwards. I have made my bed. Now I lie in it. And I have made it with others in mind. Maybe not MI37, but…

I reach into my pocket, pull out my cellphone. I dial.

"Hello?"

"Aiko," I say, "we need to meet."

47

Aiko's apartment is surprisingly cozy considering it belongs to someone who spends their spare time hunting down supernatural horrors. She's decked everything out in sunny yellows and soothing greens. Polaroid snaps of London are scattered like barnacles over bookshelves and CD-racks. A rainbow of pushpins tack more to the walls. A few faces appear again and again, Malcolm and Jasmine among them. A young Asian man appears in them frequently too.

Aiko emerges from one of London's customary nutshell-sized kitchens holding two mugs of tea.

"Your boyfriend?" I say, tapping the young man's face on a nearby picture.

"Brother. So... no, that'd be a bit creepy." She hands me the mug. "The position of boyfriend is currently vacant," she adds. "No time for much outside of the Weekenders, and Malcolm's a little old for me."

I'm worried we're heading toward Cheshire cat territory, which is something I really cannot deal with less than an hour after throwing a badge at Felicity, but Aiko just sits down in an armchair opposite me with a slight sigh. So, apparently I'm an egotistical fool as well as all the other types.

In fact, Aiko hasn't said much since I phoned her and laid out my current employment situation. She told me to come over, and when I did asked me if I could take my shoes off, and if I wanted sugar with my tea.

Now finally she gives me an appraising look.

"You have any idea what you're doing?" she asks me.

I think about that. "Not really, no."

She nods to herself. "You've got balls, Agent Arthur. I'll give you that."

"I threw my badge at her," I say, contemplating the depths of my tea. "Actually flung it at her face."

"Your boss?" Aiko checks. "Your girlfriend?"

I nod.

"Bold, Agent Arthur. Definitely bold."

I think about it, and, no, my tea mug is definitely too small to drown myself in.

"Hey," Aiko sets down her tea, "chuck us your phone, would you?"

My wariness perks its head up again. The last thing I need is Aiko making a phone call to Felicity. "Why?" I say.

Aiko rolls her eyes. "Look, Arthur, let's face facts here. You have clearly thrown your chips in with us Weekenders at this point. It's a little late to stop trusting us."

She has a definite point. A sharp one. For better or worse now, I am a Weekender.

Every single time they've been involved in an MI37 operation one of our people has died.

Clyde's words echo up at me. That's me now. On the outside looking in.

I throw my phone over to Aiko. She catches it one-handed, flips it over and yanks the battery, then she fishes the SIM card out. She folds it neatly in two.

I almost object, but then I realize what she's doing. This is thriller movie 101. Remove methods of being traced. And cellphone triangulation is number one on the list. Still...

"I think just turning it off works, as well," I point out.

Aiko shrugs apologetically. "Malcolm's drills on this stuff are pretty thorough."

Drills? He makes them break other people's cellphones on a regular basis?

"You're not going to try to cut up my credit cards, are you?"

She shakes her head. "Though I will want to seal them in a bag full of water and freeze them."

I close my eyes. This is what it's come to. But this really is the only way I see forward. I start to dig through my wallet for the cards. Then the doorbell rings and I dump it, seizing my pistol.

Aiko stifles a laugh.

"What?"

"Calm down, Agent Arthur," she says. "It's just Malcolm and Jasmine. I called them as soon as I got off the phone with you."

She gets up, answers the door, ushers the pair in from the hallway. Malcolm lands on the couch next to me. Jasmine perches on the couch arm on my other side. Cozy takes a definite step toward cramped.

"You actually, genuinely, positively quit MI37 today?" Jasmine even pulls off her headphones to hear my response.

"Yes."

"To be one of us?" Her eyes are virtual saucers.

I glance to Aiko and Malcolm. They give me nothing.

"Oh my God." Jasmine explodes with radiant joy. "I think I love you."

"Erm." She's joking. Please let her be joking.

"Jasmine," Malcolm warns.

"Totally platonic. Totally. Totally." Jasmine lays a hand on my shoulder. "Totally," she says again, looking at Aiko this time. I try to keep my imagination under control about what that look means.

"First things," Malcolm says, mercifully changing the subject.

"I know this!" Jasmine bounces up and down on the arm of the couch. "Cellphone. Credit cards."

An almost parental smile crosses Malcolm's lips.

"Already working on it," Aiko says.

"So, second things," I say. "The Russians." Because that's it. That's the nub. And it's the same problem I faced with MI37. Except... and suddenly a feeling of liberation creeps over me. Because for the first time we can really address the problem. Now we can focus.

"Chernobyl," I say. "We need to go to Chernobyl."

I realize I have the attention of the whole room. And it's not derisory attention either. It's a heady moment.

"That's where this all started," I say. "If we're to find these guys before the seventeenth, we have to go back to square one. The real square one. There are answers there." God, there have to be answers there.

A contemplative silence.

"Wow, Arthur," Aiko breaks it, "you sure know how to turn a girl's day upside down." But she's smiling.

"Won't we, like, melt or something if we go there?" Jasmine asks. "Or, like, have mutant babies one day or something."

Except... "It's not radiation," I say. "It's pockets of disturbed space-time. That has to be it. So as long as we avoid those—"

"Oh well, that shouldn't be a problem at all then," Aiko says. The grin has a sarcastic edge now.

"We have to go." I genuinely believe it. "I don't know what else we can do."

Next to me, Malcolm shifts his weight. The couch trembles. "One problem," he says.

Oh God, this is how it begins. The niggling doubts, the slow chewing away of resolve. And can't we just—

"Passport," Malcolm says.

Not what I was expecting. But, "Oh shit, yes," I say. Because traveling under my own name would probably mess with the whole incognito thing.

"You don't have like fifteen secret identities?" Aiko looks disappointed.

"My car doesn't even have ejector seats," I tell her.

Aiko shakes her head sadly. "And you call yourself a secret agent."

"He's perfect." Jasmine pats my arm defensively. Not that needing to be defended by a teenage girl probably helps my standing here.

"I might know a guy," Malcolm says. "Knows a guy who knows a guy."

A false passport. Jesus. Again the enormity of the day's actions swamp me. I'm totally adrift. I don't even know where I'm sleeping tonight. I don't have clothes for tomorrow. It's not like I can just go back to the hotel.

Shit and balls.

"What sort of turnaround for the passport with a Russian visa?" Aiko asks Malcolm. She's all business now, talking shop. And they're actually pretty good at this, I realize, no matter what the rest of MI37 claims.

"Tomorrow morning should be doable. You got the camera?"

"Sure." Aiko nods, steps out of the room.

"Camera?" I'm trying to play catch up. I'm used to being on the official side of secretly bringing down supernatural threats.

Jasmine rolls her eyes. "Malcolm's mad for passports. I've got, like, four now."

Malcolm gives Jasmine a withering look.

"What?" she says. "You have a mad-on for them. You know it."

"Language," Malcolm rumbles. Jasmine just grins.

And she's a teenager. A teenager with four false passports. And I'm about to blithely drag her off into God knows what danger.

"Do your parents know you're here?" I ask her. There's probably a way to ask that question that doesn't make me sound older than Father Time, but I can't figure it out.

"Oh," Jasmine waves a hand. "My parents haven't known where I am for about four years now. I live in a commune."

"Ah." And how do you respond to that? Part of me wants to march her to a phone right now and demand that she call them and tell them where she is. Except I don't know the story, I don't know why she's here. Her parents could have done terrible things, anything.

It's like my first day back at MI37, starting over again, misjudging people again.

I feel nostalgic, and sad, and a little like an idiot.

Aiko re-enters holding a massive Polaroid camera with four lenses. She sees me examining it. "What can I say?" She shrugs. "I had a brief bout with kleptomania while working at a drugstore as a teenager."

So I stand, I smile, and blink in the aftermath of the flash.

"All set," Aiko says, handing the pictures to Malcolm. She turns to me. "You should probably lay low tonight. So I was thinking the best thing would probably be for you to sleep here with me."

"Oh rrrrreally." Jasmine rolls the word around her tongue like hard candy.

And oh crap, maybe my imagination wasn't running away with me. At least Jasmine thinks it wasn't. And this is the last thing I need. I don't even—

And then the doorbell rings.

Everyone freezes.

I close my eyes. That didn't take long. Still… "There isn't—" I look at all three of them, "—a fourth Weekender I don't know about, is there?"

In answer, Malcolm reaches to his waistband, beneath the back of his shirt. He produces a large, matte black pistol. "You all get in the kitchen."

I look at the kitchen. That place is tiny. It's a totally impractical plan. And… Jesus. No. I am not having Malcolm shoot any of my former co-workers. Not today. Not ever.

I put my hand on his gun. "If it's MI37, I'll go quietly," I say. "You all just get to Chernobyl. Get this done."

I step toward the doorway.

"Arthur." Aiko catches my arm. But she doesn't go any further than that. There's nothing much else to be said. I pull away.

It's almost a relief to be out in the corridor. Heading out of the fire back to the familiarity of the frying pan. Still, I pause in the hallway, take a few deep breaths. It was fun while it lasted. And hopefully the Weekenders will prove more effective than I have. Hopefully they can finish what I've failed to start.

I close my eyes, swallow hard, and open the door.

48

"Devon?"

She stands in Aiko's doorway, sheltered beneath a large, floral umbrella. My mouth opens. I have no other words.

"Ah," she booms. "There you are. Marvelous."

They sent Devon? To bring me in? I mean... I like her, but that's kind of insulting.

"Well come on." She looks at me expectantly. "Invite me in. It's raining cats and dogs out here. Well, not real cats and dogs. Terrible, bloody mess that would be. Pet bits everywhere. Hazardous to one's health. At least—"

"Come in," I say, regaining some control over my jaw. I move out of the way of the door. I'm still trying to put everything together in a pattern that makes sense.

"This isn't my..." I wave a hand at the hallway.

"Well obviously it's not your place," Devon says. "You don't even live in this city. I mean, you could have some love nest secreted away, but even so this apartment is owned by Evan Walter Young—who isn't young as it turns out—and rented to Aiko Maria Futsawa, neither of whom are you." She pauses. "Unless you live a much different life than the one I imagine you to have. Which, given my history with that sort of thing, may actually be more likely than I'd thought." She pauses again. "You don't dress up as an Asian woman on the weekends, do you, Arthur?"

I work my jaw a little bit more, still trying to catch up with events so far.

"Not that there would be anything wrong with that if you did." Devon misreads my silence. "I'd just be surprised Shaw would go with that is all. She doesn't seem like the type."

"No," I finally manage. "No, I do not cross-dress on the weekends." Not something I expected to have to explain today of all days.

And this is, of course, the moment Aiko pokes her head around the door.

"I'll leave you two to it then," she says and ducks away.

I try to find steady ground. "Devon," I say, "what are you doing here? How did you even find me?"

"I may be new, Arthur," Devon puts her hands on her hips, "but it's not the hardest thing in the world to find out someone's address. I can use a computer. Sort of have a doctorate from Cambridge on the very subject. Not that I like to parp on my own trumpet." She stops, looks left. "That sounds terribly dirty, doesn't it?"

"Devon," I implore her, praying for sanity, for a short swift answer, "please, what are you doing here?"

"Oh." Devon looks momentarily, and uncharacteristically, nonplussed. "Did I not say that?"

"No!" I regret the way I say it as soon as it's out of my mouth. "Sorry. It's been a long day."

Jasmine's head appears. "You sure you're all right?"

I whirl on her, catch myself in time. I breathe. "One minute, please."

Jasmine's head disappears. I look back to Devon. "Please?" I say.

"Oh right, yes, well."

And then Devon lapses into silence.

I'm on the verge of pulling my gun on her just to get an answer when she says, "Sort of inspired by your lead today. Might have followed it a bit."

"Wait." That sounds like... "What?"

"Sort of quit MI37 today." She nods to herself.

Oh holy crap. I try to sort through that in my head. Not a

good day for the home team. "How did Felicity take it?" I ask. It surprises me that that's still my first thought.

"Well," Devon keeps nodding, "sort of haven't told her yet."

"What?" Devon is apparently a master of postmodern, non-linear storytelling.

"Well," Devon says, "I'm not very into the whole confrontation thing. Makes me very uncomfortable. Like tights. Never liked the things. I mean, what's the point? Isn't that why God invented pants and socks? Tights are just a useless version of long johns as far as I can tell. And long johns are quite possibly the work of the devil. But, anyway, yes, quitting is always a bit of a silent affair for me. A sort of not showing up until they catch on. Which I'm sure they haven't at MI37 yet, given as it's only been about an hour or so, and I technically quit at the end of the work day. But that doesn't make it less so, Arthur. My commitment to quitting is absolute. Like when I gave up herbal teas. Except that was for Lent. Funny name for something. Sounds like I lent all my herbal teas to someone else. But I didn't. I just stockpiled them and went hog crazy on Easter. Drank so much I nearly ended up in hospital. Had to pee for twenty minutes straight at one point. Not my finest hour. Or third of an hour, I suppose. So maybe not exactly like when I gave up herbal teas. But hopefully you get the analogy."

She breaks for breath. Or for confirmation. I just sort of whirl about in the verbal stew, until I find some meaning to grab onto.

"So, you're not going back to work tomorrow," I say. I think that's what it all boils down to, but I'm not sure because so many words were used.

"Not on your nelly," Devon confirms.

"But…" and maybe I missed this, "what are you doing here?"

"Oh." Devon slaps palm to forehead. "Did I miss that bit again?"

"I did." That's about as certain as I can be.

"Probably me," she says. "Well, you know, your lead, I mentioned that. I thought it was marvelous. Didn't want to limit myself to just quitting. Not that I want to bill myself as some sort of strange Arthur Wallace groupie or anything. Always put stock in the idea of being a strong independent woman. Except, as it turns out, that woman was rather more co-dependent on her utter shit of a boyfriend than she liked to think, but that's neither here nor there, though if you ever feel the urge to remove Clyde's spine and beat him to death with it, I will again be happy to follow your lead."

A momentary breath. I'm still none the wiser.

"But," she says, "I mean, I'm not totally convinced by a theory that's twenty-five years old myself. Theoretically impossible, my Aunt Fanny, I say."

Wait… Wait… She's talking about…

"This whole space-time magic thing. Makes a lot of sense to me. Just sort of wanted to be in on that action. And that action seemed to be with you. So I figured you'd be with the Weekenders after what Felicity said. Did a little bit of messing around in the records, found an address, and skedaddled over here. Simple really."

God, I… I… I hug her. Big, and fierce, and maybe, though I will deny it later, with a tear in the corner of one eye. Faith, belief, whatever Aiko wants to disparage it as, someone else has it in me, and it's quite brilliant.

"Thank you," I say. "Thank you so much."

Devon looks rather nonplussed. "Oh. Well. You know."

Malcolm's head appears. He looks tired and put-upon. I hold up a finger. His head retreats.

"Erm," I say, and realize that just because it's selfish to ask something that's not going to stop me, "what exactly did Felicity say about me quitting?"

"Oh." Devon examines her feet. "Not some of the nicest things. There may have been use of the phrase 'rogue agent'—"

—which actually sounds kind of cool and I like—

"—and slightly more of the phrase 'selfish shit'—"

—which I don't—

"—and some instructions to arrest you on sight, and some threats that the same would happen to us if we tried to help you. And then Coleman was terribly unpleasant about it all, saying things like, and remember I'm only quoting, but things like, 'good riddance,' and 'nice pick, Felicity,' and stuff about how you were both, well, he used the f-word, which I personally don't like to use. Unless I'm watching my college play *University Challenge*. Which, well, let's say they're effing bad at it. So that's acceptable. But he said you were both a bit effed. And then he was about to make some horrible innuendo joke, but Felicity punched him in the chest and he needed to go and lie down."

It's probably wrong that my first thought is that I wish I hadn't quit today just so I could have seen that. Still, it's good to hear that MI37 hasn't become any more functional in my absence. It makes it easier to think I made the right decision.

"So," I say, "you're in with us then."

"Rather looks that way." She gives me an almost shy smile.

Both Jasmine and Aiko appear at the doorway. "Has she arrested you yet?" Aiko asks.

Devon looks shocked at the very thought.

"Not exactly."

49

DOMODEDOVO AIRPORT, MOSCOW, OCTOBER 13TH

Despite the fact that I am producing enough sweat to drown an African bull elephant, Moscow passport control gives the passport of Mr. Henry Jarvis Junior nothing more than the most cursory of inspections. Devon, now traveling as Mrs. Wilhelmina "Hillie" Jarvis, receives a similar level of scrutiny. I'm not sure if I'm more troubled by the ease with which we can violate international borders, or by the horrendous names Malcolm's forger came up with.

Aiko, Malcolm, and Jasmine are waiting for us after we push through the final set of doors and into the arrivals lounge. I try to lead us to a quiet spot, but I find the crowds hard to navigate. I always imagine airports to be soulless places, but there's something distinctly foreign about this one. It's as if someone made a copy of Heathrow and something was lost in the process. I know rationally that it's just a cultural reference issue, but that doesn't help me feel any less lost.

Lost, and so far I've managed to penetrate about twenty yards into Russia. My comfort zone is several thousand miles and three days behind me. I keep hoping Clyde will come round the corner and say something that makes me smile and lets this tension out of my shoulders.

Except it feels like a long time since Clyde said anything like that. These days, he's more likely to try and hack the security system and set off every alarm in the place. So maybe it's a good thing he's not here.

"Who's this contact we're meeting again?" I ask Malcolm. It turns out he has some sort of global network of men of ill repute. I'm not sure if I'm reassured by that or not.

"Nicky should be here." Malcolm doesn't look at me when he replies, just keeps scanning the crowd. "He's reliable."

"It should be noted," Aiko says, "that Malcolm's definition of reliable is a little looser than most people's."

"Still alive, aren't you?" Malcolm says without looking around.

Aiko shrugs and doesn't elaborate further. Still I am not reassured. This is the man we're relying on for transport and weaponry. It's tricky to wear a shoulder holster while traveling coach on a false passport. Plus, personally, I like to leave talk of our drastically shortened lifespans until after the first day of a new mission.

"I don't, you know," Devon starts, "want to be a Debbie Downer on everything. Or a Devon Downer. That'd be more appropriate in this case. And I've no desire to malign all the Deborahs of the world. I've known two Deborahs and both were very cheerful women. Except one of them when I ran over her cat. But that was very much a one off. For both of us. Don't make a habit of vehicular pet maiming. That'd be a terrible thing. But what I meant to say is, do we have a plan B should this chap, Nicky, decide he'd rather not turn up and help us?"

"He's reliable," Malcolm repeats.

Devon looks at me. "No then," she mouths at me. I nod.

I'm not sure MI37 missions ever went smoother than this. Still, Felicity valiantly tried to give the impression that they did.

But I'm trying not to think about Felicity. What she's doing. What she's thinking.

I mean, I know the relationship is over. You don't throw your badge at someone, and quit on them, and expect to then go home with them and enjoy a cup of tea while you both watch the sitcoms. I get that.

I just wish we could. When this is all over.

Assuming, of course, that when this is all over the world still exists.

"There he is." Malcolm interrupts my mental muddling. His meaty finger points to a hunched figure in the crowd. The figure has a grease-stained New York Yankees cap pulled down over his eyes and he's wearing enormous aviator sunglasses that almost entirely cover his pock-marked cheeks. He sees Malcolm pointing at him, and ducks back into the crowd, head low.

"Not," Devon says, "exactly how I'd define reliable-looking."

"Reliable," Malcolm rumbles. "Not respectable."

Which is about as much as I suppose we can hope for. We cross over the room, tailing Nicky's greasy wake through the crowd. His appearance doesn't seem to have affected Jasmine's enthusiasm in the slightest. She is practically skipping.

Nicky is waiting outside standing next to… well, I suppose it's a minivan, but it looks closer to a pile of sculpted scrap metal painted lime green by a lackluster monkey. The sort of thing Fred Flintstone would have had to upgrade to if he and Wilma had decided to have more kids.

"You come now," Nicky says. "Nikolai take you to private airport now. Very hush-hush. Very good. You like it there. Very nice."

He smiles and I kind of wish he hadn't. I haven't seen that shade of yellow since I helped my dad take up the linoleum in my grandmother's basement.

Nikolai opens the minivan door. "Very good ride," he tells us. "You like very much. Like Cadillac."

I'm reasonably sure Cadillac could sue for slander over that one, but someone has to bite the bullet. "Shotgun," I say.

VNUKOVO AIRPORT, MOSCOW, ONE HELLISH HOUR LATER

I spill out of Nikolai's car about two seconds before the contents of my stomach do.

"You like very much!" His smile is very wide. Like a shark's, I imagine.

Aiko clambers shakily out of the back seat and helps me to my feet.

"Not exactly a TV-style secret agent, are you?" she says.

"I'm better when my stunt man stands in for me." I almost manage a smile, but I can still taste my airplane food and I decide against it.

"Plane this way!" Nikolai shouts with far more enthusiasm than seems required. "You like very much! Cadillac of planes!"

My stomach lurches again.

We've parked a fair distance from the terminal and Nikolai leads us away. Mist makes everything seem loose and unreal. I still lean on Aiko for support. Devon stays close, unsteady on her feet. Jasmine and Malcolm weave after us. Parked planes hulk to our left and right. They all look far too heavy to ever lift off the ground.

All except one.

"Tell me," I say to Aiko, "please, that that's not our plane."

"Oh no." Jasmine shakes her head. "That's so not cool."

It is as if rust has accreted over the years, flaked off some great iron behemoth in the sky and happened to collect, through a freak geological event, into the shape of a plane. Seeing it, I can kind of see why Nikolai called his minivan a Cadillac. It's all about frames of reference.

"Come on!" Nikolai shouts. "All fuel and ready to go. Like Icarus we go!"

"No." Aiko shakes her head. "He did not say that."

Jasmine turns to Malcolm. "M," she says, "I love you, but I'm going to kill you."

"No," Devon says, "this flight is going to kill us all."

"Very nice," Nikolai purrs. "You like very much."

50

SEVERAL THOUSAND FEET TOO FAR OFF THE GROUND

I've always been a big public transport fan. Buses and trains make a great deal of sense to me. The maximum number of people in the minimum number of vehicles. Reduced emissions, a protected planet. Everyone's happy.

Planes and I have always had a more tenuous relationship. It's the whole turbulence thing. If there were trains that thrashed up and down like moshers at a Metallica concert there would be a public outcry. But apparently when you're thousands of feet up in the air with nothing below you but a fatal landing, we as a society are OK with it.

And, in my defense, when the turbulence is causing the plane wings to flex up and down like a bird's, I think the terror might be justified.

It doesn't really help that every time we survive a particularly bad bout, Nikolai releases the flight stick to give us a thumbs-up while the nose of the plane dips toward oblivion.

At least Aiko, Jasmine, and Devon all seem equally disconcerted so I don't feel like a total coward. Devon is being particularly vocal about it, with her usual eloquence and volume. It turns out that when it comes to epithets, she is more creative than Shakespeare.

"Invertebrate, neck-breathing, fecal-festering, bile-soaked, intestinal parasite," is not an insult one forgets quickly, even if you are fearing for your life. Malcolm watches us with something between bemusement and disdain. There again, he's been overly cheerful since we got on board and Nikolai showed him a giant sack of budget-priced Russian firearms.

Nikolai's enthusiasm continues unabated. "We enter Ukraine now," he tells us after a few hours, conveniently tipping the plane on its side so we all tumble towards the windows and get a great look at the earth coming up to meet us.

I put my head down between my knees and breathe slowly. *This is worth it.* I repeat the mantra in my head. *This is the right thing to do.*

Except, if I'd stayed with MI37 and the world had ended, at least I'd have been standing on it when it did.

I have to believe I couldn't have convinced them. If I don't believe that then I'm the stupidest man on earth.

"We enter restricted airspace now," Nikolai tells us with an exuberance usually only displayed by men discovering they're about to receive unexpected sexual favors. "Very nice!"

"Wait," I say. "Restricted by whom?"

"Nice syntax," Aiko says, which seems to be missing the point.

"Ukraine military," Malcolm says without batting an eyelid.

"Restricted like they'll send us an angrily worded letter about it?"

Malcolm doesn't seem to want to answer that one.

"They're going to shoot us down, aren't they?" I say to Malcolm. Nothing from Malcolm.

"Aren't they?"

Still nothing.

"They're going to send up planes to shoot big holes in us. Aren't they?"

He has the decency to at least shrug.

"MiGs incoming now!" Nikolai seems on the edge of clapping. "Very nice!"

"Oh my God," I say. "We're going to die. Jesus. MI37 may have fucked pretty much everything else up, but even they could arrange a basic bloody flight."

"Hey!" Aiko seems genuinely offended. I am too busy fearing

for my life to really worry about that right now.

"You be calm, shouty man," Nikolai says. "You no worry. I am..." He contemplates the instrument panel and the plane veers wildly to the left. "How you say?" he asks. "I no be harmed."

"Invincible?" I say. "You're invincible?" It's a testament to the weirdness of my day job that I have to weigh up the likelihood of that statement being true.

"Doesn't seem totally likely, does it?" says Aiko, seeing my expression.

Devon appears to be praying.

"You see now!" Nikolai shouts gleefully.

There is a noise like a weaponized coffee-grinder suddenly blaring into life. Then the windows fill with fiery streaks and Nikolai yanks on the flight stick like he's trying to snap it in two.

The plane reacts as if struck by a fist. People and possessions fly through the air and spiral away across the fuselage. I land upside down in a seat staring at my feet.

"You see now!" Nikolai bellows. "Ukraine pilots very bad."

Thunder roars around us. Nikolai cranks on the stick. Then the whole plane shudders. There is a terrible metal grinding. Our defensive spiral becomes a shuddering half spin through the air.

"Lucky hit!" Nikolai shouts, dripping derision. "Hit me now, eater of shit!" And with that he puts us into a plunging dive. I'm relatively sure the only reason I don't shriek like a six-year-old girl is because my stomach collides with the back of my throat and shuts off my air.

Devon screams, and then her body slams into mine. Together we tumble, head over heels for the cockpit, for the far-too-thin sheet of glass separating us from empty, parachute-less space. Only the back of Malcolm's head stops our descent.

Behind us, another crackle of thunder, and suddenly wind roars. Two neat holes, one on either side of the fuselage, gape as a massive round punches through the plane.

"He not bad, this guy," Nikolai muses.

I try to clamber over Malcolm, try to make sure that I get a chance to end Nikolai's life before the Ukrainian bastard shooting at us does it for me.

Nikolai counters my murderous impulse by pulling more Gs than I can overcome. I slam back, mash my spine against the far wall. I am pinned there, Devon half on top of me, Aiko splayed next to me, her body at a ninety degree angle to mine.

And then, suddenly, level. Suddenly sagging to the floor. The only sound the rattle of our wings and the howling of the wind against our plane's new perforations.

"See, I lose him now," Nikolai says. "Nothing to... Oh shit."

I don't even have time to form a suitable expletive before a plane seat drives the air from my lungs. I sag over it like a child's toy—deflated and discarded.

"This..." Nikolai suddenly doesn't sound quite so confident. "This may not be so good actually."

And then the tail of the plane disappears. A great ripping tear crashes through the body of the plane, and then all that is between us and a Ukrainian MiG fighter jet bristling with missiles, machine guns, and other assorted instruments of death is air.

51

All I can think, and this is probably unfair, is that if I somehow get out of this, once I have murdered Nikolai, I am going to murder Malcolm as well. "Reliable," my left arse cheek.

"Hold on! Hold on!" Nikolai is screaming at the top of his lungs, but it sounds like a whisper against the roar of the wind that claws and chomps at the ragged tail of our aircraft.

Down we go. Down and down. I watch suitcases, holdalls, and light reading material fly out into the desolate European sky.

A cloud swallows us. Nothing but screeching white behind us, lapping at us. I cling to a chair roughly bolted to the rusted floor. My feet fly up above me, flapping in the screaming turbulence. And how long will these bolts hold? Will any of this hold?

"Hold on!" Nikolai keeps screaming it. And I don't know if he's yelling at us, or the plane, or at the world itself. One more second. Just one more to live, to try and rectify this absolute fucking disaster.

Blackness laps at the corner of my vision. If I pass out I'll let go. I can feel my fingers slipping. I want to look, to see if everyone else is safe, to see who we've lost. But I don't dare move my head. I need to concentrate on this seat. I need to make it my world. My anchor. I need to pour my will into it. Hold on. Hold on.

Down.

Down.

Out of the cloud. And the ground below us is so close. It's right there.

And then it's flung away. And my feet slam against the floor of the plane. And my teeth rattle. And I slam my head against the floor. And everything seems to be spinning, but maybe that's just me. And Nikolai is cheering, shouting wildly. And the wind is still howling, still trying to drown him out. But somehow it all feels a little bit less like I'm going to die.

Not enough less. But a little.

"OK," Nikolai screams. "We land now. No more in the air time. Party over."

And the plane lurches like the hand of God swatted it, and we plummet down and I release the last of my breath in what has to be my worst attempt at my last words yet. One long drawn-out syllable.

"AAAAAAAAAAAAAAAAAAAAAAAAAAAAAAAAAAAA—"

The ground comes up like a fist. Nikolai lets out a grunt like he's been headbutted by a warthog. The plane bucks, tilts up, remembers half of itself is missing, and slams down to earth. I fly up. Everything flies up. A nanosecond of weightlessness, and then the plane leaps up to meet us, to carry us down to dead, dry dirt once more. Up, down, up, down. The back of the plane rips over the ground, over dirt and chunks of tarmac, vomiting up sparks, screaming at the universe. A seat breaks free from the fuselage, rolls down and away. It strikes the ground, spins, splays open, spills its stuffing in a messy tangle. Another chair scatters away. And the bolts on the one I'm still clutching, still have seized in a death grip, they rattle and shake as the floor of the plane quakes and bucks.

And then finally, slowly, shuddering, the plane rolls to a stop.

We lie there. Smoke and dust billow quietly around us. Someone is sobbing, and I'm trying to pry my fingers loose from the chair so I can see who it is, see if they're hurt, but I can't let go. I can't. My breath is ragged, my heart a wild galloping beast.

Hold on. Hold on. I just need to hold on a little longer.

Of all the ways this job has almost killed me that was… well, the second worst. Probably.

Not that this is even a job anymore. What is this? A calling? A hobby?

Jesus. This is what I'm choosing to do in my spare time.

"You…" Malcolm's voice from the cockpit breaks the silence. "You OK? Everyone OK?" Even he sounds shaky.

Finally I let go of the seat. It takes a while to stand up though. My legs are trembling violently. Everything hurts. "Yeah," I say. "Yeah, I think I'm OK."

"I… I… I…" Jasmine doesn't get any further than that.

"Just a moment. I just need… Just a moment." Aiko isn't faring any better than us.

It's Devon who's crying. I take a step towards her.

"We land!" Nikolai shouts with glee, seemingly oblivious to all. "Very nice." He claps his hands. "You like very much."

And I find that, despite the shakes, despite the last dregs of adrenaline rattling in my body, I still have the wherewithal to step up to the cockpit and lay him out with a single punch.

52

PRIPYAT, UKRAINE. AN HOUR LATER

It's probably not fair to say that everyone has calmed down, but we have at least achieved the status of rational human beings again. Devon has cried herself out. Malcolm has finished obsessively searching for every piece of lost luggage, no matter how damaged. Jasmine is starting to talk again. Aiko has finished barking orders at everyone. And Nikolai has stopped threatening to have the Russian mob rub out me, my family, and anyone I may have said hello to during my tenure on this planet. And I have recovered from totally losing my shit over no longer having a way to fly out of this hellhole and finally accepted Malcolm's promises of "an exit strategy" without threatening to resort to violence.

It's a desolate bloody place we've landed in. What's left of the plane lies on an old road, a thoroughfare that is now more weeds than asphalt. Gray buildings, ragged and sharp-edged, stare blindly down at the ruins of their city. Every window in the place is shattered. The whole place looks shattered. Like whatever happened here took the city and broke its back. It is a city gutted, all its viscera on display.

Even Mother Nature has been halfhearted in her attempts to reclaim the place. The trees are straggly things, anemic arms reaching desperately for the heavens. The vines clamber halfway up the walls and then seem to lose their sense of urgency. Dead gray strips of leaves hang down like discarded thoughts.

Malcolm is going around handing out guns like penny candy. We lost Nikolai's giant sack of weapons, but fortunately by that point, so much of its contents had spilled about the fuselage that we have enough guns lying around that no one goes empty-handed. I even get another shoulder holster.

"All right then!" Aiko claps her hands. "Let's get going!" She's talking too loudly, too brashly.

"It's OK." I reach out a hand to her. "We can take a moment."

"No." She shakes my hand off. Then she stops and looks at me. "Please," she says, and her voice almost breaks, "can we get out of here?" She takes a breath, it sounds loose and too long. "Come on," she says, the false brashness back in her voice. "Let's get moving, people!"

So we pull together our remaining bags, dust off our wounds, and start walking.

TWO MILES DEEPER IN

Finally I see it. I'd expected it earlier, and had almost lost my faith. Had almost started to believe this was all for nothing, that I'd been blown out of the air for nothing. But then: proof. This is the correct path. For all of its terrifying implications, we were undeniably right.

The deer paces slowly out into the road before us. It lowers its head, nibbles at a weed, then raises its head and looks at us. After a moment it moves slowly on.

Copy after copy of the deer drags after it as it moves. A concertina of flesh. It stops to eat again, and one by one the multiple hindquarters fold into the whole.

Wonder and horror in equal parts leave me speechless. There is something majestic about it. Something awful.

"Woah," Nikolai says, summing up the moment as best he can. "That is some pretty fucked up shit."

He takes a step toward the animal, and it lurches into movement, leaping up and away. It multiplies as it does so, copy after copy of its own body hesitating momentarily before leaping after the first. Like photographic stills laid over each other. It bounds away, trailing its elongating body, disappearing into a long-abandoned office building.

"That's it," Aiko says. "That's what you saw at Trafalgar Square, right?"

"Yes." I nod. "Yes that's it."

"Residual temporal-spatial disturbance." She smiles and holds up a palm. It's a confused moment before I high-five her. "Proof, Arthur. Not belief. Just there. Just happened."

I smile.

"So." Jasmine looks worried. "It just, like, wandered into a pocket of space-time crazy and that totally happened to it?"

"Pretty much." I nod.

"So," Jasmine persists, "we could totally walk into one and become, like, creepy monster us, right?"

"It's on the continuum of possibilities," Devon responds.

"So, you, like, totally have a way to spot those, right? Because I am really so not about ungluing myself in space and time."

"Erm." Devon turns to me.

"Erm," I say.

"Totally reassured, guys. Totally."

ANOTHER MILE

"There." Devon points. "That building there."

Things have been getting decidedly weirder the closer we get to the Chernobyl power station. The fountain that flowed backwards was desperately strange to look at. And there was the massive flock of birds caught in an infinite spiraling loop above a high-rise of cheap housing. The crumpled bag of crisps caught quivering in mid-air spitting out potatoes that melted to seeds on the ground. We've taken wide berths around these phenomena. So far everyone appears to be attached to the same space-time continuum they arrived in.

The same can't be said for our surroundings. As we've moved toward the edge of Pripyat, closer to Chernobyl and the epicenter of the explosion, the levels of dilapidation have been increasing. The buildings are coming more and more to resemble giant piles of rubble.

But the building Devon is pointing at is remarkably whole.

"Reinforced structure." Malcolm nods.

"Which means?" Aiko looks perplexed.

"Government building," Devon and Malcolm say in unison.

Aiko and I get to the conclusion of that thought at the same time, but she's the one who gives eloquent utterance to it.

"Pay dirt."

53

The building reeks of mold and wet cement. The walls are covered in graffiti—skulls, roses, jagged Cyrillic letters, and amorphous blobs in drab shades of red and green and brown. None of the bright Day-Glo colors that London's disenfranchised use to tag its public spaces and vehicles. But apparently we're not the first people to make it this deep.

Whatever branch of the Soviet government occupied the building, they left in a hurry. There are rusted filing cabinets wrapped in thick mutant strains of ivy—all stalk and no leaf. Smashed computer monitors litter the floor. Bookshelves spill their former occupants, providing rotten shelter for rodents. The place is a monument to abandoned bureaucracy.

Winston would fit in here. He'd hate it, but he'd fit in.

I wonder if I'll ever see Winston again.

It's funny how it leaks in. The realization of what I've done. Of what I've left behind. Who.

I wonder what they're doing back in London. If they've worked out how to get closer to the heart of this. I wonder if I'm on a wild goose chase.

But the temporal effects are here. So the truth is here. It has to be here.

We go deeper still. Malcolm leads. Nikolai trails at the back.

His exuberance is significantly dampened.

"This is not being so awesome now." He tries to reason with us.

"It's where we need to be," I tell him curtly. Now I don't need to rely on him for transport I find I don't nod and smile so much.

We come to a stairwell. Tiles are peeling off the walls, collecting in small shattered piles at the corners of the landings.

"We split up?" I ask.

"Have you never even seen a horror movie?" Aiko looks at me like I'm insane.

And the truth is I've seen many, but I've never met anyone else who seemed to think they provided legitimate strategic advice. In fact, if I'm applying Hollywood logic, the best bet is running away very fast. The serial killer traps you on the roof. The giant monster lurks in the basement.

Maybe there is something to that logic after all.

"Down," I say, letting randomness supersede Hollywood's life lessons.

So down we go, to a landing with a great white stencil that reads α-1. A door leads onto the basement floor. The stairs carry on, descending into darkness. The sound of dripping water is louder down here.

"Sweep this floor?" Jasmine looks to Malcolm for confirmation. He seems to be fulfilling a role that lies somewhere between surrogate parent and drill sergeant.

"Sweep the floor," I confirm as Malcolm nods.

It's dark. Medieval dungeon dark. In a few places the ceiling has given way and light filters in. But all it reveals are more filing cabinets, more derelict computers, more rotting books. The place is a maze of little rooms with no clear purpose. One resembles a surgical theater. One looks more like a dentist's.

"Where do we start?" Devon has managed to tear open one filing cabinet drawer. It's stuffed with papers written in an illegible hand. She leafs through them. "There's so much."

I check my watch. The little box showing the date says the 13th. Four days counting today. Except we'll need one to get back to England. Three. Well, three assuming Malcolm's exit strategy doesn't involve hiking the whole way, or wrestling down our own wild horses to ride back to civilization.

"We just start," I say. "We have to. Pick a point and begin there."

"Just at random?" Devon looks dubious.

I shrug. "I don't see anywhere obvious to start."

"You all so crazy." Nikolai has found a lump of rebar from somewhere and is holding it defensively, like a club.

"Devon and Malcolm, start going through files." The plan forms in my mind while I speak it. "Aiko, Jasmine, Nikolai, and I will sweep the rest of the floor. Make sure there's nothing weird here."

"Nothing?" Aiko looks dubious.

"Nothing weird *and* dangerous," I modify.

Malcolm is nodding along.

"Once it's clean we go down. Rinse and repeat. Once down is clear we go up."

Three days. Three long laborious days. But no one questions me. I clap my hands. Back the way I did when I gave my team a pep talk back at the Oxford police station. "Come on people, let's get to work."

WITH DARKNESS FALLING

We settle in for the night in a room nestled in α-1. It's large, high-ceilinged. Rusty hulks of degraded electronics outline broad corridors. It reminds me of some post-apocalyptic NASA control room. The floor slopes down to a waterline—a nearby stream was redirected at some point and now flows through the building. It tumbles through the ceiling in a small waterfall. We can hear the sounds of it gurgling down into the deeper basement levels a few rooms away.

Malcolm made a campfire of sorts. There's enough food in our remaining luggage to pull together a rudimentary meal.

Devon is perusing a foot-high stack of folders we lugged up from the next floor down, β-2. "A little light reading," she called it. "Time flies when your nose is pressed hard into some profoundly trippy Russian magico-scientific texts."

Nikolai is still nursing his piece of rebar. "You people all so crazy. Reading files. Talking time travel. What make you…" He looks to the dimness of the ceiling searching for the right English phrase. "…so sick in head?"

Aiko laughs. I join in.

Devon looks up from her folders. "Ex-boyfriend," she tells Nikolai. Then she looks at the rest of us. "I dare any of you to come up with a worse reason than that."

"I here because of you," Nikolai counters.

Devon contemplates that. "OK," she nods. "You win."

Aiko, who's been trying to make a bed out of clothing from the suitcases, finally lies back and says, "I think the government term for it was a low-level zombie event."

I lift my eyebrows. Zombies have never come up before. She's not looking at us, toying with her hair. "I was temping at a place. Apparently one guy had recently lost his wife. Tried to summon her ghost, or soul, or something. He had her corpse in his office closet. It was really fucked up. I don't know what he was doing exactly. But it didn't go right. I was in the office supplies closet. About the only person who didn't lose their soul. It's pretty hard to fend off zombies with office supplies." She draws a breath that isn't quite steady.

Jasmine shifts over closer to her, holds her hand.

Personally I am being colored impressed. Binder clips versus a hunger for human gray matter. Not exactly what I'd call fair.

"And they didn't recruit you to MI37 after that?" I say.

Aiko shrugs. "The conspiracy theory thing. People judge."

I shake my head. Despite everything, I still have a lot of love and respect for Felicity Shaw, but that was a very, very bad call.

Jasmine looks over at Malcolm. "Can I tell…?"

"No." Malcolm shakes his head violently. He reaches into an inside pocket and pulls out a small brown vial of pills. He thumbs off the lid.

"I saw something I wasn't meant to see," Jasmine says cryptically. "I'd met Malcolm at AA."

My eyebrows give another bounce. Not even old enough to legally drink and she's already a recovering alcoholic?

"Jasmine," Malcolm barks. He is, apparently, not all about the sharing.

"I wasn't there for me." Jasmine misses Malcolm's point with the practiced ease of a teenager. "Just moral support for a guy from the commune."

Malcolm still glowers. I don't think he was there to support someone else.

"And, hey," Jasmine nods at Malcolm, "I just figured, like, Malcolm needed some support too."

I glance over at Malcolm. He looks a little mollified. "But that wasn't the start for you?" I prompt him.

"No," he says, and it's clear that's about the most we're going to get.

Nikolai has wandered away, down by the stream with a pile of discarded 3.5-inch floppy disks that he's skipping over its gently burbling surface.

"But still," he shakes his head, "I no understand. Why not turn, run like fuck? Why stay? Why still fight?"

I think about that one. It had seemed to make sense at the time. These days...

"It's like you say, Nikolai," Aiko says from her nest of sweaters and jeans, "we're sick in the head."

Nikolai shakes his head in disgust. "You people crazy. When I get new plane, I no fly with you no more. We leave here and I walk away. I like that, it very nice."

God, I can't help but laugh at that. I really can't. In the heart of one of the greatest disasters in human history, in the heart of one of the greatest disasters in my personal life, and I'm bloody laughing. I think Nikolai was right about us.

Maybe Nikolai isn't so bad.

Then the water starts to froth and boil.

"Vl—" Nikolai starts to say something, the first words I think I've heard him say in his mother tongue since I've met him. And I find I'm oddly curious to find out what they'll be. Except I never will.

It is massive. It explodes out of the water in front of him. Something impossible. Something my mind tries to deny. A great coagulated blob of catfish. A thousand of them. A thousand mouths ballooning wide. Two thousand sopping mandarin mustaches, flicking him with spray.

It descends on him—a mass of scales and slime. It envelops him, cutting him off, burying that native word. And I don't understand. I don't understand what is happening here.

Nikolai is gone even as the event starts to register, as we start to move. There's just a writhing mass of fish on the floor, retreating back into the water, shrinking down into the depths.

Malcolm grabs a gun off the floor, starts firing. I grab for my shoulder holster, but I've taken it off to sleep. The thing is never comfortable at the best of times. It's lying on the floor next to me. I wrestle with straps and buckles, and then think, *fuck it*, and just fire through the bottom of the holster. But the fish has gone. It's too late. Bullets kick up sharp plumes of spray in the water. But there is no blood. No returning of our guide.

"What the fuck? What the fuck?" Aiko has her hands in her hair, is on her feet, pacing toward the water, then retreating back. "What just happened?"

"Get him!" Jasmine yells. "Get him back!"

I stare at the dark water, the flickering reflection of the fire's light. Black water. And how deep can it be? What else lurks there?

I get up, walk toward the water.

"Don't." Malcolm's voice is definite. "Get away."

"No!" Jasmine shouts. "No, he has to. One of you has to."

"So we're down two?" He stares at her without mercy. And he's right. He knows he's right. And when Jasmine knows too she starts to cry.

"Shit," I say. Plain and simple. "Shit."

"Does it ever stop?" Devon's voice is small in the large room. "Does it ever get better? I just think I could deal with this all a little better if I thought one day I won't be terrified. If I thought one day we might win."

And I know the answer to that. I know that a few days ago I felt like I saved the world. And now... I get to go another round with a different set of lunatics fresh to the fight.

But when are you OK with trying to stop bad things from happening to people?

So I lie. I stand in the center of a nuclear bomb blast crater and tell her soon everything will be OK. And then we pack like crazy, and we move to a room without water. And I lie down, and I close my eyes again. But I do not go to sleep. Not tonight.

54

We say words for Nikolai in the morning. Malcolm leads. He has the whole "ashes to ashes" speech memorized. Which is a little morbid, I think, but this is basically a funeral so it doesn't seem like the time to point that out.

Jasmine makes a cross from two pieces of scrap metal. "Like they're from his plane," she says. Personally I just hope he wasn't Jewish, or Zoroastrian, or something.

Devon doesn't say much. She stands at the back, and returns to her files with a certain vengeance. We've uncovered what seems to be about half a forest's worth of files and we can't reasonably expect her to go through it all, so Jasmine joins her in the reading. Malcolm stands guard. They pick a room where the water hasn't permeated and steer clear of the stack of chairs in the corner that is constantly spilling and then reconstructing itself.

Aiko and I head down the stairs and sweep β-2. The time anomalies seem to be getting fewer and further between as we go deeper down, but the increasing gloom counteracts any good feelings that inspires. It's too easy to populate dark corners with the unfolding flesh of the imagination.

When we're done, we head upstairs for lunch. Devon looks up

from some files. She is gnawing on a strip of jerky. Malcolm seems to have packed a lot of jerky.

"These look like personnel files." She flips around the folder she's holding so we can see. The paper is spotted with dots of black mold, but a photo is clearly visible. She holds up another. Another picture. A middle-aged-looking man with a severe haircut and a military uniform. "All sorts of chappies and chappesses. Vladimirs, and Ivans, and Natashas. Charming names the Russians have. Like they all live in ice castles and snowy forests. Instead of horrible industrial poverty. Ah well."

"Wait," I say, because she wandered away from an important point there. "Personnel? Staff?"

"Seems like it," she says. "This looks like dates of employment. Security clearance. Some sort of general description." She points to spots on the page.

"So," I smile, "if our boys and girl are from here, they're in those files, correct?"

"Oh yes." Devon grins. Then her face falls a little. "But didn't that…" She considers her word choices. "Didn't Tabitha," she says the name as if it leaves a bad taste, "look back at KGB files?"

"How far did she look back?" I ask.

Devon's face really lights up for the first time since we met Nikolai. "Only ten years," she says. "That useless little tart!" The insult is uttered with absolute glee. "Oh, I cannot wait to…" Then she trails off. "Oh wait," she says, "we quit."

"Has a way of sneaking up on you, that, doesn't it?" I keep on finding the fact around dark basement corners. Along with questions about what Felicity is doing, what she's thinking, what her response to my leaving has been. Is she looking here? Does she know about the plane being shot down? Does she think we're dead? Has she shed a tear?

"You keep harping on that," Aiko says, "and I'm going to start taking offense." The edge I've managed to avoid in the darkness is back in her voice. I do my best to ignore it.

"We should focus on these personnel files," I say, wrestling the subject under control. "Find our Russians. Find out everything we can about them. Anything."

"Already on it," Devon says, opening folders and discarding them rapid-fire.

"You need my help?" I ask Devon.

She shakes her head. "If you don't mind, it'd probably be better if you keep exploring. Well, when I say better, it'd be better for me. Because you can bring me the files instead of sending me down into Creepsville to find them. I wonder if there is a Creepsville somewhere. Probably is in America. They have all sorts of silly names. Towns called Gavin and all sorts. I saw it on Google Maps once. Mind-blowing. But yes, if you could bring stuff to us, that'd be fabulous."

Aiko is still eyeing me. "Trying to ditch me, Agent Arthur?" The edge is still there. I'm beginning to think it's not just dark corners I have to fear.

CREEPSVILLE

Considering how much we lost in the plane crash, Malcolm's packing must have been remarkably thorough. We had enough Maglites left over that both Aiko and I are wielding one, and there's a spare one up on the ground floor. Malcolm even gave me spare batteries. He even gave me a fanny pack to carry them in.

Aiko is starting to make me wish he hadn't.

"No," she says, "it's a good look on you. You should wear it more often."

"It's not a fashion statement. It's practical." This is the sort of defense my father would mount.

She nods. "It's stating how practical you are." She pauses. "Among other things." She fails to stifle her smile.

"I am fully aware that it looks stupid." I am not going to get flustered about this. I am not. That would help no one.

"I never said you look stupid."

"Not explicitly, no."

"You want me to be explicit?"

It is getting harder and harder for me to deny that this is flirting. Not that there should be anything wrong with that. I threw my badge at Felicity. We're done. Except every time I think about how much I'm enjoying the verbal sparring, I find myself thinking about Felicity cutting off parts of my anatomy I'd prefer stay attached.

There's a free-spiritedness to Aiko that's been absent from every other girl I've managed to date. They've tended to be serious, sensible women. Something about being a policeman seemed to scare off the girls less concerned about social norms.

But Aiko... well, she's insane of course. She believes in Zurich-based finance gnomes, and assassination conspiracies, and television studios with sets of the moon built inside them. And she spends her weekends putting her life, and quite possibly the lives of others, in danger. It's as if she's in an actual fight with all that is sensible and smart.

And that's tempting in a way that it's never been before.

"We should focus," I say, more to myself than to her, truth be told. "There could be very bad things down here."

"You mean aside from your fanny pack."

"I'm beginning to think," I say, mounting what defense I can, "that you're just jealous. All this obsessing over the fanny pack. You just wish Malcolm gave it to you."

She tries to stifle a laugh and fails. It's an infectious sound.

We are standing, I realize, closer than the width of the corridor or the pool of light cast by our flashlights really requires. I flick my eyes down at her hand, and hope she doesn't notice. It is very close to mine.

I swallow several times. Felicity flashes through my mind again. Her hands. And what would they do if I took other hands? Do I even want to take someone else's hands?

I...

I step away from Aiko, maybe more quickly than is necessary. I push on a door handle.

"Let's try this one." I know I sound flustered even though I'm trying not to.

"What's the matter?" Aiko asks. I can still hear the smile in her voice. "Worried I'm going to try and grab that pack off you?"

Her hand touches my shoulder as I open the door and take a sharp step into the room, sweep my flashlight around it in a swift arc.

"Arthur?" Aiko's hand is still in place.

"Holy…" I sweep the flashlight around the room a second time.

"Arthur?" The humor is draining out of Aiko's voice.

"Do you see this?"

"You're standing in my way." The humor has gone now, but I'm paying far more attention to the room than I am to that.

I step further in. The closest analogue I can think of is Ogden Beauvielle's storage room in the basement of the MI6 building. His collection of artifacts from the world's secret history.

There are vases, and golden plates, and broken crates spilling straw and crockery. But there is more than simple riches. There are bell jars of fluid, mysterious anatomies floating in them, twisted things that don't seem entirely like plants but can't be described as anything else. There are half-unfurled maps of continents I don't recognize. There is a row of tiny shrunken heads, all grinning at me.

"Holy…" Aiko echoes me. Whatever was on the cusp of happening between us is gone now. And if I wasn't so distracted I'd have to decide if I was happy or sad about that, but fortunately I can just let it slide.

We move slowly through the room, lifting the lids from crates, peering into narrow spaces on shelves, beneath dust-crusted tarpaulins. Each new discovery draws a gasp, an expletive. There is a stuffed frog as big as a recliner, a whole crate of jeweled skulls. And then hanging on one wall… I stop.

"Oh that's cool."

"What is it?" Aiko spins around, brings her flashlight's beam to bear on the wall in front of me.

I pull the sword off the wall. The handle is wrapped in worn tan leather straps, a dirty bronze ball marking its end. The hilt is unremarkable and plain. The scabbard though—that is something else entirely.

It glistens ruddy gold in the flashlight's beam. Deep, intricate shadows etch a tree, a garden, figures around it. The detail is astounding, each leaf carefully carved, each vein upon each leaf. I could lose myself in that picture.

"There's an inscription." Aiko points.

I examine the tiny text running around the scabbard's edge. I expect a Cyrillic alphabet but it's in a Roman one. Not that that helps me.

"*Eiecitque Adam et conlocavit ante paradisum voluptatis cherubin et flammeum gladium atque versatilem ad custodiendam viam ligni vitae*," I read. Whether it sounds like that's what I've read or not, I'm not sure.

"I think that's Latin," Aiko says.

"You understand it?"

"A few words." She squints at the sword. "*Vitae* is life, definitely."

I nod. Even I got that one.

"Erm, *cherubin*, I think, refers to..." She squints even harder, puzzled. "Angels?" She shrugs. "Which would mean Adam could well be the biblical Adam. That matches up with where it says *paradisum*."

"I don't remember Adam having a sword." I probably would have paid more attention in Sunday School if he had had one, though.

"No, but the cherubs do if memory serves." She nods to herself. "The warriors of heaven armed with swords of fire or some such."

"Swords of what?" My eyebrows soar along with my hopes.

Aiko's mouth makes a little "o." "You don't think?" she says.

I wrap my hand around the sword's handle. "Only one way to find out."

Aiko looks at the crates. "There's a lot of wood in here."

But I'm beyond caring about silly things like fire safety. This could be a flaming sword, damn it. After all the crap I've put up with, I at the very least deserve a flaming sword. I tear the scabbard away.

And of course there is no flame. Just a dull steel blade reflecting Aiko's flashlight.

And then... A shimmer.

"Was that...?" I hardly dare hope.

And then flame. A great gout of it consuming the blade, billowing up to the ceiling. Aiko shrieks and leaps back, crashing into boxes. I yell too, almost drop the bloody thing, but somehow I keep hold of it in a mad fumble of numb fingers. The flame has settled to a steady burn, writhing up the blade to the tip where it spills away into nothingness.

"Holy shit." Aiko stares. "That is the single most fucking cool thing I have ever seen."

I'm grinning like a child. I look at her. "This totally makes up for the fanny pack, doesn't it?"

55

GROUND FLOOR

"No freaking way!" Jasmine leaps up as we enter the room. She tears across the space between us and stares, mouth open, at the sword.

It is, seriously, my favorite thing ever.

"That is so totally badass." She's holding the sides of her head as if trying to contain the awesome sight before her. "Can I touch it?" Jasmine asks. "Can I? Can I? Please."

"Sure." I let her take it. She wields it above her head with wild abandon, leaving a fiery contrail in her wake.

"We're all going to die," Malcolm comments mildly from where he's sitting, field stripping a pistol. He looks notably less full of girlish excitement.

"Man," Jasmine says, still dancing in lethal circles, "and I thought it was exciting when we found our Russians in the personnel files."

Which stops me for a moment. "Wait... we... we did... what?"

I stare over at Devon who is looking rather smug. "Well," she says, "as previously mentioned, the whole self-trumpeting is not my preferred musical genre, but we've got them I think. Thought I'd let you have your moment with the sword, first. Didn't want to be the raincloud over that parade. I prefer to be associated with skinnier metaphorical images than rainclouds anyway. Of course, sometimes it's unavoidable. And well," she pats her hips, "not exactly like I'm going to hide behind Kate Moss any day soon, is it?"

I smile. "Kate Moss was never my type anyway."

Devon's eyes immediately flick to Aiko.

That's going to be trouble. I just know it is.

But... There is still no time to really deal with that. Or work out how to deal with it. We just found our Russians. "Show them to me," I say to her. "The files. Please."

She hands them to me one by one. "Ivan Spilenski," she says. It's the tall bastard from the British Museum. The ringleader. "Joseph Punin." She hands me the next and it's the round little man from Trafalgar Square. "Urve Potia." A third file. Proto-Lenin. "Ekaterina Kropkin." The angular blond with Terminator-eyes. "Natasha Wiloski." The woman Winston trod on.

"It's them," I say. "We were right. Totally right. About everything." I'm staggered by it. The monumentality of my vindication. I could take this to Shaw now. I could show her this. I could rub it in Coleman's face.

Except... Do I want to take it back to MI37? Can I trust them not to dismiss this? Not to screw it up?

I glance over my shoulder at Aiko. It's an unconscious move.

"The files are cross-referenced," Devon says. "Some stuff we have, some I don't think we do yet. More exploring for you, you lucky devil." Another quick glance at Aiko. "Or maybe you enjoy it."

I'm not touching that with a ten-foot barge pole. "What do we have already?" seems like the quickest way to change the subject.

"Well, here in personnel there are a few more files." She hands me a stack more. The first five I don't recognize. One name stands out, though. Katerina. The woman who scoped out Big Ben. She looks more Asian than Russian to my untrained eye.

Then one I do recognize. "Leo." The teleporter who almost killed me at Trafalgar Square. "Leo Malkin," his file says.

I stare at that face. The bastard. He doesn't look happy here either, his straw-blond hair combed down from a severe parting on the left of his scalp. The sort of cheekbones I wish I had. Good-looking and bent on world destruction. I am totally justified in hating him.

But as I stare at the photo, an oddity strikes me. "How old are these photos?" I ask.

Devon shrugs. "I... I guess they must pre-date the explosion here. So, thirty years at least."

"None of them look like they've aged a day. Leo here should be in his sixties, maybe pushing seventy." I scan the file for something that resembles a birth date. "Holy crap," I say, "this guy was born in 1947." That's impossible.

"They've been affected." Aiko has come over. She peers over my shoulder to get a look at the photo. "They must have been here when the blast happened."

"But they look..." And then I think about how they actually look. And they have changed a little, all of them. Bits and pieces encased in metal. "You're right," I breathe. And then it starts to make sense. Why they're referencing "the West" and "the USSR." "They're from the eighties," I say. "They're time travelers."

No wonder they want to turn back the clock. Thrown from their nation's supposed moment of triumph into a future where Russia has capitulated to capitalism and America is the world's lone superpower.

What's more, they're living proof that intradimensional magic is possible.

"So." Devon stands back a little. "Is that it? Can we go home?" I notice her look toward the ceiling where the sound of dripping water is louder.

I could rub this in Coleman's face.

Could I...?

And still, is that the point of this? Do we need MI37? Do I want us to need them?

And I have to try to rise above all that. I have to try and think of the big picture. Of all the lives, not just some of them.

"Is it enough?" I ask Devon. "Can we find them based on this information?"

"I..." Devon's brow creases. And it's written plainly on her face, what answer she wants to give. It's the answer I want her to give. "Maybe..." she says. "It's all in Cyrillic though, and I only know three words in Russian, and they all mean beer. And that's in spite of a state education system that thinks giving you a pitiful understanding of French is enough of a concession to cries of xenophobia. Still, the numbers are helpful…" She shrugs desperately. As if she thinks a solution will settle there if she can only get them right. "I don't know. I… I don't think so."

I look at the date on my watch. Three days until the deadline. And everyone's looking at me. No one wants to be here. Everyone's thinking about Nikolai.

God, why did I ever fret about Felicity trying to undermine my role as field lead again?

"We stay," I say. "More research. Make sure we get what we need." I look at the disappointed faces. "This is the best and only opportunity we're going to get."

They nod slowly, one by one. Devon last of all.

56

"This is insane." Devon looks up from the papers she's poring over. "Utterly mad."

Lying in a discarded government building less than a mile from the epicenter of the Chernobyl explosion, it takes me a moment to realize she means the papers she's holding.

"Science that defies the laws of reality often seems to go that way," I say.

"No." She shakes her head. "It's more that these groundbreaking experimental thaumato-scientists could not carry the remainder from one division to the next to save their own lives. Literally." She shakes her head. "No wonder they blew the place up."

She's been going through papers since before sunup. The Cyrillic still baffles her, but apparently most of this is math.

"It's all here," she says. "It's pretty transparent even, once you understand some of the underlying concepts. But the math is horrendous."

"Their electronics are pretty solid." Jasmine, lying on her stomach, looks up from a circuit diagram. How a seventeen-year-old runaway became so familiar with such diagrams I'm not sure I want to know. I worry that Malcolm may have been involved.

"Does any of this help us?" I ask her. "Does it get us closer to finding them?" I don't mean to be an arsehole but I'm starting to feel the time crunch.

"Well, not directly," Devon says.

I take a calming breath before I do an impersonation of Felicity losing her shit.

"What it might tell us," Devon carries on oblivious, "is why we're seeing these particles of residual disturbed time and space."

And that does actually sound important. Because without those particles all we have to worry about are the Russians destroying history. Which, while not a total win for us, is significantly better than them destroying all of creation. I'd take it.

"Could you do anything about it?"

Devon's eyebrows go up. "I hadn't really..." She blinks a few times. "I really don't know, truth be told. Maybe. Doesn't look so hard. Like skiing. Just point yourself downhill and go. But, of course, all sorts of potential for limb loss just waiting to leap out at you."

"It doesn't look so hard?" Working with Clyde has taught me to navigate these conversational waters and to cling to the seemingly relevant.

"Did I say that?" Devon looks a little panicked.

"Totally." Jasmine looks up from her diagrams to nod assent.

"Bugger," Devon curses. "Well, I mean, it's largely about electromagnetic forces. But there's some stuff to do with electronic representations of syllabic constructs which I'm a lot fuzzier on."

"Is that what this is for?" Jasmine looks up again. I just thought they were messing about with speakers. She taps the circuit diagram.

"Oh." Devon shrugs, and for a moment the memory of having this sort of conversation with Clyde is almost overwhelming.

What is he up to now? What is Felicity doing?

"Well, I suppose, if I redo the math to work out the discrepancies in their initial calculations, then figure out how to do it all backwards, then feed it into their syllabic algorithm, which seems essentially sound..." She drifts off into mumbling for a few minutes.

"It depends," she says finally.

"On what?"

"How willing Jasmine is to sacrifice her headphones in the name of dubious science."

Jasmine clutches the massive tin cans still strapped to her ears. "I'm warning you," she says, "I've got a gun."

TWO HOURS LATER

Even though we've swept it thoroughly, the pitch blackness of δ-4 is still unsettling. Aiko and I shuffle back toward the stairs, let our flashlights explore every cracked floor tile, every inch of mold. The degradation is worse down here. Half the filing cabinets are rusted shut. Those I could open were usually filled with rotten mush, or had been bored through by rodents long before I arrived.

At least I hope it was rodents. There's really no telling down here.

We reach the stairwell and I look down. Nothing but pitch black oblivion. "How deep do you reckon?" I ask.

Aiko flicks her flashlight down. It illuminates a few more flights, a few more landings, then darkness swallows the beam. "Depends how many flights it takes to get all the way to hell."

For a minute I let my fingers play on the hilt of my flaming sword. I've threaded the scabbard through the strap of Malcolm's fanny pack. It is not—nor will it ever be—*my* fanny pack.

"God I hate this place," Aiko says. She shudders slightly. And considering the abandon with which she was pillaging the remaining paperwork five minutes ago, it all seems a little odd. "Gives me the creeps," she says. And she takes a step toward me.

Oh. I see.

I wish I was someone cooler than I am. That I could exchange girls like I do coins.

Except, then I'd be as big an arsehole as Coleman. So maybe I don't. But it still doesn't help me out here and now.

My awkwardness is rapidly becoming a palpable entity in the stairwell. And I'm the one that feels like the third wheel.

"Arthur," Aiko says. She places a hand on the center of my chest. She doesn't go on.

"Aiko," I say. I'm copying her, to be honest. I have no idea what else to say.

"What the hell is that?"

Not exactly where I saw this conversation going. She pulls her hand away, steps back. And do I have a growth or something?

Then I hear it. An ugly wet scraping sound. Something heavy being dragged across the ground. A dull grunt at the end of it all.

"Seriously, what the hell is that?" Aiko is going for the gun stuffed into the waistband of her pants.

For one psychotic moment I worry that it is somehow Felicity, enraged and monstrous, coming to slap me for even contemplating a dalliance here.

That would be... Yeah, that would be insane.

Slowly, I pull the sword from its scabbard. Flickering yellow light fills the stairwell.

"Let's go upstairs," I say. "Really, really carefully."

"How about we run up the stairs like the bat out of hell itself is on our heels?"

Which, given all that we've seen so far, might actually be what is going on here.

"Sounds like a plan." I turn on my heel, toes skidding across the dull cement of the basement floor. But it's already too late.

I hear the soft crash of the thing's body against the stairwell wall. I bunch my knees.

An enormous weight sledgehammers into my back.

I sprawl, fling my arms out wide so I don't impale myself on my sword. I even take the opportunity to grind my jaw against the ground. I spray spittle laced with a side order of blood and pain.

"Oh sh—" Aiko's expletive is cut off by the floor.

I struggle onto my back. Try to look at what's handing us our arses today.

I wish I hadn't.

It's like a clipping error in a video game. Three frogs, stacked imprecisely on top of each other, each one seated within the one below. Four legs are planted squarely on the ground, eight wave ungainly in the air. One squat face stares at me. Two more sprout painfully above and behind it, mouths twisted, features distorted.

It's roughly the size of an ottoman. Either the footstool or one of the Turkish sultans if he was bent down. Doesn't matter. Too bloody big for a frog if you ask me.

"All right, you—" I start, clambering to my feet.

A tongue whips out of the face staring at me. It's about the breadth of my arm and the length of my nightmares. I take it full in the face. It feels like being bitch-slapped with a brick wrapped in snot.

My feet bid farewell to the ground. I arc like an acrobat. I land like a sack of shit.

I take a break from the fight to stare dazedly at the ceiling waiting for the pain to subside to the point where I can breathe again. As fun as that is, though, there is absolutely no way I am letting something as revolting as a mutant frog eat me. Some sort of killer wolf with fangs and a tail of fire: maybe. But I so do not want to be the guy remembered for getting noshed on by a giant amphibian.

I roll toward it, which, while it minimizes the threat posed by the tongue, turns out to be a mistake with a flaming sword. Instead of coming up with a swing and a battle cry, it's more of a hop and a yelp.

Froggy slams me in the gut with another tongue-slap.

"Are you—?" I hear Aiko ask over the rush of the breath leaving my lungs. But I have had it with being embarrassed by this thing.

I lunge breathlessly at the creature, sword stretched out wildly in front of me. It's not a move of great elegance or finesse, but I'm making up for that by being too close to bloody miss.

Except I do.

My sword hits empty air. There's no frog there. The stairwell is empty.

I hear something land behind me. I almost have time to turn before—

Thwack. Something slimy collides with the side of my head. I collide with the wall. I stare groggily at the frog.

"It teleports?" I ask the world at large. "It bloody teleports?"

I go at it then, a mad dervish. I heft the sword above my head, whirl it in huge circles. Flame crackles like an angry halo.

I hit space. Space again. Empty space. Each time I close, the frog moves. Its tongue slaps me, knocks me this way and that. I am drenched in frog spittle. I yell, let my rage out at it. My frustration. If I could just chop off the end of its tongue. So I could jam it up its irritating, teleporting arse.

The tongue catches me under my chin, a perfect oral haymaker that lifts me off my feet and plants me against one wall.

The frog and I regard each other from across the stairwell. I swear the bastard thing is smiling.

"You know what," I say, "as cool as this sword is—"

I lever myself half off the ground.

Its tongue sits me right back down.

"Screw it." I just yank out my gun and shoot the bloody thing.

Three short thunderclaps. Holes appear in the frog. Blood sprays, decorates the wall. The frog dances and rolls. Then lies dead and still.

Slowly, painfully, I get up off the floor. Aiko, who seems to have escaped the whole incident remarkably slime free, looks at me apologetically. "I was totally with you on the sword thing," she says. "Would have been awesome. But, well…" She shrugs. "Maybe the fanny pack is more your speed after all?"

She's making light, but her hands are shaking. And I should take the joke in the spirit it was intended, but all my battered pride will allow me to say is, "Oh shut up," as I start to hobble up the stairs.

57

"A giant teleporting frog?" I am not sure if Devon is more disdainful of the quality of monster I am fighting, or my inability to do so proficiently.

I look at her sourly. I swear I can hear Jasmine snickering in the background.

"Oh, Arthur, I'm sorry." Devon seizes me in a bear-crusher of a hug. Considering the residual frog spit covering me, it's pretty decent of her.

"No, I'm sorry," I say, once I can get air back in my lungs. "Just... being beaten up wasn't the most fun."

I'd been so excited about the sword too. I was looking forward to my Errol Flynn moment. Swinging on a chandelier and diving over a grand staircase.

That said, considering how this stuff normally goes, I'd be lucky to get a bare bulb and a stripper pole most days.

"Would it cheer you up if I told you I thought I could blow up disrupted space-time particles?"

I weigh this information. "How big of an explosion do they make?"

"Very small individually. But if you get a big pocket it could make quite the boom."

"Let's find a *really* big pocket."

"Att-a-boy."

α-1

We're in the room where Nikolai died. Devon pauses at the small cross we made for him, mutters something under her breath. She's holding a tangle of wires and circuitry attached to a naked speaker.

Aiko, Malcolm, and Jasmine have come along for the show too. Jasmine is headphone-less. She regards Devon's messy little machine with something like hatred.

"The headphones were a worthy sacrifice," I tell her.

"You, like, totally realize that frog was karma, right?" she asks me.

Devon looks at her sympathetically. "Would you like to blow something up too?"

Jasmine grimaces, then shrugs, defeated. "Sure."

Devon holds out the wires to Jasmine. She takes the messy thing, then examines it, turning it over several times. Finally she looks up. "Like, how does it work?"

"Well," Devon says, "you point the speaker at the disturbance." Jasmine sorts the apparatus out from the tangle, and grips it delicately in one hand. "Then you take those buttons in the other." Jasmine organizes an accretion of circuitry into her left hand. The wires connecting the two parts make it look something like an electronic nunchuk. "And you press play."

Jasmine looks at her. "That's it?"

"Wait," says Aiko.

Jasmine huffs angrily.

Aiko won't be distracted. "So if this works," she says, "then it's going to cause the disturbed space-time particles to detonate?"

I nod, keen to get to the exploding part. "Thereby posing less of a threat to the Chronometer and random bystanders."

"Blowing shit up poses *less* of a threat?"

Aiko's quizzical expression gives me pause for thought.

"Well," Devon intercedes, the proud parent defending her child, "it's a question of degrees. An explosion, in general terms, is not a wonderful, happy, shiny thing. Not the sort of thing one puts in a box, wraps in paper, and gives to a child, for example. Well, excepting certain children in the class of Mrs. Bradmoor around twenty-three years ago. Maybe Kenneth McWhirter, for example.

For him and his derisive comments about a girl's enthusiasm for chocolate custard, an exception could be made. But, yes, as I was saying, in general terms, that's a no-no. But here we're dealing with a more specific case, sort of a sliding scale from, say, nothing going wrong at all, to explosions, all the way to ungluing parts of people in time and space. And also, while I don't want to be seen as the squeaky wheel demanding some oil, maybe we could all consider that I just retroengineered this from what was, quite frankly, some shitty math, written in a language that I don't actually speak, so maybe a little slack is in order."

We all contemplate that for a moment. "All right then." Aiko nods. "Let's blow some shit up."

Jasmine crosses the room until she's about five paces from the water. "Is this good?" she asks.

Devon nods.

Jasmine presses the button.

The thin sheet of plastic over the speaker ripples. At first I don't hear anything, but then there's a sound like muttering, like a record played backwards. It's an ugly sound, tinny and raw. Jasmine makes a face.

"Is this—" she starts.

A ball of fire fills the air above the pool of water from which the catfish emerged. There's a percussive clap that rocks Jasmine back on her feet and ruffles my hair. Steaming drops of water spray about the room.

"Yeah!" Jasmine whoops.

But the fire hasn't finished. A flickering flame lingers in the air, racing up the height of the little waterfall. It spits and sparkles, fiery strands of light spinning away and fizzling out.

"Oh shit," Devon says.

We all turn to her.

"Why—" I start, and then the next explosion knocks me off my feet.

Water sprays across the room. I see something unfolding out of the water, massive and on fire. A shapeless blob of scales that expands and expands out before collapsing into nothing. Then suddenly bursts into existence again, still wreathed in fire. And it's gone before it hits the wall.

Trails of fire are racing up and down through the hole the waterfall fell through.

"Shit, shit, shit." Devon is cursing as she picks herself up.

"What's happening?" Malcolm is not in the most amused mood.

"It's propagating." Devon is already moving toward the doors, the stairs up. "The particles of disturbed space-time are too densely packed. It's like we've lit a match in a gunpowder factory."

"And we didn't think of this before we tried out the device?" Aiko is frozen by her outrage.

Devon is framed in the doorway. "They're undetectable particles." Devon is talking with her hands, and her hands are saying "Panic!"

"You know," she adds, "you really should be running away right now."

Another boom emphasizes the point. The floor shakes. We run.

We hit the stairs. More blasts, both above and below. The floor shakes. I rattle between wall and banister. The rusted thing creaks ominously. I think of teleporting frogs and find my balance.

We hit the first floor just as part of the ceiling gives way. The world becomes a stinking, rasping cloud trying to erase my lungs. I cough and spit. The sound of collapsing concrete races after me. I lose sight of Aiko in the swirling clouds. I call out and hear nothing.

Another explosion. More felt than heard. I pick up the pace. A wall looms out of nowhere. I crash into it, spin away, smash through a doorway. The room is clear but blank. Dead end. I back up. A blast spits fire at me, knocks me flying. I land on the floor. It's not soft.

Another doorway ahead of me. A chance for an exit. I pump my legs, push my body toward it. Another explosion. The wall around the door quakes, ripples like water.

The door comes down, heavy concrete lintel smashing inches in front of my feet. I skid to a stop, graze my nose on rubble.

There's more smoke than dust now.

Another explosion. Another.

And what a stupid bloody way to die after all this.

I spin around, try to retrace my steps. A window. I just need a window. Anything.

Another explosion. Another. Another.

I'm choking, coughing, blundering. I'm down on my hands and knees.

Something massive and gibbering scrambles out of smoke towards me. Some horror of fur and flesh, its form liquid and malleable. It's past me before I can even figure out what it used to be.

Another explosion. Another. And then one more. It must be in the room next to me. As it lifts me off my feet, I think about that. Try to locate its point of origin. As I sail through the air I realize I was next to a door, and wonder if the thing was ripped off its hinges, if it's going to hit me before I'm mashed against a wall. With adrenaline going, you really can think about a lot of things. About Felicity. About Aiko.

Glass shatters around me. I try and work out where it came from.

And then falling. And then the ground. Wet, and muddy, and not at all how I expected it. And then the smoke is pouring away from me. Pouring up into the sky.

The sky.

I can see the sky.

I am lying on my back, outside, staring at a window I just smashed through, staring at a Russian government facility, on fire and collapsing. And above it: the sky.

Strong hands grab me under my shoulders. I let them pull me away, let my head loll, my thoughts slowly arrange themselves back into something like cohesion.

"Thanks, Malcolm," I manage to say as my feet bump over the twisted asphalt.

"Not quite a compliment," Aiko replies.

I twist in her hands, almost forcing her to drop me. And it is her there. "You're strong for your size," I manage.

"Still not sure if that's a compliment."

I think I might have a slight concussion, but I start to laugh. Aiko laughs too. It lets a little of the terror wash out.

She drags me to where the others stand. We make a small tight knot, looking back at the damage we've caused. The building comes down piece by piece, collapsing in upon itself, choking the endless basement levels.

Slowly, carefully, Jasmine hands Devon back the little knot of wires and circuit boards.

"Well," Devon says, "on the plus side, we know it works."

58

A ROAD, SEVERAL HOURS LATER

It is not a comfortable or easy walk through the shattered city of Pripyat. It is not fun slogging down the roads that come afterwards. Jasmine and Devon complain more than me. Malcolm less.

When we hit the first village, Malcolm assures us he will get us a ride. I half expect him to tell us that he knows a guy who knows a guy, but it turns out that he has a fanny pack on that's full of hundred-dollar bills. Then he removes half of its contents. Apparently that's our much touted exit strategy. And apparently Antonina, a savvy-looking local woman, knows a good deal when it walks into her grocery store.

One extortion later and she leads us to a truck that looks like it comes from the same trash pile as all of Nikolai's vehicles, and tells us the ride to Kiev—home of the nearest international airport—will take a while. Then she sits up front in the cab, her eight-year-old daughter beside her, and I sit in the truck bed and see if my bruised bones can be physically shaken from my body.

At least, I think, as a pothole in the road lifts me six inches out of my rough seat for approximately the nine billionth time, there is a plan.

KIEV

It's almost three a.m. when we check into the hotel. I was expecting a student motel with fifteen to a room, but apparently Malcolm is picky about where he sleeps.

"If I'm going to spend a third of my life doing it, I'm going to be comfortable," he informed Antonina after rejecting her first five hotel choices. This apparently convinced her that she should have tried to get more money from us, and we have to walk the last fifteen blocks.

The clerk, though, is a friendly fellow, more so than seems reasonable at such an hour; and being more bonesore and world-weary than I feel anyone should ever feel, I take advantage of this to pressure him into opening the bar for me. He pours me a double of some mystery whiskey and then, mercifully, leaves me alone.

I sit in the half-light of a single lamp, and try to work out what's eating at me. We're not doing too badly, truth be told. Sure I've taken some knocks today, the worst of them possibly on my posterior, but we've still got two days before the deadline. We're closer than we've ever been to ending this.

Maybe I'm just tired.

But then the real reason walks into the bar.

"Mind if I join you?" Aiko doesn't wait for me to reply. The desk clerk scurries over and she points to my glass, which may not be particularly wise, but a silent minute later she has her own. She takes a sip and sighs.

"Quite the trip," she says, nodding to herself. "Quite the trip."

"Yes," I say, fully aware of how monosyllabic I am. This sort of thing seems to reduce me to caveman levels of verbalism.

"So." Aiko looks up at me from her glass. She's changed into a pair of dark green cargo shorts and a loose white T-shirt proclaiming "I shot Kennedy." It hangs off one shoulder. She has very smooth skin. "Why did you come to the Ukraine, Agent Arthur?" Aiko asks. "Business or pleasure?"

Oh Lordy.

It is, in the end, a question about the future. A question that extends beyond the Russians' deadline, about life after the seventeenth. Assuming there is life beyond then. And I have been sticking resolutely to the short term.

But here Aiko is, and she's asking me where I stand. When the chips have all fallen where they may, am I with MI37 or the Weekenders? With Felicity or her?

I look up at Aiko. She is a pretty woman. A clever woman. A good woman. A good human being. She makes me laugh. I admire her.

But…

Jesus.

It's all true of Felicity too. Except, that makes them sound the same. And they are so not the same. There is something so very fundamentally different about them both.

And I know, I can be certain that I belonged with Felicity. I felt that, albeit fleetingly. She was the person I wanted. But now? Who am I now? Who is she now? And does that even matter? Because, surely, regardless of whether the world survives, I don't think our relationship will.

So surely there's no real question here.

Except… Jesus, why can nothing ever seem sure?

I begin to realize it's been quite a long time since Aiko asked her question.

"Maybe," she takes a substantial swig from her whiskey, "I should put it another way."

I remain resolutely noncommittal.

"I like you, Arthur," she says. "I think we both know that. We both do now." Another gulp of whiskey. "And I think we both know that your girlfriend doesn't like you anymore. So," she finishes the whiskey, "the only thing I don't know now is whether you like me."

Oh crap. And it's all so simple when she lays it out like that. All so easy. Logical. Except logic doesn't seem to apply to my life anymore. Maybe it never has when it comes to the heart. And now I have to figure out how to explain that, when I can barely explain it to myself.

"Aiko—" I start.

She closes her eyes, shakes her head. And even the tone of my voice is enough.

"There is one other way I can put this," she says. She stands. I think she's going to leave. And part of me feels like an ass for having pushed away such an obvious opportunity, and part of me is so relieved I have to suppress the accompanying sigh.

And then she leans in and she kisses me.

Her lips touch mine. Soft as a breath. My mouth opens slightly, as much shock as... well, at least half shock. She slips my bottom lip between her two. My breath is caught. What if I am caught...?

Caught by who?

And then she pulls away. My breath so short it's an actual little person.

"I—" I start.

"Think about it," she says. "But, speaking selfishly, it'd be nice if you made your mind up soon."

She gives me a smile, a beautiful smile, then turns and leaves. I stay sitting, staring at the empty whiskey glass, at the smudge her lips made on the glass.

And if I made the right decision or the wrong one, I honestly don't know.

59

THIRTY-FIVE THOUSAND FEET ABOVE THE NORTH SEA AND DESCENDING. OCTOBER 16TH

"So," Devon leans across the aisle of the 757 and gives me a conspiratorial wink, "I am assuming you have a terribly cunning plan for when we land about how to find these dastardly Russians."

Terribly cunning might be exaggerating the extent of my planning. The ratio between terrible and cunning has been somewhat negatively affected by the fact that I've spent a large portion of the flight failing to not think about either Felicity or Aiko. The latter of those women has spent the whole flight sitting directly in front of me, not turning around once. She has pulled her hair into two small pigtails. I have studied them to the point where I could now pretty much write an algorithm for their movement in response to turbulence. On other subjects I am less edified.

"We need access to the full KGB files on our Russians," I whisper, looking up and down the aisle for any stewards who seem overly interested in our conversation. There are, unsurprisingly, none. "We have their names, some associates. But we need things like aliases. Or known contacts. Or safe houses. More about them, about how they operate in London."

"So," Jasmine leans over from my other side, "like who has the KGB files?"

I grimace. Not because I don't know where they are, but because, a few days ago, I walked out of that building swearing never to return.

"MI6," I say.

"Oh," Jasmine says. "Like, shit."

"No chance you can hack into those files is there?" I ask Devon.

"I can't hack anything," she says. "That's Tabitha's game. And Clyde's." She wrinkles her nose. "The sort of underhanded, unpleasant thing that dirty little people who can't keep their hands out of the cookie jar would do if you ask me. Legitimate computing needs not good enough for them. Doesn't matter how many years of good service the old computer may have given them. Once the odd part needs trading in, and there are new models on the showroom floor. So it's time to trade in, apparently. No need to let the old computer know. It'll figure it out. If its processing speed is up to it."

Air stewards are starting to look our way now.

"It's OK." I pat her hand. I'm not sure what else to do. "It's fine."

"You can't just, like, ask one of the old MI37 folks to do it for you?" Jasmine asks.

Devon almost spits into the aisle.

"Relations were strained last time we spoke," I say. "And there's this whole thing with them needing to arrest us both. And we don't know anyone at MI6. And I doubt anyone Malcolm knows is suicidal enough to want to break into Vauxhall Cross."

"Are you saying, Arthur," Devon looks at me, "that we are, in the common parlance, screwed?"

In front of me, Aiko's pigtails bob. I pause. Because what I suppose I'm really doing is laying the groundwork for asking Devon to do something really unpleasant.

"There is one person I can think of."

"Who?" Devon is watching me warily. She can see the shadow of the trap closing over her and is trying to work out if she has time to escape its clutches.

"Kayla would do it," I say. "If you asked her."

Devon is very quiet.

"Who's Kayla?" Jasmine asks. "Is she the grumpy goth one, or the one with the awesome sword?"

"She's the one," Devon replies, "with the awesome sword and an alarming preponderance for treating me like a pre-pubescent child. You bloody ask her." This last statement is stabbed in my direction.

"She wouldn't do it if I asked her. She's not one hundred percent fond of me."

"I shouted at her a lot," Devon protests.

"She's the forgiving sort."

"She's the sort to stab people long before the forgiving process has a chance to begin," Devon comes back.

Which is a fair point, to be honest, but not one likely to get us closer to Devon begging this favor.

"She'll forgive you," I say, as convincingly as I can, "precisely because she has an enormous affinity for you."

Devon regards me as balefully as she is able. "You know," she says, "I think I'm beginning to see why Kayla doesn't like you."

LONDON, 8:36 P.M.

Bushy Park is not one of London's better known royal parks. It's a gem though. A beautiful ocean of green in the urban mix. That is, right up until sundown. At which point it becomes a bit large, and out of the way, and full of suspicious shadows.

I fight monsters for a living, and I'm still enough of a city lad to jump at a deer crossing the path in front of us.

Still, Devon informs us that one of the many things I don't know about Kayla is her love of taking evening strolls in Bushy Park whenever she's in the city.

Aiko, Devon, and I wait by the large fountain at the park's heart. Aiko and I still haven't really talked since the evening in Kiev. And yet it's Devon who is the tense one. I think she's starting to regret agreeing to this entire plan in fact.

And then, around quarter to nine, I see a round-shouldered figure slouching towards us.

"That's—" I start.

"Yes." Devon nods. She swallows several times. I don't know if her face is in the shadows by accident or design; I don't know what emotions are brewing.

She steps out into the pathway. The plan is for her to make first contact, and then, if she thinks it's important or helpful, I'll step up too. Patting her legs three times is the best signal we could come up with. Malcolm seemed to not think much of it, but he didn't go as far as offering his own.

I'm not sure how into subterfuge Malcolm is. I get the impression he'd rather kick in the doors at 85 Vauxhall Cross and see how things went from there.

Devon walks slowly toward Kayla, mirroring her shuffling gait. Neither of them seem anxious to get very far very quickly. Then Kayla looks up and abruptly stops. I can see her looking at Devon. Devon catches the change and stops too. They stand looking at each other.

Then Kayla moves. I barely catch it. The barest suggestion of movement, and then she's fifteen feet from where she started, standing tight behind Devon's back.

60

"Oh shit." Aiko fumbles in her waistband for another of Malcolm's illicit guns.

I put my hand on her arm. Then I hesitate for a moment because I've had the audacity to physically touch her. And then I get over myself a little.

"That's not necessarily aggression," I say. Then I think about it. This is Kayla after all. "Well, it's probably aggression. Everything's pretty much on a sliding scale with Kayla. But this isn't so bad for her."

"But if it turns bad…?" Aiko tries to pull her arm out of my grasp.

"Then we'll all be dead before you get the gun up," I say.

Aiko doesn't look exactly happy about that. But it's hard to be happy when confronted with the fact that if Kayla wants to kill you, she just will. On the plus side, it does add a frisson of danger to staff meetings that is usually inherently lacking.

Kayla and Devon remain a frozen tableau for a few seconds more. Fortunately Kayla seems to decide against impaling Devon, so it's good I read Kayla correctly on that one.

Then Devon reaches out her hand and slaps her thigh three times.

Personally I'd imagined it would happen a little more naturally, and not like a moment of jazz hands in the middle of something that resembles a hostage negotiation.

Still, I pick myself up off the bench, give Aiko a hopeful smile, and head in their direction.

"Hello, Kayla," I say.

She barely even looks at me. Devon gives me a look that is less than encouraging.

"Will you help us?" I ask Kayla.

The shrug is a bare flicker of movement.

I'm honestly not sure what that means. I wait for further information but it doesn't come. "I..." I say.

"No." Kayla's monosyllable is barely audible.

Right then...

"Will you tell Coleman you saw us?"

Another minimalist shrug.

"Come on, Kayla," I say. "Please."

Not even a glimmer of anger from her. Not even a spark. She stands there as near to lifeless as she can be.

"No," she says eventually.

I let out a breath of relief. Now this is just useless, not actually hazardous.

"Why not?" Devon asks. She's still standing with Kayla behind her. I wonder if Kayla bothered drawing her sword. I doubt it. I don't know what she'd fight for right now. It's as if everything has been taken away from her, out of her.

"You don't want my help." I have to lean in to catch the words.

"Well of course I do," Devon snaps. "I'm here bloody asking for it."

Not quite the gently-gently approach I'd have taken. Kayla doesn't even respond to it, though. Just stands there staring over my shoulder.

I just need to snap her out of it, to...

Sometimes words come into my head and I wish that they didn't. Because they're usually not awesome for my chances of survival. But... Hell, it's been a good week for stupid things.

"What would Ophelia want?"

Finally Kayla makes eye contact. It's like staring at an event horizon.

"To be alive," she says. Each word is a tombstone falling. And

I have nothing to come back against that with. I know it's not my fault Kayla's daughter is gone, but it doesn't make the unspoken accusation any easier to deal with.

Kayla stares at me a moment longer, then drops her eyes. We all stand for a few moments longer. A frozen tableau.

"Come on," I finally say to Devon. "Let's go."

Devon hesitates then steps away from Kayla. Kayla makes no move. We walk away. We're almost back to the bench when Devon looks over her shoulder. Kayla is still standing there, frozen.

"You couldn't save your daughter," Devon calls, "but now you have the chance to save the whole world." She stands and watches for any effect the words have. If they have one, I don't catch it.

"Waste of time." Devon shakes her head.

THE LAMB AND FLAG, 9:17 P.M.

"Well now we're proper fucked, aren't we?" Aiko counts off the ways on her fingertips. "Can't get into MI6. Can't get the aliases. Can't find the Russians. Can't stop them."

At least she didn't have to use both hands.

"What if we gave the files to Shaw?" Devon asks.

"No." Aiko slaps her hand down on the table. She looks around the rest of the group, eyes coming to rest on me. "No, right?"

I want to agree with her.

I want to disagree with her.

I...

"We still can't trust them," I say. In the end, that's the heart of the problem. "Not to do the right thing. And not to do the right thing right."

I put my head in my hands. "No one will let us into MI6." I talk at the table. "So we have to break into MI6." It's an absurd thing to say.

"Well that's just being plain silly," Devon points out.

Except, God, I don't know another way. I think it's what we have to do.

We have to break into MI6. A mad plan. God, I don't even know where to start. We'd need... An ID badge. A disguise, probably.

Wait... Is that it?

Balls, I suppose. We'll need really big ones of those.

I look up. Nobody is looking as if a lightbulb has gone bright in their mind.

"Who could we steal an MI6 ID from?" I ask.

Aiko's eyebrows perform a quite athletic leap up her forehead. "Seriously?"

"Our timeline runs out at six p.m. tomorrow. That's less than twenty-four hours. At this point I'm willing to try anything."

"What about, like, your girlfriend?" Jasmine says. "Couldn't you go, be all like, 'take me back' and swipe the ID out of her pocketbook while—"

"—she's calling for back-up?" I complete. I shrug, trying to ignore the fact that Aiko is giving Jasmine dirty looks. "I mean, maybe. But she's pretty sharp. And I don't know if any of us could really pass for Felicity even with a disguise." I scan the table. "Wrong body types."

"Disguise?" Malcolm contemplates this.

"What about that unutterable shit, Clyde?" Devon asks. "Just put on a mask and try to shag every little whore that comes within six feet of you and nobody should be able to tell the difference."

"Clyde's seven feet tall," I point out, "and capable of hiding behind broomsticks."

More silence. More contemplation of the wood grain.

"You're about Coleman's height," Devon says into that silence.

"I'm nothing like that arsehole." It's a knee-jerk verbal response, but I'll stand by it.

"No." Devon apparently won't. "You're actually fairly similar builds. I mean he's got a bit of a paunch on you, and that godawful mustache, but it's fairly obvious Shaw has a definite 'type.' Like me and men who look exactly like Patrick Swayze. Except I'm never their type, it seems."

A type? Coleman and I are the same type? Felicity's type? Even Devon's waffling at the end didn't take the sting out of that one.

I take a drink and try to let the red drain from my vision.

Flop, flop, flop.

I take a few more sips for good measure.

"But," Aiko says to me, "don't you and Coleman sort of despise each other from the bottoms of your souls? He's not going to just give you his ID."

Which is very true. Except...

I look at Devon.

"Oh no," she says. "Me and my bloody mouth."

"What?" Jasmine looks from me to Devon and back.

"Coleman doesn't hate everyone in MI37," I say.

Aiko's eyebrows bounce back up. Jasmine's join them.

"I won't do it." Devon is shaking her head, waving her hands, physically leaning away from the suggestion. "I can't. There is no way on earth."

"The greater good, Devon," I say. "The fate of the very world."

"You made me sacrifice my headphones," Jasmine adds, apparently unafraid of the more personal guilt trip. And more power to her for it, I say.

"All you have to do is flirt a little bit with him." I emphasize the word "little," try to make the pill easier to swallow.

"He keeps his ID in his pants pocket." Devon can't keep the horror out of her voice. "How am I meant to get that?"

I try to suppress any sort of visible blanching at that thought, but I'm not sure how successful I am, because Devon throws up her hands and says, "See!"

"The greater good," I say weakly.

Devon looks at me. "First Kayla. Now this? You know, Arthur, I think there's a chance you're no better than Clyde."

61

ONE HOUR LATER

As unrealistic as it may be, I did sort of imagine that Coleman would live in some sort of fetid swamp alone with other bottom feeders and amphibious scum.

On the other hand, a flat in Knightsbridge seems relatively close.

I was a little worried we'd have to go through the phone book looking up every Coleman in London, but fortunately the arrogant arsehole had given Devon his card. On it he wrote, "Any time. Any position. xxx." I am again reminded of my loathing for this man.

"I hate you all," Devon tells us. Which seems a little unfair considering we splurged on a new dress for her, along with new shoes and a bottle of dubious champagne.

Jasmine picks a rogue tag free from the dress.

"OK." Aiko holds Devon by her newly bared shoulders. "Remember. Get the key card, then get it out of the apartment however you can. Dropping it out of a window is preferential."

"You do realize you're asking me to remove his pants."

Aiko shakes her head. "Not necessarily, no."

"You want me to reach into his pants pocket while he's still in them?"

I throw up a little in my mouth.

"Yeah," Aiko nods, "get him to take them off."

"Then leg it," Jasmine adds.

"If I end up having to Bobbitt him," Devon says, "I want you all to swear you'll defend me in court."

"To the ends of the earth," I promise.

"I still hate you."

She steps out of the car and marches toward the door as purposefully as her new heels will let her.

We sit tensely across the street, watching as she rings the bell. She speaks to a grate. She pushes the door open.

"Must have buzzed her up," Aiko says.

None of us say a word.

Devon disappears through the door. Extra lights come on, brightening the third floor. Coleman's floor. The lights having flared, dim but do not go out.

"I feel like we've done something awful." Jasmine is squeezed into the back seat between Aiko and Malcolm.

"Me too," I say.

"Me too," Malcolm rumbles.

We all turn to stare at him.

"What?" He shrugs. "I do."

I look at the three of them cramped together in the back of the car.

"Does one of you want to sit up here in the front? We could be some time."

There are some very rapidly exchanged looks. The amount of subtext to seemingly everyday interactions is getting out of hand.

"It can be Aiko," I say, because it's easier to just do that at this point.

Jasmine arches one eyebrow very high indeed. "Did you two—?"

"No," Aiko and I say at the same time.

"You didn't know what I was going to say." Jasmine looks forlorn.

"Yes they did," Malcolm rumbles as Aiko gets out of the car and comes up to sit beside me.

"You know she likes you though, right?" Jasmine says.

"Jasmine," Malcolm rumbles.

"Jaz!" Aiko snaps.

I close my eyes. The more things change…

"Yes," I say. "I know."

"And what?" Jasmine asks. "You don't like her back?"

My eyes stay closed. "No," I say. "I like her very much."

"So what's the problem?" she asks. "Why haven't you—"

"Jasmine."

"Jaz!"

"I have…" And how do I put it into words? "I have a… prior commitment." That doesn't sound right.

"To the ice queen?" Jasmine is incredulous.

"Let it go, Jaz." At least Aiko sounds as embarrassed as I feel.

And why won't I let Felicity go? What is the problem? Even if I don't have an answer for Jasmine, or even one for Aiko, shouldn't I have one for myself?

I miss her.

That's it. In a nutshell. I miss Felicity Shaw. She made me happy. Making her happy made me happy. I miss that.

God, I didn't just leave because she was making me unhappy, but because I was making her unhappy too, and it was killing me.

Shit. I think I really like Felicity Shaw.

What a stupid bloody time to realize that.

"Just seems stupid is all," Jasmine grouches from the back seat.

"The heart is stupid all the time," I say. Not loudly. Not really for her. For myself. A little bit for Aiko.

"That's what I keep hoping." She gives me a soft smile.

And here and now is really not the time for this conversation.

I look up at Coleman's flat. At the clock in the car. Five minutes elapsed. Jesus, only five. It's going to be a long night with this crowd.

Which is when one of Coleman's windows suddenly flies open. Devon is there waving frantically. A tiny white rectangle flies out of her hand and away into some bushes below. She waves twice more, and then suddenly, violently, disappears back inside.

We all stare.

"What the hell?" Aiko bursts the silence.

"She got it," I say, staring in disbelief at the closed window. "She already got it."

"His pants are down already?" Jasmine seems caught between disgust and admiration.

"We should get her out." I'm worried. That is not a healthy timeline for pants removal.

"No." Malcolm is definitive.

"She could be in trouble up there." Malcolm is too big for me to add, "you bastard."

"We have a signal," Malcolm says. "If she's in trouble she'll let us know. That wasn't the signal."

"She's not a trained field agent!" I snap back.

"If you'll forgive me," Malcolm studies his hand momentarily then meets my eye square on, "I think she can handle herself as well as some trained field agents I've met."

Ouch.

There again...

"Just go and get the bloody card already," Aiko says. "Quicker we get you to MI6, the quicker we get back here for any necessary extraction."

I hesitate, hand on the door. They're right though. We're committed. If we don't pull this off, the world ends tomorrow. Time to go all in. I open the car door and go to get the bloody card already.

85 VAUXHALL CROSS

The biggest chance of disaster, it seems to me as I cross the lobby of 85 Vauxhall Cross, is that I'm going to sneeze this ridiculous fake mustache off. It itches like a bastard.

The paunch is a little better. Some of Malcolm's old socks held in place by reams of gauze to give that natural, I've-been-drinking-pretty-solidly-for-twenty-years sort of look. The effect isn't exactly flawless, but it is frightening how little else needed to be done to make me stand up to at least a cursory glance.

Which is all the guard gives me. Though that isn't as relieving as I thought it might be. Defense of our realm and all that.

Sweat coats my palm as I swipe the ID before the metal scanner. There's a dish for me to empty my pockets into. I do so. Keys.

Spare change. The flash drive Jasmine gave me to copy the files onto. My wallet.

Oh Jesus, my wallet.

My wallet with its clear plastic pocket and my Arthur Wallace driver's license on full bloody display. I turn it over carefully, place it face down in the tray. I glance back at the security guard at the door. And fortunately the whole eyes-in-the-back-of-the-head thing is still an unrealized security feature.

But he must have some MI-sixth sense, because he looks back at me as I look back at him.

"Let me help you with that." He takes a few steps over.

"Oh," I start, and realize I sound nothing like Coleman. I try again. "Oh," I say in the new voice, then realize this guy doesn't know what Coleman sounds like and talking to him in two voices is probably not increasing my chances of looking like a regular employee. So then I just say nothing, which I'm not sure helps anything either.

The guard takes the tray. The wallet rocks slightly on the bulge of change. I watch the lip of the driver's license. Don't drop it, I pray as the guard transfers the tray from one side of the gate to the other. Don't spill a thing. Don't try to hand me anything. He lays it down. The wallet rocks one more time and lies still.

I let out a sigh of relief and then try and stifle it. The guard is still right there, looking at me.

"Thank you," I say in my Coleman voice. I figure I've committed to that now, and take a step toward the metal detector before catching myself.

My gun.

God, the last thing I need is the guy to wand me, to detect the strange unwashed sock odor emanating from beneath my shirt.

I pull my pistol from my shoulder holster and hand it to the guard. I compose myself, straighten for the metal detector.

I glance over at the guard. He is looking at my gun. A quizzical expression is on his face.

"Is there a problem?" I really don't want to know the answer to that question.

The guard drums his fingers on his radio.

"This gun, sir," he says. "Not exactly standard issue, is it?"

62

Oh crap. And no. It's not a standard-issue pistol at all. It's the dodgy black-market pistol of dubiousness Malcolm gave me. Something to do with the bullets being difficult to trace and filed-off serial numbers. Not something that sounded astoundingly legal.

"No," I say to the guard, unable to bluff in the face of such overwhelming evidence. "Not standard issue at all." I have an urge to plunge through the gate and just see how far I get. I manage to suppress it, though.

"Get a special dispensation for it, did you, sir?"

"Yes." I swallow and sweat harder than any innocent man ever would. "That's exactly what I did."

The guard grimaces. I almost soil my underwear.

"Been trying to get one for my Browning forever," he says. "Don't really like the action on the ones they give us." He shrugs. "Above my pay grade, I suppose." He gestures to the metal detector. "If you'd just step through."

I almost pass out with relief. I almost skip through the detector. I have enough trouble just keeping the grin off my face.

I'm in.

* * *

OUTSIDE COLEMAN'S OFFICE

There is a surprising amount of activity still going on in 85 Vauxhall Cross considering this is a government building, for people on government salaries, but MI37's borrowed offices are mercifully quiet.

I wonder if everyone is out together. Do they have a lead? Are they way ahead of us?

I want to know, I realize. I want to know how all of them are doing. Is Clyde dealing better with being a mask? Is Tabitha? Is Felicity using my face as a target down at the practice range?

I especially want to know about Felicity. If only I could see a way back to her.

I swipe Coleman's security card to unlock the office door and quickly push through. His desk is a large, ostentatious thing. Dark wood, severe edges. The sort I'd expect Wall Street villains in Oliver Stone movies to have. There are large official certificates on one wall—like the ones doctors always seem to have in excess. He has a bookshelf along another wall, heavy with thick leather-bound tomes that seem a mismatch with Coleman's brash impatient demeanor. At least they do up until I touch them and realize it's a thin veneer of spines over a wooden frame. He didn't even bother buying real books he'd never read.

As much fun as exposing Coleman's flaws is, though, I'm wasting time. I sit down in the high-backed leather chair behind his desk. His laptop is still plugged into its docking station. I'm tempted to just yank the whole thing and run. But the whole point of this is to try and be undercover. Stopping the Russians will be hard enough without being actively chased through London.

I flip open the monitor, press the power button, wait.

For the password box to pop up.

Shit.

I stare at the blinking cursor.

Double shit.

Hacking. What do I know about hacking?

Man, as much as I like Devon, I sort of wish Tabitha or Clyde had gone rogue instead, right now.

JONATHAN WOOD

The only thing I know about hacking is what Clyde told me. That way too many people use… Wait…

I type 1-2-3-4 into the little box. I press enter. The screen blanks to an innocent blue. I hold my breath.

The box reappears. It kindly apologizes to me but that is not the password.

Triple shit.

I think about Coleman. What do I know about him? He doesn't strike me as being the most computer savvy of men. 1-2-3-4 isn't too unlikely a password for him. But if not that, then…?

I try a-b-c-d, but to no avail.

Coleman thinks highly of himself. I'm staring blankly at all the framed certificates. He thinks he's clever. He would do something he thinks is clever. Except it won't be really.

If I was an idiot who wanted to prove his smarts, what would… Something comes to me.

But no…

And what if I only get three tries at this password? That's how it works sometimes. If I screw up, I'm done for. I can't believe I wasted a chance with a-b-c-d.

I quickly ransack drawers looking for a piece of paper, anything, any scribbled notes. Nothing. There's only a single fountain pen in a drawer and a single legal pad with a quick sketch of an improbably proportioned naked woman on it. That's it.

I stare at the blinking cursor one more time.

Something an idiot like Coleman would think is clever.

Oh screw it. Nothing ventured…

I type it in, slowly. 4-3-2-1.

I stare at the four asterisks. So bloody stupid.

I hit enter.

The box disappears. The screen is pure blue.

And then folders appear. An MI6 logo appears. Outlook starts booting up.

I'm in. I'm actually in.

Jesus, not only do I look like Coleman. I've figured out how to think like him. Is this how I'm going to be in ten years? I need to find someone to kill me if that happens.

There again, who am I kidding? I'm never going to survive ten years with this gig.

I see the database I want and start with the clicking. After five minutes of frustration and butting my head against a wall, I finally notice a little search box some designer bastard decided to make as unnoticeable as possible. I pull a note with the names we discovered in Chernobyl out of my wallet, and start typing.

Ivan Spilenski gives me a hit straight away. A grainier photo than the one from the Russian files, and from a worse angle. It lists him as deceased, so that could explain why Tabitha had trouble finding him. More hits on Joseph Punin, Urve Potia, and Ekaterina Kropkin. More on their associates.

I look, but the bastard designer doesn't seem to have given me a way to save individual files, which renders my flash drive useless. I start clicking on the "print" button.

Next up is chasing the links the files have in common. More known associates. Mission files. Counter-intelligence operations. I click print again and again.

Only Leo Malkin is missing. The teleporter who beat me up. Either a nobody or somebody too good to make our radar. I am very worried he's the latter. My ribs ache just thinking about him.

The printer grudgingly spools out sheet after sheet. I check my watch. I've been here half an hour now. Devon should be out of Coleman's apartment, in with the others. Which means the chances of Coleman discovering the theft of his card are starting to go up.

I check my printing queue and curse loudly. Apparently even inanimate objects Coleman owns are out to get me. I'm going to be here another fifteen minutes at least.

I close my eyes and take a breath. No one knows I'm here yet. It would take Coleman a minimum of fifteen minutes just to get here from his house. I'm OK. It's going to be OK.

And then someone rattles the handle of his office door.

63

One hand goes to the butt of my pistol. The other checks that my mustache is still in place.

How the hell did Coleman get here so fast? Something must have gone wrong with Devon. Why didn't the bastards call me? Unless they're all in the clink now. Oh God. It was all—

"George?" says a voice from the other side of the door. "George, are you in there?"

Not Coleman's voice.

So much worse.

Felicity.

My heart hits my feet, tries to rebound. Fails.

Oh Jesus. Two options flash through my mind: truth or bluff? And can I really bluff Felicity? But can I really trust her with the truth?

God, I wish I could.

"Err," I rumble, trying to hit Coleman's pitch. "Don't come in." There's too much at stake for the truth.

"You've locked the door, George," Felicity snaps.

I don't remember doing that. It must do it automatically when it closes.

Felicity sounds tired. She must be under a lot of pressure. A lot of it must be due to me.

"Just getting changed from the gym," I lie. Coleman ought to go to a gym even if he doesn't actually.

"I'm fine missing out on that," Felicity says, with an enthusiasm that warms my heart. "I just wanted to double-check the attribution in the third email blast about our so-called solar flare. Last thing we'd need is to have to apologize for a typo."

And that tells me the route they've gone. Spring the EMP on the British public and claim it's a solar flare. Which means there's been no traction finding the Russians. Which means that how I respond to Felicity's statement is very important for the future of the world as we know it.

I go with a grunt.

In my defense, I think it's harder to get more dismissive than a grunt. I wait. The printer keeps chugging. Has she gone?

"Did you have a chance to look at the damage projections for the blast?"

God, she's bloody tenacious when she wants to be. And admittedly that is a charming feature, which I have to say makes me feel a certain amount of fond longing, but seriously now. I have no bloody idea if Coleman did or not. I grunt again.

"It's a lot of collateral damage."

I massage my skull. And *now*, of all times, she wants to have a conversation?

I consider grunting again, but if I do then it's going to sound like Coleman's taking a dump in the trashcan. I need to shut this down fast.

"It's happening, Felicity," I say as gruffly as I can. "Sooner you just accept it the better."

Fight it, I want to tell her. *Fight for what you believe in. Fight Coleman tooth and bloody nail. Just do it later.*

"I accept it, George. I just wanted to make sure you acknowledged it." She's telling him this is on his head. Not hers. Politics. Always with the politics. Which is totally what you want the players to be primarily concerned with in an end-of-the-world situation. Yet another of Coleman's little gifts to MI37.

God, I just need her to go. Which, if I'm going to stay in character, means being as big an asshole to her as possible. Which is, of course, so much fun when what I really want to do is fling open this door, fling off my mustache, and start on the apologies.

She thinks it's Coleman, I tell myself. *She's going to blame him.*

"Eyes on the prize, Felicity," I burble in my pseudo-Coleman voice.

Another pause. Success?

"You know, George—"

Oh crap. Her tone really doesn't make it sound like success.

"—I have had it up to here with your insinuations about Arthur."

Oh double crap.

Well, on the one hand I did manage to be an even bigger arsehole than I was intending to be. On the other, this promises to be about as entertaining as a colonoscopy.

"I *am* committed to the success of this mission. My *team* is committed to its success. We are keeping an eye on his movements. We're pretty sure he's left the Ukraine—"

Jesus, when did MI37 get so bloody efficient?

"—and is likely to be here. The psych profile predicts that it's likely he'll try to interfere with the EMP. We *are* prepared for his appearance. We *will* take him down."

OK, so my ex-girlfriend basically just announced she's willing to shoot me. In fact she's going so far as to insist upon her willingness to do it. As break-ups go, this is probably not going to make my top three.

I grunt again. The noise comes as much from me trying to deal with the body blow of information as it does from any attempt to maintain my charade of deception. Silence from the doorway. Behind me the printer continues to chug.

"You know what," Felicity says. "Fix the damn email yourself." There's unexpected emotion in her voice.

God, if I could just open the door, could just tell her...

I hear footsteps walking away, heels clacking down the corridor.

Crap. Balls, and shit, and just crap.

I sit in Coleman's chair and wait for the final sheet to spill from his printer.

* * *

FIFTEEN MINUTES LATER, OUTSIDE

I flip open my phone. I stare at Aiko's number. I stare at it for longer than I intended.

Felicity is willing to shoot me. I'm not wholly sure if she's happy about it, but I'm not sure if that's really important.

I don't think shooting me has even crossed Aiko's mind. At least not seriously.

God, I don't know what I'm thinking about. I'm always bemoaning other people letting personal crap get in the way of saving the world and look at me. I just need to make the call, get picked up, get out of here.

I push buttons, put the phone to my ear.

"You got the stuff?" There's no preamble from Aiko.

"Got it." We're all business. Right now that's a good thing. "Devon get out OK?"

"I don't know."

And apparently I've run out of good things already.

"How the hell do you not—?" I start.

"Flat tire," Aiko snaps back. She sounds tense. "We're stuck in the middle of Grosvenor Place. Malcolm's changing it as fast as he can."

"So she could still be in there with Coleman?" I'm still too close to MI6 headquarters to shout it, but I come pretty close. The "Oh shit" signal is a double bump of the lights in Coleman's apartment. It's a signal that requires people to be there to see it.

"She may be."

Jesus. Devon is not a physical girl. And Coleman is a big guy.

"She'll remove his testicles before he gets a chance to do anything." I don't know if Aiko is trying to reassure me or herself. I don't take the time to figure it out. I'm already running.

64

KNIGHTSBRIDGE

I wilt onto Coleman's street. My lungs are on fire. My legs, rubber. Bastard couldn't live any bloody closer to the Underground station, could he?

I sag against a car. But I need to keep going, I need to... I stumble forward, bounce off the car's neighbor. Its alarm blares into life. Flashing indicator lights highlight the sweat dripping off my brow.

The lights in Coleman's apartment are still turned low. No sign of Devon. No sign of any of the others. I glance down at my watch. Twelve-fifteen p.m. She had his ID in about five minutes. That's almost two hours of Coleman without his pants on. I can't believe that's a good thing.

I cross the street to his building's door. I've given up running for more of a shuffling hobble. I need to think of something that will convince the bastard to buzz me up. No, screw that, I just need to smash the glass in the door and open it myself.

Except someone's done that for me already.

Oh, we have so definitely left good very far behind.

I shoulder open the door, pull the gun out of my jacket. And for about the first time in my life, I'm actually premeditating murder. If he's hurt Devon, I'll kill him. Actually kill him. And I'll do it gladly.

I crash up the stairs, panting, huffing. I slam into one wall then another. My gun echoes hollowly against wallpaper and plasterboard.

Coleman's door. The lock busted. Splinters and the exposed bronze of the lock. And what the hell?

But I can't stop, so I don't stop. I stagger through, try to suck in air, try to focus. I try to get the breath to call Devon's name, but I can't.

A staggering footstep forward. And there's a body. A body face down on the floor. Someone standing over it.

And Devon. Devon sitting on the couch.

Wait…

Wait… I… On the couch?

Kayla stands in the middle of Coleman's living room. Stands over Coleman's comatose form.

"Finally," she says derisively. "The feckin' cavalry."

65

COLEMAN'S LIVING ROOM, 12:58 A.M.

"I'm telling you," Devon says, upper lip firmly stiffened, "I'm fine."

Aiko stands across the small living room, staring at Kayla. "But," she says, "you said no. You said you wouldn't help."

Aiko, Malcolm, and Jasmine arrived two minutes ago and chaos is still busy reigning.

"I said you didn't want my help." Kayla is as gruff as can be anticipated. "Didn't say I wouldn't give it."

"Oh, Kayla," Devon says from the couch, "of course they're surprised. It's not like you overwhelmed us with your enthusiasm."

Kayla looks away, her face guarded. For a moment I think that's going to be the full extent of her response. Then she shrugs. "You said I didn't save my daughter."

"I said you could save the world."

"I don't give a feck about the world." Kayla spits onto Coleman's carpet.

"You sure he's going to stay out?" Malcolm pulls his head back from the doorway to the bedroom where we laid Coleman's unconscious body.

"He'll stay out." There's an element of professional pride in Kayla's tone.

And Coleman, and the fact that he did something to make Kayla attack him, brings me back to the beginning of this conversation. "You're sure you're OK?" I ask Devon again.

Devon's smile is still shaky but she waves a hand as Jasmine and Aiko advance in step. "I'm fine."

"You want to talk about it?"

Devon looks around the small room. For some reason we've not turned the lights up fully yet, and everything feels too close and overcrowded. She grimaces. "It was…" She looks up at Kayla.

Kayla lets her gaze drift away from Devon's. It comes to rest on me. "Followed you after the park," she says with another shrug. "After what Devon said. About my daughter."

"I don't understand," I say. Not that I'm objecting to Kayla's presence. It's just it would be nice if something actually did make sense for once.

"Never feckin' do." Kayla grimaces. "It was what hit home. Someone else I care about going off with you. And I thought, well, maybe some things are worth fighting for."

Well, at least Kayla's low opinion of me is good for something…

"Plus," Kayla says, "Coleman's a prick."

Devon shifts on the couch. "He didn't touch me," she says. "I don't want you to think that. He'd just been… Just been talking and pacing and drinking for over an hour. And drinking blended malts. My father would have beaten a man for having blended malts. That said, my father didn't take his lithium very often. But then he… Well, I was on edge. And someone should really talk to that man about personal space issues. And I think at one point he might have sniffed my hair, which I don't care what Hollywood tells you, is always creepy. I mean, it's hair. It's hardly an erotic bloody tool. It sits on top of your head and gets greasy if you don't wash it.

"So, yes, I was not at all comfortable, and then… well, he offered me the whiskey, you see. And it was a blended malt. I said that. And you have to understand, in a way, how profoundly wrong that is. And, well, it was probably silly of me to scream about it. But I did scream. And then the door crashed open. And then there was Kayla. And then it was all over."

There's a satisfied smile on Kayla's lips. "Good enough excuse," she says.

"He offered you whiskey?" I ask, just to clarify exactly why we have broken and entered this house.

"A blended malt, Arthur," Devon implores. "That's just not right."

I stare at the others. Aiko is still looking confused. "But how did you get his ID in under five minutes?"

"Oh," Devon gives us a small smile, "apparently Coleman prefers silk pajamas in the comfort of his own home. Left his other pants on the bathroom floor."

The sight of Coleman, unconscious or no, in maroon silk pajamas will haunt me until the day I die.

"Now," Devon reaches a hand out to me, "could you just give me the files. That's what this was all about anyway."

It's a quick, efficient way to force the room's attention onto me.

"Shit, yes," Aiko says, flicking her eyes my way. "How did it go? You get everything?"

I pull the stack of papers from under my shirt where they've been nestled between my skin and my paunch of Malcolm's socks.

"Any problems?"

And how exactly do I describe my exchange with Felicity to Aiko of all people? I don't even know how to describe it to myself.

"Nothing significant," I say. Saving the world before personal crap. Plus now it's almost past one in the morning and I'd rather skip any extraneous matters and get down to business.

"So," I say, "Devon looks at the papers, we find the bastards, and make plans about how best to hit them very hard in a place that hurts."

"That's your plan?" Kayla looks at me as if I'm a half-wit.

"It's a little more nuanced than that."

"Better be." Kayla looks over the Weekenders with an appraising eye. "You're outnumbered, out-trained, and outgunned."

"I know," I say, ignoring Malcolm's sour face. "We need MI37 too."

"You say." Malcolm can't quite hold in the bitterness.

"Hush." Jasmine taps his arm.

"You realize," Kayla says, "Shaw's probably going to feckin' shoot you on sight?"

And God, I do now. "It's a risk," I concede. But we have to try. The Russians are just too powerful for us to go up against them alone. "We just have to convince them of the truth."

"Because that's gone so feckin' well for you so far."

And she does have a point. But... "Every time we've encountered the Russians," I counter, "it's been on their terms. We've seen what they want us to see. They've been prepared. This time we draw them out. We catch them off guard. We get them to show us what they don't want us to see."

It's hardly Sun Tzu. But it's my plan, and I have a certain amount of pride in it.

Malcolm steps up. "A controlled first contact operation with both the Russians and MI37," he says. Which I think is what I said.

"So you define the second engagement." Kayla nods.

Malcolm nods.

"A controlled environment," Kayla says. Something in her body language has changed. Less confrontational. And she and Malcolm seem to have found a common language. They move closer, speak lower, sit down on the couch, fire suggestions back and forth with increasing rapidity. Jargon and acronyms I can't follow. Next to them, Devon sits, head buried in the papers I printed out. Jasmine balances on the couch arm next to her. I glance at my watch. Less than seventeen hours until the Russians make their move.

"We're running out of time, aren't we?" Aiko has slipped up next to me.

"Yes," I say. I can't see the point in denying it.

"You think there's time for this?" She nods at Kayla and Malcolm.

"I think we have to make time."

She looks at me. "This is the bit where we consider having to live this day as our last." She puts a hand on my arm. "*Carpe diem*, Agent Arthur."

We will take him down.

"Well this is interesting."

Devon's boom seizes the attention of the room. And, seriously, can I not catch five minutes to think about this one?

Aiko takes a quick step away from me. Jasmine is looking at us.

"What's interesting?" I ask quickly.

"Oh," Devon says, looking up and remembering she's in a room full of people. "Well, I was just thinking that maybe this might be useful." She holds aloft a sheaf of paper. "Old protocols on how the Russians used to contact each other. They really did drop personal ads into newspapers. I just assumed that was your standard Hollywood tomfoolery. Always had these images of spies accidentally turning up to first dates when they expected nuclear plans or some such. But no, the codes are all here. 'Single white female' is one sort of meeting. 'Desperately seeking' is request for a mission status update. That sort of thing. Different papers even mean different things too. All divided up by geographical location and everything. It's all very Machiavellian. Which I suppose shouldn't be unexpected. Spies after all. It's not like they're going to send each other instructions in Hallmark cards with love and kisses."

Suddenly Aiko is not the only woman in the room I am considering kissing.

"But there are hundreds of newspapers in London," Aiko says. "It's bloody huge."

"Oh yes." Devon nods. "They've subdivided London a lot."

"So how do we know which papers to use?" I ask.

Jasmine looks up from a piece of paper she's been staring at. "Would, like, this list of safe houses be helpful?"

This place is threatening to become a regular smooch-fest.

There is much calloo-ing and callay-ing at this. Spirits rise slightly. Even Kayla seems like a functional member of a team again. I should fail to defend her friends from lecherous old men more often.

In the end, the list narrows it down to six locations. "The *East London Advertiser* should cover us," Devon concludes.

Suddenly it feels as if we have momentum, as if this might actually be achievable. "Can we make the morning edition?" I check.

Jasmine taps at a smartphone. "Yeah," she says after a while. "Might, like, cost a bit extra, but there's a nine a.m. edition we can probably get in, if we submit something in the next few hours."

I turn to Kayla and Malcolm. "And you. This plan. You can

work something out within the next few hours?"

"Feck you," Kayla says.

"I'll take that as a yes."

They sit down, get to work. Jasmine and Devon go back to their papers, searching for extra clues. I stand at the center of the room.

Aiko is looking at me. It takes me a moment to recognize the look in her eyes. And then I realize what it is. Admiration.

66

As it turns out, you can't save the world from time-traveling Russians without getting your feet wet. And unfortunately my rain boots are back in Oxford so it's time for my feet to get a soaking.

We're in an old, river-soaked, industrial barge house. The roof's rusted through and a couple of rotting hulks are slowly sinking into the Thames mud. The barge house itself sits on the edge of a small island in the middle of the Thames—Lot's Ait—caught between the brilliance of the Kew Royal Botanic Gardens and the grungier end of Brentford. Around us trees and duck shit threaten to swallow the building entirely.

I turn to Jasmine. "How did you know about this place again?"

She shrugs noncommittally. "I, like, grew up around here. Kind of."

I look over my shoulder, across the thin stretch of water back to the city. "You mean your parents live…" I nod in the direction of civilization.

Jasmine shrugs again. Part of me wants to push it, but I can't see much point to antagonizing her. And anyway, while I'm no expert, the responsible adult thing is probably not to worry about Jasmine's past but to save the present from total annihilation.

"The place I was talking about is down here." She points to some stairs at the back of the barge house. I flash back to the stairs in Chernobyl and hesitate. But that's hardly the heroic thing to do, and I'm trying to keep on the roll I've been on since last night. I follow her. Aiko, Malcolm, and Devon trail after us.

"I played here when I was, like, a kid. Was easy enough to get over when the tide was low. Been under contract for development for, like, years, but nothing ever happens. Good place to smoke, and, you know, stuff."

I try not to be visibly middle class about that statement.

"But yeah, there's this bit." She waves her hand around.

A small basement area squats at the bottom of the stairs. A few rusty shelves, some amorphous lumps of rust that were maybe once tools, rotting wooden planks. The floor is a stew of river silt and decomposing leaves. The smell puts me in mind of open sewer pipes.

"So this place totally floods at high tide," Jasmine says. "Almost killed my friend Jimmy back when we were, like, eight or something."

It's a revolting little space. Cramped, dirty, and likely infested with vermin.

I look to Malcolm.

"Perfect," he says. He pats Jasmine on the arm.

"You're sure you can rig something up to seal the doorway?"

Malcolm ducks his head out of the basement and looks up. "Roof should do," he says, nodding.

Which seems a bit much to me, but we're way beyond subtle at this point.

I look to Devon. "And Kayla will hold up?"

Devon shrugs. "I think knocking Coleman out did her good."

I check my watch. Just over seven hours until the deadline. Just over four until high tide. And I actually have a plan.

"OK," I say, "let's get to work."

LOT'S AIT. 2:46 P.M.

I am now officially nervous. I can tell by the way I've checked my watch eight times in the last three minutes. And by the sweat.

"You're sure your phone gets reception?" I ask Aiko.

"Shockingly my phone has remained entirely functional in the thirty seconds since you last asked me." Aiko is moving from sympathetic to the point where I'm honestly not sure she'd be totally upset if Felicity shot me.

Which, of course, we may all get to see in a minute.

I check my watch.

Aiko's phone buzzes. She glances down. She looks back up. "Right on time."

God, I hope I don't get shot. Like Aiko said, this is potentially my last day on earth. I'd hate to spend it bleeding everywhere.

Aiko's phone buzzes again. She checks the message. "They're crossing the river."

Malcolm provided us with some waterproof industrial lights, the ones that come complete with protective orange cages. He set up a small generator for them outside and ran the wires in. Now, his job as our spotter complete, he starts it. The lamps blaze to life. Hopefully that should make the basement a more tempting lure. My plan's a bit buggered if they fail to come down the stairs.

"Is Coleman with them?"

I worked out what Kayla had to say very specifically before she called Felicity, but there are certain elements of this plan I just can't control.

Aiko re-checks the message. "Malcolm doesn't say."

My stomach lurches. That would really screw the pooch.

What a horrible phrase…

Aiko's phone buzzes again. "Incoming," she says.

Devon and I step into the middle of the room and raise our hands.

The first thing down the stairs is Felicity's gun. She follows shortly afterwards.

Behind her come Tabitha and Clyde. She's got her laptop open. He's got an AA clenched between forefinger and thumb.

Kayla brings up the rear. "There they are," she says. "Feckin' told you." And she's come through. Everyone has. It's up to me now.

I stand there, water starting to lap around my ankles, and look Felicity full in the face for the first time since I threw my badge at her.

She looks… God, she looks everything. Violent, and beautiful. Like someone who betrayed me. Like someone I should apologize to, who I should demand apologies from. Too much history has been compressed into too few days. It's only slightly reassuring that she looks as confused as I feel. And how is she going to play this?

"You're back," she says finally. A small statement. Not confrontational. Not exactly. But not welcoming.

I want to say something dashing and cool about her postcard being in the mail, but I'm too busy being scared shitless.

"Yes," I say. Which should win points for lameness if nothing else.

"From the Ukraine," she says.

"We went to Chernobyl."

"Told you he would," Tabitha says mildly.

"Was it worth it?" Felicity's asking about Chernobyl, but she's asking about more than that too. Her eyes momentarily flick over my shoulder to Aiko who's standing back in the shadows. My stomach lurches again, and I have the urge to protest that nothing happened, but too much is riding on the next five minutes.

The water laps above the edges of my shoes, a cold rush soaking my socks.

"I'm still waiting to find out," I say. I don't really enjoy being the cryptic asshole, but I have to play this so damn carefully.

"You realize you're going to jail?" Felicity snaps at me. "Both of you." She looks over at Devon. "That's the best thing that can happen to you at this point."

"I'm going to look at my watch now," I say. I can't afford to go off script here, no matter how much I want to. We've worked out the timing of this down to the seconds. "I'm going to do it very slowly."

"I'm not fucking around here, Arthur," Felicity snaps. Clyde and Tabitha shift uncomfortably. Behind them, very quietly, Kayla is drawing her sword. I really, really hope she doesn't need it for…

I look at my watch. Less than five minutes. The water is above my ankles.

"I'm going to take five steps backwards," I say to Felicity. "If you come down here, I will give you a list of six addresses. The Russians are likely at one of them."

That causes Felicity to pause. She seems irresolute between anger and sudden hope. I'm sure it crosses her mind to just shoot me and take the addresses. "What are you playing at, Arthur?"

I take a step back. Devon steps with me. Felicity keeps the gun trained on me. We take another step in unison. We keep going until we're in line with Aiko. Five and a half steps. Close enough.

"The others," Clyde says abruptly. "The black man and the girl. Where are they?" He's still using that short, curt voice that doesn't seem to be quite his.

"Arthur?" There's a warning edge to Felicity's voice.

I was really hoping they wouldn't notice that. "They're outside," I say. I don't have a good answer prepared.

"I don't know what you think you're doing, but I am not walking into a trap. I am not as stupid as you."

So we're back to anger apparently. Felicity is wearing thin. I want to reach out to her. To reassure her.

"Please," I say, "get off the stairs." I'm asking as nicely as I can.

Felicity looks at me very hard.

"I promise you," I say, "the last thing on earth I want is for you to get hurt."

Beside me Aiko twitches her head slightly. But I just can't afford to be delicate about everyone's feelings right now.

Behind Felicity, Tabitha, and Clyde, unseen by them, Kayla shifts her grip on the sword. But I really don't want to do this with violence. I don't want judgment clouded here. The MI37 crowd has to be alert. They have to see.

"Show me the list," Felicity says.

Slowly I reach into my pocket and pull out the printout sheet. I glance at my watch as I do it. Two minutes.

Aiko's phone buzzes. Felicity twitches the gun in her direction. Everyone seems to flinch. But the gun stays silent. Slowly, Aiko opens up the phone, examines the screen.

"They're early," she says.

Shit and double shit.

"Please," I say. "Get off the stairs."

"Who's here, Arthur?" Felicity asks. "Tell me what's going on."

"I promise you," I say it again, "if you just get off the stairs and come over here I will happily allow you to arrest me in five minutes' time. I will cuff myself."

Devon looks at me askance. And I am admittedly way off script with that one.

Aiko's phone buzzes a second time. "They're in the boat," she says.

"Arthur?" Felicity wants to trust me. I know she does.

"Please." I'm not above begging.

Felicity screws up her face. The gun is back on me, and it doesn't waver for a second.

"Fine." She doesn't sound happy but I don't care. She has acquiesced. She takes a step forward into the watery stew. It's reaching up to her calves. She grimaces as the Thames soaks through her suit trousers and ruins her shoes.

"This better be worth it."

"I know," I say.

The ghost of a smile on her lips. Just the ghost of one. But maybe, if I die today it won't be at her hands.

We stand in a small huddle at the back of the basement, just out of the pool of light cast by the work lamps. Kayla has her sword still out but held down, the blade turned so it doesn't reflect any light.

"Give me the list, Arthur," Felicity says.

I have my eyes firmly on the basement stairs.

"One minute," I say.

"Don't make me shoot you, Arthur." And I'm not the only one who's willing to beg today.

"I didn't know a better way to do this," I say.

"Do what, Arthur? What the hell have you got me—"

But she never finishes the sentence. Because that's when the Russians enter. Summoned to this space at this time by a coded message in the nine a.m. edition of the *East London Advertiser*.

They're in a tight little group. Bunched together. If I'd choreographed it, I couldn't have gotten it better. Well... I'd probably have gotten rid of the crackle of blue fire around Ivan Spilenski's right hand, but aside from that...

Everything hangs very still for a moment. Everyone trying to work out what just happened, what to do next. All except me, and Devon, and Aiko. We know exactly what's going to happen.

Ignorance would probably be better.

Malcolm detonates the explosives.

67

The thunderclap of the explosion blows the Russians violently into the room. Bodies and legs spray plumes of white froth. There are curses in English and Russian. A scream. The spit of sparks. I try to take a step back, lose my footing. The water froths madly, messily. The lamps skitter, cast wavering beams of light. Everyone is shouting and staggering. I'm down on my knees. Someone leans on my head, almost pushes me under. Whether it's friend or foe, I have no idea. I kick out and away.

The stairway is a bright rectangle of white light. A silhouetted figure races toward it.

A great thundering creak from above. An ugly tearing sound. The water swirls. A sequence of blasts, like bombs, one, two, three. Everything quaking. I'm down again. Water closes over my head. Everything blurred and muted.

I break the surface. Gasp, blink, stare at the rectangle of white light. Watch it disappear.

A cry. A shout. A violent, "*Nyet!*"

Bodies scramble and splash in the wallowing half-light. I thrash backwards. My gun is a sodden lump against my chest. The water is halfway up my thighs now. Rising quicker and quicker. But it's the equalizer. The Russians won't want to be throwing lightning bolts in this much water. And I still have my ace in the hole.

I reach a shelf on the back wall. My fingers scramble along it. *Don't have fallen into the water. Don't have got dislodged by the blast.* And there it is.

I seize the scabbard. I pull out the sword. Flames burst into life.

"Oh," I hear a thick Scottish brogue come from my left. "You have got to be feckin' kidding me."

And sure, this is primarily a way to prove to Felicity et al that I was right about the Russians, but if I get to take some of the bastards out now then I'm not going to complain.

A shape lurches through the water towards me. I have no idea if it's friend or foe. Then one of the remaining lights glints off metal that encases a hand. Joseph Punin. I swing the sword like a cricket bat.

The impact runs up my arm like an electric shock. My hands ring. I stagger back, hang desperately onto the sword. Rotund, little Joseph hangs onto the other end. The blade is encased in his massive metal glove. I tug at it. The glove spits sparks, and Punin crashes toward me.

People shout, yell all around us. I slosh in water up to my waist. A flash of light blinds one of my eyes. There's a loud crash. A muzzle flare, or Kayla's sword? Electricity? The Russians powering a spell?

Blue light envelops Punin's free, flesh hand as he closes on me. I skip back faster.

"Fry me and you fry yourself, you little shit." God, I hope he understands English.

Either he does or he works it out on his own. Because he mutters a few words and the electricity turns into a crackling ball of fire.

"Oh shit."

I heave on the sword again. Metal screams again. More sparks. I kick at Punin's legs, my own moving slow through the water. But I catch something. Punin grunts. I wrench the sword again. He goes down, water swallowing the flame-wreathed hand. There is a spit of steam and the flame goes out.

Another wrench on the sword. It comes free. Punin's glove fragments. Shards of jagged steel erupt out, arc into the rising Thames swill.

Punin screams.

Flesh folds and unfolds from the hole I've ripped in his glove. Jags of bone explode and evaporate. Branching arterial trees spraying blood in brief fountain spurts. He staggers back, clutches the wound.

More screams around us. More cries.

"Get them!" Felicity bellows. "Put them down!" I hear the report of her gun. She must have kept her gun drier than I kept mine.

Clyde is muttering nonsense syllables. Something crashes through the water. A body flies backwards. The water rises. Up above my belly button now. Screams in Russian.

Suddenly the room is lit by a lightning flare. I see Ekaterina Kropkin limned in white light, a massive spark linking her to one of the wires powering the work lamps. And then nothing. A hole where she was. Gone.

Teleported.

Right before the eyes of MI37. So they saw it. So it was undeniable. So they know. They know I've been telling the truth.

"What the fuck?" I hear Felicity say.

And oh God, it worked. This plan worked. I could cry.

More lightning flares of light. Five more Russians. Five more disappearances.

The room suddenly seems very quiet. Just panting breath and the splashing of water.

"What in God's name...?" Clyde starts.

"Teleportation!" I yell. I scream the word. I can't help myself. "Don't you dare fucking doubt me now! Don't you even dare."

We stand there. The seven of us staring at each other. Me, Devon, and Aiko—the true believers on one side; Felicity, Clyde, and Tabitha on the other—our potential converts; Kayla stands in the middle—not really giving a shit either way.

"Space-time magic," Felicity finally says. She looks at Clyde and Tabitha.

Nothing from Clyde. But Tabitha shrugs. "Wrong. We were." She shrugs again. "I guess."

Felicity looks back at me. "This was all planned? You intended it to go down this way?"

"Pretty much." I feel abruptly modest. I realize I'm holding a flaming sword. I slip it back into its scabbard, not quite meeting her eye.

"And you didn't think that maybe telling us they were coming so we could set up something to actually capture them might be helpful?"

"They can teleport!" I throw up my hands. This is not exactly the praise I'm looking for. "You were looking to arrest me. I had limited options."

Felicity weighs all that. "And trapping us all—who, I might add, can't teleport—in a room where the water level is rapidly rising. That was in the plan too?"

I wave my hand. "Malcolm's going to get us out. Just keep away from the staircase. He's going to blow a hole for us to get through."

Felicity is actually starting to look impressed. "You figured this all out?"

I pat my breast pocket, still just above the waterline. "I've got six addresses right here. We're pretty sure they're retreating to one of them right now."

For a moment Felicity actually lets a smile through. And for a moment it actually feels like the sun is shining.

Clyde has his head cocked on one side. "Police are coming," he says. "Five minutes."

"You get wireless down here?" That stuff is bloody ubiquitous. I smile at Clyde. It is good to see him even if he still doesn't seem himself. "And hey."

"Hello." Clyde sounds distracted. And even if I did just prove him totally wrong in a pretty grandiose way, I did hope for something a little warmer than that.

Next to him, Tabitha grimaces.

We stand. We wait. The water rises. I take the list of Russian safe houses out of my breast pocket just in case. I can hear Devon's teeth starting to chatter.

"This man, Malcolm…" Felicity starts.

"He knows what he's doing," snaps Aiko. But she doesn't look as if she has full confidence in her own words.

"Shouldn't he have stopped the generator?" Clyde says abruptly, addressing no one in particular. "Your wires are frayed. If the water hits them there might be enough power to electrify it." He tilts his head on one side. "And us," he adds as an afterthought.

"Might be?" I ask.

"Willing to find out. You are?" Tabitha asks.

And she has a point. A sharp one.

I look at the wires. We've got about eighteen more inches before that disaster. By which point I'll be swimming.

"It won't come to that."

The water continues to rise. I look at Felicity. She looks right back at me. I try to think of something to say, something to encompass the totality of what I need to express. Something more than, "How *you* doin'?"

"Nice sword." Tabitha breaks my concentration.

"Picked it up at Chernobyl." I try to play it cool. It's not my strong suit.

"Good trip?"

I think about that. "Our plane got shot out of the air by a jet fighter."

Tabitha nods. I was sort of hoping for a bigger reaction. I look to Felicity. She's just shaking her head.

"It was bloody terrifying," I point out. Still nothing.

"Speaking of terrifying things," Devon cuts in to the witty banter, "I don't mean to doubt Malcolm, but I'm treading water now."

"Call him?" Tabitha suggests. She's swimming too.

"My phone got wet," Aiko says.

"Feck this." Kayla starts marching toward the staircase.

"No!" I call after her. "If he's up there with explosives then that's both of you turned into meat wallpaper."

Aiko looks at me. "Meat wallpaper?"

I shrug. "Sometimes I don't think before I speak."

"Sometimes?" Felicity sounds incredulous.

Not exactly an expression of desire for our continued relationship, that.

"Can someone at least please do something." Devon is hanging onto a shelf. The water is only twelve inches from the wires. It's almost up to my chin.

"If I skewer Malcolm, it's his own feckin' fault."

"Police are three minutes away," Clyde adds to no one in

particular. He sounds like the talking clock.

Kayla sloshes towards the steps.

The explosion lifts her off her feet.

She flies back through the water. A great white spray swamps the room. Water slams over my head. I gasp in a great ugly mouthful. It laps against the back of my throat, and I gag, convulsing under the waves. My arms and legs spasm, driving me upwards. My head breaks the water. Chaos reigns once more.

I dive toward the spot where I assume Kayla must have gone under. I collide with something. A tangle of limbs. I head for the surface and for a moment I can't find it. Waves slosh around me. I panic, kick. I break the surface. I've got one of Kayla's arms. She's unconscious. When I finally manage to get out of here I am going to give Malcolm a stern bloody lecture on the nature of tardiness.

And there he comes now... except why is he coming down here? Why is he coming down the stairs backwards? And who on earth is he firing that massive assault rifle at?

68

"Back!" Malcolm bellows, between bursts of rifle fire. "Fall back!"

Despite his urgency, this proves an unpopular suggestion.

Devon is the first to reach him, floundering through the sloshing water. She barrels into him and his shots go wide. Ricochets ping off the stair rail.

"Back!" he yells again.

"We've got to get out of here." I surge forward, struggling to keep Kayla's head above the water.

"What's going on?" Aiko yells at the same time.

"The generator!" Devon is shrieking. "It's going to fry us all."

Malcolm keeps on firing, blocking the stairway, even as Clyde tries to pilot his angular body past him.

"Speak!" Tabitha barks at him. "Inform!"

"Sit rep, major!" Felicity's voice slices through the madness like a flaming sword through a time-traveling Russian's space-glove.

Malcolm comes up short, almost flinching to attention before hunkering down against the stair rails. "Russians," he says. "Still engaged."

Balls. That was not exactly the plan. They were more meant to flee in terror. Maybe I'm overly keen on the tactical withdrawal as a strategic option.

"Positions?" Felicity snaps at him.

"Ten, one, and two," Malcolm barks back.

At that moment lightning arcs through the doorway. The concrete lintel sprays shrapnel. Devon shrieks.

We're crowded in the mouth of the stairs. I'm treading water now. I glance back. The water is two inches from the wires.

"We better do this fast," I say.

Felicity nods. "Malcolm, take point. Suppressing fire. Clyde and I will flank out behind you. Arthur, can you use that sword?"

"Erm," I start.

"He can't." Aiko apparently has no compunction about eviscerating my pride.

"What I thought," Felicity says.

Did no one else see me take out Punin? That was all me.

"Arthur, you and Aiko take a defensive position inside the stairwell with Tabitha and Devon. Keep Kayla safe."

Another lightning bolt slams into the doorframe. Rubble flies. And I'm not about to turn down a job out of harm's way. Aiko and I nod in unison. Devon is sobbing now.

"We move in five." Felicity holds up her hand, fingers extended. "Four." One finger down. "Three." Another. "Two. One. Go! Go! Go!"

Malcolm charges forward, screaming, firing, the gun juddering and blasting in his hands. Felicity and Clyde follow hot on his heels. Felicity has her gun held out, Clyde his bare hand. The cavalry.

I heave Kayla up. Aiko heaves Devon back as she makes a leap for the stairway opening. The world in front of us explodes in noise and light. Fire blossoms. Lightning crackles. Figures flit back and forth through space.

We're on top of the building's roof. Malcolm brought the whole thing down—a jagged corrugated blanket over a thick layer of rubble. Our exit is a splintered hole punched through cross beams and metal sheeting by a small shaped charge.

I don't know where it is Malcolm shops, but something tells me it isn't the local supermarket.

He hunkers behind a large steel beam, fires blindly across the Thames. His bullets chew up the riverbank. Felicity squats beside him, head bowed. Clyde has scrambled to the far side of the building. He takes cover behind a chunk of collapsed wall and spits out batteries from beneath his mask.

Even the way he moves has changed.

"Where's Jasmine?" Aiko is lying flat on the stairs beside me, eyes peeking above the top riser, water lapping against her shoes. "She was up here with Malcolm. Where's she gone?"

I scan left, right, trying to find her.

"Oh shit. Oh no."

"What?" Aiko looks at me.

I point. At the far edge of the collapsed building, on top of the remains of the roof, Jasmine lies flat, hands over her head as bullets whistle above her. She's totally exposed. No cover. And her leg... Below the knee of her jeans, her left leg is a bloody ruin. I can't even see the foot.

"Fuck!" Aiko brings her hand to her mouth.

It feels like my heart has stopped. It's only a matter of time before the Russians hit her. Or we do by accident.

"Oh Jesus... Her leg." Aiko seems overwhelmed.

She's only seventeen. She's just a kid pulled into this horrendous fucking mess. And this was my plan. I put her here. I brought her here. Her goddamn parents probably only live a mile away. And I brought her to a firefight.

"I'm going to go get her," I say.

Aiko looks at me. "Are you fucking crazy?"

"I have to." I don't know how else to put it. This is a simple necessity. And I cannot live knowing I didn't try to help her. I just can't.

"You keep your arse right here and hunker down like a sensible—"

I don't hear the rest. I'm busy running.

69

I make it about six yards. Something flares past me, grounds to my left. A massive shock runs up my leg, lifts me into the air like a rag doll. I somersault in the air. The world spins. I come down on my back.

Corrugated aluminum does not a comfortable landing make.

I roll over, groan. Blood dribbles from my mouth. I don't know what I bit. Maybe everything.

"Arthur, what are you—?" Felicity is yelling at my back. But I can see Jasmine. I have to get to Jasmine. I stagger up and forwards. I half hurdle, half dry hump another girder. I roll. Another blast of something or other. I'm bucked up into the air like a lightning-powered donkey kicked me in the gut. I fly with all the grace of a sack of potatoes.

That may be slander from the sack's point of view.

I'm out of cover now, an open stretch of metal between Jasmine and me. Even the walls have dropped away. Jasmine's shouting something, waving at me, but my ears are ringing, and I can't hear a word.

I make it to my feet, stumble forward. A flash of white light to my side. A Russian appears. I spin. A fist comes at me, connects on my jaw, sends me sprawling backwards.

Not this again.

Another flash. A boot to my midriff, floors me properly this time. God, I hate teleporters.

The air above my head is shredded by bullets. I turn, groggy. Felicity is emptying a clip into the air around me, buying me time.

Goddamn, she looks hot right now.

I need to focus. Jasmine. I need to get to Jasmine.

I roll, get to my knees. She's just yards away.

A flash of light. The Russian. Leo. His straw-blond mane wild. His face a picture of pure spite. He stands over Jasmine.

I launch myself at him, as hard and as fast as my shaking legs will propel me.

Lightning lances from a nearby wire, slams into Leo, through him, plunges down. Jasmine arcs her back, screaming. Her howl bubbles up out of frying lungs. I am in the air, caught in midair. Closer, closer, time a fraying piece of string. And I am going to kill—

A flash of light. The Russian, Leo, disappears. Nothing. Thin air that I sail through. My hands clutching no throat, tearing at nothing.

I slam onto the metal next to Jasmine.

Next to Jasmine's corpse.

No.

No. No, it can't be. I shake my head, try to negate reality.

She's barely recognizable, blackened, twisted, caught in the final convulsions of agony.

No.

I pull the gun from its holster. And fuck these people. Fuck them all. Fuck my shitty shooting. Fuck water-soaked bullets. I am going to execute every last one of these motherfuckers.

I pull the trigger. Nothing. I slide back the action on my pistol, watch the sodden round spill down. I fire again. Nothing. I eject that bullet. Again. Again. Damp rounds litter the air around me. Lightning sears the air. The wail of sirens rises. Again. Again. One bullet flies out of the gun. I see the dust it kicks up against the wall some of the Russians are crouching behind. Again. Nothing. Again. Nothing.

Fuck this gun. Fuck this shit. Fuck those fucking Russians.

I wrestle the sword from its sheath. I remember the howl of agony on Joseph Punin's face. I am looking forward to seeing that expression again.

I stride forward, over the metal roof, over the mud, into the swirling, rising water of the Thames. And fuck cover. Fuck bullets. Fuck magic. I don't care if they hit me, I am coming for them.

She was just a child.

Jesus, she was just… Jesus.

The police sirens are a banshee howl now. A keening wail of grief given up by the world for Jasmine. I am fighting the current, fighting reality, fighting for vengeance.

A policeman bellows, his message lost in my rage and the static from the bullhorn.

A flash of light. Another. Another. The Russians retreating, driven back, and away.

"No!" I scream at them. "No!" Stay and fight me, you fuckers. Stay and let me carve out your hearts.

But they're gone. The police are here. Men and women in black, armed-response uniforms—thick padded vests and faceless helmets. They level rifles at me.

I stand in the river, and raise my hands, and I weep.

70

Felicity takes care of it.

She shows the police ID cards. She speaks to the people in charge. She calls their superiors, wrestles with jurisdiction, fights in pissing contests.

To be honest, I don't really care.

They have to pry Malcolm off Jasmine's body. He hangs onto her corpse, keening to himself. Tears streak his big face. They come to him quietly and he takes two policemen out, big fists plunging into guts and faces. It takes Aiko, struggling through her own tears, to let them move his arms away. He seems to have no strength for that.

I feel hollow. I stand there, staring at the little black bag they've sealed her up in. It doesn't seem right. Nothing seems right.

We put the world back wrong.

Or maybe the world has always been wrong. And maybe we just didn't fix it when we had the chance.

Maybe now is the chance.

I try to seize hold of that, to turn grief to anger, to light the spark that drove me into the river, that led me shivering and shuddering to here, wrapped in a silver blanket.

A shadow falls over me. I look up. Felicity.

"How are you?" she says.

Jesus. Felicity. I don't... her and me... now, here, on top of this...?

"I don't know," I say. "I don't know." I hear myself echo the phrase.

"Were you right about everything?" she asks. I realize she's serious, and if this were any other time I might smile at that.

"Not everything," I say. I'm still looking at that little black bag.

"About the EMP? About the Chronometer?"

"Yes," I say. "I'm right about that."

"We have to stop them," she says.

"Now?" I don't want to move. I don't think I can move. The ember of rage is still trying to spark, but I'm too sodden with grief, the fight washed out of me and gone downriver towards the docklands and the English Channel.

"It's four p.m.," she tells me. "Two hours left. And we have traffic to contend with."

"And we'll find them?" I ask. I want to be sure.

"Yes," she says. "Once I get back to Vauxhall Cross, I'll get clearance, redeploy the troops we have ready for the EMP blast. We'll have those houses raided in under five minutes. Those Russian bastards won't be able to teleport without landing in a field of lead."

I look over at Aiko and Malcolm, wrapped together, fused in grief. "What about them?"

"Even if I wanted to, do you honestly think I could keep them out of this fight now?"

It's said with kindness, with heart. I look up at her. At a good woman.

She puts her hand on my shoulder. "I was only ever trying to protect people, Arthur. I swear."

It's not wholly true. She was trying to protect herself too. Trying to protect her job. But it's not wholly untrue either. And this is an apology. Of sorts. And here, now, intimate with loss, I am willing to be the bigger man.

"I know," I say.

She smiles at me then. Not the powerful woman in a suit, not the director of MI37, but Felicity Shaw, a woman I know, a woman

I admire, that maybe I... I don't know.

"Come on," she offers me a hand, "want to go see how big of a new arsehole we can rip in Coleman?"

I take her hand, stand up, and from somewhere inside me, I even find a smile.

85 VAUXHALL CROSS. 4:57 P.M.

We march into MI6 like a storm cloud. The police cars that delivered us sit outside, lights still revolving, painting the lobby in the colors of urgency.

The security guard that fell for my Coleman disguise is on duty. He looks at the influx, blanches, and rushes forward.

"Can I see—" he starts, but Felicity bats him away with her ID.

"I am Division Director, Karl," she says to him, "and you do not want to fuck with me today."

And in that moment... I am so totally going to try to get back together with her if I get the chance.

The metal detectors squawk as we push through. Karl the security guard doesn't.

We march down the corridors. Felicity leads, Clyde close behind her, his long legs and swift body propelling him rapidly. I take third position, Tabitha next to me, Kayla behind, Malcolm and Aiko taking the rear.

It was a quiet, tense ride over. It's a quiet, tense walk. Tabitha is balling and unballing her fists. She talks a lot of smack, but she usually doesn't let things get to her this way. She didn't even know Jasmine.

"You OK?" I ask her.

She doesn't say a word, but her eyes flick to Clyde.

So not Jasmine then. "He's..." I start, but I don't know how to finish.

"Worse," she says. "Lot worse. Since you left. Not blaming you."

It doesn't help me feel less guilty to hear that.

"Withdrawn," she says. "Always," she hesitates, reaching for the word, then she taps the side of her head, "connected."

I look at his tall back, head held high, hair swishing under the two leather straps holding the mask in place. "Does he…" I struggle to put the concern into words. I'm not even sure I should. "He understands what's going on, right? He's still… connected," I use her word, "to here, to now?"

"Yes." Tabitha nods, but her face twists. A foreign emotion invades her features. She looks helpless. "But distracted. Other stuff. Too much of it." She shakes her head. "He never was any good at multi-tasking." The fondness that breaks through into the last statement only seems to make things worse. She grimaces again, tries to fix the scowl back on her face.

"Maybe," I start, "after all this is over… it'll be easier. He'll have time to process everything."

"Maybe tomorrow," Tabitha says, "reality won't exist."

She always was a chipper girl, Tabitha.

We round a corner and come into MI37's section of the building. It has changed significantly since I was there last night. About fifty women and men have been crammed into the space. They huddle around laptops like hobos around trashcan fires. If hobos wore the off-the-rack suits preferred by myself and others on a government salary.

Coleman stands in the middle of the room barking at people.

"Tell that fuck from Channel Four he can stick to the script or I will personally crucify him. On a real fucking cross." He spins. "Where's my bloody five-minute warning broadcast?" Spins again. "Why the fuck hasn't the Prime Minister called back? The urgency here is not hard to fucking understand." He spins again. He sees us.

"You!" He points at Felicity. "I realize you have managed to bungle every damn operation leading up to this moment, and you can count your remaining days in this office on your pinky fucking finger, but I thought you might have the brain cells required to—"

He stops mid-harangue. His eyes fix on me. "You." His voice drips acid. He wheels back to the crowd of agents behind him. "Jennings, Smith," he barks. "Arrest this blithering fuck. With extreme fucking prejudice."

Two agents stand and stare at our group. Apparently the description "blithering fuck" isn't enough to make me stand out from the group. I don't know if that speaks to the poorness of Coleman's descriptive powers or of the quality of company I keep.

"No." Felicity's voice is razor sharp. "Sit down and pay attention."

Coleman doesn't move a muscle, but the blood flows to his cheeks.

"The EMP is over," she says. "It's done. It's a broken plan. It endangers more than London, more than England, more than the western world, more than the whole world. It's over. Now you," she points, "Jennings, was it? I need—"

"You shut your fucking trap, woman." Coleman is the color of an overripe tomato.

"No." Felicity doesn't even blink. She takes a step toward him. "Understand this: your plan is over, George." She doesn't raise her voice but everyone can hear her. "You're over. You'll be packing your bags. You backed the wrong horse. Arthur came through. He was right. He has the proof." She points to a chair. "Now sit down, shut up, and be a good little boy while your career goes away."

Coleman visibly quakes with rage. I think he's going to hit Felicity. I think if he does I might run him through with this goddamn sword.

Somehow, using some resolve I didn't know he possessed, Coleman brings himself under control.

"Arrest her," Coleman barks. He doesn't even bother naming agents to do his dirty work. "Arrest them all."

Behind me, I hear the slight noise of metal over metal. Kayla draws her sword.

The mass of agents blanches.

"You are relieved of duty, George." Felicity is no less insistent. "You two," she points at the two agents Coleman wanted to arrest me, "escort Co-Director Coleman out of here, please."

"In your fucking seats," Coleman barks, not that any of the agents look any keener to carry out Felicity's order.

Coleman and Felicity stand in the middle of the room staring at each other. It feels like a recreation of the experiment in which nuclear fission was discovered.

A telephone on the desk behind Coleman shatters the silence. He seizes it so hard I'm surprised the receiver doesn't crack in his grip.

"Yes?" he hisses into the mouthpiece.

Suddenly his whole demeanor changes. He stands up straighter, puts his shoulders back. He even sucks in his gut. "Yes, sir."

I exchange a look with Felicity. She looks as nervous as I feel. A happy, comfortable Coleman is not a good thing for us.

"Ready to go, sir," Coleman says. His smile is a broad, smug stain on his face. "Yes, sir. Of course, sir." Three bags bloody full, sir.

He hangs up. He lets the silence drag out.

Felicity, clearly sick of his shit, opens her mouth to speak.

"Do you know who that was, Felicity?" Coleman cuts her off. He is prim with pride.

"Escort him out of here. Now, please." Felicity is still talking to the agents. One or two of them shift their weight. They're the ones unable to see the expression on Coleman's face.

Coleman keeps on looking smug. "It was the Prime Minister, Felicity." He rolls the title round his mouth like hard candy. "He just gave the final go-ahead on the EMP blast. Authority from the highest level."

And that is us pretty much screwed right there. The wind sags out of Felicity. She knew she was beaten, I think, she just didn't know how badly.

Coleman turns to the collected MI6 agents. "Arrest them."

For a moment we just stand there. I don't think any of us know what else to do. The EMP is going to go off. The Chronometer is going to be exposed. We are just totally screwed.

An agent steps toward Felicity. He looks apologetic, still deferential. "I'm sorry," he says. "I'm going to have to ask you—"

And no. Just no.

My fist whips out and shuts him up. He staggers back, falls, lands in a tangled heap. Coleman's jaw drops.

"Oh hell yes," Aiko says from behind me.

If only one bold move of defiance could somehow cancel out the mass of armed agents whose friend I just punched.

"Time for us to move," I suggest.

"Kayla! Clyde!" Felicity barks. "Cover our exit."

Kayla's sword is up in less time than it takes Coleman to think of shitting himself. Clyde's body gives a violent ripple, and every screen on every computer in the room goes blank. With trembling fingers he eases a battery up under his mask. Not to be outdone I pull out the flaming sword. Shock and goddamn awe.

The MI6 agents look very upset. But now they also look nervous as hell.

"What are you waiting for?" Coleman froths. "Get them!"

Despite their nervousness, more than one of them pulls a gun.

"Tactical retreat," Felicity mutters.

Clyde stretches out a hand, mutters to himself. This time it's not him who shudders but the reality around him. A great invisible tidal wave of force sweeps through the room and smashes into Coleman's operations center. Papers, laptops, and agents fly like dice rattled in a shaker. Coleman is barreled over, arms flapping like his bright red tie.

And then the bullets come.

"Faster tactical withdrawal!"

That, apparently, is the fancy technical language for, "flee."

We turn and hoof it. Shouts, barked orders, and bullets careen after us. We spin down one passageway and then another. We thunder past men talking quickly into walkie-talkies, tear away from doorways blocked by gaggles of anxious-looking civil servants.

"Arthur," Felicity says to me between pants. "Sword. Fire." She nods at the ceiling.

"What?"

"Alarms. Sprinklers." She pants again. "Set off."

I stare at the flaming sword still clutched in my hand, stare up at the ceiling. Every ten yards, a little gray nozzle perches between strip lights. I catch on, raise my sword. And I bring the rain.

We're splashing through puddles as we reach the exit. The lobby is full of milling sodden people. Security guards try to form a line but anxious men with half-drowned laptops keep pushing past. The place is a mad turmoil of panicking humanity. Behind us, the shouts are getting louder.

"Clyde!" Felicity yells. "A hole!"

He stretches out his hand and makes one. Personnel fly like bowling pins. I wave my sword around as imposingly as possible.

One guard fires. Kayla's sword whips out and there is the whine of a ricochet.

Oh, that trick I am going to *have* to learn.

Then we're out. Through the opening, through the doors, down the steps. The police cars still sit there. Policemen stand about looking confused. We race toward them.

"Ma'am," says an officer, holding out his hand to stop Felicity.

Out whips her fist. Down goes the officer. His partner yells, but only until the pommel of Kayla's sword cracks his skull.

"In!" Felicity yells at us. "Drive!"

There's a mad scramble for the cars. I still have the list of Russian safe house locations in my pocket so I dive for a driver's door, but Tabitha ducks in front of me.

I spin around, seize the door on the next car. Devon is sitting behind the wheel with a look of panic on her face.

"I don't really drive," she says.

"Accelerator. Floor. Now!" I so would have made an awesome driving instructor.

Behind me, people are still scrabbling into the seats. A door slams.

"Now!" a voice yells. Felicity. I spin around. There's something about the fact she chose the same car as me. Something that might be trust. That maybe could be something more.

Felicity sits in the back seat. Next to Clyde. And then... Aiko.

Oh, this is going to be a terrible race to save the world.

Devon pops the clutch, slams her foot to the floor. Wheels spin. Devon gives us all intimate feel for the g-forces available in a standard-issue police car.

By the expression on her face, I think Devon rather likes the experience. So at least one person in this car is grinning.

71

In my pocket, my phone buzzes. Screeching down the waterfront doesn't seem like the best time to take a call. Then Tabitha pulls alongside us, gesticulating wildly with her phone.

Side by side the cars peel down the road. Devon is letting out a keening yell of excitement and terror. Cars lean on their horns and spin out of our way.

I fish for my phone and smell something ugly. The flaming sword is melting its way through the passenger door. I somehow wrestle it away and settle for plunging it through the window. Collision glass shatters, spills in our wake. A thousand glittering glass beads flash with reflected firelight.

My phone continues buzzing. Tabitha continues gesticulating. Just more angrily.

Devon swerves. A car whines past, clips our wing mirror. I introduce my head to the doorframe. I come up, head ringing.

I make another attempt to flip open the phone. Instead I drop it, curse, wrestle with the scabbard; almost neuter myself; set myself on fire; pat it out; finally slot the sword away; and then beat my head rhythmically against the glove compartment while I try and get my phone back.

Finally I grab it, take the call.

"We're going," Tabitha snaps. "Where?"

I pull the list from my pocket. I stare. Six addresses. I look at my watch. 5:17 p.m.

"Address," Tabitha demands, steering violently away to avoid a motorbike's kamikaze run. I think the bike's rider was covering her eyes.

"Give me a minute."

"Reality. Not having enough time left to spare you a minute."

Devon slams us up onto the sidewalk. A trashcan explodes over the windscreen. I get to really regret having shattered the window.

Six addresses. Scattered across London. Think. I need to think.

We put the message in the *East London Advertiser*. That makes two of the addresses more likely. The first place they hit was the Natural History Museum. They're going to target Big Ben.

I really wish my sense for London's geography was better.

If I pick wrong...

If I pick wrong then we're going to need to get to Big Ben really fast.

"Thirty-five Redman's Road," I say. And then I pray I'm right.

72

The car hurtles around a corner. Our suspension creaks. Our tires scream almost as loud as the pedestrians.

"I don't want to be a pain in the whole gluteal region," Devon says, grimacing over the rim of the steering wheel. "But I actually have no clue how to get to anywhere in London."

"Next left," Felicity says from the back seat. "Then a right."

I glance over my shoulder, look at her. She's sitting, perched forward on her seat. Jaw set. Eyes ablaze.

She looks such a tremendous badass.

"I just..." I start. "When you..." Both Felicity and Aiko look up at me. And that's not helping. "Thank you," I say to Felicity. "For what you said to Coleman. When you said he'd picked wrong. I... That was nice."

Felicity glances over my shoulder at the road. Devon slings us into a sliding, trembling skid. Then Felicity reaches out, touches my hand. "How about we save the world, then have the make-up sex. OK?"

And despite it all, despite the peril, and the terror, and the absurdity of my role in trying to save the world, despite Aiko being right bloody there, God do I smile. Big enough to split my face and hurt my cheeks.

I turn to Devon. "Whatever you do," I say to her, "please do not crash." I suddenly find I have way too much to live for.

"Additional pressure is not absolutely the most helpful thing right now, Arthur." Devon attempts to force the car into a pirouette around a traffic circle. She settles for mostly just smashing through it.

A few yards behind us, Tabitha pinballs her cop car off a bus bench and a streetlamp.

"So," Aiko's voice comes from behind me like a blade. "You two back together then?"

And really? Really now?

"Too much talking!" Devon tries to pilot the car but we've taken the opportunity to leave the ground. We sail past agape tourists. We land. The suspension crunches. The police siren fights through several awkward octaves. I seek to extract my head from the car's roof.

"I believe so," Felicity answers Aiko.

I seek to extract my head faster.

"Did we ever, I mean, officially," I say, attempting to inject levity into the disaster yawning wide in the back seat, "actually officially break up?"

Clyde twitches his head at that one. Either the internet is getting to him or even he can see what an abysmal attempt to rescue myself that is.

"I did assume that when you screamed, 'I quit,' at me, you weren't only talking about the job." Felicity glances at me, and then at Aiko.

"Is there," Devon shrieks, "the slightest possibility of any of you considering that I found a polite but forceful way to tell you all to shut the hell up?"

"I did assume," Aiko says, ignoring Devon and my desperate need to live through the next minute, "that after Kiev you'd broken up."

We bounce off a curb. Horns howl in our wake. Tabitha sends her car shooting past us and levels a trashcan.

"What," Felicity's voice does the icicle thing that makes my spine seem to seize up, "happened in Kiev?"

"Nothing happened in Kiev!" I throw up my hands as best the car roof and g-forces will allow.

"Counting the kiss?"

Oh God. I was really hoping she wouldn't bring that up.

"If someone doesn't stop trying to organize Arthur's sex life and tell me which turn to take next the world is going to end!" Devon snaps.

I have to say, it's not often I hear that.

"Right in a hundred and fifty yards," Clyde intones.

Felicity, perhaps in deference to Devon's request for silence, simply stares at me with all the powers of unholy hell itself.

I wonder if it's possible to get into Tabitha's car at these sort of speeds. Hang out with Kayla and Malcolm for a while.

"I didn't…" I start. "She… me…" I close my eyes. And I thought we were past this. I thought all the personal crap was dealt with. I thought we were going to save the world. "*She* kissed *me*. Nothing happened."

Absolute silence. Like the void of space. Like traveling beyond the event horizon.

"There," Devon says, "much better. Much appreciated."

73

Devon plows on through London's streets. Traffic peels away from us, screeching. The only noise from our car is the thrum of the tires over the blacktop. Devon noses past Tabitha. Tabitha noses back.

Clyde breaks the silence. "What is our plan of action for when we arrive?"

Nobody else seems to want to answer, so I open my mouth and wait for someone to jump down my throat. When the coast seems clear, I say, "Guns blazing is pretty much the full extent of it." I think it's safe to assume the time for subtlety is over.

"And what about Coleman?" His voice is utterly emotionless. Which, for once, seems to be the best option, considering the range of alternatives available at this particular emotional buffet.

He's right too. Coleman could be after us.

"As long as we take care of the Russians then that's all that matters," I say. I don't have time to come up with contingencies

"I could have changed his mind," Clyde says quietly.

"He seemed pretty set on the whole screwing us and everything else up plan," I say. It's a little late for the rehash, I feel.

"I could have," Clyde insists.

"No." Felicity looks over at him sharply. "Remember what Tabitha said. What we all said."

I risk a glance at Felicity's face. She looks concerned.

"About what?" I'm confused now.

"Look," Devon says, "I don't want to be the proverbial broken record, but when exactly did we decide it was OK to start distracting me again?"

"Next left," Felicity snaps at her.

"I simply worked out how to reverse the upload I did to move my consciousness from my body into the mask. A download process."

And wait… That doesn't… "You can invade people's heads via a wireless connection?" I try to imagine the repercussions of that simple statement. It's… That's bad. The sort of bad that fuels CIA conspiracy theories. The sort of bad that causes people to wear tinfoil hats. Jesus… Clyde almost has more powers than bloody Superman at this point.

"But it's morally wrong, though, isn't it Clyde." Felicity has the sort of smile you wear while you talk the crazy man into putting down the gun. "We discussed that. With Tabitha."

She pulls out her phone. "We can discuss it with her now."

"Not discussed. You stated," Clyde says.

I try to be happy that there's finally some emotion in that last speech. Except sulkiness isn't the right one.

I glance over at Tabitha in her car. Kayla and Malcolm both sit ramrod straight in the back seat. The former grips her sword, the latter his enormous revolver. Tabitha stares at her phone, glances at us, swerves around a pedestrian, then gives us the finger.

"Can you use that sword?" Clyde asks me abruptly.

Devon slams the car into a hard turn. The wheels scream and screech.

"What?" I don't know why Clyde is asking me this. I don't know why he's addressing it after talking about mind-raping people. I don't know if I want to talk to him at all.

"Your sword," he speaks louder. "Are you any good with it?"

"Erm…" I say.

"He's terrible," Devon says, nerves apparently winning over verbosity as she struggles to keep the car out of a storefront.

"See." Clyde turns to Felicity. "It can be useful."

Oh God.

"No!" Felicity barks. Her hand snaps out at him, through

space, reaching, reaching… never arriving. She seems to slow halfway through the motion. I watch her hair flicking, the ripple of motion. I watch the expression of fear build muscle by muscle. The car's desperate lurch becomes a swampy slide. Everything feels slushy and awkward, time wrapped in treacle.

And then pain. Pain moving with all the speed the world has lost. Expanding. Blooming. And I'm trying to grab my head, to stop the pain from exploding beyond the confines of my skull, trying to hold it all together, but I'm so slow. Everything is slow. Everything except the pain. And the world shrinks to a pinpoint. And all I can see is Clyde's mask. And I look for a smile, for something cruel or kind, for anything. But there's nothing. Just wood and blankness. And then the pain is too much, and there's nothing at all.

74

If my head is a cake of baked pain, then the car's police siren is the knife. A pulsing wave of auditory agony that cuts through the pleasures of unconsciousness.

"There," Clyde says, "all done."

"What the fuck did you do to my head?" I scream, except it comes out more as a grunt and a gob of spit. And there is a lot of shouting and name-calling, and I'm not sure I'm really heard.

I open my eyes. I wish I hadn't. The world slaloms back and forth in front of me. It is full of screaming people and endangered pedestrians. The back of another police car looms too close.

"What the fuck did you do to me?"

I achieve audibility. Everyone turns.

"I helped." Clyde does not sound as defensive as I feel he should. "With the sword."

"We talked about this!" Felicity has her fists balled, knuckles white, arm half-cocked. "This is not a fucking gray area!"

"Are you OK?" Aiko stares at me, face pale. "Is your head OK?"

"I helped." Clyde is insistent.

"With giving me fucking migraines?" I would love to give Clyde the benefit of the doubt but he ran out of that about one mind-raping ago.

"The sword." Clyde sounds slightly hurt. "So you can use it."

"What?" Maybe it's the blinding pain, but I am not getting a clear read on his reasons.

"I downloaded information," Clyde says. "Into your brain. On swords. On how to use them. A lot of styles. You know how to riposte now."

"I don't even know what—" and then I stop. Because I do know what a riposte is. I know how to execute one. I know how to look for one. I know tell-tale signs. I know how to string them together. I know different sword types and grips that will facilitate styles that rely heavily upon the riposte. I am a virtual sodding encyclopedia on ripostes.

"Oh my God."

"You're welcome," Clyde says.

Except am I? Should I thank him? My brain was just violated in a massive and monstrous way.

"I suppose that does sound helpful," Devon says from the driver's seat. "Minus the blinding pain. Do you know anything about driving?"

"Do not encourage him!" Felicity barks.

Useful. God, is that really the word?

I look at Clyde, the world swaying and swerving behind his head as Devon fishtails round another corner.

"You're not human," I say. I don't mean to. I'm disoriented, and head-fucked, and trying to come to terms with too many things, and it's an accident. But I say it. And I mean it.

"No," Clyde agrees with me. "I'm not. I'm a mask."

"You're not." Felicity is insistent, hissing it through her teeth. "You're human. Meat. Blood. You have to remember that. God, we spoke about this."

I look again at Tabitha in the car, my eyes still watering. And does she know? Has she had this conversation with him? Does she know how far he's gone?

"I'm electronic," Clyde insists. "I am ones and zeroes."

"You're…"

"My body died. This is someone else's. I'm like a parasite."

And I can't take my eyes off Tabitha. And she can't know. She mustn't know. She's tougher than nails and twice as sharp but this would break her in two. Does Clyde know that? Does he realize?

"Could we have picked a better time?" Devon says it sotto voce, but her hushed words are another man's violent yell. Clyde died. I realize. More than a week ago now. Just none of us realized it. I finally look back at him. It's like there's a ghoul or a zombie sitting between Felicity and Aiko. Calm. Unfeeling.

Except he's our ghoul. Our zombie.

"I'm sorry," I say, trying to reach Clyde, somewhere behind his mask. "You're right. And it's been wrong to pretend you're not a mask. And it's wrong to make judgments because of who you are."

"He's a dick, Arthur," Devon says. "No matter what his corporeal state."

I'm not sure I have the nerve to insult a man who can overwrite my brain.

"You're a member of this team," I say to Clyde, ignoring Devon. "You're valued. You're a friend." I honestly don't know if that's still true. But I think it's what he needs to hear. And I don't know what team I'm officially on now, what team any of us are on, but the world has less than thirty minutes and I'm sure as hell not going to spend it trying to establish which circle I can piss in.

"We're all a team," I say. "We need to work together." I look from Clyde, to Aiko, to Felicity. "Can we work together?" We have to work together.

Nothing but silence from the peanut gallery. And I'd be the first to admit, this is a little late in the day for me to start a career as a motivational speaker.

"We're about to find out," Devon finally chips in. "We're here."

75

As a general rule, if you're trying to sneak up on someone, I've always believed that going about the business with a police siren blaring is a no-no. Maybe not something I should really have to point out, but subtleties like this can get lost in a rush.

One sneaking faux pas we do manage to avoid: ramming our vehicle through the wall of our target's house. We settle for violently dispersing our tire rubber over the asphalt and making the suspension cry uncle.

Devon slews her car round in front of the house. Felicity flings open her door, spills out, gun drawn. She crouches behind the metal door, aiming at the house's wooden one.

Kayla is already leaping from Tabitha's car, sword drawn, as it screeches towards the building's front door.

"Be ready!" Felicity shouts, clearly audible through my smashed window. "If this is the right house, they'll already know—"

There's a flash of light in one of the windows.

"Incoming!" Devon yells.

Electricity spits and crackles twenty yards down the road. A silhouette is just visible in the retinal afterglow. More flashes of light. More figures appearing.

And then further away. Retreating.

Holy crap. I picked right.

"They're running!" I yell. "They're making a break for it."

More flashes of light. The Russians are fifty yards further down the road.

"Holy shit," Aiko says.

And those Russians sure can move.

"Floor it!"

Devon doesn't need telling twice now. The engine howls, the car spasms. Felicity dives through her open door. We spin out into the road, tires shrieking, and peel after them. Tabitha's car is inches from our careening path.

Devon pushes the car to speeds that should be impossible in London. The needle of the speedometer creeps to fifty, to sixty, seventy. And we're barely keeping up. The Russians are spots of light blinking down the street, jumping fifty yards at a time.

"My coat pocket," Devon says to me, without taking her eyes off the road.

As much as I'd love to be a Dan Brown hero, puzzling out cryptic clues during the middle of a car chase is not exactly my bloody forte.

"Little more information, please."

"Teleporting Russians. Space-time disturbances. Residual pockets of danger." Devon seems not to have time for her usual loquaciousness. "We hit one, we all get turned into babies and old people. Horrible way to die. In my coat pocket. The device to clear the path."

The car hurtles after the Russians. Behind us, Tabitha and the others careen in our wake. I try to envision the myriad pockets of disturbed time and space we are rushing through. I try not to imagine having a fetal arm. To be honest I should have spent two seconds working out what Devon meant by "my pocket" and not wasted all this bloody time.

I reach in. My fingers tangle with a mess of wires. I pull it out, point the speaker out the window, and press play.

The street erupts in flame. We barrel into a floating ball of fire. I feel the hairs on the back of my hand blacken and curl.

More explosions. Little detonations spaced fifty yards apart, sometimes a fizzle, sometimes Krakatoa. We race through their shockwaves. One leaves a crater in the street. Our car hurtles through it and I am nearly flipped out the open window. Tabitha chases in our fiery wake.

People should be running. Should be screaming. Cars should be barreling over each other to escape—a Hollywood ecstasy of panic. But we sail through traffic lights, and there's no one there to honk us. We fly around a corner, tires leaving a black trail, and there are no pedestrians to scream and cower. The press of traffic that accompanied us to the Russians has abruptly abandoned the streets.

"Where is everybody?"

"I'm not certain now is the time to interrogate providence?" Devon snaps, at least as much as anyone is capable of snapping that many syllables.

"Oh shit," says Felicity from the back seat.

"What?" I spin round.

"Turn off the car!" She waves urgently and inarticulately at Devon's back.

"Are you kidding me?" Devon isn't going to be stopped by anyone.

Tabitha's car skids past us, still drifting as I see her wrench her own keys free. The Russians are retreating points of light.

"Stop the car!" Felicity bellows it at the top of her lungs.

OK, apparently Devon is going to be stopped by that. Tires squeal, the car pitches, the back wheels give out on us, drift wildly, send us spinning out in a wild circle. We swirl around like a ballerina on the blacktop.

My phone is buzzing. I stare at it as Devon yanks the keys from the car.

"Five!" Felicity yells. "Four!"

It's Tabitha's number. I flip open the phone, press it to my ear.

"His mask! Get off his bloody mask!"

"Three!" Felicity yells.

"What on earth—?"

"Clyde!" Tabitha is still shrieking. "Get it off!"

"Two!"

I reach out, grab the edge of Clyde's mask, wait for him to reach out and stop me. But there's nothing.

"One!"

"The EMP!" Tabitha is shrieking. "Get off—" Oh shit. I rip at the mask, not caring if Clyde offers resistance or not.

"Zero."

76

I expect a crescendo. A symphonic blast of electric wind ripping through the streets of London. I expect a hurricane of newspapers and trash flowing like a tidal wave down the streets.

It is not the first time Hollywood has lied to me.

Instead it is like a great hand coming down, vast and implacable, snuffing London like a candle.

Everything goes out. Every streetlamp, every light in every house, every neon sign. Not a spit or a spark. Just out, off, done. London shut down.

I'm holding Clyde's mask. My best friend is in my hand. But is he still in there?

In the distance I see a flash of light.

"They're still going," Felicity says. "The Russians are still getting goddamn power from somewhere."

"Go," I say. "Start the car. Go now."

"It's always bloody demands with you," Devon grumbles as she fumbles with the keys.

"Just go!" I yell at her. There is a chance I'm letting the tension get to me.

"I'm going," Devon says, and accelerates at a rate that would make NASA scientists proud. We rocket past Tabitha but a moment later she's hot in pursuit again.

I stare at the mask. "Did I get it in time?" I say. This is what was left of him. And it was broken, and breaking my heart, but I need it to be him still.

"You got it." Aiko reaches out a hand to me.

Felicity slaps it away. "Put it on him and we'll find out."

It's a struggle to get it on his slumped body from my angle.

"I'll do it," Aiko offers.

"I will," Felicity demands. She takes the mask, jams it on Clyde's head.

Nothing. Nothing.

He arcs, shudders, and yells. An electronic mess of sounds. And then silence. He stares at us each in turn.

"Clyde," I say, "please... just... please never cut it even half that close again." I smile as best I am able. "Tabitha will remove my balls."

Clyde doesn't respond at first. Then he cocks his head. "Unlikely," he tells me in a mirthless monotone.

And it's never going to be as good to have him back as I hope.

We scream through London. Shops are a blur. Landmarks are a streak in my vision. The battered police car rattles, almost quivers as the speedometer creeps toward the red. We eat miles like hors d'oeuvres. Behind us I can see Tabitha barreling after us. Malcolm leans from one window, shielding his eyes against the battering winds. A gun is in his spare hand.

And we're getting closer.

The flares of the Russians' teleportation grow larger, from twinkling sparks, to flashlight rays, to spotlight glows.

"Batteries," Clyde says from the back seat. "They must be carrying batteries."

I think. "How much power to make a jump?"

"Assuming they have car batteries?"

"Sure." I breathe slowly, trying to keep the adrenaline from pushing frustration into my voice.

Clyde cocks his head, trembles. "They have enough electricity to power somewhere in the vicinity of three thousand jumps, I'd say."

"Can we run them down?"

"The batteries?"

"Of course the batteries!" My cool is definitely starting to fray.

"Many potential definitions of that sentence." Clyde sounds like he's trying to impersonate HAL.

"Let's go with the obvious one."

"Average of fifty-six yards per jump. Average charge…" Clyde mumbles to himself. "Distance… Assuming taking as direct a route as… Avoiding major…" He cocks his head, straightens it. "We'd have to double the number of jumps they need to take. Approximately."

I stare at the growing blasts of electrical light racing ahead of us. Double. How do you divert someone who can blink through fifty-plus yards of space?

Visions of dropping massive cages with hundred-feet-thick walls flash through my head, but being shy of a week, five hundred engineers, and a limitless supply of lead that may not be so helpful.

"We have to distract them," I say.

"You have a plan?" Felicity arches an eyebrow.

"We have to make them stop and fight us."

"Why in God's name would they do that?" Devon takes a break from trying to choke the life from the steering wheel to sound incredulous.

But I'm picturing Jasmine again, that little black bag on the riverbank of the Thames. I picture the red glaze that overtook the world.

"They fight us because we piss them off. They fight us because we make them hurt."

77

"Get us closer," I tell Devon.

"What, in the name of all that is holy, do you think I'm trying to do? This is hardly how I idle down to the shops. I think going one-ten is, in fact, the polar bloody opposite of idling. Though of course if you have an alternate definition, or some spare dictionary upon you—"

"Faster!" I cut her off.

To her credit, Devon complies. I grit my teeth. I aim the speaker of the space-time disruptor. Fire flares and dies, rushing past us in whispers of searing air. Tabitha does her best to match our pace. We race down the streets, almost parallel.

We edge closer. Closer. But I still need to be closer.

From Tabitha's car, Malcolm starts firing. Even over the tear of the wind I hear the explosive percussion of each shot. He fires slowly, methodically. Boom. Boom. Boom. He has one hand up almost covering his eyes. The gun is held out like a new-fangled lance, the police cruiser his twenty-first-century steed. Like some knight of old come to save us. Boom. Boom. Boom.

I count the flashes of light ahead of us now. Seven. I list them off in my head. Urve, Joseph, Ivan, Ekaterina, Leo, Katerina and… the woman in the van, the one who had warned Leo he was going to hurt himself while he beat seven shades of shit out of me. I wonder who she was in the file. Who we missed. I wonder if I'll ever see her face before one or both of us die.

Boom. Boom. Boom. Malcolm ducks back into the car, reloads. I turn out of the wind, suck in a tortured breath, hold it, turn back. A Russian blinks into existence, maybe ninety yards away. We close the distance. Eighty yards. Sixty. He vanishes. Reappears, but we're closer now, on his heels. He's only eighty-five yards away now. We close. We close. Fifty-five yards. He disappears. Reappears. Sixty yards. Forty. Disappears. Reappears. Fifty yards. OK, it's on.

I twist around in my seat. "Clyde, I need you."

"How can I help you?" Clyde sounds like an ATM machine.

I lean out my open window. We're alongside Tabitha's car now. The barrel flare of Malcolm's pistol is almost close enough to warm my ear. It's like he's trying to hit air, though, and the Russians know it. We need a broader field of damage. Something they'll have a harder time avoiding.

"You remember the lion in Trafalgar Square?" I twist back, yell at Clyde as he leans out the window, wind tearing his lank blond hair into a streaming tail. "The one you chopped in two?"

"Sinsdale." Clyde is barely audible above the wind.

"How big a space can you paint with that bastard?"

Clyde's head twists. He ducks back into the car, I follow suit.

"You want me to create an area that they will teleport into?"

"Hell yes I do."

"That will cause them to be sliced in two."

And where does that moral dilemma fit in to Clyde's shedding of humanity? "That's kind of the point," I tell him.

Clyde nods. He ducks out the window, stretches out a hand, bows his head. I can't hear the words, but I see the edges of his jaw work. Then a bellow. He sags back into the car, panting. I spin, watch the points of light. Less than fifty yards away. They jump.

At the leading edge, one spark turns from blue to red. A detonation ahead of the bleeding line of disturbed space-time. A silhouette framed in red and yellow. A silhouette splitting. Two halves of a body peeling away. One up—an almost elegant arc— the other down, tumbling, rolling, ungainly and splayed, two sticks of meats sprayed over the ground. The spinning torso sheds strings of viscera, comes down, collides with the ground. Half of a Russian grinds along the ground. Devon swerves to avoid it.

Seven flashes of light, reduced to six.

Our first Russian down. The violence of the death keeps me from fist pumping though.

And then ahead of us, six flares are reduced to four. I scan wildly. Where did—

A blast of blue light to the right. A woman on the hood of Tabitha's car. I wrestle for my gun.

And then, another blast of blue. Directly in front of us, filling the windscreen, eclipsing the street. I throw up a hand trying to shield my eyes. Too late. Devon flaps ineffectively at the sun shade.

And then, there, in the fading glare, balanced wildly on top of the car's hood: the portly, tweed-encased Joseph Punin. Pummeled by wind, he crouches there, face contorted by fury. His space-glove is held way above his head. I can see fresh plates of metal roughly riveted over the old. Something that looks too much like flesh crusted around the edge. Repair work after our last encounter.

And then the time for appreciating the enemy's armament is over. Punin slams the glove through the windscreen, turns it white with cracks. He tears the glass away in one movement, fills the car with howling wind.

And if I was looking for a fight, I just found one.

78

Devon screams. The glove comes at her head. I want to go for my sword, but thanks to Clyde, I'm fully aware of how badly I'm positioned for that. Instead I punch at the man's legs.

The angle's wrong, and the wind is wild, and the distance too far, and I just graze his ankle, but Punin is balancing on the hood of a car going over a hundred miles per hour, and sometimes a graze is all it takes.

He goes down, the blow turned into an ugly flail. His metal fingers punch through the metal of the hood. He drags six-inch-long tears in the metal. He dangles there, a fish hooked.

He blinks away. Suddenly gone in a spark of light.

"Where?" Aiko shouts against the roar of the wind filling the car.

I stare around. A woman I don't recognize is clinging to the hood of Tabitha's car. Malcolm empties a magazine at her.

A thump from the roof of our car. Five fingers crash down, punch five holes in the car's ceiling. Aiko yells out.

I really need to get this sword out.

I stand, leaning my body out through the empty frame of the windscreen, pitching my body until it meets the angle my head tells me is right. I twist my hand just so. Not too far clockwise or anticlockwise. I pull with fast, firm efficiency, watching the pitch of my shoulder, my elbow. The sword comes out in a quick, clean stroke.

And, actually, this could have been worth the migraine.

Punin is tearing at the roof, punching holes. His fist comes down, almost sits in Aiko's lap.

I twist around in my seat, facing backwards, body still through the windscreen, propped up by the wind. I can see Punin towering above me. He twists, sees me. He raises his fist. I swing the sword.

A sword lances through the air in front of me. Not mine. No flames. No flash. Just sheer and deadly. It slams through Punin's fist. He screams as he is pinned to the car.

I'm already swinging. A great cleaving swipe, aimed at his midriff. Flame spits and crackles as my sword connects with his side, continues on, embeds in spinal tissue.

Punin doesn't even scream. Just spills himself out onto the road in a silent, bloody gush.

I stare across the road. Kayla is looking at me, leaning out of a car window, her hand still extended from the throw that speared his hand.

On the car hood—a bloody stain. No Russian. Malcolm is smiling triumphantly.

I stare at Punin's corpse, still flapping against the car window, pinned by Kayla's sword.

I tug my sword free, then Kayla's. Punin's body tumbles to the road, and rolls away. I discover I know the angle to toss the sword back to Kayla. She catches it. For a moment she might even look impressed. She nods at me, and ducks back into her car.

79

Three Russians down. Four to go. Four spark-haloed silhouettes racing through the night. Still on course.

And then just two sparks.

Which means…

Suddenly, sitting in Clyde's lap. Between Aiko and Felicity. Ekaterina Kropkin. Terminator eyes red with rage. She smashes an elbow into Felicity's face. Felicity's nose becomes a red smear. I yell, drive the sword at her, slicing into—

—nothing. A flash of light. The Russian woman gone. The flaming sword tip is an inch from Felicity's blood-soaked hands as they clutch her face. She bellows in pain.

"No," Clyde says clear as an alarm clock. "No."

To my right another flash of light. I spin, expect to see Kropkin lunging at me, but there's proto-Lenin, Urve Potia, on the hood of Tabitha's car. Electricity lances through the windscreen. Glass shatters.

"No!" I bellow, an angry echo to Clyde. These bastards just upped the personal ante.

I'm not really thinking as I pitch across the car, seize the steering wheel. Devon screams. I ignore her. I slam the car right, barreling us into Tabitha's car.

Hands loose on the wheel, too busy ducking, Tabitha loses

control. Her car veers right, slams up onto a curb, grates along building facades. Potia is thrown wildly up. He crashes into concrete, rolls along, his body folding at unnatural angles. He lands, becomes a speed bump for Tabitha. Becomes a mess of blood and bone.

Four down, you fuckers.

A lightning burst, right in front of my eyes, blinding me. I reel back into the chair, retinas burning. I just make out the figure in front of me, her hand going back.

Felicity is still yelling, still bleeding.

Clyde says "No" again. The same voice. Definite. Soulless.

Kropkin's hand plunges towards my throat.

And stops.

"No," says Clyde.

Her hand goes up. She clutches her head.

"No," says Clyde.

I blink, trying to clear my vision. Trying to understand. Kropkin pulls away from me, pushes herself backwards, across the hood of the car.

"Wait…" I say, not understanding, feeling that something is askew, that we have somehow deviated from life's script.

Ekaterina Kropkin calmly pushes herself off the hood of the car and under our tires.

The car thuds over her, bounces, suspension shrieking. The back wheels hit and the car flips up. We land, crash down. Bewildered. Dazed.

"What?" I ask the world. "Why did she…? Did she…?"

Words emerge from Felicity's bellowing. "You irresponsible, amoral shit!" A hand leaps out, strikes the side of Clyde's mask. His head snaps away, a bloody handprint on the otherwise blank wood.

"I don't understand," I say. But I think I do. But I don't want to.

"I helped," Clyde says, calm and savage all at once in the back seat.

"You made her?" I ask him. "You went into her head, and you made her do that?"

"The grossest of violations!" Felicity sounds as if she has a cold. I am torn between comforting her and… and… Clyde… Clyde… I feel sick. That's… And, Jesus, I know we are killing people here. I know we are fighting for our existence, for everybody's continued existence. But that's a sort of cold-blooded I can't even begin to imagine. To just reach into someone's head, to tell them to kill themselves. To know they'll do it.

"Good riddance, I say," says Devon. Who is apparently a lot more bloodthirsty than her floral patterns would lead you to believe.

"What would Tabitha say?" I ask him. "What would she think of this?"

I look over at her car. Would it be different if she were here? Would he refrain from exercising the more alien of his powers? I fear he wouldn't.

"We cannot always accommodate others," Clyde replies, quite calmly, and he turns his head quite slowly from Felicity to Aiko.

And no. No, don't make this about me. This is about more than just losing a friend. Losing friends. This is about what's right and wrong. About good guys and bad guys. About being one and not the other.

And maybe it's not just what's worth fighting for, but how you fight.

I close my eyes. "She kissed me," I say.

Felicity snaps her head around. She looks at me. "What?"

"She kissed me. I let her kiss me. I thought it was over. You and me. I thought we were done. And I let her kiss me."

"How the fuck is that relevant?"

She's angry. She has a right to be angry.

"It's not," I say. "I think that's the point I'm trying to make." I'm not sure. But I have four friends in this car, and I think I can feel three of them slipping away. But maybe this is my chance to grab onto at least one of them. "You once said I was a decent man. And I did an indecent thing. I'm trying to make it right in a decent way."

Felicity stares at me, and I can't read her face.

"I don't suppose," Devon says from the driver's seat, "that there's a chance we could save the melodrama until later and sort of focus on stopping those two bastards in front of us? I mean, I realize that I'm just some psychopath's ex-girlfriend at this point, but considering how completely my life has been crapped on over the past two weeks, I would really appreciate a little effort in making the sacrifice worthwhile."

She flings the car sideways. We spin around a car, sitting abandoned in the center of the street.

There are people on the streets now. Some cheer as we scream past them. Probably think we're street racers taking advantage. Some are busy smashing windows in stores. Grabbing and running. No alarms sound. The lights have gone down and the night people have come out. People willing to be faceless masses, to welcome the darkness. Chaos is slowly breaking loose in London.

Jesus. Coleman EMP'd the capital. All of it. He shut everything down. For nothing. For a false belief.

God, I hope we get these guys just so I get to see the look on his bloody face.

"Five down," I say. But I can no longer smile as we hurtle towards the two remaining sparks of light.

80

"Big Ben's getting close." Felicity, bloodstained and angry, is staring past me at the road.

The Russians tear toward a T-junction and we shriek after them.

"Left or right?" Devon is white-knuckled on the steering wheel.

Clyde sits stonily in the back seat, saying nothing.

The Russians are sixty yards ahead of us, Tabitha ten yards behind. Detonating disturbed space-time leads the way, and the blast of Malcolm's pistol chases us. And the yards of stone frontage approach us at an alarming pace.

"Toss up," I tell Devon.

"I've never made a handbrake turn," Devon informs us.

"Watch which way they go," I say.

"Any other patently obvious advice?" Devon snaps.

I bite back an equally catty response. One of us losing the battle with our nerves seems like enough.

A blink of light. Our tires eat asphalt. Another flare. We're running out of road.

Two flashes. One left, one right.

"They've split up!" Aiko and I—apparently the official peanut gallery—say it in unison.

"Oh shit on it." Devon hauls on the steering wheel. The brakes squeal. The tires squeal. Even I squeal a little bit.

We're up on two wheels as we make the left. I can see the curb approaching. If we hit it, we're going over.

The car trembles. I can hear the free wheels spinning madly, whining through the air.

The car comes down. Four wheels touch down. We slam up onto the sidewalk. Smash through a plastic box of newspapers. They flutter through where our windscreen should be. I scrape a bogus story about solar flares off my face.

I glance back. The rear lights of Tabitha's car retreat from us. She's chasing the other Russian. Malcolm and his deadly aim go with her. Kayla too.

I need to concentrate. To focus. On the bastard in front of us. Which one is it? Ivan Spilenski, who almost killed me at the British Museum, or Leo Malkin, who almost killed me outside Trafalgar Square? The time distorter or the teleporter?

A soft "bwoom." A movie special effect of slowed time. As all around me, everything seems to accelerate.

I try to bring the tangle of wires still clutched in my hand to bear. Try to target the ball of space.

Devon slams on the brakes. Felicity flies forward. My seatbelt snaps tight as a garotting wire. Aiko shouts. The car shrieks. Devon seizes the handbrake. I try to wrench my head around. But I know what's coming.

Ivan Spilenski, you are so going down.

Unless you turn me into a baby first, of course.

The back wheels go, screeching round. We barrel down the street sideways. Devon's precious tangle of wires flies out of my hand, somehow lands in the back seat. It snakes toward Aiko, picking up speed, heading toward the open window. The car pitches. We sail up onto two wheels again. The car teeters. The wires take off, lift up into the air. I snap out my hand, lunge against the tangential forces. I miss. The wires sail by.

A trailing wire catches around my finger. I grip tight. It slips. I grab again, catch a finger hold, squeeze. I hold tight.

The car goes over. Up onto its side. Down the street, sideways. The frame buckles. Blacktop grinds closer, closer, through my open window. Then—with a crash, with a shaking of the world—over again, onto the roof, which crumples down, shrieking, screaming, the ripped metal howling at the injustice. Gravity pulls at me, but apparently it pissed off my seatbelt at some point and that thing's not letting go without a fight.

"Oh shit. Oh fuck. Oh no. Oh crap." A stream of profanity flows out of Devon. I fear we may have broken her.

Something slams into the exposed underbelly of the car. Slams through it.

It's a slow implacable grinding. Spilenski's ball of distorted time eating out the exhaust, the suspension, the steering. Rust rains on us. Clyde kicks his legs out of its path, towards the crumpled car roof now below him.

If we'd been upright… If we'd been facing head-on… It would have torn us apart. Not that Spilenski will be hanging around now, scratching his head.

"Out of the car!" I yell. "Now!"

And this is the point where the captain ensures all the crew are safely out before he takes care of himself, except I'm going to do that after I get the hell out of this death trap.

I wrestle with the locking mechanism.

Bwoom. Spilenski rolls out a ball of distorted space-time with my name all over it.

And was it Satan him-bloody-self who designed this damn belt?

Felicity slams down onto the roof behind me. She sees me wrestling. She slams her fist at the belt mechanism.

The effect is something similar to what I imagine James Bond experiences when he activates his ejector seat. Except his car is never stuck upside down when he does it.

Staggering, barely able to see, I push out of the window. I'm on my back, head arched back. I can see Spilenski upside down. His form seems to ripple and bend.

Because I am seeing it through a bubble of distorted time. Because I am about to be hit.

I struggle against my own confusion, my own limbs. I demand my body gets its shit together. I half roll, half drag myself to the side.

The enormous gelatinous thing wobbles past me.

The police car disintegrates. Rust eats it. Parts fold up on themselves, compressing into impossibly small pieces of metal. Other bits unbuckle, spit out their rivets, collapse into shining unpainted sheets of metal as the clock turns back. A few chunks of rocky ore spatter the road.

Bwoom.

Spilenski fires at us again. I scramble up, still on all fours. An empty street in London. Lined with lawyers and dentists, real estate agents and upscale cosmetic salons. Not the sort to litter the street with convenient bits of rubble or colossal concrete barriers.

Bwoom.

I reach for my sword. My hand closes over empty air.

My sword. Still in the wreck of Devon's car. Spilenski's ball of messed up time rolling towards it.

God my priorities are messed up.

Bwoom.

I break into a run, lungs battered and screaming at me, demanding I stop this madness. My legs add to the chorus. Two yards between me and the blade. Four between me and the ball. One yard to the sword. Three to the ball. I scrabble at the sword's hilt. Two yards. One. I dive away.

Bwoom.

Some part of my brain knows how to roll without setting fire to my pants. Still, I'm thinking Clyde might have overwritten some important self-preservation urges.

I come up, lit sword in my hands.

Bwoom.

My weapon recovered, but I'm still too far from Spilenski. The closer I get, the harder his giant balls of fuck-you-up are going to be to dodge. Going up close and personal would be suicide.

Bwoom.

"Shoot the fucker!" someone yells. Either Aiko or Felicity. At least, I really hope it's not Devon.

Bwoom.

I have my pistol, but a bullet is only going to be turned into so much molten yesterday by the temporal distortion.

Bwoom.

Temporal distortion.

Devon's tangle of wires around my left hand. I seize them, take aim. Each second I spend sighting the speaker on him feels like a grain of sand slipping through my fingers. I can feel Leo Malkin edging closer and closer to Big Ben.

Bwoom.

I aim the speaker. I press play.

Bwoom.

Barely audible syllables from the tiny speaker. A tinny voice.

Bwoom.

The explosion lifts me off the floor.

81

I have heard that falling into water from a sufficient height is like falling onto concrete. I honestly don't know if that's true. I've had the good fortune of never being hurled from a sufficient height into water.

Falling onto concrete, however, from any height really, sucks balls.

The detonation throws me like a rag doll. I come down hard on my left side, arms splaying out. I roll, like a bowling ball waiting to hit the pins. My sword's gone. My chin grinds over and over. My skin tries to dissociate itself from a fool like me, to stay behind scraped over the asphalt.

I come up bleeding, bloody, raw. I've replaced my palms with lacerations, my sense of hearing with a high-pitched whining sound. Blood keeps getting in one of my eyes.

And I'm smiling, because I'm still doing way better than Ivan Spilenski.

That said, so is pretty much anybody who's not smeared over the base of a crater like strawberry jam.

I see my sword embedded in the roof of a classic red telephone booth. Apparently that's as close as this Arthur is going to get to a sword in the stone. I hobble over to it. Wrench it free.

Felicity, Devon, and Clyde all slowly pick themselves up. Their

JONATHAN WOOD

clothes are ragged, their skin blackened by ash, crisscrossed by cuts. Clyde is double-checking the straps of his mask. I hobble towards them.

"You OK?"

"Yes," Clyde says. "I am. This body is taking a beating though."

This body. Not his body. Not him. That wipes the grin off my face.

Felicity is checking her watch. "Big Ben," she says. "We have to be there. Now."

And she's right. This is hardly the time to rest on our laurels. It's just that resting on anything would be really nice right now.

Devon bends down, scoops something up from the street. Her mess of wires. Blasted out of my hand but still intact. She tosses it to me. "You'll need this."

To me. She throws them to me. And for a moment everyone looks to me. All of us moving together. All of us fighting for the right thing, the right way: together.

"Come on," I say. "Let's finish this."

82

If there's a tomorrow, I'm really going to regret this.

In fact, it is my body's opinion that no tomorrows might be a wonderful thing. It screams at me to give up. There's still time, it tells me, to get some good lying down and not hurting so much done. Some time for the good stuff.

It's a good argument, truth be told.

But it's not what Kurt Russell would do. Somehow that mad thought won't leave me. It's a spur stuck in my brain driving me on. So I put my head down, pump my legs. I suck in lungfuls of air, try to find a little more willpower, just to push a little closer to whatever the finale is going to be.

There is still a chance I have make-up sex to live for.

One more stride. One more. One more. The stitch builds in my side. One more.

We round the corner. Big Ben stands before us, vast and shadowy. The clock face is lost in the EMP-enforced gloom. There are a few uniformed policemen standing near the base of the clock tower. A group of tourists chat in German. One of them clutches an old SLR camera to his eye. Something with a strip film and cogs and gears. Old-school tech that survived the blast. He takes photographs of the city in darkness. Each time the flash goes off, I almost shoot him.

"Where are they?" Felicity peers into the dark.

"Well, I think the Russian must be in there already." Devon looks at Big Ben. "Didn't seem the sort of chap to hang around and have a good old-fashioned natter about the best way to pluck a turkey." I turn to stare at her. "Or anything else that may catch his fancy," she says, a little defensively.

"No." I shake my head. Look for straws to grasp. It can't be. "Where's Tabitha? Malcolm? Kayla?" I stare around looking for an abandoned police car, for any sign of them.

"We have to get in there!" Aiko jams a finger at Big Ben. "The others could be roadkill by now!"

Not exactly sugar-coating it for me. But still, I can't think that way. If Malkin's already in there we've already lost.

"Clyde," I say. "What about Sinsdale? That took out one of them on the way here. Can you... I don't know, booby-trap this place. Prime it with a Sinsdale spell to chop the bastard in two."

Clyde looks around. "Too many tourists," he says simply.

"Would anyone really miss Germans?" Devon asks.

Another flash from their camera. I'm tempted to side with Devon. I turn to stare at them, annoyed.

Except they're nowhere near where the flash came from.

Another flash. Larger. Closer.

"Oh shit!" I pull my sword. Flames flicker forth. "Incoming!"

There's a yell from one of the policemen at the base of the tower. Another from the Germans. Their camera clicks compete with Leo Malkin's portable battery.

Tabitha's car slews around a corner and into sight. At least two of the tires are blown. Bare rims throw up a wake of glittering sparks. A figure sprawls on the roof, clinging on. Kayla, her sword clenched between her teeth. Malcolm leans from the window. His shots are still a steady metronome beat.

Closer. Closer.

I toss my gun to Aiko. "Get ready."

"Will be," she says, steadying her aim.

My adrenaline is pushing my heartbeat up into my throat. And what would Kurt Russell do? He'd kick this guy's ass.

Flash. Flash. Leo Malkin draws closer, outpacing Tabitha's car, pulling away, pulling closer to us. Flash. Flash.

I ready the sword. Hold it high. A powerful position, my mind tells me. One of dominance. Bring the sword down, let gravity help power the swing. The flames are warm against the October damp. Sweat trickles down the back of my neck.

Closer. Closer.

I see him as he emerges from a flare of light. Yellow hair wild. Clothes torn. Bleeding from a long gash in his arm. His face: a mask of determination, rage... fear.

God, I almost feel sorry for him then, in that brief instant of connection. Out of time, out of friends, armed with only one desperate plan to try and make it all right. In some ways he's not so different from me.

Except that, well... I've never tried to screw over all of space and time just to get what I want.

And then the moment passes. He closes his eyes, mouths a few empty syllables, jumps, and—

Nothing. He lands, almost trips on the ground. He stares, bewildered. He jumps again, an almost idiotic motion. Like a child pretending he can fly. I half expect him to flap his arms.

He stares around desperately.

"He's out of power," I say it as I realize it. "His battery, it's dead."

"He's dead." Aiko lines up the shot.

"No!" I hold up a hand.

The policeman is still yelling at us, but seems to have decided to come no closer. He grabs his radio ineffectually. It's as dead as every other electronic device that was on during the blast. No back-up for him.

The Germans are still snapping away.

"Are you fucking kidding me?" Aiko doesn't put the gun away. "He killed Jasmine."

"We are *not* an execution squad," Felicity insists.

And she's right. We need to do this the right way.

We move in on him, slowly draw the circle tight. Behind him, Tabitha's car grinds to a halt. She and Malcolm step out fast, guns drawn, also aiming at the frozen Russian. Kayla leaps down from the roof.

"I could stop him," Clyde says quietly. "Make sure he doesn't do anything ever again."

"No!" Tabitha shrieks. I swear she almost brings the gun to bear on him. And did she see what happened to Kropkin? Does she suspect?

And where did my friend go? When was he replaced by the man, this thing, happily offering to overwrite a man's brain to kill him?

"He moves, he feckin' breathes a word, and I've got him." Kayla holds her sword in both hands. The encyclopedia in my head recognizes the posture. It's not one I would call defensive.

Felicity holds up her hand. "We are taking him in."

Malcolm cocks his pistol. "I don't remember agreeing to take orders from you."

Felicity snaps her gaze to him. It's the eye equivalent of Kayla's sword pose. "If you shoot an unarmed man, I *will* arrest you."

"He killed Jasmine," Aiko says again.

"And he will pay for his crimes." Felicity switches her gaze to Aiko. Aiko's eyes slip to my face. Felicity's eyes flick towards me and back.

And, suddenly, just like Leo Malkin, I know exactly what I want to fight for.

"We don't kill him," I say, shaking my head at Aiko. "We're not like him. We're the good guys." I put my sword back in its sheath.

A thin smile is on Felicity's face.

We draw in tighter on Leo Malkin. He has his hands up. He has that desperate caged look. But there's nowhere for him to go.

It's over.

"I say he's too feckin' dangerous to let live," says Kayla. "I say we feckin' end him."

"To be fair," Devon points out, "you say that about a lot of people."

"Boy bands are a blight on the face of feckin' humanity and they feckin' deserve it." I glance to see if she's joking. Apparently she's not.

But I'm not the only one who glances.

And, apparently, that moment of distraction was exactly what Leo Malkin was waiting for.

83

A syllable. Another. A bright spark.

I spin, grab for the sword. A line of white fire briefly attaches Leo Malkin to Clyde's face. To his mask. A moment of connection. And then gone.

Clyde slumps. My sword is out of its sheath. Kayla is moving. I swear I even see the muzzle flares as the guns discharge. But the world has lost its soundtrack, has gone silent as the grave.

A line of lightning. From Malkin to Felicity.

Felicity.

My Felicity.

Lightning. Bright and urgent and overwhelming. And then gone. Gone as Kayla's sword descends, as the bullets fly. Gone as utterly as Leo Malkin.

Clyde falls to the ground.

Felicity falls to the ground.

Tabitha screams.

The smell of charred meat fills my nose.

Leo Malkin is not there.

I stare. And I stare. As Tabitha howls at the world.

Because... because... but there was no power.

Except the power in Clyde's mask. The one power source that we brought to him. The one power source keeping Clyde alive.

Clyde lies on the ground. Felicity lies on the ground.

Tabitha screams.

The smell of charred meat fills my nose.

Power—stolen from Clyde. Power—electricity, lightning, that burned through the air, that lit the world, that was buried in Felicity. My Felicity. Burned into her. Scorched and blackened. And then, its last remnants, fulfilling Leo Malkin's last wish, propelling him up, up, up. Into Big Ben.

And he's gone. And Clyde's gone. And Felicity... Oh God. Oh no.

He lies on the ground.

She lies on the ground.

Tabitha screams.

The smell of charred meat fills my nose.

They're dead.

84

"No," I say. "No. Please no." And... no... I just... I try to process it. I try to understand. It's too big, too much.

She's dead.

Clyde's dead.

But... but... Felicity. Oh God, she's dead.

And, God, this can't be happening again. Someone I... God, did I love her? I think I loved her. And she's dead.

And Clyde. I can't even... What did I even feel for him? I'm still caught in the muddle of who he was and who he is, who he was becoming.

Was. Jesus.

I can't deal with the past tense. I can't...

"Big Ben." Aiko's face is aghast, she's staring at the bodies, but she's talking about Malkin, about what's left to be done. "He's in Big Ben."

And I try to care, try to give a shit about the end of the world.

She's just lying there. She doesn't even look like herself. Blackened, bloody. A rictus of pain. She died in pain. Leo Malkin killed her. He fucking roasted her.

The red is starting to fill my vision.

"It's over," someone says. And I know they're right. It's too late. I will never get to revenge this. I will never get to make this right.

The world is going to end to the soundtrack of Tabitha's screams.

"It's motherfeckin' not."

Kayla's arm is about my waist. I'm off my feet. I'm twenty feet from where I stood. The distance is increasing. There's the confused, terrified-looking policeman between us and Big Ben. He holds up an open palm.

Kayla's backhand breaks the sound barrier. He flies from our path, another useless rag doll.

Felicity's dead.

Malkin killed her.

Two other policemen are between Kayla and Big Ben. They heave out pistols. In this post 9/11 world, the London police force takes its monuments' safety seriously. She leaps, plants a foot in one man's throat. She launches off him as he drops gurgling. Her other foot swings, connects beneath the second copper's chin. He flies away, dismissed.

And I'm still in her spare hand. Still bundled up like so much luggage.

We're fighting. We're fighting for what's right.

She crashes through a door I couldn't make out in the dark. We're in a tiny black space. A yell from someone. The crunch of flesh against flesh. Something, someone, falling past me.

I don't know how Kayla's doing what she's doing. The physics of it defy me. I am lost in her violent ballet. A mere accessory of her ferocity. But I don't care. Because she's getting me closer to Malkin. Closer to his death.

And I know revenge won't bring her back—

God I can't...

She's dead...

I can't breathe.

I need to focus on the red. I need to cling to my rage. I need to make that fucker pay. Pay, and pay, and pay.

Pounding feet. More shouts. Kayla leaps, gazelle-like. Her feet fly out. Bodies spin away. Light reflects from the blade of her sword. Flat steel twangs against skulls. Bodies fall. Gunshots boom, but they never sound near, always seem to be retreating, even as their echoes rattle in my ears.

We go faster. Faster. It's hard to breathe, as if my head is jammed out the car window again. Kayla's arm makes the garotting seatbelt seem like a loving embrace. Screams. Shouts. More people now. The whirl of glimpsed violence is thicker about me.

Felicity is dead. Clyde is dead.

And I can't think about it. All I can think is that Leo Malkin must pay.

And then a sudden screeching halt. My neck cracks as the g-forces reverse. My vision blurs. I can hear Kayla panting hard, her breath short and ragged. I can hear shouts and yells, pounding feet echoing up behind us. I hear something else. A mechanical noise, repeated and repeated. The same action happening over and over all at the same time.

My vision clears.

Oh shit and balls.

Machine guns. Men and women ratcheting the action on their machine guns. Hundreds of them. That was what that noise was.

We're in the doorway of a room perhaps thirty yards wide, and twenty yards deep, and it is full. Literally full. Metal concert mosh pit full. Soldiers pack the place. Row upon row of them. An ugly crush of people. The place is hot with the sweat of them all. They wear black sweaters, and black bullet proof vests, and black night vision goggles, each head marked by two bright green LEDs.

And every last one of them has a very large black machine gun. And every last one of them is pointing that very large black machine gun at Kayla and me.

My brain tries to dissociate, to enter denial. It wonders how the night vision goggles survived. I find myself thinking that they probably weren't needed until Coleman set off the EMP. They probably weren't on at the time.

"You still got them wires?" Kayla sets me down, brings me back to reality. This is not the end of our journey. This will not stop us. We are MI37. We will not allow it. We cannot.

I glance down at my left hand. Devon's tangle of wires. Still wrapped around my fingers. Something to blow up the space-time distortion. Something to save the Chronometer. Something to blow the living crap out of Malkin with.

"Got it."

"Through there." Kayla nods at a door beyond the soldiers. Dark blue. Copper hinges. Something intricate carved into the whorls of wood. I can't make it out in the half-light.

I stare at the soldiers. Clyde's military ninjas. They stare implacably back.

Clyde's dead.

Felicity's dead.

"Let's do this."

I'm going to die. I know I'm going to die. There is no way I can fight these soldiers and live. But that doesn't matter. I have to fight them. I have to try to get to him.

And then something happens and I only piece it together as I'm sailing through the air. The sensation of a hand on my collar. Of a great force heaving me. Of my feet leaving the ground. As Kayla throws me bodily over the heads of the soldiers, kicking and flailing, headfirst toward the dark blue door and the end of all things.

85

Adrenaline is an odd chemical. When it floods the system in great quantities your perception of time skews strangely. Every detail is crisp and clear, absorbed and processed. It's like being Neo in *The Matrix*. Time slows. You observe.

If only I got Neo's reaction times too.

Instead, I watch in excruciating detail as the door flies toward my head.

My mind knows how to pull the sword, how to aim it, how to best angle it to break down the door. But the knowledge is useless.

A hundred machine guns track my path. I rotate as I fly, watch them rotate with me. I spin from headfirst to feetfirst. I see Kayla raise her sword. I can even make out her movements for once. I watch fascinated as she slices through the first of the gun barrels.

Then my feet strike the door. And time catches up with me. A compressed blur of movement and pain rushing past me, over me, trampling me.

My ankles feel broken. My head rings. The floor is cold and hard. I'm bleeding onto it.

I'm through a doorway. In the dark. Muzzle flares cast a thunderous strobe light. I wait to die, perforated by sixty rounds a minute. But the guns aren't firing at me. The guns don't seem to care.

Kayla dances on the shoulders of the soldiers. Her sword is a line of liquid fire. Shards of metal spiral through the air as she hacks away with a sushi chef's precision and efficiency.

And the soldiers fire and fire and fire, and fill the whole world with flying lead. And they cannot hit her.

But I am not here to gawp. I am not here to stare. *I have to get up*, I tell my arms and legs. I have to get up. Now. I have to turn around.

Knees trembling, I make it to my feet. The room I'm in is dark, cool, and larger than I expected. Probably most of the width of the tower. It's a mess of machinery. Great hulks of painted steel lying dead and cold. Cables and cords thick on the ground. Pipes snake to the ceiling in ropy pillars. There are great panels of dials and meters, unreadable despite the reflected light of Kayla's firefight.

The lower edge of Big Ben's clock face breaches the upper half of the opposite wall. A white crescent of filtered moonlight.

I take steps in, try to see past the metal hulks to the Chronometer. Try to make out Leo Malkin in the mess. Surely if you decide to enshrine the device that controls all of time, you actually, well, give it some sort of shrine. It seems implicit in the action.

I go deeper in. Where is he? Where is the bastard? Where is my piece of his goddamn hide?

The noise of the firefight outside seems to drop away too quickly. I glance over my shoulder. The doorway seems small now.

A noise to my left seizes my attention, gives it a good shake. I stoop low, peer around the corner of another metal hulk. Its surface is cold against my hand, gently dotted with condensation.

There, rising out of a tangle of metal cords, is something like a plinth. An industrial interpretation of an ornamental table. Hard steel edges, decorative rivets.

Sitting on it, reflecting the filtered moonlight that slants in through the clock face—a large bell jar. And inside that…

The Chronometer.

It looks like nothing else but a large golden clock, baroque in detail, its inner workings clearly displayed from its case-less back. Tiny cogs whir. Counterweights shift. Around it, pudgy little angels stroke harps.

For one of the most powerful supernatural artifacts in the world, it looks terribly like something my gran would have owned.

However, while it doesn't appeal to my aesthetic senses in the slightest, apparently Leo Malkin has a mad-on for it.

He stands with his back to me, arms raised, a massive industrial-sized wrench poised above his head.

He brings it down. A great sweeping, powerful arc. And I stare. Too late. Too late by mere seconds.

The wrench bounces off the bell jar with a dull bonk. Malkin grunts with effort. Apparently the Chronometer is protected by more than just an electric anti-magic field.

But there are spider-line cracks in the glass. This is not some impenetrable barrier. Given time, Malkin will get through.

Funny—in the house of time itself, it's the one thing Malkin doesn't have.

Behind Malkin hovers something like a heat haze. It's a barely perceptible shimmer. I'd probably have never noticed it if it wasn't turning pipes into a fine rust-colored powder.

It's spreading, rolling gently toward Malkin. He's got about two minutes before it sets his personal clock back. And I'm guessing that then there'll be about one more minute before it eats through the glass and sets to work erasing all of reality.

I look down at my left hand. The wires are knotted around my fingers. And I don't need minutes to spray him across the room.

I point them at him.

"Hey!" I yell. There is a smile stretched across my skull. I'm going to enjoy this. I'm actually going to enjoy the death of another human being. Something is broken in me, and I don't care. And I want him to know. I want him to know he is reaping what he's sown.

Malkin turns around, stares at me. His eyes go wide. And he knows.

"Enjoy hell, you motherfu—"

A flash of light.

Oh crap. Why did I have to open my big mouth?

86

My finger has to travel an inch. Leo Malkin has to travel thirty yards.

He still beats me.

The wrench buries itself in my gut, lifts me off the floor, sends me flying backwards, crashing, splayed painfully over machinery.

No. I have to… I can't let it go down like this.

He comes at me again, in a flash of light. I roll, not knowing where he's going to manifest, not knowing if he's going to reappear with his foot stuck through my gut.

It turns out it's behind me, and I am not rolling half as fast as I need to.

My upper right arm takes the blow. I feel the crack of the bone. The pain is like a lance from elbow to skull. Like someone lit a fire in my marrow. I howl.

Through tears, I see Malkin raise the wrench again.

Another shout from the doorway. Shots. Leo Malkin blinks out of existence. The air above my head shrieks as the bullets whip by.

I stagger up, clutching at my arm. It hangs useless next to me. I cannot believe this hurts so much.

Malkin better not believe that's enough to take me down. This is a Pythonesque flesh wound. I'll bite his bloody legs off if I have to.

That said, I'm totally going to use my flaming sword before we get to that point. I grab the hilt—

Something barrels into me from behind. Something angry, and large, and shouting in Russian.

I land on my bad arm. The world goes red with pain. I roll, senseless. More shots.

I'm still going to kill you, you bastard.

I pick my head up. I can see the Chronometer, a silhouette between me and Big Ben's clock face. Beyond that: a flash of light. Malkin. He looks around.

I raise my left hand. It's shaking.

I can't get my right up to press the button.

I fucking refuse to be defeated by my own limbs.

Malkin crouches low, scans the room, searching for me.

I bring my left hand to my mouth, grip the small, almost vestigial play button between my teeth. I twist my hand, straining against the tension in the wires, point the speaker.

Malkin moves a step left. Scans. Freezes. He's looking right at me.

I bite down on the play button.

Silence.

I wait a heartbeat.

Another.

And then the speaker crackles to life. Words emerge.

Malkin stands.

The explosion hurls him backwards.

87

My sight of Malkin is occluded by roiling flames. Then, through the haze: the white glass of Big Ben's face breaks. A national monument scarred. Malkin flies out into space. He flails, searching for power. Searching for a way to teleport back.

Nothing here for you, Leo. Ta-ta. Nice knowing you.

I shudder a sigh. I won. I saved the world.

I saved the world.

Shouts from the soldiers, yells, footsteps approaching. And then: A spark of light. A thin trailing streak of electricity.

Oh no. No, no, no.

A soldier throws up his hands, clutches his night vision goggles. The two bright green LEDs have gone out.

A flash of light next to me.

Oh no. Oh shit. Oh piss and balls.

I dive forward. Malkin's wrench glances off my ribs, sends me spinning and crashing, doubling up in pain even while in midair.

I land on my left shoulder. Which means I don't black out from pain. On the other hand, now my good arm feels like two tons of spare lead.

Soldiers are pouring into the room now, Kayla unable to contain their attention. More night vision goggles. More little LEDs. More power for Malkin.

A crackle of lightning, and he's on me.

I kick out with my legs. Grab for my sword. It's futile. He's behind me. I roll. The wrench slams into the ground where my head was. It raises sparks. I keep rolling. I hit my right arm. I howl, lying on my back, paralyzed.

Malkin kicks me. Hard. In the gut. I double up about his boot. No. No. No. No.

More shouts from soldiers. More electricity. Malkin blinks away.

I manage to make it to all fours. Well, to three out of four. My right arm cradled against my chest. God, I wish I was left-handed.

Another blink of light. Malkin's wrench emphasizes the point his boot made on my stomach.

Considering how long it's been since I last ate, quite a lot of food comes up.

I lie on the floor in a bubble of pain. And I've been here before. This is Trafalgar Square all over again. Except there's nobody to call Malkin off. This time he's going to finish the job.

Why won't he just die? Why won't he just rot?

More gunfire. Something ricochets near my head. And the soldiers that represent my only hope are equally keen on killing me. And they keep coming. A virtual horde of batteries for Malkin to tap.

Still, they scare Malkin off long enough for me to finally get my blade free. The blade flickers to life.

Lightning flares. Come get some, Malkin. I thrust out with the sword. It's an awkward jab. My left hand is normally busy being a paperweight. And Clyde skimped on off-hand fighting. All of which gives Malkin all the time he needs to line up a sweet shot between my shoulder blades.

He swings like Tiger Woods, like an all-star, like a really pissed-off dude with a giant fucking wrench. The pain is literally blinding. I don't know where I land. How I land. If I land. Maybe I am suspended, floating in my bubble of crushing agony.

More pain, from some directionless nowhere. Some invisible torment slamming down on me. I am distantly aware of my leg catching fire. Maybe I have been shot. Maybe it was Malkin. Maybe it was me. I don't know. I don't care. I just want it to stop. Just want him to die. And it doesn't. And he doesn't.

Somehow, through the haze, I see light. Not *the* light. Not something distant and glowing at the end of a tunnel. Something flickering and red.

The sword. Lying next to me. I scrabble to hold it. My hand jerks loosely in all the wrong directions. I'm using my right hand, I realize. My right arm. It's probably why this hurts so much.

There are more lights. White flashes that precede the pain. I concentrate on my right hand. It's like operating it by remote. It flops down on the sword hilt but the fingers won't work. It flops off the sword. Then back. The hand spasms. Distantly I scream. I grab the sword.

Howling, barely sensible, I swing the sword in a wide arc above my head.

The white flashes stop. The new pain stops. Just all the old ones to keep me company.

Still screaming, whether in rage or pain I don't know, I stagger to my feet. I sway there, swishing the sword back and forth.

A flash from behind. A kick in the small of my back sends me staggering forward. But I don't fall. I spin around, slice through empty air.

Bullets ping off machinery around me. Ricochets and half-blind shots burying themselves in the floor. Another flash. Another kick. I stagger. I spin. I hit nothing.

A flash. A punch this time. A dizzying blow to the back of the head. He's fucking playing with me. I spin. The howl is definitely more anger now. More rage. He's not there. He's never fucking there. I can't get him. He's too fast.

I have to get him. I have to.

A flash. A blow. A flash. A blow. I can hear the bastard laughing. I spin. A flash. A blow. My feet can't keep up. My adrenaline is wearing thin. I drop to my knees.

Breathing hard, I wave the sword in front of me. A flash. Another blow to the head. I can barely fucking see. I struggle round. It's ridiculous. A three-year-old would be gone by the time I make it round.

Another flash.

And I'm sick of this. And I think that maybe I'm not faster, or stronger, or more powerful than Leo Malkin. There's a slim chance I'm not even as pissed off as he is. But I think I might be smarter.

A flash of light. And I take the hit. But this time I don't turn.

Behind me, every time, Malkin? That's a pretty fucking predictable pattern.

I stab straight backward. Under my own right arm. Everything I've got left. Every ounce of hate and rage and pain. Ignoring the scream of my body, of my arm. Ignoring the building sense of futility. Thinking only about Felicity, only about her lying there, thinking only about the pain expressed by her corpse. I thrust the blade back, feel the heat and wind flicker past my body.

And then, resistance. A grunt. A scream. The grind of steel on bone.

And I scream too. My fingers fly wide, involuntary, undeniable. But there is no flash of light. No other blow. Just a slow whimpering gasp.

Finally, achingly, I turn round.

Leo Malkin is on his knees. We stare at each other. Eye to eye at last. He opens his mouth, closes it, gasps. His tongue works. And tears. He's crying. Pain or loss, I don't know.

My sword, still flaming, protrudes from the center of his chest, neatly slotted through the ribs. Thick, arterial blood sprays from his back, hissing and spitting in the sword's flames. "You…" He reaches out a hand to me. I can see the toll the action takes writ large upon his face. But the hand never makes it. It sags back down. He looks at it, at the sword slotted through his chest.

"No more time," he says. And he sags to the floor.

88

I kneel there, before Leo Malkin's corpse. I feel hollow, and used, and full of pain. All the Russians are dead. Everybody is avenged. But my friends are all still dead too. Jasmine. Clyde. Felicity.

This is the world I fought for.

I'm barely a yard from the Chronometer. From the source of all this fuss. Its protective case has been broken. Maybe in the explosion I caused, maybe a stray shot, a stray sword stroke. I don't know. I don't really care. For something meant to be essential, for something so fundamental to the regulation of the world, it seems a lot like a tacky piece of shit to me.

There are sounds of violence to my left. Kayla still fighting the guards. Unaware that we've won. Unaware that it's all over except for the copious bleeding.

I try to build the will to shout to her, to tell her to stop. But I can't.

Soldiers are breaking from the main group, are running toward me. Guns out and trained. They bellow at me.

I don't pay them much heed. I keep watching Kayla. Still fighting. Always fighting. I remember Devon in Chernobyl asking if it ever got any better. I remember lying to her.

Kayla's blade knocks a man's helmet flying. She skips around a muzzle flare, slices a gun in two.

It's never a case of winning. Never. Just a case of how well we lose.

"Stop!" I finally find the strength to yell at her. "Just stop." Be defeated, I want to tell her. There's no point struggling anymore.

Felicity is dead.

Kayla looks over at me. I swear she even smiles.

The soldier's gun goes off in her face.

Even Kayla can't dodge that. I see her body arc one last time. I see the spray of bone and blood and brain sailing out the back of her head.

Jesus. Oh Jesus.

We put the world back… we put it back… Jesus.

Kayla's dead. She can't be dead. She can't die. But she's dead.

Did I just kill Kayla? Was that me?

Oh Jesus.

Soldiers swarm about me. Everything is dark. Shadowed figures. Dull shouts barely breaking through into consciousness. Everything sludgy and distant.

This is what we saved? And who's left? Tabitha and me. That's MI37 now. Aiko and Malcolm. Devon. How long before they're dead too?

Jasmine's dead.

Clyde's dead.

Kayla's dead.

Felicity's dead.

I stare at the Chronometer. I want to smash it. I'd be shot as soon as I moved. I wish I'd let Malkin win.

Its second hand moves mercilessly on. Tick. Tick. Tick. Time—unrelenting in its march. Leaving all the might-have-beens in its dust.

Jesus.

And then it hits me.

No… No… It's too big. The thought. The audacity—it's not mine.

But this doesn't have to be the world I fought for. Not this time. Not here. Not now. Malkin was wrong. There's still time. Time itself staring me in the face, and asking for a do over.

I look at the Chronometer. At its ticking hands. So close to my own.

There's probably a better chance I'll be killed and all this will be for naught.

But… God, what the hell am I fighting for anyway? Not this. Never this.

Kayla lies on the floor, twenty yards away, what's left of her mind pooling on the floor.

Felicity lies on the ground far below, blackened and burned.

Soldiers scream at me to put my hands behind my head. To put my head on the floor.

Sorry guys, but fuck you.

I lunge at the Chronometer.

89

The pain is incredible.

I feel each bullet strike my body. Each one an individual hammer blow. A spear thrust through my gut, my arm, my lungs, my heart. I feel each muscle tear, each bone break, each organ rupture. I feel the hot spray of blood through my perforated chest cavity. I feel the burn of the bile and stomach acid as they splash against the inside of my guts. The black poison of my liver seeping down my back.

The Chronometer looms even as my vision narrows. It becomes the whole world to me. My hand reaching out, occluding its face. And I don't have the strength to reach it. I am too broken by Malkin's beatings.

But the bullets drive me forward. Even as they rob me of my strength and will. They drive me into the Chronometer.

I can't see. The pain is too much. It's too eclipsing. My world has been reduced to entry and exit wounds.

I'm dying. Hell, I'm almost dead. I don't think my heart is beating. I know I'm not breathing. Something is wrong with my throat. The building, burning pressure threatening to detonate in my skull is proof of that. I can feel blood spluttering down my chin, each cough weaker than the last.

I'm lying slumped on something, my face down in my own blood. The plinth, I realize with my remaining neurons. My finger is on something too. My forefinger. I try to concentrate on that one point. Try to push everything away. What is my left fingertip resting on?

Could it be the hand of a clock?

I don't know.

It's not like I'm going to get a chance to figure it out anyway.

With everything I have left, I push down.

09

.ekatsim a ekil ylbakramer sleef sihT .doG hO

91

Malcolm cocks his pistol. He points it at Leo Malkin's head. "I don't remember agreeing to take orders from you."

Felicity snaps her gaze to him. It's the eye equivalent of Kayla's sword pose. "If you shoot an unarmed man, I *will* arrest you."

Wait. This… This seems familiar.

"He killed Jasmine," Aiko says again.

Again? Again and again? How many times again? I think I have the worst case of déjà vu.

"And he will pay for his crimes." Felicity switches her gaze to Aiko. Aiko's eyes slip to my face. Felicity's eyes flick toward me and back.

HOLY CRAP! Oh my God, I just died. I just died. Up there. Up in Big Ben. I was shot. Everyone was dead. Kayla was dead. Clyde was dead. Shit, holy shit, Felicity was dead. And me too. I lunged at the Chronometer, and soldiers shot me dead.

I lunged at the Chronometer and everything is happening again. Oh my God. I just turned back time.

"We don't kill him," I hear myself say. I am shaking my head at Aiko. "We're not like him. We're the good guys." I put my sword back in its sheath.

Why did I say that? Why did I put my sword away? I need to kill this man.

A thin smile is on Felicity's face. And then it falters, just slightly. A distant look in her eyes, as if something is wrong.

Does she know? Does she feel it too? It's like we're on rails. Like we're caught acting out a rerun.

We draw in tighter on Leo Malkin. He has that desperate caged look.

"I say he's too feckin' dangerous to let live," says Kayla. "I say we—" Then she stops. Her brow furrows. "I say we feckin' end him." It almost sounds like a question.

And this is it. This is where everything becomes too late. This is where he kills Clyde, kills Felicity. I need to do something, need to break free from this.

"To be fair," Devon says, "you say that about a lot of people." She says it slowly, hesitantly.

Now. Now! Everything is sluggish and offline. It's like a dream where nothing works. I beat at the control panel of my own body. I just screwed time for this. I just died for this. I am not going to do it again.

"Boy bands are a blight on the face of feckin' humanity and they feckin' deserve it."

Everyone turns to stare. Everyone except Leo Malkin. Everyone except Leo Malkin and me.

92

Clyde's mask. He's going to go for—

I fling myself at Clyde. At his face.

Malkin speaks. A syllable. Another. A bright spark.

My hand connects with the mask at the same moment that it lights up. There is a crack like a storm cloud spitting thunder directly at my eardrums. Pain spikes up my arm in a jagged wave, thrusting into my neck, my chest. My fingers slip over the mask's surface. My knuckles connect. A near perfect roundhouse.

I slump to the ground. The mask flies into the air. A great spark still spitting from its heart.

The mask reaches the apex of its curve. Starts to descend.

Leo Malkin screams.

I gasp. Pain still blazes.

There is something wrong in how Clyde's mask falls. Something out of kilter in the way it twists and tumbles.

In the way it bisects.

No. No. Not again. I saved him this time. I saved him.

Clyde's mask falls in two splintered halves.

Guns fire. Kayla slices.

Leo Malkin bucks as the bullets smash into his body, as one tears through his neck, as one punches bone shards from his sternum into his heart, as one plows through the breadth of both his lungs. And then Kayla's sword stops him from moving at all.

And then, very abruptly, very painfully, Leo Malkin dies.

93

No. Not again, no.

Tabitha howls.

Then Felicity. I spin. No, this can't be all for nothing. This can't be.

But Felicity is clutching her completely unharmed body. She stares at where her hands are clasping her chest, a look of utter confusion on her face. Kayla is staring at Malkin's corpse as if she can't quite believe it. Aiko, Devon, and Malcolm all stand looking completely nonplussed.

Only Tabitha is pure in her emotion, her horror. She races to Clyde. She cups the two shattered halves of the mask. Massive splinters of wood stick out of them. Smoking circuitry.

And I screwed up. I couldn't move fast enough. Couldn't save him in time. He's still dead.

"I'm alive." Felicity's words tear my attention from the mask, from Tabitha's horror. She looks at me as if she can't quite believe it, as if she doesn't know why she should. "What's going on?" She presses a hand to her head. "Why do I think I should be dead? What the hell is going on?"

"I need to go back." I look up at Big Ben. It's the only thing I can think of. "I need to go back in there again, try this again, go back further."

"He's dead." Aiko points at Malkin. "We... I..." She shakes her head. "Why does this all feel so messed up?"

"Kayla!" I shout at her. "Take me back up to the Chronometer."

Both Kayla and Felicity look at me as if I'm insane. "The Chronometer?" Felicity asks me. "What does that..."

"I turned back time!" We don't have time for me to explain this. Clyde is dead. "But not far enough. I didn't get it together enough in time to save Clyde. I just... I saved you."

God, it hits me then. I saved Felicity. I violated time and space, and I saved her.

Felicity looks at me in utter bewilderment. And she doesn't remember. She doesn't know. She died. I died. Kayla died. And they just don't know.

And then a look of wonder fills Felicity's eyes. And then horror, and then she just stares at me.

"I died." She says it so quietly, I barely hear it over Tabitha's howls. "I died. He killed me. And I'm alive. And it never happened."

"I turned back time," I say. It sounds so small. So ridiculous. But I did it. I saved Felicity Shaw.

And she knows it.

She steps toward me. She's shorter than me. Her head comes up to my nose. She tilts it back to see me clearly, as her arms slip around my waist. I tilt my head down.

We kiss. We kiss like it's the last kiss, like it's the first. We kiss like I just broke the laws of the world just to save her life.

Because I just damn well did.

"I knew." Felicity has her hand against my cheek. "I goddamn knew I was dating you for a good reason."

I close my eyes. This. This right here is what the world is meant to be like.

94

Something bounces off the back of my head. I grunt and turn. Turns out it was half of Clyde. Tabitha is standing, gripping the other half, staring at me, eyes red-ringed, mascara streaked.

"Back," she demands. "Go. Fix this. Fix this right. Don't fuck up again."

Felicity's arms are still around my waist. Kayla is standing next to Tabitha. She has her hand to the spot in her skull where I saw the bullet enter.

"Go!" screams Tabitha. "He's dead! Make him alive!" The strength in her voice ebbs. "Fix him. Please."

And Clyde's been dead so long. He just never stopped moving. And I have gained so much. And I don't know if I can repeat the performance. And what if I don't make it to the Chronometer this time? What if I die?

I am scared, I realize. I have fought and won, and I don't know if I can do it again.

"No." It's Felicity who denies Tabitha. Maybe she too feels her own mortality. Maybe she too fears what Clyde was becoming.

"We do not casually play with time," Felicity insists. "This should never have happened once." She doesn't look at me when she says that. I have a hard time believing she is really chastising me.

Tabitha's face crumples, her mouth twists. She turns away from us. Even now, she cannot bear to share her emotions. Even now she can't let us past the barriers.

I step towards her. "Tabitha—" I say. I want to make her see. This isn't cruelty. This is just playing the odds.

Tabitha abruptly lunges at Aiko. She grabs at her pistol. Aiko yells. Tabitha slams an angular elbow into her jaw. Aiko's hands fly to her mouth. Tabitha grabs the gun.

She points it straight at me.

"Now. What about," she says to Felicity, "if I shot him? For him—would you turn it back? How fucking heartless are you?"

Oh crap. "Tabitha—" I start again.

"Kayla." Felicity's command is as short and simple as the blow Kayla deals to the side of Tabitha's temple.

Tabitha collapses like someone hit the power button.

I look at her lying there, crumpled and broken. Aiko standing next to her, still rubbing her jaw, looking pissed. Felicity is still next to me, she's put one arm around my waist again.

Felicity is alive. Clyde is dead.

Can I sleep with that? Is that a trade I can live with?

And in the end… we fight for what we can. We put the world back as best we can. We lose as best we can.

Aiko is pissed. But Felicity is happy.

Leo Malkin is dead. And the world survived.

Happy or not, I'll take those endings.

95

Felicity starts making phone calls. She looks at the hand I used to interrupt Malkin's spell. She says the burn is bad enough that she should add an ambulance to her list of calls.

Aiko and Malcolm hang around looking awkward. To my surprise Devon is the one who puts Tabitha in the recovery position. She places the two halves of Clyde's mask next to her. It's almost reverential. Kayla puts a hand on Devon's shoulder. I expect Devon to shrug it off. But she doesn't. They stay there, quiet. Finding what peace there is.

The police beat the paramedics. Coleman does too.

His BMW screeches up against the curb. He steps out and strides towards us, his mustache wobbling in time with his gut.

"What in the name of all holy fuck do you think you are doing?" He sprays spit as he yells at us. A good quantity gets stuck in the mustache and hangs there glistening. "You think that diverting police resources is somehow helpful? That distracting essential attention will somehow speed things up? What sort of dull-witted fucktards are you? Even you, Felicity? Is this some grandiose career suicide? Some swan song of incompetence?"

Felicity glances over her shoulder, away from the two policemen who are being bewildered by her clearance levels, and says, "Oh do be quiet, George."

I open my mouth to join in, to let him know how badly things are going to go for him. But then I close it. I smile. I've done my fighting. I've won what I need to. This I'll watch. This I'll savor and enjoy.

"Quiet? Quiet!" Coleman roars at the top of his lungs. "I will fucking sing from the rooftops. I will do a whole song and fucking dance routine on the grave of your directorship, Felicity. I will—"

"They're dead, George," Felicity says. She's got her back to him. So he can't see how savagely she's smiling. "The Russians. We killed them. One of them right here at the foot of Big Ben. The one location they were all racing towards. Because Arthur was right. Just like I told you he was right. But you didn't listen, did you, George? You didn't do anything to help. You just blew every electrical device in London. And you did it for no reason."

Coleman swallows very hard indeed. "You," he starts, "you haven't heard the last—"

"Yes, George," she says, "I have. So go home, write your letter of resignation, and leave it on my desk in the morning. *My* desk, George. *My* MI37."

I take the time to kiss her. Because I can, and because she deserves it. And, although it is terrible manners, I open my eyes halfway through, so I can stare at Coleman while I do it.

Coleman's face investigates the colors of the rainbow. I think he's going to settle on red, but then he shifts to purple and gets stuck there.

"This is a fucking outrage!" Coleman bellows. The police start circling. The German tourists are still there and they start snapping photographs. "You're a useless bitch!" he screams. "A fucking liar!"

He launches himself at Felicity.

She turns fluidly, bringing up the flat palm of her hand, and with an efficiency that even Kayla would admire, she lifts the fat bastard off his feet.

Coleman lands heavily on the ground. He doesn't get up.

Felicity takes my uninjured hand. She squeezes it.

"You're awesome," I tell her.

"You're not too bad yourself."

The ambulance arrives and I pull away from Felicity toward it as she continues to harangue detectives and chief inspectors. Paramedics get out, take in the scene, and move toward Tabitha. Who, I consider, may actually need the attention more than me. I stand and wait, and as I do, Aiko sidles up to me.

"I'm not good at goodbyes," she tells me.

"This doesn't have to be one," I say. Except, I can't see a way for it not to be. But sometimes lying is the decent thing to do.

Aiko gives me a sad smile. "I was wrong in Kiev," she says. "Your girlfriend does still like you."

"I like you," I say. And I honestly do. "Just not..." I shrug. It's easier not to get into specifics.

"Oh trust me, Agent Arthur, I am fully aware." Another sad smile, and then something mischievous quietly sneaks in around the corners. "Of course, I don't guarantee that you won't change your mind. And when you do, you still have my number." I will miss Aiko. Despite all the shit this job throws at me, it has afforded me the opportunity to meet some of the strongest, smartest women I've ever known. Parting sucks. "You could stay," I say. "Be part of MI37."

Aiko shakes her head. "Don't make me think less of you right at the end, Agent Arthur." She steps toward me, hesitates, then leans in and plants a soft kiss on my cheek. "There," she says. "I won't tell her about that one if you don't."

"Goodbye, Aiko."

"Goodbye, Agent Arthur."

She steps away toward Malcolm. She takes his arm. He tips an imaginary hat at me. Quietly they slip toward the shadows.

The paramedics load Tabitha onto the ambulance. Devon points in my direction. A lotion and a bandage later, they're driving away.

Devon stares after them.

"What now?" I say to her. "Back bright and early in the office tomorrow?"

"Erm," Devon hesitates. "No, I'm afraid. Nothing to do with any sort of personal feelings toward you, Arthur, you understand. Love you. Not in, well, you know, the sort of way Felicity loves you.

Totally platonic. Not at all interested in invading that territory. Not suggesting some sort of ménage à trois. Not my cup of tea at all. Far too middle class for that sort of thing. Leave it to the politicians. Power and perversity. Funny how often they go hand in hand. Like ketchup and mayo. Assuming you like mayo. Some people don't. I can't understand why. How on earth can you eat a sandwich without mayo? Which is sort of what I'm trying to say really. MI37, for me, and just me you understand, but rather like a sandwich without mayo. And you know, I did quit last week, and I really don't want to come back."

"I'll miss you," I say.

"Oh, I'll be about," Devon assures me. "Just not doing what you're doing. I mean, just because I know there are terrorists, I don't want to join MI5. And just because there are monsters, I'm not sure I want to fight them."

She smiles at me. "I'm no hero, Arthur."

I almost laugh at that, but it doesn't seem like the right moment. Instead I go with, "Stay in touch."

"Of course." She smiles. "Look after Tabitha. I think this is going to take a lot out of her."

I go to say something, to make some promise, but she's already pushing away, already following Aiko's lead into the anonymity of the night.

OXFORD. LATER

Felicity's bed. Back where it feels like everything began. Or this latest chapter of disasters. It's not the first time that I've thought I should regret having met Felicity Shaw.

But I don't. I really don't.

She sleeps on next to me. She looks peaceful against the pillow, the light breaking through the orchid leaves along her windowsill, casting dappled shadows over her cheek.

I slip out of bed. I have no desire to wake her. She needs the rest. Forty straight hours of work, on four hours of sleep, have finally caught up with her. Trying to clean up after Coleman's mess.

I should probably rest more too. But part of me really wants to double-check the world hasn't exploded in the night. That no mutants have emerged from the center of the earth. That no avatars of fear and chaos have broken through from alternate dimensions.

I root through my hastily packed suitcase, recovered from the hotel in London. My laptop is buried under dirty laundry. I heft it out.

Something silver slips out with it, lies on the floor. I stare at it.

A flash drive. Where did I get a flash drive?

It's Aiko's, I realize. Given to me so I could copy Coleman's files.

Except I never took that out of my pocket. That's still in my jeans lying crumpled at the foot of Felicity's bed.

So who else? Who...

Oh shit.

Hands shaking, I turn the computer on, jam the stick into the USB port. The laptop chugs and chimes through a million seemingly pointless start-up processes. My hands don't stop their shaking. A little icon whirs on the bottom of the screen. Then a box pops up.

"This is an executable file. Are you sure you want to run Clyde.exe?"

Oh shit.

I hesitate. This laptop is a magic lamp and I am standing here with a cloth and a jar of polish. Should I be careful what I wish for?

But I only hesitate for a moment. How can I not? I click. More icons whir. The fan on the little laptop starts to whine. A progress bar slowly fills. Then the computer pings. "Installation complete." I search the screen for an icon. "Come on. Come on." Nothing. I open the start menu. Still nothing. Trust bloody Clyde to program himself into something that no one can access.

I'm about to throw the machine across the room when a window suddenly appears. A small black rectangle. I stare at it. The screen flickers. A room appears. Something grainy and out of focus. Another flicker.

Clyde's head appears.

Really Clyde. Not a man in a mask. Not a blond giant. But a scruffy-looking chap with a tweed jacket and a straggly beard. Sitting in a gray featureless room. He blinks at me.

"Holy shit," I say.

"Well," says Clyde's head, "not the name I usually go by, but I suppose I've been called worse."

Oh my God. "It's you," I say. "It's really you."

"Well," Clyde shrugs. "I'm Clyde 2.2, actually. I thought a numbering system might be clearest. Probably a terrible idea. Cause all sorts of release confusion. But, well, the thinking, if you're generous enough to call it that, was that good old 1.0 was the one who died. So you get 2.0 in the mask. Then Tabby has 2.1, you've got 2.2, Felicity has 2.3, and so on and so forth. You know, independent paths of progress. Nature over nurture from this moment on. All that. Does that make sense, or am I making you go cross-eyed? I can never tell."

"You can see me?" Not a direct answer, I admit.

"Webcam." Clyde nods. "But the sense thing, I'm making it, right?"

I nod. It's Clyde. It's really Clyde. Words tangled and confused and hopeless. My friend.

Except, it's a copy of Clyde. And not the only one. He hasn't died. He's bloody multiplied.

But it's Clyde. Clyde is alive. Or close as he can get.

My friend is alive.

Clyde grins at me. "And did we save the world today?"

I hesitate. I look at the face of my friend, on my computer. An electronic man. Someone who can never be killed. Only deleted.

I remember Jasmine, burned and blackened on the edge of the Thames.

I remember Nikolai, eaten by a mutant catfish in Russia.

I remember London. Every light gone dark, every computer dead.

But then I glance back at the bed, to Felicity, lying there, peaceful, maybe a little aglow after the make-up sex.

And I smile, because maybe this isn't quite normal, and maybe we haven't quite put the world back the way we found it, but I think I might like it this way all the same.

"Close enough," I say to Clyde. "We were close enough."

ACKNOWLEDGEMENTS

Launching a book into the world is an exhilarating and unnerving act much like kicking a young bird out of a nest to see if it can fly. These are the people who helped me put the boot in.

Thanks to my agent, Howard Morhaim, who can shoot holes in my writing like a sniper, and then knows exactly how I should make the repairs.

Thanks too to Paul Jessup, Mark Teppo, and Natania Barron, my writing partners in crime. They are wonderful, inspiring people full of wonderful and inspiring words. They put many of them to paper, and I highly recommend seeking those words out. Plus they're total nerds, which makes me feel better about being one.

Most of all, thank you to my wife, Tami. Without her unending support, quiet cajoling, and extensive knowledge of grammar this book would never have come to be. She is the lynchpin upon which everything depends. If you enjoyed this book, you should thank her too. If you didn't, well that's my fault…

And finally, thanks too to you for reading this far. Hope you're enjoying the ride. I know I am.

ABOUT THE AUTHOR

Jonathan Wood is an Englishman in New York. There's a story in there involving falling in love and flunking out of med school, but in the end it all worked out all right, and, quite frankly, the medical community is far better off without him, so we won't go into it here. His debut novel, *No Hero* was described by *Publishers Weekly* as "a funny, dark, rip-roaring adventure with a lot of heart, highly recommended for urban fantasy and light science fiction readers alike." Barnesandnoble.com listed it has one of the twenty best paranormal fantasies of the past decade, and Charlaine Harris, author of the Sookie Stackhouse novels described it as "so funny I laughed out loud." He is continuing the Arthur Wallace novels with the forthcoming *Anti-Hero* and *Broken Hero*, both available from Titan Books. He can be found online at www.jonathanwoodauthor.com.